Finding Grace

A Novel

By

Sarah Pawley

Finding Grace

Copyright@2011 by Sarah Pawley

This is a work of fiction. All of the characters, names, incidents, organizations, and dialogue in this novel are either the products of the author's imagination or are used fictitiously

ISBN: 9781449559465

Printed in the United States of America

Front Cover Image:
1873 "Girl In a Hammock" by Winslow Homer

Other Titles by Sarah Pawley
"Oh, That I Had Wings"

To D.W. for being such a big fan

Chapter 1
"A Willful Girl"

Stones Mill, Virginia
June 1927

There were spies everywhere.

Reaching into her bucket, Grace tossed feed to her chickens. The key to fooling a spy was to stay busy...or at least, to keep up the *illusion* of being busy. Anyone, at any time, could be watching, hoping to catch her in a quiet moment. It could be one parent, or two...an older brother, or a younger one.

A woman's voice broke the quiet of the afternoon.

"Hello in the house!"

She raised her eyes for a moment, looking towards the driveway. Sometimes, spies disguised themselves as neighbors. This one was all short legs and hefty behind, with a hideous whiskered chin. Grace shuddered in disgust at the sight of Bessie Green, who lived just across the road. With a sigh, Grace muttered to herself...

If only she would stay at home where she belongs, the world would be a more peaceful place.

Her mother didn't seem to be bothered by unexpected company, and if she was, she never let on. Rachel Langdon, coming from within the house, called out to their neighbor. Slinging a cup towel over her shoulder, she gave a tired but polite smile.

"Hey there, Bessie. What brings you buy?"

"Afternoon, Rachel," said Bessie. "I thought I'd come by and sit a spell...and check on everyone while I was at it."

Grace pursed her lips in disgust. *My eye*, she thought.

Bessie seemed like a name that fit. Like any old cow, she had a tendency to wander where she didn't belong, usually making a lot of noise in the process. She had her favorite choices of subject...usually, who wasn't married yet and why, or who was guilty of breaking a commandment. Grace knew herself to be of particular interest. "Willful" was a word she'd often been called. To be truthful, she didn't mind being called that. As her favorite teacher had once told her...

Finding Grace

Never bend your head. Hold it high, and look the world straight in the face.

She knew she wasn't the bravest woman in the world. Her father's wrath could still shake her to the core, even at her womanly age of seventeen. She fought for herself as best she could…keeping her head held high, just as her teacher had told her to. It wasn't always easy. While she considered herself proud and strong, it was sometimes a hard cross to bear. Still, she did the best she could, often turning to those words in times of sadness or trouble.

The quote infused her with a sudden rush of bravery…a flash of courage to steal a few moments for herself. She knew it was a crime to delight in a bit of idleness. But she'd been praying for such an unguarded moment as this, and she could not wait any longer. Glancing to see if anyone was watching, she crept around to the back of the chicken coop. Carrying her empty bucket with her, she turned it over and put it down on the ground, using it as a seat. She looked around one more time, and reaching deep into her apron pocket, she took out a paper wrapped parcel. And eagerly she ripped into it.

Under the paper was a beautiful leather-bound edition of *Jane Eyre*. Underneath that, there was an envelope. For a moment she admired the soft brown leather of the book. Then she quickly put it aside and tore open the letter. She smiled with anticipation as she began to read...

Dear Sis,

Here's a brand new copy of your favorite book. I hope Uncle Nathan and Aunt Em got it into your hands without much trouble. I know they're pretty good about getting my mail to you, but you never can tell.

By the way, Alice says to tell you not to wear this copy out so fast, and she's smiling as she says it. Speaking of my dearest, I'm sorry to say there's nothing to report in the way of baby news. We keep hoping and praying, but it doesn't seem to do much good. Maybe if we stop thinking about it so much, it'll happen. That's the way it usually works, right? But you can't keep a woman from thinking about such things. And I'll be honest. I think about it every day myself. I suppose we'll just have to keep trying.

I really wish you could be here. Alice would be tickled pink to see you. But I know how the old man still feels about me, and you know how I feel about him. Maybe one of these days you'll find a good man and have a home of your own, and then we can figure out a way to visit. Until then, I guess these letters will have to do.

Take care of yourself and write back soon.

Your Loving Brother,
Jack

Just as she finished reading, she heard the irate voice of her mother.

"Gracie Ellen! What'd you do, fall asleep out there? Daylight is burning, girl!"

2

Finding Grace

She jumped at the sudden interruption. With a grumble, she quickly folded the letter, securing it in her pocket. Looking at the book, she found she couldn't bear to part with her new treasure. But she didn't want to leave it behind, sitting in the filth of a barnyard hiding place. So she tucked it in the band of her skirt, making sure the hem of her blouse kept it hidden. Hurrying to the house, she found her mother waiting at the back step...and scowling.

"Were you out there lazing around with another book?"

Grace could manage no answer. She could only blink, for to answer at all was either to lie or confess, and neither seemed a viable option. Silence was no great defense either, for there wasn't much that her mother didn't know or see.

"You were, weren't you?" She shook her head in dismay, her sigh a deep, frustrated sound. "You know, if you spent near as much time with your chores as you did with those old books, maybe we could make something useful out of you. Now get on in here and do what you should."

Grace nodded obediently as she hurried into the house. Looking up as she came in, she saw Mrs. Green sitting at the table, slicing apples. Knowing what was expected of her...visitors were to always be welcomed, and work was always to be found...she went over to sit in the opposite chair, politely greeting her neighbor.

"Hello Mrs. Green." Reaching for one of the apples, taking up a knife, she started to help with the cutting.

Mrs. Green didn't look up, but gave a cool and polite reply. "Hello Miss Gracie."

As she cut into the fruit, Grace stole a glance at her neighbor, catching the tiny smirk on the old woman's face. She seemed quite entertained, as though she'd caught a child stealing cookies from the jar.

Old Cow, she viciously thought. *I wonder how far her head would go back if I threw an apple at her noggin'?*

The idea was tempting. But she kept herself from it, knowing the consequences would not be kind.

The room was quiet for a moment...until the silence was broken by a metal pan falling heavy on the stove. That sound was followed by bowls dropping on the counter...and then the sound of Rachel's voice, usually calm, but now bitter and furious.

"That Miller woman. It's all her fault. She's the one who filled your head with foolishness." She leaned forward slightly, both hands resting on the edge of the counter. Then her tone suddenly softened, a quiver coming to her voice when she spoke. "Your brother would still be at home if it weren't for her."

Grace watched as her mother's lip trembled...and then, Rachel turned away, rushing out to the little storage room just off the kitchen. Mrs. Green was close on her heels. And Grace, now alone at the table, put down her cutting knife. She let out a troubled sigh.

The store room was a dusky little space, filled with mason jars, sacks of flour and corn meal, tins of sugar, and other such things. The room was quiet and dim...and Grace knew that in that room, her mother often wept in silence.

Finding Grace

While Mrs. Green tried to be of consolation out there, Grace stood up and went to the cupboard. Behind the glass was a small faded picture, tucked into a corner of the wooden pane. She took the picture out, looking down at it...and she smiled, as she always did when she saw her brother's face. They might have been twins, if not for the difference in their age and eye color. Hers were blue-grey, his were dark brown. But in every other way, they looked alike, right down to their dishwater blonde hair. But Jack was much more impressive, at least in her way of thinking. He certainly cut a handsome figure, especially in his Army uniform.

As she put the picture back in its place she sighed, missing him dreadfully. Six years had hardly dulled the sting of his loss. And she knew their mother suffered just as much, if not more.

Thinking of why he had gone...and the reasons were many...she knew that one of the causes, and probably the main one, was standing right out there in the storage room, crying. But Grace often wondered...

But wasn't her suffering her own doing?

She felt a strange sense of both pity and indifference for her mother, who suffered from Jack's loss, but had been one of its catalysts. Her utter lack of conviction, of courage...her inability to defend him, on all fronts, had driven him away. And she knew it to be true, whether or not she said so out loud.

Losing her oldest son had changed Rachel Langdon in many ways. She had once been so soft spoken, so meek. At times, she still had that way about her. But now, there was a hint of bitterness in her tone. In times past, she had rarely raised her voice. But now, at least with her younger children, she was often harsh.

Grace sighed deeply at the thought of it, thinking...

Mama, you've only got yourself to blame.

* * * * *

Later that evening, after all was done in the kitchen and everyone was spread out to talk and rest, she slipped away from the house. Following behind her was Pilot, her spotted bird dog. His was the only company she really needed. Bad a thought as it might have been...and her mother would have scolded her for it...she preferred his quiet company to that of any person. He was certainly a better soul than most.

In an alcove of trees was a resting spot. It was her own little private nook, with a hammock hanging between two trees. She knew that way out here, there was little chance she would be disturbed, and falling into the hammock, she let out a sigh of ease. Taking up her book, she read to her heart's content until the last of the daylight began to fade.

When the sky grew dark, she clutched her book to her chest, drumming her fingers absently as she looked up at the stars. The heavens were wide above...millions of little diamonds twinkling in a sea of dark blue. Those stars made her wonder at the enormity of the world...of life, and how very little of either she'd known. Her imagination was sparked. She thought of a certain passage from *Jane Eyre*. From a thousand readings of her most beloved book, the words were seemingly burned in her brain…

…Women are supposed to be very calm generally. But women feel just as men feel. They need exercise for their faculties, and a field for their efforts, just as their brothers do. They suffer from too rigid a restraint, too absolute a stagnation, precisely as men would suffer. It is narrow-minded in their more privileged fellow creatures to say that they ought to confine themselves to making puddings and knitting stockings, to playing on the piano and embroidering bags. It is thoughtless to condemn them, or laugh at them, if they seek to do more or learn more than custom had pronounced necessary for their sex…

She did not believe truer words had ever been written. In her heart, at least, they rang very true. And they gave her strength in moments like this, when she felt so isolated from her fellow human beings. She was certain that someday soon she would hear her calling and seek it out.

And she would find love…on her own terms.

Chapter 2
"An Old Friend"

Someone was staring at her.

As she stood in the back of the company store, Grace tried to ignore the feeling of someone's eyes upon her. She was used to being observed at home, but this felt different. She tried to look interested in the everyday objects around her, thinking it might distract her from the feeling of being watched.

There was lots of bric-a-brac in that part of the store...ceramic washbasins and pitchers, barrels of grooming brushes and small sets of furniture. Various pots and pans hung from hooks, along with several styles of mirrors. She came to stand in front of one, and very slowly, she raised her eyes. But it wasn't her reflection she looked at. In the mirror, she saw a man...of middling height and lean build...standing a short distance behind her. At that moment, he wasn't looking directly at her. But when she caught an upward flick of his eyes, she knew he was the one. A knot of uneasiness started to form in her stomach. She knew all of the people in this town, and he was not one of them. That was easy enough to see simply by the way he looked. The clothes he wore, while not exactly elegant, were certainly of better quality than what her neighbors had. He wore a buttoned shirt of soft blue color. His pants and shoes, both dark brown, looked new and tidy, and the rest of him seemed to match. He was clean shaven, with neatly clipped blond hair. The men she knew, with their unkempt ways and ragged clothes, looked nothing like him, and she couldn't help staring...until his eyes suddenly locked with hers.

She felt a burning of embarrassment in her cheeks, and she looked away. With her head down, she moved towards the front of the store, where her father and her brothers offered security and protection. But she wasn't quick enough. The man stepped in front of her, and she tried to make a quick retreat...until he said her name.

"Hi, Gracie."

She turned around, staring at him. She felt a strange shock at the bright green eyes that looked back at her. But what shocked her more was that he knew her by name. Her look was one of curiosity...and suspicion.

"How do you know who I am?"

A little grin rose up in the corner of his mouth. "You don't remember me at all, do you?"

Odd, how he spoke with a slight accent that was similar to hers, although it wasn't as thick. There was something stunning in his smile, and for a moment, it robbed her of speech. She managed to shake her head in response as he reached out to offer her his hand.

"Charlie," he said. When all she could manage was an odd look, he added, "Charlie Hillard?"

Her face blossomed with recognition at the name. She smiled slightly, stunned, putting her hand in his to accept his gentle shake of greeting. "Well my goodness," she said. "I'd have never guessed it was you."

He shrugged. "Time changes everything, I suppose."

She nodded, marveling at the sight of an old childhood friend. "How did you know who I was?"

He turned his eyes up a little, as if he were thinking for a moment. That crooked smile still shined on his face. "Well," he said, "Some faces you forget...some you always remember. And yours hasn't changed much."

She smiled. Her eyes were playful. "Is that good or bad?"

He chuckled. "It's good. Your face was one I always took a fancy to."

She blushed at the compliment, beaming, even as she felt a sense of foolishness coming over her. For a moment she cast her glance away, wondering where her good sense had gone. They had known each other as children, after all. He was just a few years older than she was. So why, then, did she feel so unsure of herself? She tried to speak, to break the awkward silence, though her voice was low and shy.

"You look so different, Charlie."

His reply was a proud smirk. "I know. People can't call me pudgy anymore. The Army took care of that."

Her eyes shined with interest. "You're a soldier?"

"I was," he replied, nodding his head. "But I served my two years, so now I can move on to other things."

"So what brings you back here? How come you ain't in Richmond?"

Charlie's face lost its cheerfulness...his mouth forming a grim line. "My father is sick. He won't live very long. Maybe a month, if that."

She felt a little pain in her heart. "Oh, Charlie, I'm sorry." She had a sudden urge to lay a hand on his arm to comfort him, but she dared not. He was an old friend, but he was also a man, and she wasn't sure how he would react to a gesture of comfort. So she refrained.

They had not seen each other since Charlie's mother had died, and his father had sent him away to live with his aunt and uncle. She only knew part of the story, and it had been a long time since she'd heard about it. But from what she could remember of Charlie's father, Walter Hillard was not the kindest of men. It was hard to be sure, because no one ever saw much of him. When he did make an appearance in town, his expression was often dark...his person usually smelling of whiskey. She had to wonder why Charlie would choose to return after all this time, especially for the sake of someone who had abandoned him. But she dared not ask him about it. It was not her place to inquire.

There was a moment of silence between them, as each tried to think of something to say to the other. It was he who spoke first.

"I should go. I have to get this medicine to my father right away." The smile returned to his face as he looked at her. "I hope I'll see you around now and then."

She nodded and smiled back, unable to get words out without making a fool of herself. What was it about that smile of his that stole her senses, making her feel so funny inside? She could only nod her head as he tipped his hat to her. Turning with a smooth stride, he walked away…and she felt a sudden sadness at seeing him go.

Her father called for her, and she hurried to follow him and her brothers out of the store. All the while, she felt as if she had wings on her feet. Her mind raced with excitement, her heart fluttering like mad. How long had it been since she'd known such a deep feeling of joy? She could not remember. She wasn't quite sure why the feeling held her so strongly. The encounter, after all, had not been anything so extraordinary or unusual, but it held her just the same, and she quickly ceased to question its existence. It would not last forever - common sense said that. But she intended to delight in it for as long as she could.

* * * * *

She felt the bowl of fruit slip from her fingers. It hit the floor…just as her father's hand struck the back of her head, hard.

"Watch your clumsy hands! Them peaches are for your Mama's dessert cobbler."

She nodded as she knelt down to clean up the mess. She knew she should have been paying more attention, the way she usually did. Most of the time, she was very vigilant in her actions, always watching to avoid mistakes. But since that morning at the store, her common sense seemed to have vanished. She couldn't stop thinking of Charlie, and she really didn't want to. He was on her mind all the rest of that day, and into the night as well.

Later as she lay in bed, she thought of how much he'd changed. As a boy, he'd been a bit heavy, and rather shy. He'd been a little clumsy too, but he had been so sweet. Now, she saw very little of that awkward boy.

It was his eyes that she remembered so well, and the way he looked at her…with that smile. No one had ever looked at her that way before. If she'd been a believer in magic, she would have sworn he'd cast a spell on her, to make her heart beat so and send her thoughts reeling this way.

Then a moment of sense returned to her, and she chastised herself for her wild thoughts and feelings.

Grace Langdon, you are the biggest fool in the world. If there were such a thing as magic, why would it be wasted on the likes of you?

She wanted to be logical…to think with her head, and not her heart. And yet, it was the voice of her heart that spoke louder. All through the night she slept fitfully, the two powers of hope and reason warring for control, until at last she came to a decision.

She needed to see him again. Judge his words, study his reactions. Only then could she begin to tame this struggle within her soul.

* * * * *

Out in the bean patch, she sat on an overturned bucket. Her back was bent low as she searched the leaves for the hateful little vegetables. Under the blazing sun, her bonnet didn't offer much protection. Sweat trickled into her eyes, and she ran her sleeve across her face. For a moment, she sat up to take a breath and to stretch her back, which ached miserably from the way she was forced to crouch down. She sighed, bending back to resume her work...and she jumped in sudden fright, startled by one of the barn cats as it pounced on a field mouse. Fury drove her up to her feet. Rocks flew from her hands.

"Devilish beast!" It would have served the wretched varmint right to have its head cracked by a stone...and it would have served her temper as well. She needed something to unleash her frustrations upon, especially of late.

It had been a week since she'd seen Charlie. After seeing him at the store, her hopes had been high that he might make an appearance, maybe drop in for supper one afternoon. But each day went by without an appearance or a word. Before long, the joy she'd felt at seeing him started to fade, and soon, her spirits were lower than they'd ever been before. Had he been a ghost, appearing for that brief time, only to vanish without a trace? She knew he was tending to his father, which of course that would be taking up all of his time. But still, she had a selfish wish that he would take time to come and visit. Heaven knew there was little chance of their meeting any other way.

It made her heart sink a little when she thought of it. Their school days were long gone, and they wouldn't see each other at church. The Langdons were Methodists, and the Hillards had always been devout Baptists, so their paths did not cross in religious circles. Trips into town were rare, so that was not much of an option. On top of everything else, Walter Hillard did not live nearby. As a child, Charlie had lived with his mother and father on a nearby farm - a beautiful place with a gleaming white house and a big red barn, set in a huge plot of rich bottom land. But after the death of his wife, Mr. Hillard had abandoned the old place and moved into a little shack high up in the hills. Now, that was where Charlie was, and for the time, it was where he would remain.

Thinking of all that, she began to wonder what had really happened to the Hillards all those years ago. She knew that Mrs. Hillard had died, but beyond that, the details were pretty vague. When it had happened, people had talked about it in whispers, so she hadn't caught much of it. She could remember her mother and someone else discussing it, but when Grace got too close, the talking ceased. Her curiosity had eventually faded, as the topic was eventually forgotten in time. But now it sprang back to life in her mind, and being a nearly full-grown woman, she felt she had the right to ask questions and hopefully have them answered.

As she set the table for supper that night, she looked at her mother, who was stirring a pot on the stove and humming to herself. Mrs. Langdon was in a good mood…a rare thing to see, but in this case, a welcome thing. That might have had something to do with the fact that, this being Sunday afternoon, the house was empty and quiet except for the two of them. Mr. Langdon had taken all the boys fishing, and Grace usually was happy to join them, but today she had preferred to spend her time alone. Now she was glad she had done so. To ease her way into the subject, she started with a bit of small talk.

"Mama, guess who I saw in town the other day?"

"Charlie Hillard," her mother answered

Grace's mouth formed a little circle of surprise.

"How did you know?"

Rachel looked slightly annoyed by the question. "For heaven's sake, Gracie. Everybody knows by now that he's back in town. And everyone knows about his father being so sick. Poor old Walter."

So there is sympathy there, Grace said to herself. Thinking of that, she wondered if this might be a good time to press for information. What would be the harm in doing so? Feeling a little bit braver now, she spoke.

"Mama," she began. "How did Charlie's mother die?"

Rachel turned down the fire on the stove. She opened the oven to take out a skillet of corn bread. She turned it over on a plate, and then turned it right side up. Grace waited with half-hearted patience, wondering if her mother had even heard the question. But she hadn't long to wait. As Rachel took a knife from the drawer and began to slice the corn bread, she began at last to speak.

"I don't know if you remember her much," she said. "You were hardly seven at the time. Charlie was about nine, and Katie was a few months away from having another child. Walter had just left the house one morning, when he heard her screaming. He ran back as fast as he could."

Grace's eyes grew wide with apprehension, and Rachel paused in her story. Wanting to know it all, Grace asked with some hesitation, "What happened?"

A sad, almost sickened look came to Rachel's face, but still she spoke.

"Katie had broken the kerosene lamp. It caught her skirts on fire and burned so fast, she didn't stand a chance. By the time Walter got to her, she was too far gone to save."

Grace sat with her hand covering her mouth, horrified. Now she wished she had never asked about it, as the image branded a scar on her imagination.

"Thank the good Lord Charlie was out playing, and didn't see it," said Rachel. "After they buried Katie, Walter went about out of his mind grieving. That's why he sent Charlie off to be with his kin. He just plum couldn't stand to raise the boy on his own."

As Grace took her hand away from her mouth, she gave an involuntary shudder.

"Poor Mr. Hillard," she said. "No wonder he is the way he is. And poor Charlie. I always knew he lost his mother, but I never imagined it was like that."

Rachel stood up suddenly, as if the topic was too upsetting to continue with. "It was a long time ago. But if you see Charlie, don't you go asking him about it. I don't imagine anything but the grave will ever set it right, for either of them."

Grace shook her head, her reply meek. "No, of course not."

What else was there to say? She felt a sudden need to busy herself, so she started pouring tea into the glasses. For the first time in a long time, she wished she didn't possess such a curious nature.

As she filled a glass, she heard the dogs barking from out in the front yard. Someone was coming up the drive. She felt her heart beat fast with excitement.

Charlie, she said to herself. Full of anticipation, trying to suppress a hopeful smile, she rushed to the front window...only to find disappointment. It wasn't Charlie at all, but just another neighbor stopping by. She let out a sad sigh, calling out to her mother.

"It's Mr. Wilson come to call."

"Come to call, and come to talk I reckon," replied Rachel.

Grace snorted in disgust. "He come to fill his belly full, that's what it is." She didn't bother trying to hide her sarcasm...which Rachel immediately chastised.

"Don't be ugly. It's our Christian duty to be neighborly."

Grace huffed. *Neighborly*, she thought. *That old fool is just looking for a handout wherever he can get it.*

She watched as he came near the porch, his bald little head reflecting the sun. *Troll*, she thought. And then she saw his attention was caught by something. A moment later she heard her father's voice calling.

"Hey Jim, where you been? Come on in the house and sit a spell."

A noisy camaraderie soon erupted. There was male laughter and bellowing, followed by heavy treading on the floor and the scraping of chairs as the men clamored for a place around the table. Mr. Wilson sat himself down in a chair and, without pause, snatched up the glass of tea before him. Tilting his head back, he downed the contents of his glass in several loud and slurping swallows. He wiped his mouth with the back of his hand, and letting out a loud breath of air, he looked up at Grace. With a smile, showing off what few teeth he had left, he pushed the glass at her in a silent demand for more. Silently she obliged...but the moment he turned away, her lip curled in disgust.

Nasty old coot, she thought. *Lord forgive me for saying it, but I hope he chokes.*

He said to everyone, "I reckon I just heard something mighty interesting."

Here he goes again, Grace thought, *Tellin' tales and rattling on and on*. She was still shaken by what she'd heard of Charlie's mother, and now this old fool was going to dominate the whole conversation at the table. It made her want to scream and curse.

They paused to say the blessing. And then it began. He didn't even take a moment for the Amen to sink in before he started talking.

"It seems old Walter Hillard kicked the bucket last night."

She gasped aloud at the news. But her little noise passed without notice...the conversation carrying on as if she were not present. Seeking comfort, she looked to her mother. But Rachel seemed more concerned with seeing that plates were full, although she did manage a few words.

"God rest his poor soul."

While she gave that small comment, Mr. Wilson continued with his own talk.

"Charlie is still up there at the house, from what I hear. His aunt and uncle came and had the body down to the undertaker. He'll be buried tomorrow morning, over at the Baptist Church."

As he spoke, he went on heaping food on his plate. Grace watched him in disgust as he stuffed food in his mouth, looking very much like a fat-cheeked squirrel. The way he was acting, he could have been talking about the weather instead of the death of a neighbor. She wanted to walk over and slap him across his ignorant head. With a last hope of respect for the dead, she looked to her father...who, with an unmoved expression, held out his glass to be refilled.

"I heard tell that old Robert Brown is a real fire and brimstone preacher. He shakes the rafters when he's up at the pulpit. I wonder if he'll give the eulogy."

Mr. Wilson pursed his lips. "I hope not. All them fire and brimstone types get up there and spew the gospel for two or three hours. Land sakes...the man in the casket is dead. Throw dirt on him and get it over with."

Grace's mouth opened slightly. Disgust was written in every line of her face. And the revulsion only deepened as her father, giving a careless shrug, gave a last comment on the subject.

"We'll be there to pay respects." He took a deep drink of his tea. And as he put it down, his face broke into a smile.

"You should have been down in the holler with us, Jim. I caught me a trout like you wouldn't believe."

They started rattling on about fish...talking loud, laughing and telling tales. And that was the end of their mourning over the Hillards.

She was suddenly ashamed of every adult at that table, especially her mother. Women were supposed to be comforting and healing, but Rachel seemed indifferent. Grace had the urge to jump up and curse every one of their wretched souls. She wanted to run out the door and ride all the way over to the Hillard place to tell Charlie how much she cared...how she wouldn't forget him as everyone else had.

But now was not the time. If she went running off like a mad fool, embarrassing her folks in front of company, there would surely be hell to pay. Not that she cared a bit for their opinions at that moment. It was the consequences that she dreaded - having to come home and be berated, maybe even switched, and then having to hear about it every day until the end of time. No, she would have to slip away quietly, after everyone was stuffed full with their supper and too sated to care what she did.

Chapter 3
"Broken"

After the meal was cleared away and the dishes were washed, she slipped quietly out the front door, moving towards the barn. Her mother was a good way off across the yard, tending her rose garden. From the back of the house, there was a hum of male voices and laughter, the sound of metal clanging against metal, and the occasional thud of something heavy hitting the ground. They were all wrapped up in a game of horseshoes, so even if the house had caught fire, chances were they wouldn't have noticed. Safe from fear of discovery, she got on her roan mare and rode off toward the house in the hills.

She had only been to the house once, and that had been by accident, when she and her brothers had been out hunting and came across it. They had thought it was haunted, and until recently, she had agreed with them. Who blamed them for thinking it, when the place sat so far back in the woods, and was kept in such a neglected state? She knew differently now, but the place still had a spookiness about it.

As she dismounted and tied her horse to a tree, she stood rooted to one spot, looking at the little house and wondering if she should just turn around and go home. The place reminded her of Ferndean Manor...the hidden home of Mr. Rochester in his reclusive state. Standing there, she half expected to see a man emerge from within, dark and brooding, to stand broken and silent in the yard. But there was no one. How could she be sure Charlie was even here? There was only one way to know. Taking a deep breath, she walked up to the front door, and after a moment of hesitation, she lifted her hand and knocked.

No one answered. She waited, and tried again, but still nothing. If this had been the door of another house, she might have given up and left. But there was something about this place that held her in its grip. She had been nervous before, but now that she was here, curiosity worked its way through her. She looked around for a moment. Slowly she took to walking along the little front porch, looking in one window and then another. As she looked through one of the glass panes, she suddenly noticed a movement from within. Wiping the window and cupping her hands around her eyes to block the sunlight, she looked again.

There was Charlie, sitting in a chair at a little table. Quickly she went to the door to knock again, calling out.

"Charlie, it's Grace."

She waited. When still he did not answer or open the door, she took hold of the handle and, slowly, opened it herself. The table sat just inside the room, and sitting silently at it was Charlie. He didn't even turn to look at her when she came in, nor even as she slowly approached him. When she came close to the table, she noticed the jug of whiskey sitting in front of him. Seeing it, she felt a quake of fear run over her nerves. Still, she spoke to him with what courage she could find.

"Charlie?" she said, hoping he would at least look at her. Then again, maybe it was better if he didn't. But maybe he would at least talk to her. Her eyes moved from him to the jug, and then to the half-empty mason jar he held in his hand. She did not have to ask what the clear liquid in that jar was. It suddenly bothered her that he would be drinking, even under these circumstances, and she sighed heavily.

"What are you doing, Charlie?"

His speech was loud, bold…a little slurred from the drink. "What does it look like I'm doing? I'm working up the courage for the funeral tomorrow. I saw one parent buried when I was nine. Now that I'm ten years older, I get to see the other one buried. That's logic, ain't it?"

His brash tone and cold words stung. But the sting was brief, for she was sure it was the drink that was talking more than he was. Someone had to do something for him, and she felt compelled to be the one. She reached out to take the glass from his hand. But he jerked it away from her reach.

"Don't touch that!" He held the glass close to himself, and taking the jug from the table, he placed it safely and securely at his feet. "My father drank himself into the grave. And you know what they say about fathers and sons."

He was scaring her now, the way he was talking. But with her fear, there suddenly came a burst of frustration and anger at him. Men were supposed to be pillars of strength, but when it came right down to it, they were just little boys who had to be told what to do. Or they had to find their courage in a bottle, of all places. It frustrated her to no end. It also bolstered her nerves, and in a swift move, she snatched the jar away from him, dodging his attempts to snatch it back. Going to the front door, opening it, she pitched the glass out in the front yard.

Behind her at the table, Charlie rose unsteadily to his feet.

"Who the hell do you think you are? Barging in here and trying to tell me what to do. I'm a grown man. I don't need no little girl like you telling me how to behave." He started to stumble toward her. "I'm going to throw you out of this house right now."

She took a step back from his approach, suddenly afraid of what he might do.

What had she gotten herself into? She prepared herself to run. But just as he neared her, he suddenly stumbled in his footing. He fell to the ground with a flailing of limbs, landing face down on the floor, and instinctively she jumped out of the way. He lay unmoving where he fell, and for several long moments she just stood there, looking down at him.

It cut her heart to the quick to see him there, in a state of helplessness and stupor. Suddenly she didn't care how angry he got, or even if he cursed and shouted at her. She wasn't going to leave him like this. She went to him and knelt on the floor beside him. She tried to help him up, but he pushed her hands away, as she had thought he would. But there was no anger in him now. She saw only shame and embarrassment, and it showed in his voice when he spoke to her.

"I can get up by myself," he said, his voice low. He managed to rise, but didn't get to his feet. He sat on the floor, hanging his head and muttering to her. "He didn't even know who I was. He forgot about me, just like he did before." He looked at her for the first time, and his eyes were hollow and sunk.

It broke her heart to look at him, but she managed to hold back her tears. He didn't need her sorrow, when he was so deeply buried in his own. Her attention was all she could give.

"In almost ten years," he said bitterly, "No letters. No visits. Nothing." His voice shook, with pain and anger all at once. "But I got through everything just fine without him. Aunt Mary and Uncle Robert took me in and raised me. Do you know how hard they worked to bring me up right? When I got into trouble at school, Uncle Robert would take me home and put the fear of God in me…to teach me to do right. My father never did that. But I never needed him anyway. I finished school without his help. I served my two years in the military just like every good man. I ran a whole company of men on my own. I didn't need him for any of that, did I?"

She shook her head, unable to speak for the lump in her throat.

"I hope he burns in hell," he said.

She saw a tear roll down his cheek. Then, before she had time to react, he put his arms around her and buried his head in her shoulder. He began to cry like a little boy lost, and she didn't know what to do. All she could do was sit there, holding him gently in her arms.

* * * * *

His tears had ceased. But now, his head was a heavy weight on her shoulder. She tried to stir him, but he only mumbled incoherently. He was still conscious…but she was sure that wouldn't last for much longer. She took his arm, draping it around her shoulders, and after much coaxing on her part, she managed to get them both to their feet.

It's like dragging the dead weight of a carcass, she thought, as she moved with him to the little bed in the other room. Once she had him on the bed and let go, he fell into a heavy heap, out cold. She tended to him as she would tend a child, adjusting his head on the pillow, pulling the blanket over him. And then, for quite some time, she just sat on the edge of the bed, looking at him.

Her mind was a jumble of confusion. He had spoken of his father with such bitterness - almost with pure hatred. Why, then, had he come back to take care of him? More confusing still were her feelings for him. It wasn't the same as when they were kids, when he'd almost seemed like one of her brothers. It would be silly to think of him that way now. Just being near him, even when he was in this state of mind, she felt something more. Was it love? She shook her head in denial at that notion. Love seemed too strong a description, for they hardly knew each other anymore. And yet, she cared for him deeply. Something within her wanted to care for him, to give him the affection he needed so much.

But who was she to be his savior? She looked down at his handsome face, soft and peaceful in repose. There were probably other girls, other women, who cared for him too. She would be a fool to think he didn't have someone out there waiting for him. If there was a woman in his life, she'd likely had many years to know him and grow close to him. She had known this man less than two days. She sighed, feeling a pit of sadness opening in her stomach.

A knock came at the door, startling her out of her daydream, and she hurried to the door to answer it. At the threshold were a man and a woman, both of middle age. She didn't recognize them, and they didn't recognize her, from the stunned looks on their faces.

"I'm Robert Brown," the gentleman said. "This here's my wife Mary. We're looking for our nephew, Charles. We left him here a little while ago so we could see to his Daddy."

Grace's expression brightened and she smiled slightly. "Oh, the Aunt Mary and Uncle Robert that Charlie was talking about. I'm mighty glad you've come. Come in, will you?" She stepped back and let them pass into the dimly lit house. "I'm an old friend of his. I'm Grace Langdon. I just came up here to give condolences." She led them into the little room where Charlie slept. "I found him in a real sorry state. He's sleeping it off now, thank goodness."

Mary sat on the bed beside him, reaching over to feel his forehead.

"Poor boy," she said. "I just hope he's in decent shape for the service tomorrow morning."

Robert scoffed, and as Grace looked at him, she saw him shaking his head.

"After all the trouble we've gone through for that boy…all the Sunday learnin' we've tried to put in him, and he's just like his Daddy. A worthless drunk."

Unsure of what to say, Grace simply asked the first question that came to mind.

"Are you going to stay here with him?"

Robert shook his head, his tone vehement.

"No, no. We're taking him out of this den of evil. We're staying over at the boarding house until after the service. And it's better for him if we just get him on out of this place."

She didn't have to ask why. One could almost feel the haunting in the house. It had spooked her from the first, and now that the sun was sinking quickly, the spookiness was even stronger. She looked out the window at the fading of the day, and suddenly it occurred to her that she ought to be getting on her way quickly. She could do that now, and feel secure, knowing that Charlie would be taken care of.

"I'd best be on my way home," she said. "Thanks for tending to him. God knows, he'll need it. We'll all be praying for him."

Robert just nodded his head. Mary was pulling Charlie to a sitting position, and as Robert went to assist her, Grace quietly made her way out the door. She crossed the yard to her horse…and hoped that with his aunt and uncle caring for him, Charlie would be just fine.

Now she just had to worry about herself.

It would be dark by the time she got home. Chances were pretty good that her Mama and Daddy would be waiting up for her, probably with a switch in hand. They wouldn't have taken kindly to one of their youngsters running off and not saying where they went, especially when they came home so late.

But what of it? she thought.

She'd been in trouble before. Not often, but enough to know what came with being in trouble. And right then, she didn't care what they did to her. She would take it as it came, no matter what, for it would be a small price to pay for what she'd done. Charlie had needed her, and that was more important than anything.

As she rode up to the house, she noticed quickly that only one light was burning. The lamp on the porch was the only one lit, and that seemed strange to her. If they were waiting to punish her, there would be lights burning bright in the living room, for that was where they would be sitting up. Had they actually gone to bed, and left the light burning for her? No, that seemed too far-fetched. It would be too kind, at least where she was concerned. Then she heard a familiar sound far off in the distance…the sound of coon hounds bawling, and she realized with relief that the men and boys were off on a hunt. She breathed a sigh of relief at her good luck, and quickly she put her horse in the stall and made her way to the house.

As she got near the porch, she saw in the dim light that her mother was sitting in the rocking chair. Rachel looked at her as she came near.

"You went up to see Charlie, didn't you?"

Grace lowered her head, her voice low. "Yes."

"He was in a bad way, wasn't he?" said Rachel.

Grace nodded. "His aunt and uncle came to look after him. But I don't know if that'll be enough."

Rachel sighed. "With the Lord's guidance, he'll be just fine."

Grace wanted to believe that was true. But after what she'd seen and heard, she wasn't so sure. Still, miracles happened every day, didn't they? Someone above had certainly been watching out for her this night, and before she went to sleep, she remembered to send up a prayer of thanks…and a prayer of peace for Charlie's broken soul.

* * * * *

There was something especially morbid about Walter Hillard's funeral, or so it seemed to Grace. All of these people, who had hardly seen or spoken to the man in ten years, were suddenly mourning his death as if he were one of their own. It made her angry just thinking about it, and she had to bite her tongue hard to keep from cursing at every person around her. Only one person had the right to mourn here… and that person was Charlie.

Finding Grace

How different he seemed this morning. Gone was the raging and disheveled thing of yesterday. And gone, too, was the broken little boy who had cried on her shoulder. What a puzzlement he was. She looked at him, standing silent and stoic by the grave. Even from the distance where she stood, she could see no tears in his eyes, no pained expression, no gestures of any kind.

How he must be holding it all inside, she thought sadly.

His lips did not move to "In the Sweet By and By," as the crowd was singing all around them. His mouth was set in a grim line, and she wanted so badly to go and stand at his side. For a sudden impulsive moment, she started to do just that. But then she held back. She would not make fools of the both of them. There was a time and a place for boldness, and this was not it.

Finally the service ended, and the crowd began to thin out. One by one they turned and walked away - her family included, and Charlie was left to stand alone. She knew, because she turned around to look at him. It was then that she broke from the pack, not caring what anyone thought, and she walked over to stand near him. She wanted to say something profound... something healing and comforting. But her tongue seemed tied in knots, and all she could do was stand there. It made her feel like a useless fool, and she turned to make a retreat.

At the same moment, he turned to her.

"Thank you for being there last night." There was a small pause, as if he didn't know what to say next, and he seemed flushed with shame. "I must have looked like such a fool."

She was tense...her nerves quite on edge. It caused a reply to bubble forth that she had not wanted to say out loud... but it escaped her lips before she could quite catch it.

"You did," she said. As soon as she said it, she cursed herself for her stupidity. "I'm sorry, Charlie. I didn't mean that."

But he just chuckled slightly. "It's all right," he said. "After all the two-faced talk I've heard today, I could use a bit of honesty." As the smile faded from his face, he sighed deeply, still looking at the grave in front of him. "I don't know why I ever came back here," he said. "I should have known things between me and him would never change."

"You had a right to hope," she declared. "It's only natural."

He gave a snort and smiled again, but bitterly this time, and he looked up at the sky, his eyes dancing coldly. "Maybe you're right," he said. "Or maybe I really am a fool." He turned sharply and walked away. His Aunt and Uncle stood by their car, waiting for him, and he went to them without a backward glance.

* * * * *

She felt miserable. The sway of the buggy, jostling everyone back and forth, only made her more so. The progress home was always slow. Her father never rushed the horse, for anyone or anything. Under normal circumstances, the trip wouldn't have bothered her. But today, she just wanted to jump out of the buggy and run home. She didn't feel like crying, which never did any good. She just wanted to be alone, to think and breathe. She would have done anything to find solitude, especially at that moment, when her little brother was trying to hang over the back of the buggy. Their mother gripped Robert by the shirt collar and forced him into his seat, scolding him.

"We just come from a funeral, boy. Sit down there and have a lick of respect." To emphasize her point she whacked him on the back of the head, and he started to cry.

The sound grated on Grace's nerves like nails on a chalk board. If she had been a little more daring, she might have reached over and slapped him herself.

Up in the driver's seat, John turned his head and glared, his voice calm but deadly serious.

"Boy, you better quit that sissy crying or I'll give you something to cry about."

Suddenly, Grace's loathing shifted from her brother to her father. John Langdon didn't give second warnings, and when he said quit crying he meant it. The next thing to come from him would be a vicious switching, sure to silence anyone into submission. And the thought of it made her furious.

Robert may have been a terror at times, but he was just being a boy. Why did the man have to always be a tyrant?

When they got home, Rachel had barely stepped down from the buggy when she started barking out orders.

"I've got to get supper started," she declared. Her eye caught sight of fourteen-year old Thomas. "Get on down to the barn and do the milking." Then she turned to her daughter, who had barely made it half way across the yard. "Gracie, don't forget to feed the chickens."

Grace felt a fire of rage shoot up her back. It radiated through her arms, traveling down to her fingers, which she clenched into tight fists. It burned its way into the muscles of her face as well, and she clenched her jaw tightly, fighting back the urge to scream. How long had she been doing that same stupid chore, along with all the others? Since the age of six, if she remembered right. Had she ever not fed those devilish birds? Why did she have to be reminded, every day, of every month, of every year? It was enough to drive her out of her mind.

Good God, why can't they all just disappear? For just a few blessed hours, at least.

Inside the coop, she grumbled to herself as she reached for the bucket. She filled it with seed and lugged it outside, and the chickens came flocking around her feet in anticipation. When she had scattered it all, she did what she had done so many times before. Turning her bucket upside down, she sat on it and watched the birds as they clucked and pecked around her. Sitting there, it was quiet for the moment. And because she was alone, if only briefly, she dropped her head in her hands and rested.

She thought of Jack at that moment. *Lucky devil.* He was the manager of a railroad station, where he worked five days a week. He was home by six each night, and he even got to go out and have fun sometimes on the weekend. In his letters, he told her how he and Alice liked to take in baseball games and go to movies. On

Sunday afternoons, they liked to play golf or tennis. She knew nothing of tennis or golf, but she did know one thing. The two of them enjoyed their lives, and they always took time out for fun. Much as she loved her brother, she couldn't help but be jealous of him when she thought of his life. How she envied his freedom...the freedom to love and live, just the way he pleased.

"Gracie?" called a voice.

It was her father's voice, deep and commanding, and it was enough to make her jump up in fright and knock the bucket over. She stammered for an excuse, but to her surprise, her father held up his hand to silence her. His voice was calm and soothing. A rare thing, but genuinely welcome when the occasion rose, and after the day she'd had, it seemed a true blessing indeed.

"Supper's almost ready," he said. "You'd better get on in the house and help your Mama."

She nodded obediently, and he walked away. She reached down and picked up the bucket, and as she did, she wondered at the fickle nature of life and fate. One minute cruel, the next minute kind. A person could only hope there would be more of one than the other.

* * * * *

She fell back into her usual routine quite naturally. If there was one small consolation in working, it was that it helped time to pass, and it kept the mind occupied...most of the time.

She still thought about Charlie and his troubles, and quite often she wondered what he was going to do now that his father was gone. There wasn't anything to keep him here. He'd most likely go back home, and if he did, she didn't know what she would do with herself. Not that he was a great part of her life. But his being back had given her a purpose. In a strange way, and despite the sad circumstances, he had given her something to look forward to. Life would seem so empty without him, more so than it was already.

It had been just over a week since the funeral, and as she'd expected, there was little mention at all of the Hillards, living or dead. She did hear one tiny bit of news. Walter Hillard had actually left a will. But who knew what was in it? They weren't likely to know, unless by some chance they ran into Charlie, but that wasn't likely, seeing as how they almost never went into town. Even that old blabbermouth, Jim Wilson, wouldn't know something as secret as the contents of a will. And so, she seemed resigned to her fate...to languish in this lonely life, and no matter how many times she read her favorite books and sought comfort from them, they just didn't seem to help anymore.

It was late Saturday afternoon. The boys were out hunting. Mrs. Langdon was in the garden, and Mr. Langdon was away from home, seeing a friend. As for Grace, she went on a fishing trip of her own. It was something, other than her books, that gave her peace of mind. And at least she had Pilot. If she didn't have a good human companion, at least she had a canine friend to rely on...and he was quiet, which she was grateful for. After a day dealing with rowdy brothers, a calm companion was quite welcome.

They wandered down to the riverbank, where their little rowboat was tied. Pilot didn't have to be encouraged to get in. He bounded from the bank right into the bottom of the boat, sat down, and waited patiently as his mistress got in and readied the paddles. Grace smiled as she looked at him. He couldn't wait until they got into the deep water where the ducks gathered, and she knew that as soon as they rowed out and dropped anchor, he would not be able to resist. And sure enough, that's what he did, jumping over the side and into the water with a yelp and a splash. She just let him go. When he got tired, he would be back. She picked up her pole, cast her line, and waited for a bite. All was quiet and serene, except for the sound of honking ducks and the water that her dog was paddling. For the first time in a long while, she felt quite content in body and mind.

Until she heard a voice, calling from across the way.

She rolled her eyes skyward, hoping to heaven that whoever it was would just go away. But after a moment of silence, the voice called out again. It was a male voice, probably one of her brothers. She couldn't be absolutely sure until she looked...and she didn't want to look.

"Hello out there!" the voice called.

She tried to ignore it. But her curiosity had a way of getting the better of her, and reluctantly, she turned to look. Her eyes widened with surprise, pleasantly so, when she saw that it was Charlie who was calling her. Like a blindsided fool, she lifted her hand and waved slightly. For a moment she just sat there, staring. Then, he called out to her again, his voice playful.

"What? Do you want me to swim over to you?"

For a moment she felt quite the fool. But she was never one to stay that course for long, and she smiled a little to herself as she replied, "What's good for my dog is good for me."

She reeled in her line quickly, put her pole down in the bottom of the boat, and rowed over to him. Pilot, seeing the boat move, paddled not far behind it. When they got closer, she saw that Charlie was carrying a fishing pole himself, and a little tremor of anticipation traveled down her spine. Before she could say anything, he spoke first.

"I was just at your house looking for you. Your Mama told me you were fishing down here, so I thought I'd join you.

She took his fishing rod as he handed it to her, and carefully he stepped into the boat. Pilot, who was never one to be left behind, followed right after, sitting himself down at Grace's knee.

They rowed back out, and when the dog jumped back into the water after the ducks, Grace was suddenly nervous at the realization that she and Charlie were quite alone. It didn't matter that they had spent many hours by themselves before, for that had been as children. Now that they were grown, the rules of the game had changed considerably, and she wasn't at all sure how to play. All she could think to do was ask a few questions. It seemed the most logical way to ease the tension.

"How've you been?" she asked. It seemed like such a dumb question, but she couldn't think of anything else to say.

He shrugged. "All right, I guess, all things considered. Did you hear he left me the old place? All the bottom land?"

"Really?" she asked. She smiled. "That's sure good to hear." She sobered a little, as she thought sadly of the father and son relationship that was so badly broken. "So then, maybe he didn't forget about you after all."

Charlie was silent. The brightness was gone from his face, the way it always was when they talked about his father. She didn't want to see that gloom every time they were together. There were happier things to talk about.

"So you're staying here for a while, are you?"

"I am," he replied, the shadows passing away. He seemed to brighten once again.

She smiled happily, her face warming. "I'm glad." To that, he shook his head in agreement.

"Me, too." Then he looked at her, and flashing that smooth smile of his…the one that sent a charge up her spine…he inclined his head slightly towards her, his voice soft.

"Besides. I wouldn't want to leave good company."

She blushed deeper, flattered in the notion that he was talking about her. She didn't want to be trapped into the honey of his words, but somehow, she just couldn't help herself. His voice and words had a power she didn't understand. Or maybe, she just didn't want to.

The afternoon passed quickly. They talked of old memories, of his time in the service. He even offered to teach her how to drive. She'd never ridden in a motor vehicle before, and he laughed as he told her how nice it was to drive something without looking at the back end of a horse. They laughed often, and the time flew by as they talked of many things and went on catching fish. It seemed too soon that they had called it a day and were headed back to the house.

"You're quite a fisherwoman," he said, pointing to the large trio of catfish she held at her side. "You must have learned that from Jack. I remember how he used to take us fishing all the time."

Her expression sobered at the mention of her brother, and it didn't go unnoticed.

"I heard what happened, why he left and all," he said. "Aunt Mary and your Mama kept in touch through the years." He paused, and said gently, "You still miss him a lot, don't you?"

She could have given in to gloom. It was tempting, the notion of pouring her heart out to him…to let him be a hero, as men liked to be. How wonderful it would have been to hear soft, soothing words of comfort. That kind of attention would have been so heavenly. But she didn't want to linger in sadness. There had been too much of that lately. So she kept herself together, replying with a cool expression and a slight smile as she thought of her beloved brother.

"I miss him every day," she said. "But he's married now, and he's happy. That's what really matters."

He nodded his head. She saw it from the corner of her eye, and in that small gesture, they both sensed that a change of subject was due. It was he who initiated it, with a question.

"So how come you're not married yet? You're seventeen. A lot of girls your age are old married women, with at least two or three kids."

She smiled, and with a little laugh, she sighed. "Mama and Daddy wonder the same thing. So do all those old pea hens down at church. They'd have me marry old man Wilson if it meant I'd have a house full of babies. Can you imagine me with him?" She gave a shudder, to which he chuckled. Then he looked at her curiously.

"So you won't ever get married then?"

"Oh I didn't say that," she replied quickly. "But I want something special." She thought of the guide to her life, the book she loved most.

"Have you ever read Jane Eyre?" she asked.

He shrugged and shook his head.

"It's the most romantic story in the world," she said. "Jane is a poor, plain little woman. A governess, with no money and no family that wants her. She works for a dark, mysterious man, Mr. Rochester. He has a big secret he's keeping, but I won' tell you what it is, in case you ever read the book. To make a long story short, they fall madly in love. There are problems along the way of course, but in the end, they live happily ever after. And that is what I want."

He chuckled at her story. "You do know it's just a book, don't you? In real life, nothing ever ends with a fantastic happily ever after."

She shrugged. "Maybe not. But it's the notion of finding your perfect mate that just makes my heart skip a beat. People can love like that, if they want to. Just look at Jack and Alice, how happy they are together. That's what I want. I want someone who will love me with their whole heart and soul. When I fall in love, I'll give everything I've got, and maybe more. So why shouldn't the man I marry do the same for me?"

She waited for a wonderful response, something that would send her senses reeling. She wanted to hear him tell her what a romantic she was. She longed to hear great warmth in his tone…admiration for her passionate nature.

Instead, he snorted. He scoffed, letting out a great laugh, as if to say how stupid he thought she was. Then he shook his head at her, his smile and words both belittling her.

"You spend too much time reading stories."

His laughter stung…very deeply. She didn't know why it should bother her, but it did. She examined him closely, looking for some sign of tenderness or maybe even regret. But all she saw was him grinning, shaking his head. *Maybe he doesn't realize he just hurt my feelings*, she thought. She waited a moment, and at last he seemed to realize she was staring at him. His expression was almost blank, clueless as he was.

"What?"

She shook her head. "Nothing," she replied.

But it *was* something. A strange, sinking feeling is what it was. How it hurt to be laughed at, when she had opened up a little part of her soul. She wanted to ignore the hurt that had begun inside. She wanted to be unmoved by his ridicule, but it made her eyes sting with tears. She turned her head away, clenched her jaw, and took a deep, calming breath. The tremor of sorrow passed...and a feeling of frustration took its place. His question disrupted her thoughts.

"Why are you so quiet all of a sudden?"

Obviously, laughing at the wrong moment was something he did not understand. *Just like a man,* she thought, *To be so thoughtless.* She wanted to say so to his face, but she forced the words back. She gave him a quiet reply. "Sometimes there's just nothing to say."

He shrugged, and in that little gesture she saw no caring, no remorse that he had hurt her feelings. He was simply moving on to the next subject, no questions to be asked. She wanted to tell him how he had just broken the magic spell for her, but he spoke before she could think of how to say it.

"Maybe I can think of something to talk about," he said. He stopped in his tracks to look at her, his face becoming more serious. "What would you say if I asked you to marry me?"

Shock overwhelmed her. His question was so unexpected, to say the least. A marriage proposal? She was certain he was only teasing. He had to be. It was all a joke, meant to tease her. Nervously, she started to chuckle. It was her hope that he might laugh a little too, and then she would know he was only being silly. But he did not laugh. He wore a slight smile, but it was a half-hearted kind of gesture, as if he was bothered by her amusement.

"Did I say something funny?" he asked.

At his tone, she felt a twinge of anxiety, and perhaps a touch of fear. There was something unsettling in the way he spoke. But she brushed off that feeling of foreboding, and tried to draw out the humor in him. "You always were a fooler," she said, putting on a smile.

They were now within distance of the house. She hoped to get to the security of her family, before he said anything else about marrying her. Even if it was a joke, it made her uncomfortable. The way he'd looked at her, and the way he'd not laughed along with her, made her feel strangely tense. She was thankful when one of her brothers came walking hurrying towards them. For once, a brother was a very welcome distraction.

"About dadgum time you two got back," Matthew said. "Mama and Daddy were about to send the hounds to sniff you out. They want you to stay for supper, Charlie." The two of them walked away, leaving her a few steps behind. And she had to say she was happy to have the moment to herself.

The idea of marrying Charlie made her very uncomfortable. Yes, he was her friend. And yes, she had wanted him at their supper table. But now, there would a sense of tension in the room, and she wished there could be some way to avoid it.

She looked at Charlie and Matthew, walking in front of her, and it angered her to think of her folks' sudden generosity. Not so long ago, Charlie had hardly been spoken of. Now they were inviting him to supper like he was one of the family? Something just didn't seem right.

With a shake of her head, she forced away her suspicions. Folks were always coming and going at the house. Now that Charlie was back in town, he was a neighbor, and wasn't it the right thing to do, inviting neighbors over to eat sometimes? As for the whole nonsense of she and Charlie getting married, she had to laugh at herself for getting so carried away. He'd always been a bit silly as a boy.

In all likelihood, this was just another one of those kinds of times.

It *had* to be one of those times.

* * * * *

The men were talking of fish. What else would the subject be, when they had it on their plates? Usually, fried catfish was one of her favorite foods. But not tonight. She found she had no appetite. And the reason for her loss of hunger was sitting right across from her.

She watched Charlie as he ate his supper, and she wondered if he knew how awful he looked. He talked with his mouth wide open, letting everyone see the food he'd just chewed up. And he was loud…obnoxiously so, shouting and carrying on just like her father and her brothers. They were all trying to talk over each other as they told their fishing stories. It was enough to make her sick. He dressed well, and his intelligence seemed to show in the way he spoke. Why, then, were his manners so atrocious? She didn't know why she felt such disillusionment with him, and she felt guilty for having such shallow feelings. But she couldn't help it. Her only hope now was to get through supper, and then, maybe she could make up some decent excuse to escape to an early bed.

Her father tapped the tabletop with his hand, commanding attention, but Grace only half-listened. What he said was usually directed at the boys, so it wasn't of much concern to her. She leaned her head in her hand, looking away as her father spoke.

"Yesterday morning, I ran into Charlie here while I was on my way to work. He had something real important to ask me. Now, he has something he'd like to ask our little Gracie."

She whipped her head around and a bolt of panic shot up her spine. It seemed in slow motion that she watched Charlie stand up, wiping his mouth with a cloth. She knew what he was going to say. She knew it as if she was saying the words herself, but she prayed it not to be so. She pleaded for help from heaven for it.

Dear Lord, please don't let him say what I think he'll say…Please Lord, get me out of this.

"I've been gone a long time," he said. "But you sure can't forget where you come from, or the people you left behind." He came walking around the table, and in a moment he stood at her side. Slowly he reached out to take her hand. She wanted to jerk her hand away, so unnerving was his touch. She wanted to turn and run away. But she was rooted where she stood, unable to escape, trapped like a rabbit in a snare…and then the moment was upon her.

Finding Grace

"Grace Langdon, will you be my wife?"

For the first time in her life, she thought she might faint. She wanted to. *If I could go out of life now, without too sharp a pang, it would be good for me,* she quoted silently. But there was no such mercy, and she felt every eye in the room on her, waiting for her answer. She looked at them, then at him. She knew just what they expected. She knew what Charlie expected. But the answer she gave was her own, bubbling up from somewhere within, almost involuntarily.

"No," she said, shaking her head. "I can't."

There was a collective gasp...And then the whole room became silent as the grave.

Chapter 4
"Friends and Enemies"

What happened next? She hardly knew, for it was a quick blur. She only knew that in a flash, Charlie had whisked her outside, away from her shocked and wide-eyed family. When he looked at her, his expression was serious, with no hint of softness. His eyes were cold...his tone low, but sharp.

"You're fooling with me, aren't you?"

She looked at him, shocked by the sound of his voice. Something inside of her hoped he was only teasing. But a little warning voice whispered that this was no game. Still, she tried to keep her own voice light and pleasant, hoping he would soften his manner. Her words trembled with a nervous attempt at levity.

"You're the one who's fooling, ain't you?"

She laughed again, but he said nothing. And the longer she waited for him to reply, the more she realized he was quite serious. Her mouth turned down in a fretful line.

"Charlie, I can't marry you. It's just about the silliest idea I ever did hear of. It's crazy."

His reply was firm. "What's so crazy about it?"

She didn't know how to answer. Just a little while ago, they'd been sharing a lovely afternoon. But now, he was starting to make her nervous. His green eyes, which had so moved her, now shined with repressed anger. It was frightening to see. But she spoke as bravely as she could.

"Charlie, we can't get married! We hardly know each other."

His brow furrowed. "We've known each other all our lives, Gracie Langdon. How much more familiar do we need to be?"

She tilted her head back, as if pleading to heaven for help. Her voice had a tone of frustration in it, and when she looked at him, her eyes pleaded for his understanding.

"Charlie, we were kids together. You've been gone all this time, and now you come back and just expect to marry me at the drop of a hat?"

He looked at her, his expression growing darker...and she realized that he meant just that. He wanted to be married and he didn't want to wait. She slowly shook her head in denial.

"Charlie, I don't want to get married," she answered, more forcefully now. "I'm not ready."

His response was bitter. "Not ready to marry me, is that what you're saying?"

She shook her head. "I'm not ready to marry anyone." She sighed, feeling the need to heal where she had wounded him. "It's not that I don't care about you. I *do* care, a lot. I always have. But I don't love you, Charlie. Not the way two people should love each other, especially when they talk about getting married."

He took to pacing back and forth. "You think I don't love you?" he asked.

With a groan of frustration, she pressed her hands to her face. "Charlie, how can you say you love me? Love takes time to blossom. We knew each other a long time ago, but we're grown up now. We ain't the same people we used to be. If you think on it, you and me are strangers in most ways."

He took a sudden step forward, gripping her arm.

"I'm not good enough for you. That's what you're thinking, isn't it? You're just like your brother. Too good for anybody who came up with you. I've heard what they say about you...that you turn away every man that comes to call. What makes you so high and mighty?"

His words cut her deeply. But they also made her temper rise. He reminded her of so many other men in her life...how they had tried to use fear and power to intimidate and control her. It was infuriating to think he was trying to do the very same thing. She yanked her arm from his hold.

"What is wrong with you?" she demanded. "One minute you're as sweet as pie. The next minute, you're as mean as a snake. It makes me wonder who the *real* Charlie Hillard is."

He sneered. "I could say the same thing, Grace Langdon. You treat me good one minute, and the next thing you know, you're throwing a marriage proposal back in my face, looking at me like I was some kind of toad. All this time I thought you really cared about me. Turns out, you're just like everybody else. Uncle Robert was right...all of you women are liars."

"I never lied about anything!"

His lip curled. "You're a two-faced bitch, Grace Langdon."

If she'd had a good stick at hand, she would have walloped him senseless. Instead, she shoved him backwards as hard as she could.

"Charlie Hillard, you ain't worth the gunpowder it would take to shoot you! Now get off of my porch and out of my sight!"

He snorted. "I wouldn't stay around here if you got down on your hands and knees and begged me." He turned towards his car, cursing her as he went. "You're a fool. And God help the fool who gets stuck with you."

He was half way down the drive when she rushed down from the porch to snatch up a rock. With a mighty pitch she hurled it at him, gaining great satisfaction when it hit him in the back. He glared at her, and with a snort of disgust he fled, his car spraying up rocks and dirt in their angry wake as he drove away.

* * * * *

Now that he was gone, her hurt came forth in a great wave, demanding full sway. Silent tears began to roll down her cheeks. She angrily brushed them away, feeling shameful for wasting tears on him, but she couldn't help it. All she wanted to do now was go to her room and hide, cry out her hurt into her pillow, and be done with it. By the morning, she would never have to give another thought to him. She turned back towards the house…and ran smack into her father. His face was flushed dark with anger…and suddenly he grabbed her by the arm, shaking her.

"What in the hell is wrong with you?"

She couldn't speak. She opened her mouth, but found she could not utter a word, and a fearful chill began to run down her spine. Her father's grip was fierce, his steps much too swift, as he pulled her up the steps and into the house. She stumbled slightly at the second step, but he took no notice as he opened the door and yanked her in with him. Her brothers were all gathered in the front room, clustered around the window, and they turned to stare at the two as they came in. But their father wasn't playing games.

"Get to bed, or I'll knock the fire out of every one of you!"

They scattered like rats, and he moved into the kitchen. Pulling out a chair, he forced her into it. She looked up and saw her mother, sitting at the other end of the table, while her father stood over her, his expression dark.

"Girl, what kind of fool are you? A man puts his pride on the line, asking for your hand, and you run him off like he's some kind of varmint?"

Her voice was small as she answered, trying hard to force back tears.

"It wasn't my fault. You should have heard some of the ugly things he said to me." Surely they would understand when she told them what they hadn't heard. "He said awful things to me. He said I never cared about him. But that's not true. I cared more about him than anybody."

Rachel spoke up, coldly. "Well you have a fair way of showing it. He come here and gave you the chance for something better, and you spit in his face."

Grace's voice squeaked. "But Mama, I don't love Charlie. I can't marry a man I don't love, especially one like him."

"Oh for Pete's sake!" cried Rachel, rising up from her seat, her chair scraping the floor loudly, and Grace jumped at the sound. Rachel walked back and forth for a moment, cradling her forehead in her hands, shaking her head. Then she froze, folding her arms. She looked at her Grace with an icy glare.

"Did you know he could've had his pick of any girl in this county?"

Grace didn't see what that had to do with anything. "What does that mean to me?" she asked.

Her father stood over her. "When he gets married, he gets all the land his father left. That don't mean just the old shack in the woods. That means the big house in the valley, and the two-hundred acres of good bottom land that goes with it. And you just threw away the chance to have every bit of it."

Grace felt a numbness taking over her body. So that was why he was in such a rush to marry her. He had said his father had left him the house, but he had left out the part about needing a wife to acquire the property. And now, it seemed her own family was turning against her. No matter that Charlie had lied to her, had treated her so meanly. If they could get rid of her, like a burdensome cow they no longer needed, then they really and truly would. She was just another mouth to feed, and the best way to get rid of her was to give her to a man in marriage. All of her life she'd known what is was to be of small value, but she never believed they would stoop so low as this. It hurt so badly it made her breathless. And it lit the fire of anger in her belly. That anger had served her well before, and it came to her aid again, as she lifted her chin in defiance.

"I don't care about how much land he has," she said, her voice low but strong. "I won't marry him."

Her father snorted in disgust. "You're about as stubborn as an old mule. And dumber than a box of rocks." He knocked over a chair as he stormed off, disappearing around the corner. A moment later there came a loud clap like thunder, as the door to the back bedroom slammed shut.

She jumped at the sound…and turned to the only person left in the room. Looking in her mother's eyes, she pleaded silently for some understanding. How could they do this to her? She was their daughter. They were her parents. How could they be so cruel and hardly blink an eye in the process? But there was no sympathy in her mother's eyes. Only a kind of weariness, as if she was tired of the whole matter, and had washed her hands of it. It hurt so deeply, like a knife plunging in her heart, that Grace rose up from her seat and ran from the room, out the front door. Her mother followed a few steps behind. She knew it from hearing her call.

"Gracie Ellen, where do you think you're going?"

She kept running, weeping wildly as she went. It would serve them right if she never came home again. They were human, after all, and still her parents, and they would wonder before long where she was. She wished they would get worried. She wanted them out of their minds with worry, after all the heartbreak she had just endured. But deep down she knew it wouldn't be heartfelt concern. It would only be another bother and a reason to be angry, as if she were their employee and not their blood kin. Their betrayals made Charlie's seem kind, and she wondered how she would get through another day without feeling the poison of her father's words.

Nearing the river, she began to slow down, and soon found herself walking slowly along the bank. That was when she heard a movement behind her in the brush, and a moment later, Pilot emerged and came to her side. She knelt down beside him and buried her nose in his warm fur, comforted by his friendly presence. How sad it was that, once again, her only loyal companion was her dog. She held his great head in her hands, looking into his loving eyes. He wagged his tail and gave her face a lick, and for the first time in a long time, she smiled. She wiped away her tears and sighed, and she and her dog walked together along the water.

The moonlight bounced beams off the water, so beautiful and peaceful...so different from the turmoil in her heart.

What was she to do now?

If she went home, they would have the satisfaction of thinking she was bound to them in some way...that because she was their daughter, she was their property, and they could do with her as they wished. If they wanted to give her away to Charlie, what was to stop them? They could pack her up and toss her out. Some senseless, stupid part of her soul still wondered if they were capable of such treachery. But suddenly she thought of Jack...and it became clear that, yes, they were quite capable of such vengeance against one of their own.

It was growing cool, and her light summer dress made things colder. She rubbed her arms in an attempt to warm them, but it wasn't any use. With great distress, she realized that she would have to go back home, for shelter if for nothing else. What other choice did she have? She couldn't stay out all night...at least, not in this way. She'd slept out on the ground at night, on coon hunts and all. But in this thin dress she wore, and without supplies or weapons, who knew what might happen?

And as much as she hated to admit it, there was a tiny part of her that wanted to go home.

In spite of all that had happened, there was no real hatred in her heart. There was great bitterness and spite, and yet she couldn't help but wish that when morning came, everything would be forgiven. But then, what if they didn't care? What if they really did do the unthinkable, and tried to force her into a marriage with Charlie? Maybe it was not so unthinkable, after all. She thought again of Jack, and how their father still hadn't forgiven him for the way he'd left home in a fit of rage. He had been their son, and their firstborn, and yet he was an outcast in his father's eyes. She was just their lowly daughter. So what hope did she have now?

That was when the idea came to her. It was something she'd tried once before...although, at that time, it had ended with disastrous results. But maybe the time had come to try again.

She could go to Jack, her beloved brother. She hadn't seen in all these years, and all because of her parents' thick-headedness. How she would get there, she wasn't quite sure yet. But oh, how she adored the idea of seeing him again.

Still, the idea of leaving home was frightening. She'd hardly been beyond the borders of the county in her life. How would she even know where to start? For several long moments she debated with herself about what to do. And then she decided,

I will go home. I'll give them a chance to make it all right.

She felt weak and broken for thinking such a thing, but God help her, she wasn't capable of hating anyone...not even them.

When at last, she returned home, she didn't bother coming in through the front door. She didn't want them to see her, just in case they happened to be waiting up. Childish as it was, a part of her took some vengeful delight in the idea that they might be worrying about her, though she knew it wasn't likely. So, she quietly slipped in through her open bedroom window, and a weariness fell upon her as soon as she was in bed. Her last thought before she fell asleep was the hope that in the morning, all of this had been only a very bad dream.

* * * * *

The morning broke, and her routine came to her without fail. She deliberately avoided seeing her folks, hoping that they might seek her out instead, and offer something of an apology. Or at least, they would offer some understanding, and accept the fact that she would not be marrying Charlie. She could only hope, as she filled her egg basket and made her way into the house.

In the kitchen, her mother was emptying a pan of biscuits onto a plate. She glanced over at her for a moment, and said nothing as she turned back to what she was doing. Grace felt the sting of rejection, but refused to let her mother see the tears that welled in her eyes. She turned to go, and saw her father standing in the doorway of the living room. Their eyes met, and he looked her over once. His mouth was set in a firm line…his tone was cold.

"I knew you'd come home when you got hungry."

With that, he turned around and walked out.

She wanted to break down and cry at his harshness. And then, the tear of pain became a tear of anger. While the little angel on her shoulder told her to forgive and forget, the little devil on her other shoulder whispered in a darker, stronger voice.

Forget these fools. They don't give a damn about you. Why don't you just pack up and get the heck out of here while you can?

She set her shoulders, determined, and she replied to herself, in a voice equally strong and determined.

I will. And I'll never look back.

* * * * *

The dawn came, and lying in her bed, she stared blankly at the ceiling. She thought of Jane leaving Thornfield in the middle of the night, and the words played silently in her head.

I knew what I had to do, and I did it mechanically.

She longed for that kind of strength, the kind of strength and faith that would lead her on her way. But she was weak, and she knew it from the knots that tightened in her stomach. The passing of the night had somehow lessened her resolve to run away, and now, she was overcome with guilt at the thought of abandoning her family and the only home she'd ever known.

Despite the hardships of this life, and the hurt of the night before, she was proud of who she was and where she came from. It was her home, the only one she'd ever known, and she knew nothing of the world beyond it, except what she'd read in books. She had desperately longed to get away and see the world, but now that the moment of truth had come, she was simply petrified. She was so tempted to stay, to give in to her weakness and do what, deep down, she knew she would someday regret. Here at home, harsh as things could be, it was safe and secure.

But then she thought of Jack, and how he had fostered in her an independent and strong spirit. She thought of Jane, too, of course. That great lady was just a character in a book, to be sure. And yet, she had been the mentor that had guided her through so many of the lonely and uncertain times in her life. This moment, like so many before it, was when her mind drifted to Charlotte Bronte's beautiful words for guidance.

...Laws and principals are not for the times when there is no temptation. They are for such moments as this, when body and soul rise in mutiny against their rigor; stringent are they; inviolate they shall be...

The words started a flow of strength and courage coursing through her frame, and though her fear still lingered, she at last rose...knowing that she must begin, and see it through.

She went about her chores as she always did. Breakfast was a silent affair, with her brothers unusually quiet around the table. That was not surprising, considering Mr. Langdon's sour expression, which was obviously held over from last night. The boys were wise enough not to provoke him, and Grace gave silent thanks that there was no mention of Charlie or of anything else that had been said. She ate breakfast quickly, helped clean the kitchen, and stole a few moments to slip away to her room.

From under the bed she took out of bag of old flour sacks. None of their clothes were ever bought in a store. They were all made from these cotton bags, which she and her mother would cut and sew into new shirts and an occasional dress just about every month. Now, one flour sack made a traveling bag for her, and into it she put the few items in the world she possessed. A few dresses and her nightgown, some under things, and her boots. Those she would wait to put on, for if she wore them now, someone would certainly catch on. Shoes, especially boots, were expensive and only allowed to be worn in certain circumstances, such as on a rainy, muddy day. Today was hot and humid, so shoes would be suspicious. There was a pair of pants there that she had taken from the laundry and a hat as well, which sat just underneath the bed. A disguise was something she'd known she would need from the first. The two men who worked at the depot were brothers she's seen around town. But they were not fellow church members, so she did not see them often. Still, they might have recognized her from somewhere, and that she could not risk. She added her books to the collection, and now there was one small thing left to retrieve for her escape.

Quietly, she went to the front room and opened the little stand beside the sofa. It was a drawer full of junk where all manner of things were thrown, including an old pair of her father's eyeglasses. Why he kept them instead of throwing them out, she hadn't the foggiest notion, but now she was glad for it. Carefully popping the lenses out of the wire rims - she would be blind if she kept them in - she put the frames in her pocket. Who would notice the glasses had no lenses? No one would be looking that closely, she was quite certain. Knowing that her mother would soon be wondering what she was doing, she quickly went out to tend the garden. Later that morning, as she sat picking beans from the bush, two thoughts came to her mind. One was when and how she would go from here. There was a train that left town at five o'clock in the evening. But how would she get away from the house without being seen? That she didn't know yet, and the idea of going still terrified her, so she put it out of her head and refused to think about it at that moment. The other thought was just how she would pay for a ticket.

Good Lord, she hadn't even thought of that until now. She hadn't a cent to her name, and there was no way she could ask her folks for the money. She knew where they kept cash. Being superstitious, and very untrusting of banks, they kept their funds in mason jars buried in the ground, down at the bottom of the cliff where the spring ran. She knew where to find it, but God help her, she wasn't a thief. She already felt her soul was in jeopardy for not honoring her mother and father. If she added stealing to her list of broken commandments, there would surely be a spot in hell saved just for her. At the thought of it, her head fell in her hands, and she sighed deeply. Then she folded her hands in prayer.

Dear God, forgive me for these sins, she said in silence. As she thought of it, the bravery that had started her going seemed to flee. It seemed that all of her plotting and preparations would be for nothing if she couldn't even manage a simple train ticket, so now, what was she to do?

All through the afternoon she fought a battle with herself, torn between self-preservation and the unbreakable bond she had for her family. It didn't matter what they did to her. Whether she stayed or went, they were all a part of her, and they would be until she drew her last breath. There had to be another way, but for the moment, it was beyond her grasp.

"Lord, help me," she muttered out loud, bending her head in frustration.

A moment later, she heard the dogs barking from the front yard. She took out her watch, and seeing that it was after four o'clock, she realized it must have been her father and brothers coming home. She felt a sharp pull in her heart when she realized that the five o'clock hour was fast approaching. If she was going to act, it would have to be soon, come hell or high water.

She had just picked up her basket of beans when her mother called to her from the back porch.

"Gracie Ellen, come on in here!"

There was something unsettling in her mother's tone. When Grace slowly made her way to the kitchen, she realized then what that strange tone was for. Mr. Langdon sat at one end of the table, his face and clothes still dusted with black soot. Mrs. Langdon sat down beside him, and from the look on her mother's face, Grace realized that something was not right. They had plotted something for her...she just knew they had...and she was almost afraid to hear them speak. He pulled out a chair, pointing her to it.

"Sit down Gracie."

She did, but was prepared in an instant to jump up if need be, the fight or flight response throbbing strong in her veins. Her father stood over her, scowling.

"You're the only girl. So by God, we're going to do what we have to do for you. We ain't gonna be around forever, and we've got to be sure you're tended to."

He paused, looking at Rachel, who had her eyes fixed on the table before her. Both avoided their daughter's eyes. And at last he came to his point.

"I've talked to Charlie, and I told him you'd marry him."

Without thought she bolted up, fear driving her.

"No I won't! I won't marry that man!"

Her arm was suddenly snatched in a vise-like grip. Her father pushed his face up close to hers, his eyes black with rage.

"What did you just say to me?"

She cried out again. "I said no!" Madness had gripped her, splintering open a shell of submission. Even as her father took her other arm, pinning her painfully with both his hands, she did not relent. Something within her had been released, and it made her wild. "I won't be bullied into anything!"

Her father's face twisted with anger.

"You'll do whatever the hell I tell you to!"

She felt herself being shaken like a ragdoll...but she heard her own voice, screaming like one possessed.

"No I won't!"

A violent backhand to the cheek knocked her down to the floor...and for several moments she lay there, stunned by the blow. She had never been hit in the face in her life. She'd been switched on the back, and on the legs, but she'd never been struck in the face. The shock of it made her ears ring. Her eye felt like it might burst from pain, and for many moments she remained on the floor, paralyzed.

But a rebellion started to rise inside of her, and the voice of her literary mentor came to her, wise and powerful.

...I was conscious that a moment's mutiny had already rendered me liable to strange penalties, and like any other rebel slave, I felt resolved to go all lengths...

Her mother had come to her side, trying in a useless way to comfort her. But suddenly she pushed those hands away and ran, dashing into her room and slamming the door behind her as hard as she could. She knew it would infuriate her father, but even if it was only for a moment, she felt delightful revenge in the sound of his fist pounding on the locked door, unable to get in.

"You open this door or I'll bust it down!"

The moment of victory had passed. She knew he meant what he said. When he got past that door, he would drag her out of the house and switch her to within an inch of her life.

There was only one thing to do now.

Grabbing up her flour sack, she rushed to the open window as her father started ramming the door with his shoulder. She slipped out and hit the ground running, tearing across the corn patch and down the hill toward the spring. Finding the spot at the cliff bottom, she dug into the ground like an animal tearing up earth, and at last found one of the mason jars filled with money. She muttered to herself as she stuffed the bills in her pocket.

"God, forgive me for this. Don't condemn me to an eternity in hell."

She threw down the jar, rushing up the other side of the hill away from the spring. Moments later she was in the woods, running again as fast as her legs could carry her, toward the distant and lonesome sound of a train's whistle.

* * * * *

She clutched her bag closely. Looking down, she saw her own hands trembling. It was beyond her control...but she knew where it came from, without a doubt. The same terror gripped her senses and made her heart hammer against her ribs. For a moment, she wondered if she might be insane for doing all of this. With trembling fingers she reached up and clutched the little silver cross that hung around her neck, praying.

"Dear Lord, see me through this."

She jumped when the train whistle suddenly blew. A moment later the train began to move and she nearly jumped up, ready to cry out for them to stop and let her out. She could still go home... there was still a chance to go back and make everything right. But something kept her from it.

I could not turn, nor retrace one step. God must have lead me on, she recited in her head.

From those words, she felt a deep faith and power that calmed her a bit.

A higher power was leading her, she was certain of that. How else could she have gotten this far?

She sat back in her seat, watching out the window as the land swept by, and she realized that with every passing moment, she was being drawn farther and farther away from everything she knew in the world. It wasn't long before she knew that the moment of return had gone by, and it became a matter not of what she had left behind, but of what was to be found ahead.

When she thought of how she'd gotten here, on this train, it almost made her laugh. She had stopped in the woods and thrown on the trousers, tucking the hem of her dress into the waist. She'd twisted her braid up and tucked it under the hat, put on the boots, and finally put on the glasses. At the depot she had been terrified of discovery, but something had moved her forward anyway, right up to the window where she nervously asked for a ticket to Chicago. She put her money down on the counter, and waited with quaking nerves to see what would come about.

And then, it was over and done with.

Finding Grace

The agent took her payment, handed her the ticket, and that was that. He hardly even looked at her, probably because he was busy talking on the phone. Maybe it was the distraction, or just pure luck. Whatever the case, there had not been the slightest of trouble, and now, here she sat.

Strange, how that small part of her quest had been so quick and easy, when the idea of it had given her such trouble. She might have thought it over a little more, but there were other matters on her mind now. Rifling through her meager possessions, she found one of her books...a copy of *Pride and Prejudice*. She opened it to the middle, where there rested a small envelope. She looked at its front and read the address...

Mr. and Mrs. John Langdon
5739 Lincoln Avenue
Lincoln Park, IL

She had no real idea where Lincoln Park was or just how to get there. She had seen it on a map many times before. She'd pointed it out to herself, so she knew it was within the city limits of Chicago. Her imagination had gone wild, thinking of what it must be like to go there. But now she wondered...how on earth she was going to find it out there in the real world?

These details were driving her crazy, and she realized she had two choices. She could either sit there, continuing with this madness...or she could push the thoughts aside and think of other thing. She chose the latter of the two.

As she looked out the window, she thought of Jack and Alice. What would they think when she suddenly showed up at their front door?

She hadn't written to them. There just hadn't been time, as fast as all this had happened. When she suddenly appeared out of the blue, would they welcome her? For a moment she had her doubts. But then she shook her head at her silly fears. Jack and Alice had always loved her. They had often invited her to come and stay with them for the summer, but that had been impossible. Her folks would never have allowed it, as opposed as they were to Jack and Alice as a married couple. Besides that, they wouldn't have let her take a trip anywhere, especially by herself. And so, she had always written back and politely declined. She smiled now as she thought of what their faces might look like when she arrived. Suddenly, a different kind of anxiety came over her. One of excitement, of hope...and wonder at what the future held in store.

* * * * *

She was nervous about leaving her seat, for fear that someone might take it from her. So she sat quietly in her place all through the afternoon, reading to pass the time. But her body had its natural requirements, and eventually, they became quite demanding. She felt like a fool not knowing what to do, but despite her embarrassment, she forced herself to seek help from the porter as he passed by. Her voice was small.

"Sir," she said, "Will the train leave without me if I step outside for a minute?"

He smiled kindly and shook his head. "No Miss, not if you are quick. You have a few minutes before the next departure."

She rose and stretched, and with much caution, she moved to the door and stepped down to the ground. The porter stepped down a moment later to tend to something, and though she was ashamed to ask the question in her head, she could not help herself.

"Is there a place where I can go..." She stopped mid-sentence, mortified. "Is there a..."

She stopped again, and found she couldn't utter another word. But the gentleman seemed somehow to read her mind, and he spoke kindly.

"There is a lavatory on the train, Miss. It's in the last car. You'll see the small door when you get back there."

Her eyes widened in surprise. She thanked the man, and went in search of what she called, in her head, an indoor outhouse. It was little more than a wooden bench with a hole in the bottom, and it served its purpose. There was even a little wash stand with soap and a bucket of water to wash her hands. As primitive as it would have been to some, she was amazed that such a thing existed. She wondered what happened when the train was moving, but right away she chastised herself for such a dirty thought. The train whistle blew, and the cars began moving as she made her way back to her seat.

As she sat back down, another basic urge began to rumble through her - in her stomach. She hadn't eaten anything since noon, for she'd run off before supper, and now her hunger was quite strong. But what could she do? She'd heard of dining cars, and she was sure there was one on this train, but she was completely ignorant of how to get there. Besides, there would probably be ladies and gentleman travelers there, and they would not want to see a poor little country girl like her. So she sat in her seat, the car dim now with the night outside, and only a small light shining above the doorway. She leaned against the window and tried to rest, for now she found herself getting sleepy as well as hungry. She was just about to doze off when the porter came by, and she jumped nervously when he stopped close to her. She looked up at him as he reached out to her, handing her a blanket.

"This will keep you warm for the night. And I thought you might be hungry as well, so I brought you something from the store room." He handed her an apple, and she smiled gratefully at him.

"God bless you, sir," she said sweetly.

He nodded and smiled back.

"It's just part of my job, Miss. If you need anything else, just let me know."

He moved quietly away, leaving her alone, and after savoring the sweet taste of her little meal, she pulled the blanket over herself and let the swaying of the train lull her to sleep.

Chapter 5

"A Journey"

The sun shined against her eyes. She opened them slowly, blinking against the harsh light of day. Then, looking out the window, her eyes widened in awe at the new world before her.

It was the third day of her journey now. So far, everything she'd seen outside her window had been somewhat familiar. High rolling green hills, low lying valleys…thick clusters of dark woods. But this morning brought a very great change.

She had never seen such flat plains…vast stretches of land crowded with row upon row of young, bright green corn stalks and mounds of soybeans. The fields seemed to go on forever, reaching out toward a vast expanse of blue horizon. The land was only broken here and there by a bright red barn or a pretty white farmhouse. She'd never seen such wide open spaces. Though she had lived her whole life on a farm, this was nothing at all like the cropland back home.

The porter walked by, bidding her good morning as he went. He was such a kind man, bringing her fruit to keep her from going hungry, and inquiring after her to see if she needed anything. When they'd changed trains the day before, he'd helped her along, kind gentleman that he was. This morning, she asked only a question of him.

"Sir, where are we now?"

He smiled politely. "We've just come into Illinois, Miss. We'll be in Chicago by this afternoon."

Jack had once described all of this to her in a letter. But until now, she had never been able to quite picture it. As the hours went by she kept watching through the window, seeing how things gradually changed from open farmland to small towns, and then to little villages. There were other changes around her that she didn't much notice, like the number of passengers that grew around her with each stop. She was too busy gazing out the window to pay them much attention. Soon the buildings began to be closer and closer together, and they began to rise up in height until some of the structures cast shadows on the windows, forcing her to crane her neck up so she could see the roof tops.

Her mouth gaped at everything she saw. She was so mesmerized that when the train was suddenly thrown into darkness, she let out a cry of surprise. It came to her that they had gone into a tunnel. The dimness was so eerie that a shiver ran up her spine. Moments later, there came a strange, almost ethereal light. The train began to slow, and then with a crying of the brakes, it came to a stop...and the porter called out.

"Chicago, Union Station!"

Her heart did a summersault as she realized that this was the end of the line. She had arrived. Suddenly, she was afraid to get out. The car had become almost comfortable...secure, in its way. It had kept the unfamiliar world out, for a time. But now she had to go and face it. Even the porter, who had been so good to her, could be of no help now. So she took a deep breath, picked up her bag, and rose to her feet. She made her way to the door, following the other passengers out. And as she stood in the doorway of the car, the shock of reality hit her full force.

Good heavens, what have I gotten myself into?

She stepped down to a long and wide cement walkway. Looking up, she saw the source of the soft white light. It came from a frosted glass ceiling, and she stood staring at it for several moments, captured by its beauty. Turning her eyes from it, she watched the movement of passengers all around her...and there were so many people to see. Everywhere there were moving bodies, more people in one place than she'd ever seen in her life, all moving to and fro. And what strange, fascinating people they were to watch.

The gentlemen were dashing, some wearing banded straw hats...others with handsome fedoras. Their clothing looked like the kind she'd only seen on Sunday mornings. There were no overalls or tattered shirts here. The men wore neat looking slacks and fine button up shirts, some covered with thin vests and others with suspenders. How tidy the gentlemen were...most of them clean shaven, though some wore a small mustache. But not one of them had a scraggly face.

Even their shoes...not mud-encrusted boots, but fine leather loafers...were perfect, and she could see why. Nearby, there was a boy kneeling down with a rag in his hand, buffing the extended foot of a man reading a newspaper...and she smiled.

No wonder their shoes shine so brightly, she thought. She'd never seen anything like it.

If the men were incredible to her amazed eyes, the ladies were even more so. From head to toe, the women were like a flock of brightly feathered birds...so elegant, so colorful. They seemed to preen for all who might be watching. Some had cute little rounded hats that came down low over their foreheads. Other hats were wide-brimmed and decorated with ribbons or feathers. The dresses were of the brightest colors and loveliest fabrics, many of the collars trimmed with fur or beads. Nearly every female neck was festooned with a long strand of pearls, most of which hung down to the waist. The ladies clomped by in thick-heeled, buckled shoes of various colors, but it was their bare knees that stunned her the most. In all of her life she'd never seen such high hemlines, falling just above the knee itself and exposing a scandalous amount of stocking clad leg.

She thought to herself, *If Mama and those old biddies at church could see this, they'd fall plum on their faces with shock and shame.* And on that thought, she smiled again, thinking how very funny it would be to see such a thing.

Someone bumped into her, bringing her back from her musing. The man apologized and went on his way, but the incident suddenly made her remember where she was. There was a loud humming from the many voices, the rattling of baggage carts rolling by, the hissing of the train...a hundred other sounds she couldn't distinguish. Another person pushed past her, and she realized that by standing in one place, she was only causing trouble. Following the flow of the crowd, though rather more slowly than they, she looked around for she knew not what. She saw a man in uniform...one who looked like another porter or maybe a conductor. Quietly she went to him, seeking directions. He pointed her down a hall, and giving him a small word of thanks, she went the way he had shown her.

Her feet froze, her head came up, and her mouth fell open wide at the sight before her eyes.

The Great Hall was enormous. Decorated in white marble, with great columns in the middle and a set of stairs rising up on one side, it could have been the hall of a king or queen. Voices echoed in the air, making her feel as though she stood in some great and magnificent church, so vast and open was the room and its ceiling. Without quite knowing what she was doing, she began to move about as if she were in a trance, her neck craned up in awe.

Suddenly she backed into someone. A suitcase dropped, popping open, its contents falling on the floor. Her cheeks flushed red with embarrassment and fear. A lovely young red-head...maybe she was in her mid-twenties in age...was the other party of the accident. Impeccably dressed in a red skirt and a dotted white silk blouse, she was a quite a beauty. But there was nothing beautiful about the words coming out of her mouth.

"Why don't you watch where the hell you're going?"

Grace stammered an apology. "Excuse me ma'am. I'm awful sorry. Let me help you with that." She knelt down to assist, but the woman snatched her things away.

"Keep your grubby paws off of my stuff! I'll get them myself!" She started to mutter as she stuffed things back into her suitcase. "Of all the stupid, clumsy little idiots..."

Then a man's voice interjected. It was a deep, soothing voice...and it was full of sarcasm.

"Problems, Victoria?"

Grace glanced over, seeing a shiny pair of gentleman's shoes. She was so flustered with her mistake, so busy trying to help, that at first she didn't look up to see who the speaker was. She listened and watched as Victoria screeched up at him.

"It's about time you showed up, Henry! I've been waiting here for a good half hour. I just had the worst trip of my life, and now this, on top of everything else." She gestured to her bag as she closed it. With a huff she rose to her feet.

Grace felt mortified as she stood. She turned to look at the gentleman...and jumped back slightly, startled at seeing his eyes. They were the palest blue eyes she'd ever seen in her life...like two blue chips of ice. And yet as cold as they were in color, they seemed to burn like fire as he looked her up and down, examining her. And while he looked at her, she did the same to him. His was an imposing man...tall, dark-haired, lean but muscular. Dressed in tan trousers and a crisp white shirt, with a close-fitting brown vest, he had a striking air of importance about him. Too important, she seemed to realize quickly. His lip curled slightly. When he spoke, his voice was deep, and rather thrilling. But it had no hint of warmth as he addressed her.

"Don't I know you?"

She blinked, startled by his question. She shook her head. And still he stared at her, his gaze burning right through her.

"What's your name?"

She opened her mouth to reply, but Victoria broke in.

"What difference does it make who she is, Henry? I want to get home, if you don't mind."

She tried to gesture him toward the stairs. But he just turned to look at her with that chilly expression of his.

"Victoria, has anyone ever told you that patience is a virtue?"

There was contempt in his voice, and in his look. Grace bristled at his rudeness. What was wrong with him? And why wasn't Victoria standing up for herself? She seemed like the kind of woman who wouldn't take that kind of behavior from a man. But Victoria just rolled her eyes turning her head away with a huff. Grace looked back at Henry, and she saw a little flicker of satisfaction in his eyes. Apparently, he was happy with the results of his reprimand. Then he turned his attention back to her.

"What's your name?" he asked again.

Briefly she wondered if she should give him an answer, as rude as he seemed to be. But she found herself answering anyway.

"Grace Langdon."

For a moment he seemed to ponder the name. "Langdon," he said at last. "That's where I've seen you. Do you have a brother named John?"

Her eyes widened in anticipation of his reply. "You know Jack?" For a moment she forgot about his rude way of being...until he answered her with a shrug.

"Maybe I do...maybe I don't."

Her eyes widened in surprise as she wondered...

What kind of an answer is that?

There was a moment of silence following his reply, as she watched him reach into his pocket to take out a piece of candy. Why did it seem he was deliberately being slow in unwrapping it, and why was he delaying in saying more about Jack? She could tell by his expression that he was just being mean...purposely withholding information just to annoy her. And it was working.

Speak! She thought. *Speak, you big bully!* And at last he did.

"He's my neighbor. I believe I've seen your face in a picture or two. The resemblance is remarkable, I have to say."

Victoria rudely interrupted. "Oh, swell!" she snarked. "It's such a small world, isn't it? We all know each other! Why don't we just take the little bunny home, Henry? Let's adopt her!"

She moved her hands about, and then brought them together in a mocking sort of clap. For a moment, Grace found something pretty in the way she moved, almost like watching a little dance. But just as quickly as she had smiled, Victoria drew her mouth into a serious, angry frown, and her brown eyes blazed.

"Henry, I am tired and hungry. And if you don't take me home right now, I'll just wave down a cab and get there myself." As she had before, she challenged him with her stance and her eyes, her hands on her hips.

Grace shifted her glance to Henry to see what he would do. And she wasn't so surprised when he rolled his eyes slightly in annoyance.

"Ishkabibble," he replied.

Ishkabibble? she thought. *What's that?* She had no idea what it meant. But she guessed it was his way of dismissing someone, as he started to turn away from them both. But he paused for a moment to look at her again, lifting his hat to her. Then he turned and walked towards the stairs, leaving the two of them alone.

Grace wasn't sure what to do...especially when she turned to look at Victoria, whose face was red with rage. The woman looked like she might explode. Would she have a screaming fit, or go on the attack? For a moment, Grace wondered if she would be on the receiving end of a slap. But Victoria just stomped her foot, cursing the man who had left her standing there.

"Son of a bitch," she muttered, snatching up her suitcase...and she hurried after Henry.

Grace stood there for a moment, bewildered by the both of them. She saw how Henry turned just at the bottom of the stairs, waiting for Victoria to catch up with him. When she did, he reached out to take the suitcase from her hand. Suddenly they became the most civil of couples, as Victoria hooked her arm in his, letting him lead her up the stairs towards the door. What a strange pair they were! But she could only spend a moment wondering about their odd behavior. Suddenly she remembered where she was...who she was trying to find.

I can't let them get away, she thought. *They know where Jack is.*

She rushed for the stairs to follow them.

Out on the street, she looked left...looked right. And there they were, just down the sidewalk. They were about to board what looked like a trackless train car, and she hurried towards it. She caught up with them just as Victoria stepped onboard. She called out to Henry, and right away she saw how his blue gaze fell on her, as if to ask...

What can that creeping creature want now?

She even heard him mumble a complaint when he saw her coming.

"Oh, for the love of Christ."

His curse shocked her. His look almost kept her from speaking. But she gathered her courage, saying what she needed to say, despite his off-putting manner.

"Can you please help me get to my brother?"

She saw how he turned his head away slightly, as if she were annoying him. But she would not let him deter her.

"I'd be so obliged," she added, hoping he wouldn't turn her away.

43

He looked at her again, seeming to think about it. He was silent for a moment...until the people standing behind them in line began to grumble. He muttered something under his breath. For a moment, she thought he would indeed tell her to go. Instead he stepped back a pace...and gestured for her to board the car.

Finding a seat just in front of Victoria, she watched Henry as he came to sit beside his unhappy companion. Of her, Grace took little notice. But watching Henry, she realized she was obligated to him, and not just for letting her follow him onboard. She had seen him pay her way. And whether she thought him good or bad, she knew it would only be right to acknowledge his help. After all, he was the one who was helping her get to Jack, and for that, she really was grateful. Awkwardly, she turned to him, clearing her throat nervously before she spoke.

"Thank you, sir, for your help." She wanted to say more. She had the words on the tip of her tongue. But suddenly he cut her off with a sharp remark.

"Yeah, yeah," he muttered. Leaning his head back against his seat, using his hat to cover his face, he let out a loud sigh...making it clear he wasn't interested in speaking to anyone, especially her. Victoria didn't seem bothered by his behavior. She took an emery board from her clutch bag and started filing her nails.

Grace turned around to face forward, unnerved by him. Victoria's rudeness she could tolerate, because she'd never really valued the opinions of other women, be they familiar or unfamiliar to her. But there was something about the rudeness of men that got under her skin. Self-importance ran through their veins, it seemed to her, and this Henry fellow wasn't doing much to change her mind about that.

What a snob that man is, she thought to herself. *Mister, when you get me to my brother, I'll be done with you, and you'll be done with me. Then we can act like we never met.*

Rather than wasting further time in thinking of him, she looked out the window, seeing the cityscape as it went by. It was all so new, so exciting. It only grew more fascinating as they moved with the flow of pedestrians and drivers. The streets were crowded with cars and trucks. Horns honked, engines puttered. Smoke belched from tailpipes. There was even the occasional clip-clop of horses hooves, brought on by horse-drawn wagons, which were a welcome sight to her eyes. But all traffic, be it live or motorized, had to dodge the hulking streetcar as it went, plodding through the middle of the street like a ship on the sea, sending pedestrians and vehicles scattering in its wake.

As they went along, the city heights soon gave way to small brick residences with neatly trimmed little lawns and hedges, lined up along white paved sidewalks and cobblestone streets. It was all so pretty to look at...like something in a picture book. Her stomach began to knot with anticipation as she imagined reuniting with Jack and Alice. Looking down at her hands, she realized they were shaking a little. Taking a deep breath, she willed herself to be calm. And before she quite knew it, the short journey had come to an end.

Henry and Victoria stepped down from the streetcar. Grace quickly followed a few steps behind them, though neither one looked back. She wondered how far they would go along, but she didn't have much time to think about it. They turned up a walkway towards one of the little houses. Victoria quickly went inside, while Henry stopped at the mailbox. Grace stood a few feet away, looking at the house across the street.

Jack's house, she realized.

She reached into her bag for her envelope, reading the address again...wanting to be sure that she had really gotten this far on her own...that it really was her brother's house she was about to cross over to. It was beautiful to look at, with its flower-filled window boxes and manicured lawn. But it didn't seem possible that she was really here. She stood rooted to her spot on the sidewalk...until she suddenly heard Henry's voice, sly and sarcastic.

"You won't get anywhere just standing still."

She turned to look at him, but he had his mail in hand, already heading for his front door. She curled her lip in distaste, muttering...and almost wishing he would hear.

"Well thank you so much for your help." Then she added, in a slightly lower voice. "Grouchy bastard."

For a moment, she compared him to Fitzwilliam Darcy, the seemingly cold and snobbish hero from *Pride and Prejudice*. But then she took it back. Darcy was one of her favorite characters, a man who really wasn't the cold-hearted beast he appeared to be. She wouldn't give Henry such a distinction, and she was glad to see him disappear into his house.

On one point, however, she agreed with him. She wasn't getting anywhere just standing on the curb. She took a deep breath, looked both ways, and crossed the street.

* * * * *

She stood at the door, her heart beating wildly. After a moment of hesitation, she knocked the little brass ring. She stood for several moments, nervously shifting her weight from one foot to the other. Then the door slowly opened...and before her stood Alice.

Alice. Her beloved sister-in-law. Once her cherished friend and teacher. She was just the same. Statuesque, with jade-green eyes and a soft, pale complexion. Her hair was shorter now, styled in a wavy bob. But it was just as flaming red as it had ever been. Alice stared at her for a long moment, as if she were looking at someone she thought she knew, but wasn't altogether sure.

"Can I help you?" she asked.

For a moment Grace was troubled. Then, she seemed to remember how she looked. The trousers she was wearing...the hat on her head. Quickly she took it off. Her long braid fell down against her shoulder. She took off the glasses and asked, "Don't you know me?"

A stunned look came to Alice's face...and then it was replaced by a great, loving smile. Grace felt arms going around her, warm and tight, as Alice squealed with glee.

"Gracie! Is it really you?" She grinned, merriment twinkling in her eye. "Well of course it's you. There for a minute I wasn't sure. But now that you've got those silly glasses and that hat off, I'd know that face anywhere. Come on in the house, will you?"

She didn't wait for her to follow. She took her by the hand, pulling her in. The moment the door was closed, questions tumbled forth.

"What are you doing here? Did Jack know you were coming?"

Grace shook her head. "No, he didn't know. Nobody knows I'm here." She paused a moment, shifting her eyes. "I ran away from home."

Alice's mouth fell open in shock. But she smiled. "Did you really? My word, Gracie. You came all this way by yourself?"

Grace nodded, and Alice shook her head, smiling with an expression full of wonder.

"I don't know what to say," she replied. "I feel like I'm in the middle of some crazy dream or something."

There was a moment of awkward silence, as if neither of them knew what to say to the other. Then they both giggled.

"I feel so silly," Grace said. "I've known you since I was a little girl, but I feel like I'm standing here with someone I just met."

Alice let out another giggle, taking her by the hand.

"We can fix that situation right now."

Grace smiled as she was led through the handsome woodworked foyer, past a finely furnished living room and a set of carpeted stairs, and into the kitchen.

"I was just about to start supper, but now you can keep me company while I do it. And while I slave away over a stove, you and I can do some catching up."

Grace smiled, nodding. "That's fine by me, as long as you let me help. I won't just sit by like a clove on a baked ham, thank you very much."

She looked around at the bright, airy kitchen...admiring the white painted walls and smooth, polished wood floor. She put her bag down in a chair, searching the room with enchanted eyes. Her voice was soft.

"Oh Alice, what a pretty place." Slowly, she ran her fingers over the granite countertop, marveling at its smoothness. She felt silly for doing it, but she couldn't help opening the doors to the hanging cabinets, swinging them back and forth. "It must be just grand to have all this space for things, right here at your fingertips. Not like the one old cupboard at home."

Still in awe, she moved to a bay window that looked out on the back yard. It was a small property. But it had a neatly trimmed lawn, a little row of yellow flowers along the back fence, and a little vegetable garden. She smiled at its quaintness.

"Your yard is as cute as a bug's ear. Jack must be glad there's not much to tend to."

Alice nodded. She stood at the stove over a simmering pot, chopping vegetables and dropping them in.

"After working at the Dearborn Station all day, managing his crew, he doesn't have the time or the energy to go out and work like an old mule. He works Monday through Friday, eight to five. It's a marvelous thing. Not like back home, when everyone is up at the first crack of dawn. Jack doesn't spend the whole day buried in the coal mine, or working in the fields like an animal."

As the memory of such things still stung fresh in her mind, Grace's smile faded. She hung her head a little. It wasn't her intention to bring a mood of gloom. But Alice seemed to sense the change of feeling in the room.

"I'm sorry if that came out sounding wrong." Her voice was gentle...apologetic. "I don't want to sound like I'm putting down everybody back home. I love my people, and I'm proud of where I'm from. But it's so sad to me that being born there is like being born a caged bird. You're confined to this little space. You can't spread your wings and take off, when you know there is this great big world out there, just waiting to be explored. All you can do is flutter your wings in frustration."

Grace smiled...a familiar sense of fascination coming over her. It was the same fascination she'd experienced as a child, listening to Alice as she taught her lessons. She had always spoken with such passion...such beauty. But more intriguing, perhaps, was how Alice hardly noticed her own mannerisms and way of speaking. She didn't speak with the intention of impressing anyone. But all the same, that was just what she did.

Not wanting to lapse into pure sentiment, she walked over to the stove where Alice stood. Looking about, she found herself captivated once again by the simple things around the kitchen...things that, to anyone else, might have seemed menial. But to her, they were all objects of immense fascination. She looked at the stove. A familiar thing...and yet, so different.

"I never saw a stove like this before. Where do you put the wood or the coal for the fire?"

Alice shook her head. "You don't need either one. It runs on gas that's piped through the ground. No chopping wood. No soot, no cinders. No carrying buckets of stinking, dirty coal and messing up the nice clean floor. And if you think that's wonderful, come look at this." She turned, moving a few steps to the refrigerator. She opened the door. "Isn't this just the bees knees? Jack just bought it for us a few months ago. Before that, we used to have an icebox, and there was a pan under it that used to overflow all the time if you didn't empty it. We used to come home and there would be water all over the place. Thank goodness for modern technology."

Grace's mouth was slightly agape.

"I would have been happy with the icebox. The only cooling we had back home was the root cellar or the cold shed down at the creek. Or the snow in the winter. Remember? And here's a little bit of winter right here, whenever you want it. If that don't beat all. There's even a little light in there, so you can see what you're looking at. That's as handy as a pocket on a shirt."

Alice smiled. "That it is," she said. "But I've always wondered. Does the light stay on or go off when you close the door?"

They looked at each other, both pondering one of life's little mysteries.

After they closed the door they went back to the cooking. They talked of many things. Of how Grace had come to be there...and of Charlie. When his name was mentioned, Grace's tone took on a sad and bitter note. When the tale was done, Alice shook her head, sighing in amazement.

"My word," she said. "Wait until Jack hears about all this. And when he hears about Charlie, he might just flip his lid."

They sat at the table now, each of them quiet for several moments. Then, Alice's expression became soft...almost guilty. "Don't be mad at me for saying this, but...I feel a little sorry for Charlie."

Grace's eyes widened. Was this a betrayal? It certainly felt that way. But Alice was quick to offer comfort, and an explanation.

"Don't take offense. I'm not saying that he should have talked to you the way he did. Men have a primal fear of the word 'no', and Charlie was acting just like any man would. You know that's how they are when they don't get what they want. But on the other hand, you have to remember what it was like for Charlie as a little boy. His father rejected him, like a baby chick being kicked out of the nest too soon. That had to have traumatized him something terrible. And when you turned down his proposal, it was like he was being rejected all over again."

She didn't want to hear this explanation, even coming from Alice. Her pride was still shaken, her feelings still hurt, even after the short passage of time. Deep down, she knew Alice spoke with wisdom. She always had. But she didn't reply to the statement. She just sat quietly, and they both seemed to sense that a change of subject was needed.

"Are you still teaching three days a week at the University? I know you wrote to me about it."

Alice nodded. "I am, and I love it. Right now we're on summer break. Your brother hates it, though. He always has." She sighed, leaning her head in her hand. "You know, I love Jack more than life itself. He's so wonderful...so smart. And he likes to think of himself as a "modern man." But he still has some of those old ideals in his head. Do you know, the first fight we had as a married couple was because he told me not to work? But I no sooner got through to him with that before he was making other demands...telling me I should quit as soon as we had children." She paused for a moment, sighing. "Well we've been married for six years. And as you can see and hear, there are no little feet pitter-pattering around."

She sighed again. For a moment, Grace thought they would now fall into a sad spell at the mention of children. After all, Alice and Jack had been married for quite some time and still had no babies, even though they wanted them badly. She looked at her sister-in-law, expecting to see a frown. But instead there was a little smirk on her face. She was intrigued.

"What?" There was a long, quiet moment. And then it dawned on her. Her eyes grew large. "Are you..."

"I'm not sure yet," Alice replied, trying to hold back a smile. "My doctor's out of town for the next two weeks, so I'm planning on seeing him as soon as I can."

A shadow of sadness crossed her expression. Grace watched her, sensing what she was thinking of. Alice frowned.

"I don't know if I should get my hopes up. I lost the other two so early on, and I've had a few false alarms. So I'm trying not to get too excited. I haven't even told Jack yet, because I don't want to say anything until I'm sure."

Grace reached out, giving her hand a gentle pat. "Keep your hopes up. You never can tell."

They smiled at one another. Then, from out in the hall, a clock struck the half-hour. Alice turned towards the sound.

"It's five-thirty already. Jack should be home any minute."

As if on cue, the front door opened. They looked at each other, Alice putting a finger to her lips. She rose to her feet, going out to greet her husband...and Grace felt her heart begin to flutter, filled with anticipation. She could not remain in her chair, sitting still. Creeping close to the doorway, she remained out of sight, but listened carefully.

And then she heard that beloved voice...one that was as familiar to her as her own, even after all these years. It made a tear come to her eye. She listened, hearing him talk to Alice.

"Honey, I'm home. And it's Friday, which means you get to spend two whole days with me. Doesn't that make you the luckiest woman in the world?"

She couldn't resist stealing a glimpse of him...just a small one. Peeking around the corner, she watched as he put his arms around Alice, kissing her. They stayed in each other's arms for more than a few moments, exchanging soft little presses of their lips, until Alice pulled back in his embrace. She smirked up at him.

"You came home to me, fella, so think of yourself as the lucky one."

Grace listened to the sweet little sounds they made as they went on with each other. For a few moments she wondered if Alice had forgotten about her. Then she heard Jack speak.

"Supper smells good. What are we having?"

"Don't worry about that now," Alice replied. "We have a visitor staying with us."

There was a pause, and Grace heard Jack grumble.

"A visitor? Oh honey, I ain't in the mood for visitors. Tell whoever it is that I have some awful disease, and then send them the hell back home."

Grace smiled, watching as Alice punched Jack in the shoulder.

"Don't be such a rat. Besides, you'll never believe the surprise I have for you."

This was the moment. Alice took Jack by the hand, pulling him forward. But just before he entered the room, he brought both of them to a halt, turning to look at her. He tried to keep his voice low as he griped.

"You know I hate surprises."

Ignoring his complaint, Alice gave him a determined little push, making him scoot forward into the kitchen. He turned his head to look...and at last, Grace was looking him in the eye. She took in the sight of him, seeing him...the real him, not just a picture…for the first time in six years. And he looked back at her, his mouth slightly open in shock. She had imagined their reunion. She'd imagined tears and loving embraces. And now, she waited to see if her imaginings would come true. But he just stood there, looking at her. He looked over at Alice…and then back at her again, dumbfounded.

"What are you doing here?"

She blinked, unsure of what to say or what to do, baffled by his reaction. She looked over at Alice, who sighed and rolled her eyes.

"Boy, sometimes you just gripe my cookies." She reached up, backhanding him hard across the upper arm. "You haven't seen your sister after all this time, and this is what you do? You knucklehead. Give her a hug or something, will you?"

He finally seemed to wake up, coming to hug her. And as she hugged him back, she felt the strength of their bond growing stronger by the moment. How wonderful it was to be so near him again. When at last he let go of her, he held her at arms length, looking her up and down.

"I'm sorry if I acted so dopey just now. I just can't believe you're standing here in my own kitchen. So, what are you doing here? And why in the world are you dressed like that? If Mama saw you in pants, she'd have a fit."

He smiled with the same lopsided grin she knew so well. It made her almost giddy to see it again.

"Look at you," he declared. "All grown up. I can't hardly believe my eyes."

She grinned. "Look at yourself. You're shined up like a new penny."

He took a slight step back, holding his arms out so she could get a better look at him. In his white dress shirt and black vest…his grey slacks and shiny black shoes, he looked every bit the city gentleman. How different he looked! So different from the country boy she used to know. But she felt quite safe in knowing that no matter what he looked like on the outside, the same old brother was still there. And she couldn't have been happier than she was at that moment.

* * * * *

During supper and long after, they talked of her long journey from home…of all that had happened. Just as she'd expected, Jack was upset over everything he heard, and he wasn't afraid to say just what he felt.

"Some things never change. Just one little difference in your thinking, just one little behavior that's different than theirs, and they want to tie you to a stake and burn you for witchcraft. And Charlie…" He paused, snorting bitterly. "If I ever get a hold of him, I'll put a boot in his ass."

Grace smiled, looking over at Alice, who was smiling as well but shaking her head. She rose to her feet, picking up her plate. She smiled over at him.

"You talk about someone who never changes, you big ape." Coming around to where he sat, she reached out to run her fingers through his hair. "I still love you anyway, hopeless as you are." She bent down slightly, leaning forward to give him a sweet kiss.

Finding Grace

Grace was smiling as she watched them together. She looked at Jack, who was openly admiring his wife, watching her as she went to the counter to get a slice of cake. There was a dreamy expression on his face…the slightest smile on his lips. But after a moment he seemed to realize Grace was watching. She saw him squirm, his face turning slightly red.

It almost made her giggle to see the changes in his expression…bolding admiring his wife one moment, and then embarrassed to be caught in such a moment of sentiment. He was just the same old Jack he'd always been. Tough and protective, but tender, and just a little bit shy at times.

"Funny that you ran into Henry and Victoria," he mentioned, clearly wanting to take the direction away from himself.

Hearing their names, Grace's smile fell a little. It was hard to hide her sarcasm. "They're not the nicest couple in the world, are they?"

Alice smiled and shrugged. "Victoria is an actress, so that makes her a little temperamental. Her folks were in show business and she's always been a little Princess. At least that's what I've heard."

"And now she works at Henry's nightclub," Jack chimed in. A grin came across his face as he lifted his glass of tea, pausing just before it reached his lips. "You might say she's at his service, in more ways than one."

She wondered at that smirk on his face. When Alice threw a napkin at him, Grace could see her smirking a little herself, even as she scolded him for his comment.

"You shouldn't talk about that, you know."

Grace looked eagerly between the two of them. "What?"

Alice sighed. "Well, since your brother already flapped his gums, I guess there's no use in keeping quiet." She leaned in close, speaking in a low, almost secretive voice. Grace eagerly leaned in to listen.

"Victoria and Henry are lovers."

Jack leaned forward, speaking in his own low tone of voice. "Very unmarried lovers."

Grace's mouth fell open a little, her eyes growing wide. She'd heard whispers about such things before. She'd even known that some of her neighbors supposedly did such things. But she'd never been openly exposed to such a subject. It was shocking. She spoke softly, just as they did.

"They really live together like that? Do other people around here know about it?"

Jack shrugged. "It's nobody's business, if you ask me. But I don't think in this one case that people pay it much attention. You see, Henry was a war hero when he got home. He came back from Europe and everyone looked on him like a big shining star. So, most people ignore his little indiscretions."

Little indiscretions? she thought. She couldn't believe he would talk about it like that. Alice just shrugged.

"Personally, I never could decide if I minded or not. And I'm still not sure."

Grace blinked, not understanding. "Why's that?"

Again, Alice shrugged. "Well for one thing, he's not exactly sweet to his women. He had a few others before Victoria, and he treats them more like pets than people. I'm surprised he doesn't keep a rolled up newspaper in his hand to whack them on the nose when they get out of line."

Grace smiled at that observation…one that seemed to be spot on. Henry had certainly seemed to treat Victoria, and herself for that matter, with an air of disdain.

"But then," Alice said, "There's another side of Henry that most people don't see. Sometimes, he can be so sweet and generous. When we were first getting started, he offered us this house to rent. He even paid for our wedding reception and sent us on our honeymoon."

Jack nodded. "He helped me land my job too. I wouldn't be where I am if it wasn't for him. So whoever he shares a bed with is his own business, not mine."

Grace felt her cheeks flush with embarrassment at such talk, but she didn't shy away from it. Actually, she felt a naughty kind of delight in hearing such adult conversation for the first time. It made her feel as if, for the first time, she was really being acknowledged as a grown woman.

A comfortable silence fell over the room as they all sort of smiled and looked at each other. Then, she tried to stifle a yawn, which Alice took immediate notice of.

"My word, look at us," she said, "Keeping this girl up so late. We should be ashamed of ourselves, Jack." She rose to her feet, and Jack and Grace followed.

Out of habit, Grace began to gather up the dishes from the table, but Alice stopped her.

"Leave that where it is," she said. "Dishes can wait until the morning. Let's get you upstairs to your room." She gave her a little push towards the hall, and Grace smiled, shaking her head. The three moved up the stairs, Jack bringing up the rear and turning off lights as he went. Grace looked around, admiring all the lovely things surrounding her, in particular the lighted wall sconces.

"It feels funny not needing a coal-oil lamp. All these modern things sure are nice."

"They are swell," said Jack, and as they paused at the top of the stairs, he turned to look at her. His expression was quite serious as he gestured a finger at her. "Another modern convenience is the telephone. And first thing in the morning, I want you to call down to Doctor Smith's house so he can tell Mama and Daddy where you are, and that you're all right."

Grace smirked at him, giving a little mock salute. "Yes boss. Whatever you say."

"Little Miss Smarty Pants," he said. "I wonder where you get that from." He grinned slightly, giving her a little peck on the forehead. "Good night, baby sister." Then he looked at Alice, gesturing his head towards their room. "Are you coming to bed?"

"I'll be there in a minute," she replied. She and Grace watched him vanish into the bedroom. After he closed the door, Alice opened the door across the hall from theirs. She switched on the light.

Grace took in a little breath as she looked around. She smiled.

"Oh Alice, this is the prettiest bedroom I ever saw. It's nearly too good for the likes of me."

Alice just shook her head.

"Silly goose. It's just another room... nothing special. But if it makes you happy, that's fine with me. Come on in the bathroom. I don't think you've ever seen one before, have you?" Grace followed her into the room next door...into the white and blue tiled bathroom. She looked around, her expression full of wonder. Sparkling clean, shining with fine fixtures of ceramic and brass, it seemed to be a showcase all on its own. Most impressive was the enormous claw-footed bathtub. Alice went over to it and turned on the faucet. Taking a small bottle from the nearby shelf, she poured a bit of liquid under the running water.

"You've had such a day. The best way to end it is for you to enjoy a nice, hot bubble bath. You've never had a hot bath, have you?"

Grace shook her head. "I still can't believe you've got water running right into your house, and without a pump. That's really something."

Alice just smiled again. "There's soap here, and the little pitcher on the floor to rinse your hair when you wash it." She looked around, and then she suddenly snapped her fingers. "Oh gosh, I just thought of something. Be right back." She ran out of the room, was gone for a minute, and came hurrying back with garments in her hands. "Here, wear these. They're Jack's, but he won't mind. I wear them sometimes myself."

Grace unfolded the thin navy blue shirt and pants. "What are they?" She'd never seen anything like them.

"They're cotton pajamas," Alice replied. "They're perfect for summer sleeping, and a hell of a lot better than those old flannel nightgowns, and I just know that's what you brought with you."

Grace smiled, but didn't answer. She didn't have to, for her sister-in-law knew her better than most anyone. "Thank you," she replied sweetly.

Alice pursed her lips, waving away the gratitude. "No thanks required, sis." She took the pajamas and set them aside for her. Then she turned back with a big smile. "Well, I think I'll leave you to it. I've had a long day myself, and I think I'll turn in." Suddenly she gave a little bounce of excitement, and threw her arms around her. "I'm so excited to have you here! We're going to have so much fun. I can't wait!"

With another little bounce she made her way towards the door, but Grace stopped her for a moment.

"You're sure I won't drown in there?" She pointed towards the mountain of bubbles that was rising in the tub. But Alice just smiled.

"I think you'll be safe." She closed the door behind her, leaving Grace on her own.

For the first time in days, she was completely alone. She looked around, and the first thing she did was to go over and shut off the faucet. Not because the water would overflow...though it had, indeed, reached its limit...but because she wanted to see if she really could control the thing. There was an odd kind of pleasure she found in managing the flow of water, turning it on and off again and again for several long moments. But after a short time playing, she made herself stop. She could have happily kept on, but felt a little silly for doing it, so she ceased and went on with her task at hand.

In the bedroom, she put her bag on a chair and rifled through it, finding her hairbrush. Carrying it into the bathroom she placed it on the sink, and shutting the door behind her, she took in the silence…the complete privacy the little room provided. Taking off her boots and socks, she set them neatly by the door. One by one she removed her garments, putting them neatly in a pile beside the boots. Then she turned to look at the bath. It seemed a little scary to see the big white tub, deep with water and high with bubbles, but she told herself not to be so ridiculous. If Alice had told her to do it, she would. It was only water, after all. She'd taken baths before, even though they'd been taken in the water of the spring, or just out of a bucket or a wash basin. This couldn't be so bad.

She stepped one foot over and slowly tested it. The bubbles were cool to the touch and smelled like lavender, which she liked very much. Then her foot touched actual water and she yanked it back briefly. She'd never felt hot water except on her face and hands, and it took several more tests before she found herself able to put both feet in and stand there, letting the heat radiate up her legs. Finally she made herself bend her knees, and slowly sinking down, she adjusted to the feeling of hot water all over her body. *Lord*, she thought with a sigh of pleasure, *Alice was right. This is heavenly.*

But even in the midst of such delight, she knew she had little duties to perform. Only this time, it was a duty to herself and not to her entire family or anyone else. After several days of traveling, she was sure she smelled quite ripe. Jack and Alice would have been too polite to say anything, but she could imagine what others would have thought. Especially Henry.

She didn't know why he'd popped into her head, but she couldn't stop thinking about how rude he'd been. Not that she cared about his snobby opinion. And what was he to her anyway? The feelings of a womanizer meant nothing to her. In fact, there were very few people whose opinion she cared about at all. But she did care about herself, and after all, cleanliness was next to Godliness, or so she believed. She cleaned herself up quickly, scrubbing herself from tip to toe, and giving her head and hair a thorough wash and rinse. Then she sank down in the water up to her neck, closing her eyes and relaxing, her obligations filled for the moment.

As she lay there, she kept seeing those cold blue eyes of his. For a moment she tried to push his image from her head, but it remained stubbornly implanted, and soon she gave up fighting it and let her mind wander. There was something strange about that man. Not that she feared him. But his look was so harsh it made her uncomfortable, while fascinating her at the same time. There was not one hint of softness in his appearance, starting with those eyes that seemed to pierce right through her, and moving on to other little things about him. His mouth, for one….thin lips set in a very angular lower jaw. His nose was hawkish and a bit long, but not ugly. It only added to the masculinity of his face. That seemed to be the thing about him…the lack of gentleness in any of his features. Maybe if he smiled, it would soften him a little. But she hadn't seen him make any attempt at that, and so she couldn't know if it would make a difference or not.

She sighed, and looking down, she saw that the bubbles had long dissolved. The water was growing cool as well. With great reluctance, she reached down and pulled the plug. She stood up in the tub, wringing the water out of her hair. She reached over and took a towel from the ring on the wall, wrapping it around herself. Just as she started to step out, the last of the bathwater was going down…and suddenly there came a demonic kind of sound from the bottom of the bathtub. It was the last of the water being sucked down the drain.

She practically jumped over the side, so terrified was she by the noise. In all sincerity, she thought it possible to be taken down with the bathwater, so she quickly got out and stepped away from the evil sounding thing. She might have pondered it further, if it weren't for the fact that she was suddenly freezing cold. She dried herself quickly, stepping into the pajamas Alice had given her. How odd it felt not to have a dress hem brushing her calves. But it wasn't unpleasant, not at all. She found the pajamas quite comfortable, just as Alice had said they would be.

As she went into her bedroom, she flipped off the light switch…then flipped it on, and off, and on and off again. She still couldn't get over the amazement of electric lights, among other things…and she was sure there were many other discoveries yet to be found.

As she sat on the edge of the bed she braided her hair, using the same tattered ribbon she'd been wearing for days. She saw how it was beginning to fray. Maybe she could ask Alice for some new ribbons tomorrow. She and Jack had been so good to her. They would probably give her new ribbon and a lot more, and without expecting anything in return, generous souls that they were. But she was determined to pay them back for their kindness, one way or another. The thought was a fading one, though, as both the wear of travel and the heat from the bath were suddenly taking a toll on her senses.

She pulled back the soft blue comforter, folding it neatly at the end of the bed, for it was too warm to need much cover. The sheet would be enough, and she slipped under its softness. Reaching over, she turned off the light…and unable to help herself, she pulled the little chain several times before finally letting the room settle into darkness.

Her last act, before she fell asleep, was to clasp the little cross at her neck and to send a prayer to heaven, thanking the good Lord above for guiding her on her way.

Chapter 6
"A New World"

Morning, she thought. *It is morning. Time to rise.*

Sitting up, rubbing her weary eyes, she wondered for a moment why everything was so silent. That danged old rooster never missed a day.

But then she remembered that there was no rooster. No fires to be lit, no water to be fetched. Looking around her new room, hearing the absolute silence, she realized that she wasn't bound to those kinds of drudgeries anymore. Her time was now completely her own, perhaps for the first time in her entire life, and it made her smile with contentment.

Stretching like a lazy cat, she fell back on her pillow where she remained for some time, just staring at the ceiling. There was an inkling in her head that she could lay there as long as she wished. No one would care if she did.

But laziness was not in her blood, even now.

Throwing back the sheet, she swung her legs over the side of the bed. How strange and soft the carpet felt on her bare feet, so different from the bare wood floor she was used to. She crunched her toes in the material as she walked to the chair to fetch her clothes. As she dressed, she suddenly wished she'd had the time to make more clothes for herself. Her wardrobe was scanty at best, and most of what she did have was worn and faded. But it was all she had, so it would have to do. As she put away her pajamas, she suddenly had a thought.

If there were no chores, what did a person do at this hour of the morning?

Then another thought came to her...a memory, of something Jack had once written to her about in a letter...

Dear Sis,

Today I saw the funniest thing. I'd heard tell that they bring eggs and milk to your door here, every morning, and today I learned it's really true. At dawn this morning, a man in a white uniform came up to our front door and sure enough, he brought with him a basket of eggs and a jar of milk. Mama sure would be pleased to have something like that. One thing though - the milk sure tastes different than the stuff old Bessie used to give. It has kind of a sweet taste - pasteurized, they call it. Just one more thing to get used to, I suppose...

Her curiosity went wild as she thought about it. Slipping quietly from her room, she made her way down the stairs, determined to see for herself this early morning ritual Jack had described. The hall clock struck five as she opened the front door and took a look around.

The sky was soft and purple, the sun just starting to light the horizon, and the birds were chirping in the trees. Otherwise, it was very quiet and peaceful. And there was no sign of anyone, and nothing at the door. If Jack hadn't said it was so, she might have doubted that anyone or anything might be on their way. But if he had said it, she believed it. So she went to the swing to sit down, rocking back and forth as she waited.

She didn't have to sit for long.

A small white truck soon came down the street. She watched, intrigued, as the delivery man criss-crossed from one house to another, carrying his goods and placing them at each porch stoop. When he came near the Langdon house, she found she couldn't sit still a moment longer. Her curiosity was too great, and she went out to the curb to meet the driver as he approached. He seemed startled by her sudden appearance, but she paid it no mind.

She bid him good morning, sticking out her hand out in greeting. "My name is Grace. How are you?"

He gave her an odd look. But accepting her hand, he gave it a firm shake as he introduced himself.

"I'm Mike."

She smiled shyly, realizing that she might be making trouble, but unable to help herself.

"I'm sorry if I'm bothering you, Mike. It's just that I never saw a milkman before. I'll tell you one thing, we don't have nothin' like this back home. You sure are doing a service to folks around here. I hope they all appreciate it as much as I do."

He still seemed a bit befuddled, but he tried to smile as he handed her the delivery of eggs, butter, and milk. She smiled at him again.

"Thanks, Mike. I've got to get in the house and make breakfast before my brother and his wife wake up. I want to surprise them. You have yourself a good day." With her goods in hand she made her way back up the sidewalk, missing the strange look on the milkman's face.

As she came up the front step, she had a sudden feeling she was being watched. It made her think of Charlie, and she shuddered at the thought. *He's another world away*, she told herself. *He's not watching you, and no one else is either.* She laughed at herself for her silliness, and went into the house.

* * * * *

In the house across the street, the grandfather clock in the hall struck five. The sun was just showing itself out on the horizon. Lying in bed, Henry twitched in his sleep. A sheen of sweat beaded on his brow. An old foe had returned to him in the night, invading the peace of his rest…

Finding Grace

Mortars screamed...an ear-splitting noise through the black of night. Then the ground exploded in a violent upchucking of rocks, dirt, and mud. The battering of machine-gun fire was relentless and deafening...but not loud enough to block out the sounds of lives being blown away in the blink of an eye. In the cold, muddy rows of the trenches there were the cries and moans of the dying, the barking of orders, and the shouting of men in states of near madness. Grown men, torn to bits by bullets and explosions, cried for their mothers. The stench of blood and carnage, of death, was everywhere...a putrid scent that infiltrated the nostrils and never left, no matter how long the passage of time. Men gave stark, sudden cries and fell to the ground, as puddles of red mixed with the water and mud...

He gave a slight cry he woke, trembling slightly as he lurched to a sitting position. His breathing was rapid, his eyes wide. Beside him, Victoria lifted her head, her voice drowsy.

"Henry, are you all right?"

He closed his eyes, breathing though his nose until his heartbeat slowed. Over the years, he'd gotten quite good at recovering from these night terrors. He spoke as calmly as he could.

"It's nothing, Victoria. Go back to sleep."

"Are you sure?"

He hated repeating himself, but did to quiet her. "Yes, I'm sure. Go back to sleep."

She hesitated for a moment before settling back under the covers.

He rose from the bed, calm now, but unable to go back to sleep. He stood and stared out the window, watching the dawning of the day. And he started to think about the years since he'd returned from battle...how his life had been forever altered.

Once, as a young man, he'd lived a quiet and obedient life, doing just what the world expected him to do as a man. At twenty-one he'd been newly married and just out of college. He'd been ready to officially join the family theatre business and begin his adult life. But the war had called for him first, and reluctantly he'd found himself serving in the U.S. Army, fighting on the bloody fields of France.

And France had destroyed the boy in him. The man who emerged had been an empty shell, struggling to recall what it felt like to be a human being. For years after he'd found it difficult to express deep emotions. The only feelings he found himself truly capable of were rage and deep depression, and those had been so deeply imbedded in his soul that his marriage had not withstood it. Mary, once his teenage sweetheart, had never understood why he hid away in his library so many nights, sometimes sobbing endlessly. His tears made him ashamed, and they frightened her so that she began to distance herself more and more each day. In the end, the emotional strife had been too much for them both. She had ended the union and joined her family who now lived in New York.

In time, the emptiness began to dull. But the desertion of his wife had left him wary of commitments. His only commitment now was his business, which he had transitioned from a drama theatre into a bustling nightclub. As for women, he found himself a very eligible bachelor and he never lacked female attention. Some men might have taken advantage of being free of a wife, and some would have taken the opportunity to go from bed to bed. But he found that notion unappealing. He knew he was hardly a saint, but he wasn't a whoremonger either. Since his divorce he'd been with four women altogether, Victoria being the latest and the longest relationship.

He turned to look at her for a moment. She'd been around longer than any of his other lovers, nearly a year now. The ones before had lasted only a few months at most. Those women had come into his life knowing he wasn't the marrying kind. And yet, in the end they had all begged for a ring on their finger. Victoria gave no hint of looking for such a union. Maybe it was because she'd been married and divorced just as he had been. Whatever the reason, she knew what they were to each other, and she never tried to take it further. And if, someday, he grew bored with the relationship and wanted to end it, she would accept it and move on. He lived his life as he pleased. That was how it was, and she could take it or leave it.

Looking out the window now, he could see John Langdon's house. John had been his neighbor for many years, and his friend since their time together in the service. But it wasn't John he was thinking of at that moment.

As he looked out the window, he saw a little figure appear on the front porch. She went to sit on the swing. It was John's little sister, Grace. He knew it from her skinny little frame. As he looked at her he wondered…

Why in the hell is she out there at five o'clock in the morning?

He watched her rock back and forth on the swing, doing nothing in particular. Then the milkman came up the street, and Henry watched her as she hurried down the front walk and approached the driver. She stood there, talking to him.

What in the world is she doing? He wondered.

For several minutes he watched them talk, and then the two were shaking hands. Then she was taking her delivery and heading back up the sidewalk, where she disappeared into the house.

That girl is so odd, he thought. But then again, he'd thought she was strange when he'd met her earlier that afternoon, especially the way she'd been dressed. She couldn't be more than sixteen or seventeen at most. She wasn't a bad looking girl. A little on the thin side, maybe, but she had a pretty face and nice figure. Her voice was soft and shy, he remembered. He remembered too, the change in her eyes at his being so cold to her. A kind of fire and energy had lit in those eyes, and he thought of how, at the last moment he'd seen her, she had cursed him and called him a "grouchy bastard." It was strange, but he got the feeling she had meant for him to hear that.

The slightest smirk came to his lips. She was right, of course. He *was* a grouchy bastard. And he didn't feel the least bit guilty about it. But he had to admire her honesty. Because of his military service, most people felt obligated to treat him with great respect. Even Victoria, with her frequent fits of temper, was apt to sweet-talk him, especially when she thought it might get her what she wanted. But there was something refreshing about someone who preferred honesty to flattery...even if that someone was a hopelessly naive little country mouse.

What a shame she wasn't suited to his taste. She was too much of a rube...not nearly sophisticated enough. And even if she hadn't been a simpleton, she was much too young, and with an older brother to boot. That was never a good chance to take. Yes, it was too bad indeed. With a little improvement, she could have made an interesting conquest.

* * * * *

The smell of coffee, fried bacon and eggs must have drifted upstairs quickly. Not long after Grace started cooking, Jack appeared in the doorway, still in his pajamas, with his hair sticking up all over.

"I smell food," he said. "Good food. What are we having?" He came up next to her and took a piece of bacon off the plate. She just smiled at him, shaking her head.

"Just like a man, always thinking with your stomach. You can't even say good morning."

"Good morning," said Alice, who appeared in the doorway behind them. As she came near them she looked at her husband, eyed him up and down, and shook her head. "You look like something the cat dragged in." She kissed him sweetly on the lips, then hugged him and pressed her cheek to his...and she winced.

"My Lord, Jack. Your face gives me whisker burn. Go get a shower and a shave, will you please?"

"Yes, please," said Grace as she tried to suppress a smile.

Jack turned around, grumbling good-naturedly as he shuffled out. "Damn. My own house and I have to shower and shave. Why don't you put me in a frilly pink dress with my hair in pigtails so I'll be pretty enough for you?"

Alice smiled as she called out to him. "You don't have the legs, doll."

Grace giggled, delighting in the fun of teasing him, and she added her own little jibe.

"You wouldn't look right in pink. Purple, maybe."

From the hallway they heard him make a goofy, mocking kind of laugh. "Everybody's a comedian."

Grace and Alice just smiled at one another. Alice gestured at the cooking.

"What is all this? You cleaned up everything from last night, I see. And now here you are, cooking breakfast. You didn't have to do all of this."

Grace only smiled, shrugging. "It's just my way to thank you for putting up with me."

Alice smirked. "Well, you're just so much trouble." She started taking out plates and silverware to set the table. Her voice became tender.

"You know sis, I don't want to tell you what to do...but I think maybe you should make that call to home. It's best to get it over and done with, you know."

There was a long silence as Grace pondered whether or not to actually make the dreaded call.

"I'm sorry," Alice said. "It's none of my business. You make that call whenever you want. Or not at all."

Grace put down the wooden spoon she held in her hand, turning down the fire.

"No, you're right. It's best to just get it done."

Alice spoke softly. "The phone is in the living room. Do you want me to go with you, just for moral support?"

Grace shook her head. "No, that's all right. I'll manage...I hope."

In the living room, she sat by the phone for some time before finally picking it up and speaking to the operator. She gave the name and location, the operator connected her, and she waited. After what seemed like an eternity, a female voice finally connected on the other end of the line. It was Mrs. Smith, the doctor's wife.

"Hello?"

"Is this Mrs. Smith?" Grace asked.

"Who is this?"

She swallowed a sudden lump in her throat before she answered. "Gracie Langdon."

There was a pause at the other end of the line. Then Mrs. Smith replied in shock. "Is that really you Gracie? Your folks have been looking all over creation for you. Where on earth are you?"

Grace swallowed, nervous as she answered.

"I'm with Jack."

There was another pause. "How in the world did you get there all by yourself?"

"I'm sorry, Mrs. Smith, but I can't talk about it now," she said. "Just tell Mama and Daddy not to worry, will you? I've got to go now. Goodbye." She quickly hung up the phone, motivated by a fear that she still might be caught and dragged home like a criminal, where she would have to suffer for a lifetime because of her defiance. The phone itself seemed frightening at that moment, like a spy who might give her away. So she moved away from it quickly and headed back toward the kitchen, and in the hall, she met Jack. He looked at her with a serious expression, and she knew just what was on his mind and what he would ask her about.

"You called home just now, didn't you?"

She nodded. Neither one of them said anything else, and both silently agreed not to discuss the subject further. As far as both were concerned, Grace had done the right thing in alleviating her parents concern, and now the matter was closed. A change of subject was best.

"I've got to go out and get the paper," he said, but Grace waved him off.

"I'll get it for you," she said. "I could use a breath of fresh air."

She went out the front door and walked out to the end of the curb, looking around at the pretty little lawns that still shined with wet dew. The air was warm but pleasant, and the sunshine helped lift the weight off of her shoulders. As she reached down at the curb to get the paper, something made her draw her eyes upward and across the street. She didn't want to look - but her curiosity had often been a bully to her common sense, and this occasion was no different. Her eyes rose, and she saw Henry sitting on the front stoop of his house, reading the paper. For the longest time, she stood there watching him - sort of admiring the way his long legs were stretched out before him, and the way his broad shoulders were sort of slouched as he relaxed. He was wearing glasses, too. She found something oddly appealing in that.

Suddenly she shook her head. *Why am I standing here, staring like a fool?* She thought. *Thank the Lord he hasn't looked up and seen me.* She hurried back into the house with the newspaper in hand, fearful that at any moment, he would look up and meet her eyes. For some reason, the thought of that terrified her.

She didn't see it when he glanced up from his paper...his eyes watching her closely as she walked into the house.

* * * * *

At the breakfast table, there were most of the same foods and rituals that she'd had every day of her life. Some things, she supposed, were common experiences no matter where one was born. But there was no lack of new things to learn...new experiences, small as they might have been.

She'd never had toasted bread before. Spread with butter and topped with a bit of scrambled eggs, it was delicious. But it was the milk in her glass that enthralled her most. The taste was not as rich as the milk she'd had at home, but it wasn't the difference between the two that held her fascination. It was the transformation that Jack made of it. Taking a little canister from the cabinet, he sprinkled in a sweet-smelling brown powder and stirred the glass with a spoon. Chocolate milk, she found, was delightful...and Jack seemed animated by her reaction. He grinned.

"God bless Milton Hershey," he said, stirring up a glass for himself.

Alice smiled, shaking her head.

"Your brother and his sweets. You should see him with Hydrox Cookies and milk. It's ridiculous."

Jack shrugged. "Hydrox cookies are an American institution. I'm just being patriotic."

Now Alice rolled her eyes. "It a wonder that you don't look like a Macy's Day float. It's a good thing we go out all the time and stay active, or you'd be in serious trouble."

"Speaking of activities," said Jack, "I think today is a good day to go down to the lake. You should see it, sis. You *will* see it, as a matter of fact. We had lakes back home, but nothing like this. And we sure didn't have a beach at home."

Grace's expression fell, and she looked down at the table for a moment. There was something on her mind that she'd wanted to ask for the longest time, but never knew how or when. Somehow, this moment seemed to be the right one.

"Have you ever missed being home?" she asked. "Even the least little bit?"

62

Jack slowly put down his glass. He and Alice looked at each other, and then he looked over at Grace. His face was quite serious, his voice calm...and almost cold as he spoke.

"Baby sister," he said. "There are little things that I'll always miss. The music we used to play, for one. The big outdoors, for another. And I miss *most* of the family." He paused a moment, and then his eyes grew very dark, the way they had always done when he was growing angry. Still, his voice was calm. "But I don't lose sleep at night, wishing I was still there. I don't miss freezing to death in the winter, or working like a dog every day and never getting a thing out of it. I don't miss scraping up just enough food to keep body and soul together. And I'm not sorry I got away from that damned old coal mine."

As if sensing that the mood had gotten too serious, and perhaps realizing that his tone had taken on a rather dark note, he paused for a few moments. He cleared his throat, and then, a little smile came back to his face. Now his tone was almost joking in its sarcasm. "I lost the chance to die in a collapse, or from a methane explosion. Or better yet, there's always that old black lung disease, from swallowing all that coal dust. What a shame I missed out on all of those things."

Alice frowned. "That's enough, Jack."

For several moments he didn't look at her, or at Grace. Then he rose to his feet.

"I have to answer the call of nature," he said. "You two will excuse me, won't you?" He said it all rather quickly, as if he was in a hurry to get away. Then he turned and left the room.

Alice sighed...and Grace lowered her eyes, troubled and saddened.

"I shouldn't have opened my big mouth," she said.

But Alice was quick to comfort her. "Don't talk like that. It's been a sore subject ever since we left the mountains. The few times I ever did get him to talk about it, he either made jokes or refused to talk about it at all. We've gotten into a few bad arguments about it over the years. He has to be the most stubborn man I've ever known in my life."

Despite the gloomy mood that had descended, Grace couldn't help but smile a little, though her eyes were fixed on the table. "He always was like an old mule, when it came to doing what he wanted." Her face fell again, as a sad memory came into her head. "I remember how bad things got at home, especially after you both left."

Alice shook her head sadly. "I always wished things could've been different. I never wanted to break up anyone's family. I hope you never thought I was trying to do anything like that."

"Alice, you don't have to tell me that. I was just a kid, but I always thought the world of you. And I always knew that Jack left because he wanted to leave. He would have gone away with or without getting married. And now that I'm older, I understand exactly why he didn't want to stay."

"But no man should forget his family," Alice declared. "If something ever happens to your Mama, your Daddy, or one of your brothers, he'll be regretting it until the day he dies that he didn't go back home."

Finding Grace

They heard a door shut upstairs, and it was a signal to both of them to cease their conversation, at least in the presence of Jack. Grace rose to her feet and began clearing the table, and Alice stood and helped her as Jack came in the room. He stood in the doorway for several moments, watching them with a kind of suspicion. Alice looked over at him, and then she snapped her fingers and gave him an excited look.

"Honey, I just had the best idea. When we go to the lake, let's stop at Edgewater Beach." She turned to Grace and began talking with delight. "We had our wedding and reception at the Edgewater Beach Hotel. You should see it. It's so beautiful. And pink! You've never seen such a place."

Jack scoffed. "Pink. I can't believe I stayed in a place that was colored like a danged piece of bubble gum." He sat down...and then a little smile came to his face. "Then again, I wasn't exactly thinking about where I was. All I could think about was getting married."

Alice cooed at his sweet statement. "The happiest day of your life, was it?" She leaned down to kiss him...and as she turned away, she didn't see the little smirk on his face.

"When I woke up the next morning," he said, "I saw the ball and chain attached to my leg, and it scared the hell out of me."

Before the words were out of his mouth he was running from the room...and Alice chased after him, threatening all kinds of violence. Grace smiled, thinking to leave them alone with whatever they would do next...but when she heard Jack shouting for help, she couldn't resist rushing to see what they were up to.

Jack was lying face down on the sofa, and Alice had her knee in the middle of his back. She had his arm pinned behind him, gripping his wrist hard, shouting at him. "Say Uncle!"

Jack was laughing and pleading at the same time. "Help! Get this crazy broad off of me!"

Alice dug her knee in further, twisting harder on his wrist...and all the while, Grace just watched the two of them, giggling at their play.

If all couples were more like them, she thought, *Marriage might not be such a bad idea.*

* * * * *

The company store is nothing compared to this, she thought with wonder.

Marshall Field's seemed too beautiful to be a store. It was all polished brass and gleaming tile floors, with carpeted stairs that went to multiple stories. In the center of it all was a great glass dome, and looking down from the fifth floor balcony, she felt her head spin from the height.

Alice seemed quite delighted as they went along, gushing over this garment and that, trying on hats and sampling fragrances from the cosmetics counter. Grace followed quietly along, taking in each new experience.

But as they passed a set of mirrors, she looked at the reflection of her plain little self in her flour sack dress...and she wanted to turn and run. As much self confidence as she'd always had, it seemed to be sapped right out of her as she looked at her own image reflected.

After walking for a spell, Alice suddenly noticed that her shopping partner was not beside her. She went back, and saw Grace standing in front of the mirror.

"What's wrong?" she asked.

"Look at me," said Grace. "I don't belong in a place like this."

Alice pursed her lips. "Oh don't be like that. You just need some new clothes, that's all. We could have some real fun getting you a new wardrobe."

Grace shook her head. "Oh no. I don't want you spending all kinds of money on me, even if I am a sorry sight. I can make my own clothes, if I can get some material. And I'll help around the house to pay for it. I promise."

Alice smiled. "If it makes you happy to make your own clothes, then I won't argue with you. We'll find you some lovely material to work with. But you need at least one or two simple dresses between now and then. And I have to fight you on one other thing, sister." She pointed down at Grace's boots. "Those things will have to go. And besides new shoes, I just have to twist your arm about a party dress. You should have at least one fine dress, in case we go out to a classy restaurant or some other special occasion. Will you please just let me do that for you?"

Grace was hesitant. But looking into Alice's eyes, she saw how eager her sister-in-law was to please her. She didn't like the idea of being dressed like a doll, but Alice really wanted to do this kindness, and she was aware that she could stand a bit of self-improvement. Right then she promised herself that this would be the first and only time she would succumb to the temptation of vanity and spending money. Other people's money, as it was.

As if reading her thoughts, Alice laughed a little. Looping Grace's arm in hers, she pulled her away from the mirror.

"I promise, I won't try to make you into a princess," she said. "I despise the notion of a princess. But we're not peasants, are we? So why dress that way? We'll keep it simple and painless, I promise you. Just some new shoes and stockings. Maybe a hat or two. And then there are the basics, of course, like underwear." She saw Grace blush, but only smiled. "Don't be embarrassed. We're both women. We can talk about these things."

It was a bit embarrassing, picking out such personal effects. And yet, there was a kind of fun in seeing all the different garments and under things. As for picking a party dress, it wasn't at all difficult. Her eye was caught by a pale pink garment in a rose print, with a straight-across bodice and draping chiffon sleeves that came to the elbows. It was one of the prettiest things she'd ever seen, but she felt ashamed of liking it so much, when she knew that Alice would be paying for it.

"I wish I had a way to pay for this myself," she said. "I feel just awful having you buying everything for me."

Alice smiled, giving her a thoughtful look. "I'll tell you what. If you keep on keeping me company, and keep helping me around the house, it'll be worth its weight in gold."

Finding Grace

Just when Grace thought they were through with their buying, Alice came across another item of a female wardrobe that she insisted her sister-in-law needed - a swimsuit. Grace took one look at the selections and went red with embarrassment.

"Women actually wear those things in public?" She gasped, shaking her head in denial of accepting the thing. "That's a little too bold for me. I think that's the one place I'll have to put my foot down."

"Well you wear a wrapper over it while you're on the beach," Alice assured her. "And when you're in the water, no one will really see it anyway. It works better than wearing regular clothes. Remember how we used to do that when we went swimming back home? It was all well and good while we were in the water, but once you got out, it was like your clothes were plastered to your skin."

"I remember," Grace said. "But I still don't reckon I'll take one of those things. I never was much for swimming anyway."

Despite her initial reluctance, she actually found herself having a fabulous time. When she looked at herself in the mirror, dressed in her new clothes, she felt a great sense of pride in what she saw. And she had to admit that the new shoes looked and felt better than those worn out old boots. When they left the store she was feeling quite confident, and ready to take on whatever new adventures lay ahead.

* * * * *

When they came through the front door of the house, they were laughing and smiling as they put their bags down in the living room. Then they heard the sound of Jack's voice coming from the kitchen, and the sound of another male voice talking to him.

Grace felt her stomach drop. She knew the sound of those low, melodic tones, and who they belonged to. The sound of that voice rattled her nerves, and she wondered...

What is that old sour puss doing here?

She had a momentary urge to run upstairs and hide. But that seemed like the coward's way out. And she was no coward. She never had been. Henry was just a man, after all, and she'd been around men all of her life, so what was there to be afraid of? Gathering her courage, she followed Alice into the kitchen.

There he was, sitting across the table from Jack, who turned around in his seat. He smirked as he looked at the two of them.

"Did you two put Marshall Field's into bankruptcy?"

"Yes, honey, we did," said Alice. "Looks like I'll have to keep teaching after all, no matter how much you fuss about it." She bent down and gave him a kiss on the forehead. Then she looked over at Henry and smiled politely. "Good morning, Henry Shaw. What brings you over today?"

Jack looked up at her. "Henry just stopped by for a cup of coffee. We were talking, and he's invited us down to the club tonight."

She leaned down, putting her arms around Jack's shoulders. "That sounds all right to me. I think we'll take you up on that offer, Henry."

No one said anything more for several moments, and all three turned to look at Grace, who was standing just inside the doorway, partially hidden by the frame as if she were trying to avoid being seen. Jack gave her a curious look.

"Why are you hiding over there like that? Come on in here and be sociable. You remember Henry."

Grace came forward a few steps, nodding slightly. Then she looked away, folding her arms across her chest, eager to keep her hands free from nervous little gestures. She could feel Henry's eyes on her, examining her. She refused to look at him...and yet, even when her own eyes were cast away from him, she could feel his gaze looking right through her. It was shameful to think about, but his look almost made her feel naked.

He probably enjoys making a fool of me, she thought. *But he won't rile me. That would make him happy, and I'm not putting on a show for anyone, especially him.*

But even if she could keep from looking at him, she couldn't ignore that velvety tone that was his voice.

"Well," he said. "It's all of a sudden too quiet in here for me. I suppose that's my cue to leave." He rose to his feet, looking at each of them in turn. "Victoria is down at the club already, deep into rehearsals. I should probably get down there and tend to business. I hope to see you at the show tonight."

He nodded at Alice and Jack, who nodded back and then turned their attention to each other. Grace hoped that Henry would be decent enough to remain silent as he passed her by. She kept her eyes away from him, pretending to look at a spot on the wall as he came near. But as he went by, he seemed to move with a slow purpose. His arm grazed hers...his touch so warm it raised the flesh on her skin and caused her take in a breath. Without thinking she slowly raised her eyes, meeting his...and her head seemed to swim from the way he looked at her. Then he smirked slightly, his voice becoming dangerously low and soft.

"Miss Grace."

It was all he said, just before he tipped his hat to her...and then he was gone. But his tone sent a wave of slight dizziness over her, making her place a hand on the wall for support. Somehow she managed to think, asking herself...

Why am I supposed to hate him?

She tried to rattle her brain for a reason, but couldn't think of a single one.

Chapter 7
"On The Town"

Jack had told the truth. The Edgewater Hotel was, as he had said, pink. But it was elegant and beautiful, and Edgewater Beach was full of visitor. They frolicked in the water and roamed the sand, enjoying the sunshine of a late June afternoon, but Grace was not among the ones playing and cavorting. While Jack and Alice walked along the beach together, reminiscing about the place where they'd spent their first few wedding days, Grace found a spot under the shade of an umbrella, where she tried to concentrate on the open book lying on her lap.

She found Lake Michigan to be quite beautiful. It was amazing to her that such a wonder of nature would be right across the road from the enormity of a man-made city. The beach was a wondrous thing to know as well. She loved the feeling of cool, wet sand as she walked along the edge of the water, and the warmth of the soft, dry sand as she walked over to sit on the blanket they had spread out. But of all these things, she found the most pleasure in just sitting and relaxing. For days, she'd been surrounded by chaos and excitement. Now, she felt compelled just to sit in peace and indulge in a good book.

Gaskell's *North and South* had always been one of her favorites. Now it seemed funny to her how her life seemed to imitate art. Just as she'd always thought of herself as her fictional mentor, Jane, she could very well have been Margaret Hale...A girl from the country coming to the city, learning to adjust. And Henry might have been her Mr. Thornton...the cold, stern businessman who harbored a secret admiration for Miss Hale.

She shook her head at such a thought. What a silly idea. To think that Henry Shaw might be harboring a secret admiration for her. What nonsense.

She knew he wasn't the kind of man she should have been thinking about. But ever since she'd first met him, he was a constant presence in her thoughts. Her mind went back to the comparison of Henry and John Thornton. What if, by some ridiculous chance, he really did harbor a secret liking for her?

For a few crazy moments, she allowed herself to imagine such an impossible thing. Yes, his disposition was not nice. But was he really so very bad? True, he'd been rude to her that first time. But he hadn't been cruel outright. In all honesty, despite his rough manner and tone, he'd managed to be a gentleman of sorts. He'd tipped his hat to her, which was pleasant. He'd let her follow him onto the streetcar, after which he'd paid her way. He'd not been required to do any of that, but none the less, he had. And then, there was that strange moment when he'd passed her in the doorway.

He'd struck her senseless with barely a word. But what was it about him that had left her so dazed?

His good looks could tempt any woman. But looks alone had never mattered much to her. Lord knew that a handsome face did not determine a man's worth. Charlie had been enough proof of that. No, it wasn't just Henry's handsomeness that appealed to her. He had an intensity about him. It was that which she found she couldn't forget, no matter how she tried. And if by some miracle, he saw something desirable in her, she might have been the luckiest woman in the world. To have such a man would be divine.

She shook her head once again, determined to dislodge those foolish dreams from her mind.

You're a fool, Grace Langdon, she told herself. *Didn't you learn anything from the mess with Charlie? Or do you want to have your heart broken all over again?*

She was determined that it would *not* happen again. She would stay away from him, even if he did live right across the street. There were plenty of ways to keep her distance.

Then she remembered...they were going to his club tonight. What rotten luck, to start off her new resolution by taking such a chance. She couldn't lie to get herself out of it. One of her weaknesses...or strengths, depending on the point of view...was her inability to lie. She'd never very good at telling fibs. And she couldn't refuse the invitation. Jack and Alice would want an explanation for her refusal, then she would confess her dilemma, and then there would be nothing but trouble to follow, and that wouldn't do at all. It seemed she had no choice.

I'll go, she thought. *But I'll stay away from him, and keep myself out of trouble.*

* * * * *

In her room, Grace stood before the mirror, looking at herself in her new dress. Jack had told her the club was a fashionable place, so they had to dress accordingly. She hoped that she passed muster. Her hair was up in a loose gathering at the back of her head. Alice had suggested it would look more elegant that way...and as usual, she was right. Reaching up to touch the neckline of her dress, she felt a little nervous about it being as low as it was, even though it was above her bust-line. Compared to the high necked dresses she'd always worn, this was more revealing than anything she'd had on before.

A knock came on her door, and she turned to see Alice come in. Grace's mouth fell open at how incredible her sister-in-law looked.

"My word, you look so beautiful."

Alice grinned, striking a pose. Her beaded white gown, sleeveless and knee-length, showed off her well-toned arms and legs.

"You look fine too," she said. "And a little nervous. Are you all right?"

Finding Grace

Grace shrugged, turning back to look at her reflection. "I don't know about showing so much skin. Do you think it's too revealing?"

With a smile, Alice shook her head. "Believe me, it looks fine. But here…" She unclasped the silver cross and chain, setting it aside on the dressing table. Taking off one of her strands of pearls, she looped it around Grace's neck. Looking over Grace's shoulder, she smiled with satisfaction.

"That should shift the focus a bit, at least for your own eyes."

Grace looked at her reflection again…and saw that Alice was right. The pearl beads made all the difference. Putting on her new hat…a lovely bell-shaped cap they called a "cloche"…she saw that it crowned her head quite nicely, adding the finishing touch to the entirely new person she saw when she looked in the mirror. She couldn't help smiling to herself, and she thought, *I look like a lady now, and quite a fine one.*

Then a second thought came to her. *I am still me, no matter what changes on the outside, and that is what matters most of all.*

* * * * *

They rode into the city in an elevated train, or as Jack called it, "The El." It was exciting to look out the window and see the city lights twinkling, and to look down and see the lights of the traffic passing on the streets below.

Odd, but as they exited the train and made their way down the stairs to the street, she didn't feel like such a stranger. The people around her moved along as one happy bunch. Some of the men smiled at her, nodding their heads in greeting, or tipping their hats politely. It was flattering to have that kind of attention, even in very small doses. But Jack didn't like it much. He frowned as they walked down the sidewalk.

"I don't think I like how men are eyeing you. Like buzzards, staking out a wounded animal."

Alice smiled at his brotherly concern. "I think she's beautiful in her new clothes. She's the cat's meow. What's wrong with letting people look?"

"As long as they look and don't touch. Men are pigs, especially when they get a few drinks in them."

Grace stubbornly raised her chin at him. "I can take care of myself. I'm seventeen years old. I don't need a guardian. Not even you, big brother."

Alice looked at her with a grin. "Give him hell, tootsie."

Jack mumbled something under his breath, and Grace saw the wounded expression on his face.

She suddenly realized she'd never talked to him in such way. He'd always taught her to speak her mind, but she'd always spoken to him with love and respect. She saw him open his mouth as if to say something, and then he just sighed. Suddenly she felt the need to apply balm where she might have cut him.

"I'll stick close by," she said. "I promise."

That seemed to comfort him, if only a little.

Finding Grace

They rounded the corner, and for the first time, she saw the lights of the club in full view. The vertical name sign glowed with a blaze of lights, given off by thousands of tiny round white light bulbs, and trimmed in brilliant glowing red. The doors leading into the building were made of shining glass and rimmed with polished brass, with large carved handles. Jack opened the door for them, and they stepped inside.

It wasn't quite what she'd expected. There were no dancers here. No musicians. Only a flow of people heading down a corridor which led to a grand staircase. And *grand* was the operative word, for although there was none of the music and dancing she'd imagined, it was beautiful beyond words. The corridor itself was made of stone walls and a wooden beamed ceiling, and in a few places along the red carpet there were velvet benches. The lighting, warm and soft, was provided by two large crystal chandeliers at either end of the hall.

Enchanted by the beauty, she moved along as if in a dream as they made their way towards the stairs. And as they climbed the steps, her ears began at last to hear the sounds of music. It was happy and upbeat in tempo…fast and exciting…so different from anything she'd ever heard before. When they reached the top of the stairs, the music fell on her ears with all its power and force. The noise of hundreds of shoe heels stomping the floor, all at once, not only fell on her ears but vibrated up her spine.

But it was the great ballroom itself that took her breath away. With its crystal chandeliers and mosaic tiles…its ceiling of terra-cotta and outer halls accessed by beautifully wrought arches, it looked like a Spanish palace courtyard. There were even potted palm trees here and there. Most incredible of all was the dome above the dance floor. Colored a deep twilight blue, with artificial stars that twinkled, and images of clouds that were created by projected light beams, the illusion was breathtaking. Jack had to take her gently by the arm and pull her away, for she was quite content just to stand and stare, captured by the wonder of it all.

He guided her to a nearby table…covered in fine white linen, set with silver and graced with a candle centerpiece. She sat, trying her best to look dignified among such refinery. But she could not be still.

The music ended and the crowd applauded as they made their way back to their tables. A moment later the lights dimmed. The room became bathed in soft candlelight. She looked all around, smiling with awe and wonder.

How beautiful, she thought. *The most beautiful place I've ever seen.*

The curtain went up on the stage, revealing a flower garden where a man and woman stood. She watched the scene begin with the young man trying to woo the girl with various flowers, to no avail. Then he started to dance, and the girl took notice…just as Grace did. She'd never seen someone move as he did, one moment madly tap dancing in place, the next moment shuffling across the floor. When the skit was done and the curtain went down, the whole place went crazy with applause, and Grace shared in their enthusiasm.

The band began to play again, and as the crowd moved back to the dance floor, Grace watched them with great amusement. She'd never seen people move in such ways...bouncing and shaking, arms swinging and feet flying. With a little giggle, she turned to Alice and Jack.

"They look like chickens on a hot stove. What kind of dancing is that, anyway?" Alice turned to Jack, seizing his hand and pulling him to his feet.

"That's the Charleston, sister. And it's not a square dance, that's for sure. Can you manage without us for a little while?"

Grace smiled, waving them away.

"Of course. You two go on and have fun. I told you, I can take care of myself."

Jack looked skeptical, reluctant to leave her there by herself. But before he could protest, Alice rushed him out to the dance floor.

As they disappeared into the crowd, Grace smiled. It *did* look like fun. And Jack and Alice looked so perfect together...so full of joy and laughter. She couldn't recall the last time she'd seen her brother so happy. And part of her wished she could go out and join them. But she could not. Sadly, she had little ability, and little experience. And she didn't have a partner...which got her to thinking of Henry. She'd vowed to forget him. But here, in his very domain, how could she not think of him? It was where he worked...where he probably spent most of his time.

Despite her attempts against it, she found herself looking among the crowd, wondering if she might catch a glimpse of him. Surely he was here somewhere. He had to be, this being his place of business. For several moments she scanned the room, wondering if he would appear...and secretly, hoping she might look at him without his knowing it.

It felt safer that way, to watch without being watched. She could not deny how attractive he was...how he stirred feelings in her that she'd never known before.

But he was a danger to her good sense. When he looked at her, it was as if he could read her mind...and that put her too far out of her comfort zone. It was better to admire his beauty from afar. It was certainly safer, for her, to maintain that distance.

Chapter 8
"Give and Take"

Up above the floor, from one of the balconies, a pair of blue eyes were looking down on Grace. The gaze was intense...deeply focused.

The little country mouse had surprised him. He'd been so sure she wouldn't turn up. It was, after all, a place of "sinful" things...of intimate dancing and drinking. Prohibition kept him from *selling* alcohol...but he had no qualms about his customers bringing their own. His wait staff served tea, sweet drinks, and various kinds of juice and if his patrons happened to slip a bit of spirit into their drinks, courtesy of a hip flask or such, that was their business. He needed his to keep his customers happy, so he turned a blind eye to the illegal consumption. And judging from the way his place was always packed, it had worked. If anything, prohibition had probably brought more people to his door. It was human nature to get away with bad behavior, and if it brought him more money, then so be it.

Along the upper corridor he'd been walking among his guests, shaking hands with people he knew and examining the ones he didn't, looking for signs of pleasure and happiness. As was usually the case, all was content among his patrons, and so for the most part, he was relaxed. Passing along the railing above the dance floor, he happened to look down for a moment, and he recognized John and Alice Langdon.

Without hesitation his eye started searching about for the little sister. For several moments, he felt the first stirrings of disappointment. Maybe she hadn't come. Perhaps she had stayed away after all.

Then his eye was caught by a young woman in rose chiffon, sitting alone at a table. The corner of his mouth twitched slightly up.

So, he'd been wrong. She hadn't hidden herself away, fearful of risking her innocence in a den of the devil. She was here, after all. And he found that for once, being wrong wasn't such a bad thing.

Leaning his arms on the railing, he watched her for several moments. He didn't worry if she would see him or not. Unless prompted to do so, how often did people actually look up at something right above their heads? So he felt quite free to look his fill. And what he saw, he liked...very much.

She had a delicate face, punctuated by fine eyes. Her skin was sun-kissed, which was so much nicer than the current trend of being lily white. Her figure was thin, but shapely. From what little he'd managed to see of them, her legs were elegant and toned. She really was a beauty, but not in a made-up way, like so many women he knew. She had an earthy, natural look. It was attractive as hell.

He thought of that moment between them in the hallway. He'd brushed against her on purpose, knowing it would get a reaction. Whether it frightened her or excited her, he didn't really care, though he suspected it had been a little of both. For him, it had been all about the thrill. He liked the sound of that first little intake of breath...the one all women made the first time they were touched, even in the smallest way, by a man they might be attracted to. And she'd been drawn to him, whether she wanted to admit it or not. He'd seen the look in her eyes...the slight little wobble of her body as she tried to recover her senses. It was the same reaction he got from many women, and he liked it.

But it wasn't love. Hell no, it wasn't even close to being that.

He scorned the idea of being in love. He'd gone that road before as a youth, with his wife, and he vowed never to be so foolish again. This was pure, physical attraction.

Not that it was going to lead anywhere. He knew she was off limits in those ways, and he accepted it. She was much too pure...much too naive for the likes of him. But it wouldn't hurt to tease her a little, to make her see what she was missing by being so wet-behind-the-ears.

A round of applause went up as the band ended their song down below. He watched as she clapped along, clearly enjoying herself. She was in a good mood, so maybe he could sidle up to her and find a place for himself. It would be looking, not touching, so she didn't have to worry on that score. He made his way determinedly down the staircase. At the bottom, he turned towards her table. He reached up to right the lapels of his suit.

But then his hands fell away. Such preparation was useless, it seemed. John and Alice had returned to the table, and all three were engaged in conversation. Irritated by the interruption of his plans, he retreated into the shadows under the stairs.

The lights dimmed around the place, the MC's voice coming over the microphone to announce a solo performance. Victoria was about to take to the stage, and a round of applause went up around the room. Out of habit he turned his head to watch as the spotlight fell on her. She started singing a beautiful rendition of Irving Berlin's "Always." She did have a spectacular voice. That was why she was the most popular of all the entertainers that worked for him. But after hearing her sing for so long, there was little left in her performance that moved him. Just like the other acts in residence, she was part of his business, and not much more. His audience, however, was what mattered. And at the end of Victoria's performance there was a roar of applause...perfect evidence of why they made such a great business partnership. She loved the glamour and power that came with being a star. And though it was a shallow notion, he profited from her love of attention. Their professional lives mirrored their personal lives. Each got what they needed from the other, and that was fine with them both.

She soon launched into another song. She was joined on the stage by several other girls, and together they danced and sang to the beat. When they were done, the audience once again went wild. Then the band began to play again...this time a slow, romantic tune that couples swayed to.

He turned his head back to the table where Grace was sitting. Watching, he saw her rise to her feet. She said something to her brother, who said something in return...and from the look on his face, he was not pleased. But she just smiled, shaking her head. She gave him a pat on the shoulder, and slowly she walked away from the table...moving in the opposite direction of himself. He found he could not resist the urge to follow her, to see where she was headed.

The Langdons once again took to the dance floor, and he was glad of it. Now he could pass their table without having to stop and exchange polite words. As he went, he passed several familiar faces...and despite his wish to move along, he shook hands in his usual manner, giving words of courtesy to those who spoke to him. But he hardly took his eyes off of her. She strolled slowly about, looking over the architecture and furnishings with childlike wonder. He kept a certain distance, finding that he enjoyed watching her when she was unaware of him.

But after a while, he felt it was silly to keep following her in that way. What would be the harm in approaching her? He took a step towards her...but a colleague stopped him, wanting to discuss a matter of business. The distraction was momentary, but long enough for him to lose sight of Grace.

Where had she gone? He looked around, but there was no sight of her. He walked towards the end of the hall, nearing the doorway that led to the backstage area. Surely she wasn't anywhere near here. It was quite a distance from the main public area. He turned to go back.

It was then that he heard the yelling. It was coming from the backstage area, and he rushed through the door as quickly as he could.

There she was, being chastised by one of his stage managers, Hal Needham. What a twerp he was. If ever a man had a Napoleon complex, it was him. Short and stout, he felt the need to be maniacal in order to be heard. At that moment, he was unleashing his temper on Grace. But she wasn't afraid of him. Her temper was nearly as hot as his. She protested loudly.

"I wasn't hurting anything!"

Hal didn't back down, giving her a push towards the door.

"I'm tired of you two-bit floosies hanging around the backstage doors, looking for your next gig." He grabbed her by the arm, dragging her along.

Henry moved fast. Before he quite realized what he was doing, he grabbed Hal by the collar, throwing him against the wall. He sneered at him.

"What are you doing? Don't you ever touch a customer like that!" His nostrils flared. "I should send you crawling out of here on your belly!"

Somewhere in the back of his mind, he knew he was acting like a madman. It was only that thought that kept Hal from getting a fist to the face. Henry watched as Hal straightened his collar, trying to gather his dignity. Before scurrying away he gave Grace an evil look. She was watching from a distance, wide-eyed. Henry turned to her, his eyes bright with rage. He snatched her arm firmly.

"What the hell is wrong with you? Don't you know not to stick your nose where it doesn't belong? What are you, stupid or something?"

She yanked her arm away...the force of her strength stunning him. But it was her eyes, suddenly dark with rage, that stunned him. The venom in her voice was shocking. She shouted in his face.

"Téigh trasna ort féin!"

Then she fled...and he stood there, his mouth slightly agape.

She had just cursed at him in Gaelic. *Gaelic*, of all things. His own native Irish language...and he knew exactly what she had said.

Go screw yourself, was the rough translation.

A little country girl using such a foul turn of phrase? Where the hell had that come from? He just couldn't believe it.

Apparently, everyone else around him was just as stunned. Several crew members were standing around staring, some of them whispering. He suddenly came back to himself, glaring at them, his blue eyes blazing.

"What are you looking at? Get back to work!"

His command was enough to send them back to their business. Then his thoughts turned back to what had just happened...and he was angry at her all over again. He spoke out loud, more to himself than to anyone else.

"Stupid girl." But a moment later he felt a wave of guilt wash over him, making him feel a strange blend of both fury and remorse.

Damn little fool. She got the scolding she deserved.

But then he wondered why he'd acted so rashly. What had come over him? The sight of someone doing her harm had enraged him. But why? And why did he feel so bad about his actions? She'd been in a place she didn't belong, and he'd served her with the correction she deserved.

Then why was he standing alone, looking and feeling like a fool? Well he didn't intend to remain that way. The matter would be settled immediately. Right now.

He hurried through the door, looking for her, but she was not to be found. He made his way down the hall, coming across the table where the Langdons had been. The other patrons were all seated and watching a dance act on the stage. But the Langdons table was empty. Which meant that they had gone, and Grace with them. He hurried to the hall. But when he reached the top of the stairs, he stopped.

To hell with it, he thought. *I will not make a fool of myself for anyone, and certainly not for her.*

He turned back towards the ballroom, intent on crossing the hall and heading upstairs to the privacy of his office. He needed to be alone to clear his head, especially now that his tie and collar seemed to be choking him. But just as he reached the steps, he heard Victoria calling his name...and it made him spout a foul curse under his breath. In all likelihood she would be making the same old complaint, whining about one of the chorus girls. And sure enough, that was her subject when she approached him, her arms flailing dramatically.

"Henry, I can't take it anymore! That new little dancer you hired had the nerve to sit at my makeup table. I'm the star of this show, and I'm sick of these little two-bit dollies not knowing their place."

He turned on her, his eyes dark with fury.

"Hell and damnation, woman! Will you stop whining? I don't give a damn about a makeup table!" Desperately wishing to escape, he started up the steps, but she followed…raging on.

"What am I supposed to do? I need my own space to prepare!"

"Oh, for God's sake! Wear a bag over your head for all I care! Just get away from me!"

He heard her indignant little squall, but ignored it, marching up the stairs.

Reaching his office at the end of the hall he entered quickly, kicking the door back to slam it shut. His first act was to reach up and yank away his tie, throwing it down on the desk. Pulling his collar loose, he took a deep breath as he sank into his seat. Leaning his head back against the top of the chair, he took a deep breath.

Lord have mercy, he thought. His peace of mind was wrecked, and he didn't like it. Not one bit. Just yesterday morning, his life had been so set, so organized. Hell, even his way of thinking had been in perfect order. He had his daily routine that he stuck to, and a limited list of subjects that he had to keep his mind on, and beyond that, there wasn't much in life he cared to worry about. Now, he was suddenly a mental wreck…and it was all her fault.

Grace Langdon, you little witch, he thought bitterly. *What kind of spell have you cast on me?*

The last thing he wanted was to have a new woman on his mind. But his head was filled with thoughts of her. It had been that way from the first…ever since he'd first seen those stormy blue-grey eyes at the train station. It was the eyes he kept thinking of. It was said that eyes were windows into the soul, and there was something fascinating behind that gaze of hers. The girl was a puzzlement. He couldn't figure her out. She looked so serene and sweet…so passive. He recalled watching her through the window yesterday, and again tonight. He recalled the way she looked… how she looked like an eager little girl exploring her new world. But when put upon, this wild little woman appeared, looking like she could tear him apart. In his head he heard her cursing him.

Téigh trasna ort féin.

Suddenly he found himself grinning. His mood was suddenly lifted as he thought of her, now with a streak of admiration. Such spirit. Such bold honesty. How many people looked him in the eye and dared to say exactly what they thought? It was the second time she'd bluntly insulted him…this time more harsh than the first. He started to wonder…

What would she do if he pushed her hard enough?

It might be fun to find out, he thought. If he pushed her buttons a little, what would she do? He was almost excited at the prospect. The next time they met, he intended to provoke her… and to enjoy every moment of it. As a boy, he'd prodded the occasional hornets' nest with a stick, just to watch the swarm get angry. It was childish…maybe even a little bit dangerous. But what fun it was. And what was life without a bit of entertainment?

* * * * *

She stood at her bedroom window, staring out at the moon. But the beauty of the night hardly concerned her. She reached up to her cheek, wiping away a tear that had escaped her eye.

Why had she ever, even for just a moment, thought that Henry was different from any other man…from any other person in general? Maybe he'd been right in telling her she didn't belong back stage, but why did he have to be so vicious about it? He'd insulted her quite cruelly, and though she'd insulted him right back, it hardly helped her feel better.

No one in the world had ever cared for her, except for Jack and Alice. Henry was just as cruel as all the others…and she'd been a fool to hope otherwise. Then why was her heart hurting so badly?

What good was a heart…a thing so easily broken? If only she could shut down her feelings. Love and generosity… kindness and compassion. They were all empty notions, doing more pain than good. And yet they remained in her soul, imbedded like a deep root.

Well if they were to stay there against her consent, she swore she would save such soft feelings for her brother and sister-in-law. Who else had ever been worthy? No one. It seemed that's how it would always be.

Henry would certainly never get close to her heart, if she had anything to say about it.

* * * * *

The next morning was a Sunday…a welcome day, in her mind. One on which she hoped to meditate and find strength in her faith.

The pilgrimage was rather different than the one she'd known at home. The church was but a short walk away, reached in only a few blocks. She found it lovely that everyone walked there together, all dressed in their finest. The sense of community was wonderful.

Their church was a much grander house of worship than the little place she'd known back home. With its red brick exterior, two stories with stained glass, and white columns out front, it put her in awe as she stood looking up at it. But when she went in, she found the same sense of reverence that she'd known back home. She was glad to find such a familiar feeling in so much that was unfamiliar.

There were many people to meet, most of whom she remembered seeing the night before…and most of whom had been tipsy. But she was polite, keeping her thoughts to herself.

As she, Jack and Alice were taking their seats, two more familiar faces came around. Henry and Victoria appeared and sat a few places behind them. Looking at them, she recalled the notion that sinners sometimes got struck down by lightning. And wickedly she thought…

I'd like to see that for myself.

Her face flushed with anger, remembering how he'd acted. He deserved to be beaten senseless with a hymnal book. But she knew she was in a sacred place and had to behave. So she just did her best to ignore him.

But all through the service, she kept feeling his eyes on her. She tried to think of other things…tried to concentrate on a hymn or the reading of a passage. But still now and then she felt his gaze, and for the first time in her life she felt like daring to flee from a church service, just to get away from him.

When the service was over, there was the familiar ritual of people gathering outside to talk and visit. She watched from the door as Jack and Alice spoke to some of their friends. Not wanting to interfere, she took to walking slowly through the empty sanctuary, enjoying the calm and serenity that a church always gave her. Finding herself near the piano, looking at it for a moment, she could not resist the urge to sit down and play. But it wasn't a hymn she performed. It was Beethoven's *Pathetique*, which Alice had once given her to play. It had become her absolute favorite piece of music. As she played, she lost herself in the beauty of the melody…and was so engrossed that at first, she did not notice a figure approaching. When she realized it was Henry, she chose to ignore him and continue, even though he came right up and stood in front of the piano. Her brain suddenly flashed a memory of a passage from *Pride and Prejudice*…and with a smirk she quoted it, certain he would not have the slightest idea what she was talking about.

"You mean to frighten me, Mr. Darcy, by coming in all this state to hear me? But I will not be alarmed. There is a stubbornness about me that never can bear to be frightened at the will of others. My courage always rises with every attempt to intimidate me."

She smiled a little to herself and thought, *Take that you big bully.* But his reply came as a complete shock.

"I shall not say that you are mistaken. Because you could not really believe me to entertain any design of alarming you, and I have had the pleasure of your acquaintance long enough to know, that you find great enjoyment in occasionally professing opinions which in fact are not your own."

Her eyes grew big. Even as a smug look came to his face…one that said he had bested her challenge…she was too stunned by what he'd said to pay attention to his look.

"You know Pride and Prejudice?" she asked, enthralled for a tiny moment…until he replied with distaste.

"I hate it. But it was my wife's favorite book, and she used to read her favorite parts to me. Unfortunately, they're branded in my brain."

She felt her spirits sink. She looked down, and as she closed the lid on the piano, she wished that his fingers were there so she could slam the lid down on them.

"I prefer masculine reading," he said, "Like Robert Louis Stevenson and Jack London. *Call of the Wild* was always one of my favorites. You should read it sometime, instead of all that romantic nonsense."

She sneered. "Why am I not surprised to hear that from you?"

Eager to escape him, she rose to her feet and started to walk out. But before she got to the door, she heard him call out to her. When she turned to look, he was coming her way. His look was defiant and stubborn.

"If you expect me to feel guilty about what happened, I won't. And if you expect an apology, then you're off your nut, sister."

He came to stand in front of her, blocking the door. When he leaned his hand on the doorframe, looking down at her, she felt herself growing tense. That overwhelming sensation came to her again as she stood so close to him. A flood of warmth flowed from his frame to hers, and for a moment she wondered if she might melt under the heat of his gaze.

But she suddenly remembered the way he had looked last night...how he had talked to her. And it gave her fresh courage. Her eyes narrowed up at him.

"You're a jackass, Henry Shaw."

To her frustration, he only smirked.

"Sticks and stones may break my bones," he started to say. But she refused to hear anymore. With an angry shove she pushed past him, going off in search of Jack and Alice.

* * * * *

They went to lunch in town. She tried to enjoy the little diner they took her to, where she had her first hamburger and fries, and her first milkshake. But her mind kept wandering back to Henry. Oh, what a troublesome monster he was. Why couldn't he just go away?

As they were coming home, her mind was still on him. As they came up the front porch, Jack opened the screen door...and a little square parcel, wrapped in brown paper, fell out on the stoop. Picking it up, looking at it, he turned to Grace.

"What's this? Why does it have your name on it? You don't know anyone around here."

Alice smiled. "Maybe it's from a secret admirer." Taking the package from his hand, she handed it to Grace.

Jack's eyes grew. "What? Who? Open it and let me see."

But Alice scolded him. "Leave her alone. It's her mail, not yours. She'll open it when she's ready."

She guided him away towards the kitchen, while Grace went up the stairs, opening the package as she went. A moment later, she was holding a book in her hands.

It was a copy of Jack London's *Call of the Wild*.

Chapter 9
"Cat and Mouse"

Henry was in bed, again unable to sleep. But now, it was not a nightmare that kept him up...but a busy mind.

He was overcome with curiosity, wondering what had happened since she'd found the book. He'd given it to her just to tease her...to see if she could keep away from it.

But had it worked? Had she given in to temptation?

Suddenly he had a thought...a realization. Knowing what a little hard-head she was, she'd probably kept away from his gift just to spite him. It seemed like something she would do.

Stubborn little brat, he thought.

He rolled over, giving his pillow a hard thump of his hand, trying his best to get comfortable...trying to retrieve his common sense.

To hell with the book, he said to himself. *To hell with her. Who needs this aggravation?*

* * * * *

Standing at the living room window, he casually sipped his cup of coffee...and stared at the house across the street.

Two days had passed. Not once had he caught sight of her, even though he found himself looking for her more and more often. He'd tried not to do so...but found he couldn't keep himself from it.

"Henry, do you plan on sitting down to eat this morning? Your breakfast is getting cold."

He didn't look at Victoria, who sat at the table behind him. Several times over the last few days, she'd questioned his occasional moments of distraction. But his replies gave her no real information. Most times he changed the subject, as he did now. He put his cup down on the table.

"I'm going out to get the paper."

Stepping outside, he found his newspaper waiting on the step. He reached down to pick it up...and as he rose, his eye caught sight of the front door across the street. It was opening. A familiar little figure was emerging. But no sooner did she look at him, pausing in the doorway, than she stepped back again, slamming the door shut.

He shook his head. Clearly, two days time had not eased her temper...

Over a few more days, though he kept vigilant watch, he saw no sign of her. She never came out to work in the front yard, or to take a walk. He never saw her leaving for a trip into town. And he soon came to understand the reason.

She's in there hiding.

So that was the contest she played at. How typical of a woman, to make a man give chase. To play cat and mouse, as it were. And he thought to himself...

Well what am I, if not game?

What would she do if went over and knocked on the door? He was very tempted to give it a try. But as he thought about it, he realized that he didn't have a clever enough reason to go.

What should I do? He asked himself. *Ask to borrow a cup of sugar?* Actually, that didn't seem like such a bad idea. It was a tired excuse, but that would be part of the fun of it. And he almost went through with his plan.

But then he was overcome with a sense of self-loathing. He hadn't been this silly over a woman before. Not even his wife. And he wondered what washer was missing in his brain to make him act this way. He shook his head, snorting at himself in disgust.

Good God man, get a hold of yourself. Why are you mooning over a little country bumpkin? Look what you have here at home.

But that argument didn't hold much water, especially of late. Over the last several days, amidst his distraction, he'd rarely given Victoria a thought. His head was filled with thoughts of another, though he tried his best to push her from his mind. Several times he found himself looking at Victoria and thinking...

I wonder what you'd do if you knew who I was thinking about? If you knew whose face I sometimes see when I look at you, you'd lose your pretty little mind.

Just last night, after a bit too much drinking, they'd tumbled into bed and had a long, lusty night. Right afterwards he'd fallen asleep, feeling quite satisfied.

But upon waking, he'd turned to look at his partner and found he was quite disappointed in what he saw. Turning away from her, he had stared out the window for a long time... impatient for the day to arrive.

* * * * *

He felt Victoria's presence as she entered the dining room. He ignored her, concentrating on his newspaper. He knew she was standing just behind him, but still he paid her no mind. He hoped his indifference would make her throw a fit and leave the room. But it seemed she wasn't bothered. She reached up to trace the trimmed hairline on the back of his neck. She was either trying to tempt him, or hoping for something else. Perhaps she wanted money, or a favor of some kind. Perhaps she was seeking information. Whatever her reasons were, he was indifferent to her touch. He sighed deeply, rather irritated, as he spoke to her.

"Weren't you pleased last night?"

There was an amused note to her voice.

"I was more than pleased."

He felt her fingers running through his hair. To that gesture of affection, he reached up to take by the hand, leading her to the chair next to him. Then he promptly went back to reading his paper.

She pulled out her chair and sat down. He didn't look directly at her, but he could see how she was trying to maintain a cool and collected aspect. As she ate her breakfast she made small talk, most of which he didn't pay attention to. She sought information…that was her motive, he now realized. But he didn't intend to give her much to go on. Whatever his thoughts or intentions, they were his own business. From the corner of his eye he saw how she lifted her coffee cup and, with a mask of innocence, peered over the rim as she sipped.

"You've been restless these last few days. You're not getting sick, are you?"

He shook his head. "I'm fine." He continued to read his paper. Several long moments went by before she posed her next question.

"I talked to Hal yesterday. He said the two of you had some kind of scuffle the other night. Some girl wandered backstage or something. Hal said you jumped on him like a dog after a bone. What was that all about?"

None of your business, was his first thought. But for the sake of satisfying his own curiosity…to determine exactly what course she was pursuing…he chose to humor her.

"He was being rude to a guest." As he thought of Grace, he found himself getting angry all over again…and he couldn't keep the displeasure from his voice. "She was just a kid who wandered where she didn't belong. She wasn't bothering anyone. And he started acting like a fool, so I called him on it. I won't have anyone treating my patrons with disrespect."

He snapped the page of his paper…as if to tell her, without speaking, that her questions were beginning to irritate him. She knew he hated to be questioned. And yet, she kept on.

"I take it she wasn't one of the regulars. She must not have been, if she was wandering around the place that way, looking it over and getting herself in trouble."

For the first time that morning, he looked at her directly, his expression stern.

"What's this inquisition about the other night? Those kinds of things have happened before. They'll happen again. It's all part of the business, Victoria. You know that."

He kept his eyes locked on her until she looked away. From the way she sat back in her chair, he could see she would prod no further for information. Satisfied that he'd silenced her for the moment, he went back to reading his paper. There were several minutes of silence that passed before she began with her small talk again.

"So, are we going to the lake to watch the fireworks tonight?"

For the first time that morning, she had his attention. He'd completely forgotten that it was Independence Day. He recalled that today would be the annual block party. The neighbors would all be there. *Each and everyone.*

Suddenly, the day became full of promise. But he was careful not to let Victoria see how he felt. He tried to maintain a careless expression.

"I suppose we could go to the lake if you like. But before that, there's the block party to go to. And we have to be sociable with the neighbors, whether we like it or not."

To that, Victoria wilted a little. He tried not to express his satisfaction. He knew that in order to keep up appearances, he would have to take her with him. But it was his hope that she would do what she usually did, which was to find a corner and sulk. She didn't like his neighbors, who in turn didn't think highly of a divorced woman living with her lover. Out of respect for him, they treated her politely. But *her* friends were artists, musicians, and actors who lived in the Pilsen neighborhood, and she wouldn't find any of them at the party tonight. It was his hope that while he conversed with people, she would go off on her own. And then, he could talk to whomever he pleased. One person, in particular. To her sulky expression, he thought to add a little twist of guilt, just for good measure.

"I'm doing you a favor by going to the lake. You can do me a favor by going to the party. It's only fair, wouldn't you say?"

He looked at her, and after a moment he saw her frame slack in defeat.

"Very well," she replied. "I'll humor you for tonight."

A smirk, very small, appeared on his face. His thought was childish…but gleeful. *So, little mouse. The game has begun…*

* * * * *

The book sat on the top of the dresser, just within Grace's eyesight as she sewed. Since it had showed up on her doorstep six days ago, she'd kept it hidden in her dresser drawer to avoid temptation. She didn't want anything to do with Henry Shaw or his gift, and for the most part, she'd done well in forgetting him.

Except for the little matter of Henry, life with Jack and Alice was so peaceful, so content. Even the housework was more of a pleasure than a chore. It helped that Alice had her very own selection of machines to help her along. The first time Grace watched a washing machine, she saw the satisfaction that Alice took in it, and her declaration seemed to say that she hadn't forgotten how things had once been.

"To hell with washboards and bleeding fingers," she said with a smile.

Just as there had been at home, there was a back yard garden from which she and Alice gathered vegetables, but the patch was small and took no time at all to tend. Most of what they needed they bought when they went to market, which they did every other day or so.

Of all the little luxuries they had, it seemed that time was what they most enjoyed. There was no need to slave from dusk til' dawn, and in those wonderful spare moments, they all reveled in whatever idle activity came to mind. Jack seemed to take the most pleasure in his freedom. Seeing how he was, she had to wonder if he was making up for a childhood and youth spent in servitude. It wasn't unusual, especially at night, to find him walking around the house with a glass of milk in one hand and cookies in the other. He had his own chair in the living room...a large leather wingback right beside the radio...that he claimed was fashioned just for him, and he got fussy if anyone else sat in it.

"My hind end has made its mark in this seat," he often said. "If you sit in it, you'll mess up the dents."

She sometimes liked to sit in the chair just to tease him, but it was all in good fun. Life was happy, and it would have been perfect...if not for a certain person lurking just across the street.

She knew he was probably watching from somewhere, just waiting for the chance to antagonize her. But she was determined not to let him. She'd gotten quite good at sneaking out of the house, while always watching for him.

She and Alice went downtown a few times, getting lost in the huge department stores or going sightseeing. On one of their trips they'd found the material and patterns that she wanted for her dressmaking. The room where she now slept had been the sewing room, complete with a fine sewing machine, and she had kept herself busy with her work. But this morning as she'd been rifling through her dresser drawer, she'd come across the book that Henry had left.

It was so tempting to put everything else aside and read it, as much as she loved a good story. But she'd told herself she wouldn't, and with a determination to stick to her word, she had tossed it down on the dresser top.

Now while she worked, she occasionally glanced over at the book that lay just within her reach, and more than once she was tempted to go over and pick it up.

But she kept telling herself she didn't want anything to do with the gift, even if it was a book...and books were like gold to her. She wanted nothing to do with Henry or anything concerning him, and she was determined to keep her vow.

It was just after seven that Saturday morning. Jack was out playing golf with a friend, and she was in her room, busy once again. There was a knock on the door. A moment later, Alice came in.

"How's it going in here?" She came to stand just behind her, looking over her shoulder.

Grace put a spool of thread on the bobbin. "Pretty good I think. I finished this one last night." She held up the dark violet dress she had completed. "I was working on it all day yesterday."

Alice smiled, brushing her fingers over the embroidery. "You sure have a way with a needle." She looked around the room, and seeing the book on the dresser, she went to it up. Her smile became a cheeky grin as she looked at it. "You haven't read it yet, have you?"

Grace looked up for a moment. Then her eyes fell back to her sewing. "Nope. Not yet." She tried to sound casual. But Alice was too clever to be fooled.

"It's because it's from Henry. That's why you won't read it."

Grace's head shot up. Her eyes grew wide with surprise. "How did you know it was from him?"

Alice only shrugged. "It was just a guess. I figure you don't know anyone else around here. And I know this is one of his favorite books, because he gave Jack a copy of it a long time ago. So now we know who the secret admirer is."

Grace stopped her sewing, setting the material down on the machine. She turned to look at Alice, who had taken a seat on the edge of the bed. Looking almost like a little girl, she dropped down on her stomach and leaned her head in her hand, a big smile on her face.

"I saw him watching you the other night. He was standing under the stairs, and I'm sure he thought no one could see him. But I did."

For a long moment, Grace was stunned speechless. She opened her mouth, but nothing came out. Then she shook her head, quickly retrieving her material.

"If he likes me, he sure has a funny way of showing it. The few times I've seen him, he's been just awful. That's what happened the other night, when I wanted to come home so fast. All I did was take a little walk around the back stage, and he jumped all over me for it. He was meaner than a snake."

Alice sat up just a little, more interested than before. "So that's what it was. I was wondering what went wrong. Well whatever you do, don't tell your brother about that. He'll have a fit, that's for sure and for certain."

"Don't worry, I won't say a thing, if you won't. And about Henry liking me...well, I don't think he likes me the way you think. He probably just looks at me like a new toy he's found. He'd have his fun and then toss me aside like an old shoe."

Alice laughed a little. "Maybe you're right. But you know, some women don't mind that. Especially with someone who looks like Henry. He's a sight to see, coming and going." Then a naughty little glint shined in her eyes. "I like to watch him go, if you know what I mean."

Realizing what Alice meant, Grace felt her cheeks flush a little. She tried to maintain composure, for she still wasn't quite used to hearing such talk. But she couldn't help the slight giggle that escaped her. "You're a little devil, you know that?"

Alice just grinned, all innocence. "I'm a good little angel. My halo is a little bent and crooked, but it's still there."

Smiling but with a slight roll of her eyes, Grace went back to her project.

Alice rose to her feet, coming to stand at her sister-in-law's side, rubbing her shoulder. "You know, you might want to give him a chance. Personally, I think all that grumbling he does is just an act. Maybe what he needs is someone sweet like you, to bring out his better side."

A loud snort of disgust was the reply. "He's a rat, and that's all there is to it. And I never did like no rats."

"He did give you a gift. That was a nice gesture, wasn't it?"

"It was not," Grace replied. "He probably did it so he wouldn't feel so guilty. And he gave me that instead of saying he was sorry. An apology was what I wanted. Not some silly book."

Finding Grace

Alice shrugged. "Well, I still think it was nice of him. And I still think he likes you. But if you don't agree with me, then I won't push my opinion on you. You have a right to feel however you want to."

"I do," Grace replied. "And even if I did feel different, it wouldn't matter. The last thing in the world I want is to chase after someone else's man. And I won't give Victoria a reason to worry about that. That's all I've got to say." She now considered the matter closed, and Alice seemed to sense it. She did, however, have one more thing to say.

"I know you won't like to hear this. But Henry and Victoria will be around tonight, when we have the block party. If you want to stay in the house, I can think up some excuse to give to Jack."

Grace thought about it, and for one brief moment, she actually considered taking the easy way out. But then, in a flash, her mind was made up.

"I'm no coward. I'm not going to hide in here like some scared rabbit. You'll be there, won't you? And Jack will be there. I think between the two of you, I'll have plenty of protection."

Alice smiled. "If that's what you want, that's what you'll get. I promise." She gave her a pat on the shoulder, turning towards the door. "Well, I have to run into town to pick up some fruit for my pies. Jack should be back from his game in a little while."

Grace nodded and smiled, watching as Alice left.

She sat back in her chair, letting out a little sigh. She looked over at the book, again...and thought about it.

Maybe I should give in and read it. What harm ever came from reading a book? And what is wrong with accepting a present? Taking his gift doesn't mean I've given in to him.

She started to get up and go to it. But then she stopped herself. *No*, she said to herself. *I'm stronger than that. I can fight temptation.*

She turned to her work, diving into it with fierce determination.

* * * * *

By early afternoon, she nearly had another dress finished. But by now, she was growing weary of the constant sound of the sewing machine. Her back and legs were beginning to tingle from sitting in one place for so long. She stood up, stretching. A moment later there came a knock on the front door. She started down the stairs to answer it, but as she neared the front door, a sense of trepidation came over her.

Who would be knocking on their door in the middle of the day? *Maybe it's a salesman or something*, she thought. But who knew what odd people lurked about? And being alone in the house for the first time, she was reluctant to answer it at all.

I will look first, she thought. *Better safe than sorry.*

She peeked through the curtains...and saw that it was Henry standing there on the stoop. She let out a loud groan of frustration.

All week long she'd been avoiding him. But suddenly she didn't feel like hiding anymore. She paused to take a breath, to gather her courage…and opened the door. She didn't give him the chance to speak before she demanded of him…

"What do you want?"

He raised an eyebrow at her, giving her one of his devilish looks.

"Well now, that's no way to treat a neighbor. You could at least begin with 'good afternoon', or something like that."

She narrowed her eyes. "Good afternoon. Now what do you want?"

He clucked his tongue, shaking his head. "That's cold, Grace Langdon. I just came by to borrow a cup of sugar. My housekeeper needs it to bake a cake, and we're fresh out."

She flashed a skeptical look. "That's a whopper of a tale. If that's what you needed, how come didn't you just send her over to get it? Or your girlfriend?"

"Oh…them," he answered. "Well, the little woman is out shopping, and my housekeeper is up to her elbows in work. So I thought I'd save her the trouble."

Her first impulse was to deny his words. But she couldn't be for certain that he lied. And if he was telling the truth, she didn't want to make trouble for a hard working woman. So she sighed in defeat.

"Wait here and I'll get it."

She went to the kitchen, finding the cup of sugar. When she came back, he was standing inside the foyer, looking around…and it felt like a total invasion of her personal space. To have him actually standing inside the house…it was too much. She upset with him than ever, she approached him with an angry stride.

"I didn't say you could come in." She thrust the cup into his hand. "There. You have your sugar, now get on out of here."

His expression lost some of its amusement. "You know something little girl, you can be as pissy with me as you want. I don't give a damn. Because I know I was right and you were wrong. You didn't belong around that back stage. And you got just what you deserved."

His arrogance was sickening…and not just because he was partly right. He seemed to take pleasure in reprimanding her…treating her like a child. She had the urge to slap his face. Instead, she ordered him away.

"Go on home and take your preaching with you. I don't need it."

"You need something," he said, turning to go. But then he turned back. "You know what? A little while ago, I thought about stealing a kiss from you. But now that I think about it, you might be better off if I put you across my knee."

Her eyes widened slightly…but an answer came to her fast. "One would be as bad as the other."

He leaned a hand on the doorframe, looking down at her.

"Why don't you just come at me with a rusty razor blade and some lemon juice?"

She stepped forward and pushed him back from the doorway. "If I had some lemons, maybe I would." She slammed the door on him.

Marching back to her room, she threw the door closed behind her. She looked at the clothing on the machine, but decided she'd had enough of that for one day. Her mind was too full now to think of work. Falling back on the bed, she threw one arm over her eyes, sighing. *Animal,* she thought. *Threatening to beat me like I'm a child. I'd like to see him try.*

But then she thought of the other thing he'd said...about wanting to steal a kiss from her. In the heated anger of the moment, she hadn't even given those words a thought. But now, his statement swirled around in her head. It terrified her to imagine his kiss...and thrilled her all the same.

She thought back to that moment in the doorway of the kitchen, when their eyes had met. Their figures had been so close to one another, so near that she could feel the warmth from his body. It threatened, even now, to erase any dislike of him that she had in her mind.

How could one person have such power over another? Was he a magician, the way he could reach out across time and space to steal her senses? She sat up quickly, rising to her feet to pace the room.

How could she escape his torment? He was there, right across the way. There was no way to avoid him. She couldn't hide all the time. Seeing him was inevitable, and there was nothing that she could do about that. If only there was some way to get him out of her head.

She sighed, folded her arms, and stood in one spot for the longest time. Then her eye caught the book lying on top of the dresser. For a moment she hesitated...then she went over and snatched it up.

If he meant to give her this, as his way of making her think of him, then she would just use it against him.

I'll read his book, she thought. *And I won't think of him for a moment while I'm reading it.*

* * * * *

Jack and Alice came home at the same time that afternoon. When they came in, they found Grace sitting in an armchair in the living room, reading. And weeping. They hurried over to her, their eyes filled with concern.

"Sis, what's wrong?" asked Jack. "What's happened?"

She never looked up at him. She just mumbled through her tears. "It's the saddest thing I've ever read."

Jack looked down at the title. He gave her an odd look, shrugging. "I suppose it's sad, but I never cried over it." Then he looked at the cover. "Hey, that's not my copy. Where did you get this one?"

Grace just waved him away, trying to concentrate on her book. Before he could question her further, Alice stepped forward.

"That was the package that was left the other night. I had a bookseller drop it off."

Jack looked at her, curious. But she just shrugged.

"I wanted it to be a surprise."

He raised an eyebrow at her, suspicious.

"Why didn't you just tell me that before?"

She gave him a teasing smile. "Because, honey, there are lots of things I don't tell you. That's what makes us a happy couple."

Now he smiled, moving to take her in his arms. He narrowed his eyes at her. "Evil woman."

Then he whispered something in her ear that made her giggle. But she pushed him back with one hand.

"Not now, you big ox. I have pies to make. Do you want to help?"

He pursed his lips in disgust. "No way. I'll leave you to your baking, and my sister to her crying. If anyone needs me, I'll be in the back yard."

They both left the room, leaving Grace to her book once again.

Finding Grace

Chapter 10
"A Summer Night"

Overwhelmed. It was the only word to describe how she felt when she finished the book, less than three hours after opening it. It wasn't a long story for her. At just over two-hundred pages, it was half the length of the books she usually read. But it wasn't the length that had sped her along. With its heartbreaking depiction of a dog's fight for survival…its cold portrayal of human cruelty, it held her in its grip until the very last page.

She finished reading just as the noise outside the living room window started to grow. Merry voices could be heard as people gathered in the streets outside. At last she closed the book, setting it down on the coffee table with a trembling hand. Then she reached for the handkerchief in her pocket, dabbing her swollen eyes as she went to the kitchen to find Alice. She found her standing at the kitchen counter, putting the last touches on a lemon meringue pie. When she looked up and saw Grace's expression, she smiled.

"Done with your story, are you?"

Grace nodded. "I'm sorry I didn't help you with all of this. I guess I got so wrapped up I wasn't minding the time."

Alice smiled. "Don't worry about it. I managed just fine on my own. I'll give you a few minutes here to get yourself together. And then if you wouldn't mind, could you carry those pies out for me?"

Grace nodded and smiled. Alice took two pies and went out. Turning toward the sink, she ran some cool water and bathed her face, trying her best to make herself more presentable. It would not do to go out among strangers looking like a blubbering fool. And when she saw Henry, which she knew she would too soon, she planned on giving him a piece of her mind. His supposed gift had made an absolute wreck of her, and losing control of herself was not something she liked. Having collected herself, she picked up the pies and headed for the front door.

Outside, it was a warm and soft summer night. Food tables were set up in various yards, including theirs, and she went over to put the pies down among the other food. Looking around at the happy scene before her, she watched with a smile as children ran up and down the street playing games. Some were carrying sparklers…something she'd never seen before, and she stopped one of the small boys to ask him about it. He seemed quite happy to share his knowledge. Running over to a box on the stoop next door, he came back with a handful and put them

91

down on the table. From the large candle in the center of the table he lit a sparkler and handed it to her. She stared at it with child-like wonder.

"How pretty. But is that all you do? Just look at it?"

The boy shook his head. "You have to move it around. Watch me. I can do two at one time."

He lit two sparklers, dancing around until both sparks went out. Then he threw the used sticks in a bucket by the steps. Picking up two more sparklers he lit them, and took off down the street to catch up with the other kids.

Grace picked up a sparkler. Lighting it, she watched as the white fire jumped and sparked before her eyes. As the boy had told her to do, she moved the wand through the air, delighting in the brief trail of fire that glowed from it. It reminded her of shooting stars that she'd seen in the sky.

She was a bit disappointed when it quickly went out, so she went back to get another, which she watched with the same kind of wonder and fascination. When it went out as well, and she picked up and lighted another, she was so engrossed that she did not see the figure coming up behind her.

"Having fun, little girl?"

Her face fell at the sound of his voice. *Why are you tormenting me?* She wanted to ask. Instead she rolled her eyes.

"Mind your own beeswax," she snapped. But even as she said it, she knew he wouldn't listen. He took a light hold of her wrist, guiding her hand for a moment.

"Try writing your name, like all the kiddies do."

She knew he was just making fun of her…and she quickly jerked her wrist back.

"Will you go away and leave me be? Go back to your woman. I'm sure she wonders where you've gone." Walking to the step, she sat down…only to find him following, replying in his usual careless way.

"I go where I please."

He sat down beside her. And for a moment, she thought of getting up to find another resting place.

But where was there to hide, when all these people were around? The idea of running away seemed so silly when she really thought about it. And sitting beside him, she instantly felt the familiar warmth that came from him. It was odd, the kind of comfort his presence suddenly brought. She had never been close to him in this way…not for more than a moment. And for the first time, she found she was not nervous or angry. Not even was she irritated, as she'd been only a moment ago.

As they sat there with the warm and pleasant evening all around them, she found her bitterness fading away. The sparkler she was holding had gone out, and she tossed it into the bucket near her feet. They sat quietly for several moments, listening to the sound of the children laughing as they ran past.

He rose and went to the table…and she wondered what game he might be trying to play now. But to her surprise and curiosity he brought back several sparklers with him. He sat down once again, reaching into his pocket to produce a lighter. He used it to light a sparkler that he handed to her.

"Have this as a peace offering," he said.

She hadn't intended to show any feeling at all. She wanted to be distant...even cold. But it was impossible, she realized, to stay angry. The mood around them was too bright. The night was just too fine. And the simple gesture, or peace offering as he called it, seemed rather sweet. She took the sparkler from his hand, looking at it. And as she watched it spark, she suddenly thought of her youngest brother...of how he would have loved seeing this.

"Robert would sure enough have a time with this," she said. "We never had things like this to play with."

"Who is Robert?"

The sudden question made her realize her error. She didn't want to speak to him unless it was necessary. Now she had brought up a most tender subject. Talking of family could be an intimate thing, and the last thing she wanted was for the two of them to get to know each other. But it seemed it was too late to retreat, for he was looking at her...awaiting a reply. It seemed all she could do was answer, and hope he didn't try to take the conversation further.

"My baby brother," she replied.

After her sparkler went out, she tossed it into the bucket and sat still for a moment, trying not to look at him. But now that she'd brought up the subject of her brother, she felt a strange need to open herself up, if only just a little. She reached into her pocket to take out a picture. She handed it to him.

"There," she said, pointing out her little brother in the picture. She kept that photo in her pocket, always. Why she felt the need to bring it out and show it to him, she didn't know. But some small part of her wanted to express the love she had for her family.

They are my family, she thought. *No matter what happens, or how far away I go, I carry them with me always.*

Those sentiments she didn't express in words. She had no desire to be singled out as a girlish, sentimental fool...especially not around him. It was daring enough that she was sharing the picture with him.

"So who are the rest of these people?"

That sounded like a rather stupid question. Couldn't he see what was right in front of him? And then it dawned on her that in his own way, he was asking to meet them. He could see they were her relations, but he wanted her to introduce the people that mattered most to her. And she did not know why, but she felt a strange need to oblige him.

"That's Mama, and Daddy. Raymond is the oldest after Jack. Then it's James, and me. Then there's Thomas and Matthew, and Robert is the littlest."

He looked at the picture a moment longer, and then handed it back to her.

"So why are they at home and you're not?"

They had suddenly wandered into personal territory...and she was not prepared for that. It almost scared her to move towards such a subject. He seemed to be interested. He was even being rather polite and soft spoken. But how much longer would they go on before he made some cutting remark and broke the spell? The thought of it was too much, and she was suddenly regretful of bringing out the picture in the first place. She took it from his hand, putting it back in her pocket.

"It's a long story," she said. "Too long, in fact. You wouldn't be interested."

Or would you? She asked herself. A tiny part of her almost hoped he would be, for she had an overwhelming desire to talk with him about her innermost thoughts. But a greater part of her feared ridicule and judgment...the way Charlie had once made fun of her. So she felt it best not to dwell on foolish hopes. And his reply seemed to confirm her suspicions about him.

"You're right," he replied with a nod. "I don't like to chit-chat. Pointless conversation has always bothered me. I only talk when the subject is of real interest."

She found herself agreeing with him...and saying so before she could stop herself.

"Me too. That's why I like to read, since most people I know don't share my interests. Reading is a little like being with a friend you can't see." She felt her face redden, thinking that she'd just said something quite idiotic. But his reply to it surprised her.

"That's an insightful observation. You have a sharp little mind."

She looked over at him, seeing the slight smile on his face, one that turned up the corner of his mouth just a little. But she seemed to prefer that to something more grand, for it was more genuine than any smile she'd seen on his face before. It seemed to bring light to his whole being.

"You read the book, didn't you?" he asked, turning his head to look her in the eye.

She started to deny it. But then he raised his eyebrow, as if daring her to lie. And when he was looking at her that way, with those gorgeous eyes of his all soft, she found it impossible to speak.

Reading the answer in her expression, he grinned. "I knew you wouldn't be able to resist."

Strange, but his gloating didn't seem to bother her then. She couldn't believe she was even thinking it, but there was something charming about the look he wore at that moment. Still, she tried to maintain a collected aspect.

"How do you know I read it?"

He shrugged slightly. "Anyone who memorizes *Pride and Prejudice* must be bookish. I'm guilty of it myself, so I know my own kind. I knew it was only a matter of time before you gave in to temptation."

She had consented to defeat...and he knew it. But somehow, it didn't bother her. She shrugged.

"I guess there's no harm in falling for a book."

He shook his head. "Not if you have an intelligent mind. And I think you and I fall into that category."

You and I, she thought. There was something in those words that moved her. *We have connected*, she thought. *How wonderful to have found someone who thinks the way I do.* She dared to look at him, and found he was looking at her. *My Lord*, she thought.

What is that look? Why does it turn me to jelly? She didn't understand that burning gleam in his eyes. All she knew was that it robbed her of her senses. *Why do I feel as if I'm falling from a great height? And am I mad, or is he moving closer to me right now? Is his face really so near mine as I think it is? And if it comes closer, then what will I do?*

"Gracie!"

Oh Lord, that's Alice's voice calling. And it broke through to her senses, making her sit up straight and fidget her hands as she tried to compose herself. She stumbled over her words a little, but managed to say them all the same.

"Um, thank you for your book." She cleared her throat, trying to sound calm. "But I don't reckon I'll ever read it again. It's just too sad." She swallowed the lump in her throat. "I have to see what Alice needs."

"Where are you going?" he asked.

But she moved away quickly before he could stop her.

Better to leave now before something happens, she thought.

She found Alice, who was standing by the food table, pouring some lemonade…and wearing a devilish little smile.

"Oh my word, Gracie, I saw it all. For a second I thought I'd have to turn the hose on you two."

Her eyes grew wide, almost panicked. "But we didn't do anything!"

Alice just giggled. "What a shame."

She wanted to crawl into a hole and hide. But Alice put an arm around her, speaking in her comforting way.

"Oh little sister, don't be ashamed. Besides, I was watching and I came to your rescue, just like you asked me to. You're safe and sound now. Although I think you might have stirred up someone besides Henry. See for yourself."

She pointed across the yard, and Grace looked to see Victoria making her way towards Henry. And she looked fit to be tied. Grace brought a nervous hand to cover her mouth.

"Oh no, what did I do? What if she throws a fit or something? Oh Lord, it'll ruin the whole party."

"Oh, I wouldn't worry," said Alice. "She won't throw a tantrum and embarrass herself. She's too vain for that. And besides, Henry would just make her leave if she made a scene."

Picking up a glass of lemonade, she handed it to her.

"Here, take this to your brother. You look like you could use a breather."

Sighing with relief, Grace hurried off to see to the errand, and though she was tempted, she did not look back. At the porch of the house next door, she handed her brother the drink. Then she took a seat in a rocking chair in a shadowed corner. She sat and listened to men talking, as she had done so many times back home…and as she had done then, she did not participate in their conversation. Only this time, it wasn't because she was not wanted. She had no desire to talk. She only wished to hide, and with her brother so near, she felt quite safe from any female wrath.

And safe from the lure of tempting blue eyes.

How warm his hand had been when he had taken hold of her wrist. His voice, when spoken in the pleasant tone that their conversation had taken, flowed with a rich and warm feeling. How intelligently he spoke, more than any man she'd known before. And his smile. Her heart beat fast when she thought of it. As in so many moments before, her memory quoted a passage that seemed to relay what she was thinking - what she was feeling, better than her own words could describe...

He smiled at me with a certain smile he had of his own, and which he used but on rare occasions. He seemed to think it too good for common purposes. It was the real sunshine of feeling...

Perhaps it *was* the real sunshine of feeling. But her heart sank a little when she remembered that her budding feelings could never be allowed to take full bloom. Whether he felt genuine affection for her, or even just a passing interest, it did not matter. He was a man of the world. He lived with his mistress, for heaven's sake. What loyalty could there be in such a man? And if there was loyalty there, it belonged to another, and she dared not interfere with such a bond. The consequences were too great a danger.

* * * * *

Come back here, he wanted to say.

He watched her as she walked away, and if it wasn't for the fact that his head was spinning just a little, he would have gone after her. When he'd seen her rise to her feet to go, he'd had an impulse to reach out and pull her back to his side. He didn't like the way she fled so fast, as if she feared him. But then he thought about that for a moment, and smiled to himself.

Maybe she was right to fear him. He'd told her before that he'd thought about stealing a kiss. Now he knew that he wanted to do much more than think about it. Sitting beside her, so close, he'd been a moment away from actually doing it, and would have if her sister-in-law hadn't interfered. Never mind the fact that everyone around them was watching. In that moment, he hadn't seen anything else but her. He thought of her hair that fell in rich waves around her shoulders. It looked so soft, and he'd been so tempted to reach out and twine a golden curl around his finger. And what a lovely smile she had, even if she'd only given him a small one. The few times he'd seen her before, she'd always looked angry or fearful, although even then she'd been attractive as hell.

But when she smiled, it was incredible. It was like watching sunlight emerging from behind a cloud, illuminating her whole presence. And then there were her lips that looked so soft and rosy. She had a small mouth, but he found it just perfect. Her lips were a natural shade of coral pink, colored only by nature and not by some cosmetic paint. And if it hadn't been for the interruption, he would have finally found out just how soft that tempting little mouth was. Damn his luck. Maybe if he tried again, he could have another chance. Maybe he could somehow sneak her away from the crowd, sweet talk her a little. Anything was possible if he planned it right. And he was just about to get to his feet when Victoria came walking up to him. At first he didn't look at her, even though she was standing right in front of him.

"Enjoying yourself?" she asked.

He nodded. "Very much." He wasn't a fool. She'd seen him talking to Grace, and now she was here sniffing around, looking for clues to prove her suspicions.

"Are you ready to head up to the lake?" she asked.

"In a little while," he replied, rising to his feet. "We haven't even been here thirty minutes. It wouldn't be very neighborly if we just up and left, now would it?" He went to the table and poured two glasses of lemonade, handing her one. "Have a drink and take it easy. Enjoy yourself a little."

He strolled over toward the house next door, and she followed a few steps behind. Normally, she would not have stayed so close. When they had these kinds of neighborhood gatherings, she was usually content to find a quiet corner and keep to herself until he came to fetch her and take her home. But now it seemed that she wanted to keep him in her sights. How could he do anything if she was trailing him like a stubborn bloodhound?

Maybe it's better to wait, he thought. *Bide my time.* Grace wasn't going anywhere, although at the moment, she seemed to have disappeared. *Where is that girl hiding now?* He wondered. He glanced around and saw John Langdon, and thought that maybe she'd gone to her brother for protection. It seemed like a logical answer, although he knew he'd have to move with caution. If she'd told her brother something wrong had gone on, there was a good chance he'd find himself fending off an attack.

But as he approached the house next door, he was offered a smile and a handshake, and he knew he was safe for the moment. Jack was exuberant.

"Henry, where the hell have you been? We were looking for you the other night at the club and never saw you once. Where did you go?"

"Oh, I was around," Henry answered. "The place is always so busy on the weekends. Sometimes I get lost in the crowd."

Jack nodded. "I think I know the reason why they pack the place, and it's standing right there behind you." He smiled kindly at Victoria, who was looking away with an air of great distraction. Still, she managed to look at Jack for a moment, giving him a polite smile in return. "You know, speaking of talent," said Jack, "I think maybe we should get my little sister to entertain us. This is a party, after all. Now where did she go?"

Henry was wondering the same thing. It took a lot of strength not to turn his neck to look for her. It wasn't wise…not with Victoria standing right beside him. He couldn't be for certain what she'd do if he overstepped his bounds, although he honestly didn't care. But he didn't want to make a scene, for the sake of his neighbors. So he tried to maintain a careless aspect.

"Oh there she is," said Jack, moving towards the porch where Grace was sitting. "Come on out of that corner, baby sister. We want to hear you play and sing a little."

Play and sing? Henry thought. He knew she played piano. But there was more to her talents? He was instantly curious.

He watched as she waved her brother away, shaking her head. But Jack was quite persistent. He went over to her and took her hand, trying to pull her to her feet.

"Come on, sis. It's been a long time since I heard a song from you. I'll even play along with you and we'll get Alice to join in."

"Maybe we should just let her be," Henry chimed in. "She looks a little skittish to me. Maybe she's too scared to perform in front of people."

What he hoped was to provoke her. He wanted to see that bolder side of her personality, wondering if a challenge would do the trick. He met her eyes, daring her to prove him wrong. And he was thrilled when she got to her feet, following her brother back over to their yard. He gave himself a few moments pause, just so it wouldn't look like he was chasing after her. When he thought a decent amount of time had passed, he casually strolled over to the Langdon's porch, where a small crowd had started to gather.

Alice brought out instruments...a fiddle and banjo, a guitar and mandolin, which Grace took in hand, and Jack had a harmonica which he put in his pocket. They sat close together, and just before they began, Jack turned to Henry with a sharp eye, but a slight grin.

"Listen here, Mr. big shot businessman. Don't go getting no ideas after you hear this. She's not for hire."

Henry just smiled a little and held up his hands in defense.

They began to play, and right away it became clear what talented musicians and singers they were. They soared through lovely harmonies that reminded him of Irish songs he used to hear as a child. Some were fast and infectious, others were slow and sweet, and when they did a rendition of "The Wabash Cannonball" Henry and the others watching were delighted by Grace's ability to yodel.

But it was the soft, sweet sound of a country hymn that captured him and the others who were listening, leaving them spellbound. Her voice was tender and sweet, unpolished and yet oh so pure. It was a moving experience to listen to her, and everyone listening was in awe.

Except for Victoria.

No one seemed to notice that she stood off to the side with a pained expression on her face. In the middle of a song, she suddenly turned and walked away, and only Henry caught sight of it. For a few minutes he ignored her departure, preferring to stay where he was. All three of the Langdons were true talents, but he couldn't take his eyes off of Grace. Not only was her voice a marvel, but her fingers were so nimble in playing, moving effortlessly as they danced across the strings of the instrument she held. How he would have loved to remain and hear more. But he knew that he had to go, and with great reluctance he pulled himself away from the crowd and went after Victoria. He followed her into the house, shutting the door firmly behind them.

"All right, let's have it," he said. "We're in the house. We're all alone, and I know you've been waiting to rant and rave about something. So let's get it over with."

"It's her, isn't it?" she cried.

God, woman, he thought. *You don't waste time, do you?* Then he snorted, and to her question he gave his own. "Her who?"

"Don't play dumb with me!" she cried. "I'm talking about that skinny little bird over there. She's the one who has your head all a mess, isn't she?"

Lord, how he detested the jealously of women, especially a woman like Victoria. As if she had some claim on him. As if she had the right to pry into his business. And as if he was going to give her the satisfaction of admitting anything. He didn't bother to hide his contempt.

"For God's sake, Victoria. You see me talking to a neighbor and that's the first thing you think?"

"What do you expect me to think? I'm not a fool. I saw the way you were looking at her. I saw the way you were watching her while she was singing. I'm not blind, Henry!"

He let out an irritated sigh and moved past her. "You're out of your mind. And even if I was looking at her, what concern is it of yours? Who I talk to and who I spend time with is none of your business."

"It is my business!" she shouted, her voice cracking slightly. "Everything about you is my business!"

At that he turned on her, furious. "We are NOT married!"

Suddenly she shrank back a little, her eyes full of deep pain at his statement. Tears began to well in her eyes, but his tone did not soften. She had her place, and it was about time she learned it. He advanced forward a step, pointing an angry finger at her, his voice low and menacing.

"YOU are not my wife. I have never given a vow of any kind to you. But I have kept you under my roof. I have treated you as well as any man could treat a woman. I have kept company with no one but you. So do not dare to question me on anything."

He watched her, eyes blazing, and he saw her sink down to a sitting position on the sofa. She tried to turn away from him, to hide the tears that had started to spill down her cheeks. But she could not hide the sobs that came from within her. For a brief moment, he felt a twinge of guilt at what he had wrought. Then, his brow furrowed in anger and frustration.

"I will not listen to this."

He threw open the front door, and a moment later he slammed it behind him as he stormed off into the night.

Finding Grace

*****

The Great Pier was a wonder for the senses. With its long boarded walks, lit along the way with the soft light of lanterns, and the grand auditorium from which sweet music flowed, it was a feast for the eyes and ears, and Grace drank in the romance of it all. The lake looked so different at night, lit by the light of the moon and dotted with the many boats that had gathered near and far to await the fireworks that would soon illuminate the sky.

At home, July the Fourth had been just another day in their little world. She had seen a fireworks display just once, many years ago, when Jack and Alice had taken her to Charleston. Now she waited in anticipation to see them again. But it was only nine-thirty now. Jack had said that the show wasn't due to begin until almost ten, so she took to enjoying all that was going on around her.

While Jack and Alice were dancing in the ballroom, she stood near the doorway, just watching. Several young men had approached her and asked her to dance, but she had politely declined. It was exciting to have that kind of attention, but the simple fact was she didn't know the first thing about dancing. After some time of listening to the music and watching the elegant movements, she took to a nearby bench and watched the people go by. So many couples drifted along within her view, some holding hands and some arm in arm. For the first time in a long while, she felt a deep sense of sadness.

Suddenly, she felt a great longing for a companion. She had always been her own confidant and best friend, but she had the same feelings and longings as any other woman. She sighed, and for some strange reason her mind turned to Charlie.

Of all people, he was the last one she was sure she should be thinking of, but she could not help but wonder what might have been. If only he had remained the sweet, charming young man she'd first thought him to be. Maybe she would have grown to love him in time, had she not been witness to the darkness of his personality. It still hurt her deeply when she thought of the way he had turned on her...the dark look on his face when he spoke his cruel words. Why couldn't he have been the right one? Someone to share her thoughts and feelings. Someone she could confide in, and turn to when the world was cold. Someone like Henry.

Lord, why can't I stop thinking of him?

She knew it was wrong. She knew he was the kind of man that she should be staying far away from. He was dangerous, in so many ways. And yet, he was on her mind constantly. He was like the forbidden fruit that she was warned to keep herself from, but like the weakest of human beings, she found herself drawn more and more to that which she could not and should not have. What was it about him that she was drawn to? As soon as the question formed in her mind, the answer came in quick and obvious succession. He was handsome, intelligent, and charming - when he tried to be. Maybe that was where the attraction lay.

He had an intensity about him that she could not understand, and yet it was the very thing that seemed to drive her senses mad whenever he came near to her. There was something in his gaze when he looked at her...something that burned like fire. The only way to keep from feeling that burning was not to look at him, but even that was not easy when she felt his eyes upon her. When their gazes were locked, she was helpless. And in the deepest, darkest part of her soul, she longed to be weak - and discover just what it was that was lying there behind those eyes.

Looking around at the crowd, she half expected to see him among the people. He had his way of appearing out of nowhere, as he had done to her before. And though she knew it was wrong to wish it, some mischievous part of her longed for him to come and surprise her once again. She was so busy looking, in fact, that she did not see him approaching slowly from behind. He came to stand just near her shoulder, and there he stood for several long and silent moments.

She felt a presence behind her, and without turning her head she knew who it was. A smile threatened to break on her lips, but she managed to hold it back. Though she was pleased to see him, she did not wish him to know it.

He'll only gloat if he sees it, she thought. *And I can't let him make me a fool.*

She cleared her throat a little, composing herself, and then she looked up at him. "Did anyone ever tell you that you turn up like a bad penny?"

"I should be asking you that question," he replied. "You're the one who keeps turning up everywhere I go. I'm telling you, this obsession you have with me has got to stop."

She just shook her head. Despite her attempts to stifle it, a little laugh escaped her. But she'd never been good at silly conversation. And this time was no different.

"So where is your other half? I saw her leave the party, and she didn't look too happy."

He came around the bench, sitting down beside her. She moved over slightly to maintain a safe distance. He gave her an odd look for it, but said nothing of it. He looked out ahead of him, watching the boats on the water.

"She stayed at home. She and I had a disagreement, and I decided to take a walk."

"And you ended up here?"

He shrugged. "Let's not talk about her."

Her eyes grew a little larger. "Who should we talk about then?"

He turned towards her, looking at her with eyes that were warm and soft. "You."

She felt her heart skip a beat, and she had to tear her eyes away from him before she melted into a puddle. She looked out at the boats on the water, trying her best just to keep her senses.

"Why talk about me? You won't find much that's interesting."

"Oh, I wouldn't say that," he replied. "Since I met you, I have to admit you've made me very curious. Tell me some things, if you will, and satisfy my need to know."

Wringing her hands, she spoke nervously. "What kind of things?"

"Well, for one thing, you never did answer my question. Why are you here, when the rest of your family is at home?"

It was the second time he had asked her of it. And something in his voice told her he truly wanted to know...that he wasn't just asking for the sake of asking.

Over several minutes she told him her tale. He let her speak with little interruption, only occasionally giving his opinion, and when he did speak it was with a kind of warmth and concern. She was discovering an aspect of him that was very alluring...one she would never have expected.

He was an excellent listener.

It was the first time in so very long that anyone had asked her questions, or showed a genuine interest in her. She found herself feeling quite warm and comfortable with him...and the barriers around her heart soon began to fall away. When she finished speaking, he shook his head in disbelief.

"Remarkable, the way people can be to one another. If I had a daughter, I can't imagine ever forcing her into anything as serious as marriage. And as for your friend Charlie...it's a shame that your rock missed his head."

She laughed a little. Strange as it seemed, she found herself wanting to please and amuse him. Still, she was wary of him, managing to remember that he belonged to another. They could never grow close, even if they wanted to.

But she did not voice her thought. It was enough to feel it lingering in her heart. With a deep breath and a sigh, she looked at him and smiled.

"You know, you can be quite nice when you want to be.

He scoffed...but wore a little smirk. "You just caught me on an off day."

Up in the sky, the fireworks began to pop and shine. The colors burst forth in all of their fiery splendor, but she only looked up at them for a moment. She felt his eyes watching her, and when she looked back at him, he was watching her with those burning eyes of his...and she found she could not look away from him.

That smoldering fire in his eyes held her captive...and a moment later his fingers brushed her cheek, sending a tremor down her spine. Her eyes closed on their own, for she knew by some deep instinct what would come next. And then his lips brushed hers, soft and warm. Her whole being seemed to burn...her head felt light and dizzy, and she had to take in a breath when he separated from her for a moment. Then he kissed her a second time, and she felt a weakness that threatened to take over her entire frame. Then another feeling came over her...one of fear and shame, and almost of their own will her hands came up and pushed at his shoulders.

"No, I can't!" She made to rise quickly and leave. But he grasped her wrist, holding it firmly.

"Don't go yet. I promise I won't kiss you again."

"I'm sorry, I can't stay." She managed to free her wrist, and fled from him before he could detain her again.

It did not matter to her that her lips still burned from his kiss. It did not matter that she wanted to go back and be with him...to feel the fire that he had let loose within her. He was not hers to have. He belonged to another. And more importantly, she would not be lured like a moth to a flame.

Finding Grace

I won't be his next Victoria, she thought. *A heart can only handle so much damage, and I won't let him have mine to break.*

Chapter 11

"Hide and Seek"

He knew he should have left right then. But the thought was a weak flicker in the back of his mind. Instead he rose from the bench and went after her. Just as she reached the doorway of the auditorium he caught her by the arm, and the strength with which she fought him was stunning.

"Let go!" she cried, trying to wrestle her arm free.

"Stop squirming and be still," he said, but she kept on. She tried to pry his fingers off, and when that didn't work she dug her nails into his flesh, causing him to yelp in pain and release her for a moment. But her dash was short, for he caught hold of her again, this time by both arms. The look on her face was positively wild.

"Good God, woman. Will you control yourself? It's not like I was trying to attack you. For crying out loud, it was just a kiss."

"It shouldn't have even gone that far!" With a great effort she wrenched herself away, dashing behind a pillar to hide.

But this time, he didn't make a lunge to pull her back. He let her go willingly, if it would be the only way to calm her. Leaning against the opposite side of the stone column, he sighed deeply and ran a hand through his hair. Then, in the silence that lingered between them, a little smirk came to his face as he thought about what had just happened.

She looked incredible when she was riled up. And kissing her had been unbelievable, even as brief and simple as it had been. Just the touch of her lips on his had lit a fire inside of him.

He almost laughed at himself, thinking that the idea of being "On Fire" sounded like some stupid depiction in a love novel. But he knew blazing chemistry when he felt it.

If only she would stop acting like a child and admit that she felt it too.

She'd been stirred, he had no doubt. He turned slightly, so that his voice would travel and fall directly on her ear. His tone was soft, deep and sensual.

"Did you really hate it so much?"

There was a long pause, but he knew she was listening. He knew she was still there. He could feel her presence. But the reply she gave him was one he wasn't ready for.

"I'm not your pet, Henry Shaw. You have one of those at home. If you want someone to play with you can go home to her. Maybe she's ready to crawl into your bed, but you won't get that from me."

He was stunned. By the outright boldness of her statement...by what she was implying. She was accusing him of entrapment...of seduction. She thought his only intention was to get her into his bed. Such an accusation felt like a slap in the face.

Because he knew it was pretty much the truth.

Suddenly it felt like someone was thrusting a mirror in his hands, demanding that he take a look at himself. But the last thing on earth he wanted was to search his soul...and he fled from the source of conflict...from her.

Voices were nagging him as he went. Two strange, small voices seemed to whisper in his ears...like the proverbial devil and angel perched upon either of his shoulders.

Have you given a damn about any of the women you've slept with?

No, but they didn't care about me either, so what the hell difference does it make?

You would have slept with Grace Langdon, if you'd had the chance. Don't lie to yourself.

God, it was true. Suddenly he found himself grappling with shame, which was a feeling he hadn't known in so long that it scared him. If she hadn't stopped him, he would have taken advantage of her and not given it a second thought. He'd done that to other women without his conscience being pricked. So why was he now feeling like such a toad? And the answer came to him instantly.

The other women weren't innocent girls. Not that they were trash he'd picked up off the street, but they'd warmed a few beds besides his.

But Grace Langdon was pure and untouched. It was quite possible she'd never even been kissed until just now. And he'd been ready to take out all of his passion on her innocent little body. Lord, he really was a shameless snake.

He was still at war with himself when he came up the front steps of the house. When he came in, he saw right away the figure lying over on the sofa. He knew what that implied, and he had to say he did not blame her for it. If it had been himself, he would not have wanted to share the bed either. He went over and sat down in the chair beside her, and he spoke to her in a low, quiet voice.

"Victoria, are you awake?"

She turned her back to him, pulled the blanket closer around her neck. Her answer was sharp.

"Get away from me."

He ran a frustrated hand over his face, sighing.

God, I wish I was better at this, he thought. *If we were both men, we would settle this with our fists, and then go have a few drinks and be done with it.*

"Look," he said. "You may be pissed at me, and that's your right. But we've still got a business to run, so we might as well just call a truce right here and now."

"To hell with your truce. To hell with you, you selfish bastard."

He let out a defeated sigh. "Fine. Would you rather go upstairs and sleep, and leave me here on the sofa?"

"No," she spat viciously. "Just leave me alone."

He sighed again, and left her there.

Going up the stairs, he was suddenly so very tired. Not tired from exertion, but tired from all that had happened in just the last few hours. Since the end of his marriage, he'd made it a point to live a simple life. But lately, he found his life was full of complications. And he *hated* complications.

In the bedroom, he removed all of his clothing quickly, for it felt like he was being smothered by the restraints of them. He kicked the garments aside, not bothering to get near the clothes hamper. There were more important things on his mind tonight than tidiness. He slipped into his pajama pants, and felt some relief, being free of the confinement that clothing could sometimes bring.

What was he to do now? He couldn't just get rid of Victoria. Much as he would have liked to simply end their relationship, he knew it wasn't that simple. It may have been a shallow fact, but Victoria was more than his mistress. She was the main attraction of his show. It was she who the people paid to see, and if he lost her, his business would surely be in turmoil. She could just up and go if she wanted to, and some other eager businessman would be glad to take her in and make a fortune off of her. He could not let that happen.

The other problem was the one he'd left back at the pier, and his mood was growing darker by the moment as he thought of her. Naïve, decent little woman that she was. And that made him even more frustrated, and he cursed to himself, *Damn her and her decency.* If she was like other women he'd known, he wouldn't be in this lousy state of mind. He might have been in a warm bed with a warm body. But no, she was an untainted little country blossom who was making him feel things he hadn't felt in years. God almighty she was a nuisance. At first it had all been fun and games with her, teasing and provoking her for his own enjoyment. But then she had to go and weave her spell, and now here he was feeling guilty about how he had treated her. The girl had been nothing but trouble since the first day he'd met her. All he wanted to do now was forget about her and salvage what was left of his peaceful life.

He let out a breath as he went to the bed and fell down on it, and he closed his eyes and rested his face against the cool of his pillow. After a time he began to relax, and before he fell asleep he found himself thinking, *I hope she can't sleep. I hope all she can think about is me. It would serve her right, the little witch.*

* * * * *

She slept fitfully that night, trying to forget what had happened and failing miserably. All she could think about was the feel of his lips on hers, the wonderful warmth and sweetness of his mouth. Even his taste and scent. Lord in heaven, she would never have imagined that such a sensation existed, but it was there still, burning on her lips. It was as if he'd branded her with his kiss, and now it was haunting her, thrilling her, and frustrating her so badly that it made her want to cry.

Finding Grace

Flopping her head back on her pillow, she brought her hands up to her face in frustration. And words suddenly flowed into her head.

I did what human beings do instinctively when they are driven to utter extremity - looked for aid to one higher than man. "God help me!" burst involuntarily from my lips.

She knelt at the side of her bed and folded her hands in a desperate prayer, begging for guidance from above. And more words of wisdom, ones she'd once heard in a lesson at school, came to her in her hour of desperation

.Gold is tried by fire, brave men by adversity

.She knew she was brave, and strong. She'd spent a lifetime being knocked about by heavier circumstances, and this was but a small trial she had to overcome. All she had to do was focus her mind, think about all the things she'd been through in life, and remind herself that this tribulation, like all the others, would not get the best of her.

Her blood flowed with new determination, and she rose from her bed. *Idle hands are the devil's playthings*, she thought. *So I will keep the idleness from my hands by staying busy. All the time.*

It wasn't until she'd gotten half-way to the kitchen that she realized it was Sunday morning. *Oh no*, she silently declared. She knew he would be there. So would Victoria. And despite the vow of strength she'd taken, she just didn't have the courage at that moment to face them. Him, in particular. So she feigned a headache and an ill stomach, telling Jack and Alice to go on without her and not to worry. She spent the next several hours in prayer, hoping that God would forgive her for her evil deeds and understand why she had done them.

* * * * *

The next day was Monday. A new day, and a new week, and she vowed to make the best of things and keep her word to herself. She arose and prepared to start her day with determination and purpose. She washed and dressed quickly, and went down to meet the milkman. Her timing was perfect, as she heard his approach just as she reached the door. She opened it, and when he saw her, he tipped his hat and smiled. At least the day was starting off with the sight of a friendly face.

"Good morning, Mike."

"Good morning, Miss Grace. How are you?"

"I'm fine," she replied, taking the bottle of milk from him. He smiled at her.

"I really enjoyed hearing you the other night. Have you ever thought about singing in public? Like at state fairs or something? People would really love what you do."

The very thought of that made her cheeks blush pink, and she shook her head.

"Oh no, not me. I don't mind singing and playing for a few folks at a time, but I could never get up in front of a big crowd. I'd die of fear first."

He smiled and chuckled. "Yes, well, I can understand that. Have a lovely day now." He tipped his cap to her and left, turning to wave at her as he reached the curb. She waved back, and closed the door.

What an idea, she thought. She had a wild, crazy moment in which she imagined herself onstage at a place like Henry's club. Then she shook her head at her own madness. If someone ever tried to get her onstage in a place like that, they would have to throw a net over her and drag her out there, kicking and screaming. She laughed at herself, and hurried to the kitchen.

She busied herself with making breakfast, wanting to keep an occupied mind at all times. Jack and Alice didn't seem to notice any difference in her manner. At least if they did, they didn't say anything about it. All seemed quite routine at the start of this day.

After breakfast, Grace and Alice stood on the stoop and waved to Jack as he left for work. As he went, Grace's eye - betraying thing that it was - caught a glimpse of a door opening at the house across the street…and Henry was emerging. She watched him for a moment. She could not help but look, however much she wanted not to. And when he locked eyes with her, she felt a knowing thrill.

Dear God, she thought. *He's as tempting as Lucifer himself.*

Then she caught herself in that unguarded moment, and silently chastised herself for it. She turned away quickly and went in the house, with Alice following closely behind.

"Are you all right?" she asked as she closed the door. They walked back towards the kitchen together.

For the briefest of moments, Grace thought of denying that anything was bothering her. But the burden within her was too great, and Alice was much too sharp to let this pass her attention. Grace sighed, and as they came into the kitchen, she pulled out a chair and sank into it.

Alice's voice was firm but gentle. "Out with it, Sis." She pulled a chair close and leaned in to listen. There was a tense pause, and then at last, Grace spoke.

"Saturday night, at the pier, I ran into Henry. We talked for a little while. And it was nice." She smiled for a moment. Then the smile fell away. "But then…" She paused, hesitant to go on.

"Then what?" Alice leaned closer, all anticipation.

Grace buried her face in her hands, but she only hesitated a moment before she answered. "He kissed me."

Alice gasped. Then a mischievous grin slowly smiled across her face. "Did he really?" Her voice was a near whisper. She paused a moment. And then she asked, "It was your first kiss, wasn't it?"

Grace didn't answer, but a response wasn't really necessary. Alice let out an enchanted little sigh, and she gushed.

"How romantic."

Grace shook her head, almost panicking. "No, no. Not romantic. It can't be romantic."

"Why not?"

"Because it's wrong! No matter what I feel, or what he feels, I won't chase another woman's lover. I won't!" She dropped her head on her arms, and let out a shuddering sigh.

Alice's smile slacked a little. She reached out with a gentle hand, rubbing Grace on the back.

"Don't feel so bad. You can't help your feelings. And at least you know what's right and what's wrong. You're a good girl, little sister." She sat back for a moment and sighed. Then she leaned forward and rested her head in her hand. Grace sat up, and like Alice, she let her head come to rest in her hand. The women looked at each other, and a little smile began to creep up on Alice's face.

"What?" Grace asked.

Alice leaned in towards her, as if they were both conspirators in some great secret. "All moral matters aside," she said, and she could not keep a little grin from her expression. "How was it?"

Grace blushed, her hands coming up to cover her face once again. Only this time, it was a shy smile she was trying to hide.

"It made me dizzy." She let out a little giggle that she couldn't suppress. Alice smiled.

"Oh, that's so sweet. I'm so happy for you, I really am."

"Happy for me?"

"You finally got your first kiss. That's a big moment in a woman's life. And Henry, my Lord." She let out a dreamy little sigh. "He could give any woman the vapors."

For a few moments more, they shared womanly sighs and smiles. But then Grace's expression changed, coming back to the seriousness it had shown just a few minutes before.

"It can't ever be more than that. And you have to promise you won't ever tell a soul about this. It can only be between us."

"Of course, of course," said Alice. "I promise."

Grace sighed a little in frustration. "What am I gonna do? He's right there across the street. We're bound to run into one another sometime."

"Go the other way," Alice replied.

"But what if he comes after me?"

Now Alice grinned slightly. "Play opossum. Maybe he'll just sniff you and leave you alone."

Grace rolled her eyes, but she couldn't help laughing. She was so grateful to have Alice. Much as she loved her brother, words couldn't begin to describe how much she cherished her sister-in-law. If not for Alice, she would be in a very different place right now, and most likely be another person altogether. She really was, as Jack had often called her, an angel in disguise.

* * * * *

Later that morning, Alice took her down to Maxwell Street. It was a bustling marketplace with vendors of every kind, with anything and everything one could possibly think of. What started out as a serious mission of self-discipline turned into a lovely day of leisure as they strolled through the noisy market. And through the courtesy of a hot dog vendor, she had her very first Maxwell Street Polish, as it was called – a slightly spicy sausage on a bun, topped with mustard, onions, and peppers. The smell was powerful, and the taste was indescribably delicious. It seemed a bit sinful to indulge, but she was learning that indulgence seemed to be just part of the local custom, and she found that she wasn't particularly ashamed of herself, though she did have to laugh at herself for it.

"I think I might be as big as a house before long. There's more food to be found in these parts than I could shake a stick at."

Alice just smiled, making a wicked joke about the food that nearly sent Grace into a choking fit. When she recovered enough to catch her breath, she mockingly hit her sister-in-law and they laughed together like little children.

Later as they strolled along, Grace found a special treasure among the vendors. A bookseller had a stand with more books than she'd ever seen before in her life, and she and Alice stood for the longest time, thumbing through volumes both large and small. Among the many tomes, Grace came across one with a familiar author's name - Robert Louis Stevenson. It was a collection of several of his works. She held it in her hands for a long time, staring at it. Alice came to see what was in her hands.

"Kidnapped. Dr. Jekyll and Mr. Hyde. And Treasure Island." She shrugged and curled her nose a little. "Stevenson was always too dark for me. A lot of murder, intrigue, adventure…that kind of thing. Pirates, mad men. The kinds of things men seem to like. Your brother does."

And so does Henry, Grace thought. She held the book firmly in her hands. She couldn't be with him, and could hardly take the chance of speaking to him. But maybe through the things he cherished, such as this, she could get to know him a little more.

As they made their way through the lanes of the market, Alice nodded at familiar faces that they passed by. One was a green-eyed, white haired gentleman that Grace recognized as Doctor Brown…one of the neighbors from the party.

"I remember you from last night," she said, smiling. "Good to see you again, sir."

"And you," he said. "You certainly have a lovely voice, Miss Langdon. I really enjoyed listening to you last night. Maybe you could play for us again sometime?"

Grace smiled shyly at the compliment, and the sweetness of the doctor's voice. "Maybe I will." The doctor nodded and tipped his hat, then went on his way.

"That's the second person who told me that," Grace said, as they walked on.

"Well, there were a lot of folks there last night," Alice replied. "And we did put on a nice little performance. Especially you, little song bird. Maybe everyone is trying to hint at your future career. Think about it."

Grace just smiled, shaking her head.

When they got home, she found a comfortable spot on the sofa and tried to engross herself in the collection. She wanted to lose herself in it, as she had lost herself in so many books before. But try as she might, she just couldn't concentrate, and she was well aware of why. She could not help but imagine what might have been. It was beyond her control.

That night when she sat in a hot bath, there were no distractions to keep her from thinking of him, and her memory played his kiss over and over again, each time sending her heart a flutter and a thrill up her spine. It was all she would ever have of him, and she knew it. Anything more would be wrong, and even these thoughts of him she knew were wicked. And yet, something within her...the rebellious spirit that lay within... cried out that it was not wicked to think of him. Her physical being was restrained from him, but there could be no sin in being with him in her mind and heart. In those places, she was free to think and feel. And surely, there could be no great evil in that.

* * * * *

Another Sunday came much too quickly, and she knew she couldn't hide any longer. All week long she'd been slinking around to avoid him, and with Alice's help she'd succeeded, and even managing to keep Jack from becoming suspicious. But today she knew she would see him, and she could not keep from feeling the excitement and anticipation that rose up. But as she looked in the mirror at herself, she could see nothing that would betray her feelings to the world. Her eyes were a cool shade of steel at the moment - due in part to the sober grey dress she was wearing. It seemed that the shade of her eyes often changed with the color of her clothing, and subsequently, with the mood that the occasion called for. On the rare occasions for celebration, she had often taken to wearing red or purple, which seemed to brighten her eyes to their fullest shade of blue. But this occasion called for a calm, cool appearance, and the ashen dress with its simple lace trim seemed the best for that effect. She lifted her chin in a proud and determined manner, straightened her shoulders, and left the room to join Jack and Alice.

When they arrived at church that morning, they all made the usual greetings and such. The pastor seemed very pleased to see Grace, and requested that she take a place in the choir.

"Your songs of praise were indeed wonderful to hear," he declared. "We would be so pleased to have an angel's voice in our choir, one that can help lift the spirits of our parishioners and bring them closer to God."

It was not within her to refuse the request of a man of God, and so she smiled and politely accepted. It was not long before she was standing among the members of the choir, just as she had done so many times before at home. It might have very well been just the same, except that as she sat quietly in her place listening to the sermon, she could feel a certain pair of eyes watching her. And heaven help her...weak, sad being that she was...she found her own eye lifting, for just a moment, to meet the gaze that met hers.

When the service was over, and they were wandering out among the crowd, she was walking ahead with Alice when she heard Jack's voice behind her. He was talking to friends, which was nothing of importance to her. But then she heard the one voice that she did not want to hear...a voice that both thrilled and petrified her. She turned to Alice and whispered.

"What are they doing? What are they talking about?"

"I don't know," said Alice, casually turning her head to look. "Victoria is standing with them. She is probably on guard, you know. There are dangerous women about." And she smiled a little at Grace, who just shook her head.

Then, Alice's expression grew serious. "They're coming this way."

Grace felt her nerves jump, but she did not let on. She took a deep and calming breath. Looking away, she tried to look calm. Jack came to stand beside them.

"Honey, I've invited Henry and Victoria to supper tonight. We're going out for Chinese. Your favorite." He smiled, turning to talk to a neighbor...unaware of what he'd just done.

Grace turned a shade of white. Alice had to reach out and steady her.

"Breathe," she declared.

Grace did, holding up a hand to signal she was well. At least in the physical sense. Her mental state was altogether different...and she put her head in her hands, feeling a strange need to weep.

"Lord above, why is this happening to me?" In a childish gesture she could not help, she dropped her hands and suddenly stamped her foot, her frustration at its breaking point. "I feel like Lizzie Bennett at Netherfield, being forced to dance with Mr. Darcy and not being able to do a thing about it."

Alice smiled at the reference to *Pride and Prejudice*. And while Grace played the part of Elizabeth, for a moment she made herself into Lizzie's good friend, Charlotte Lucas, and quoted a bit of the text.

"I dare say you will find him agreeable."

Despite the tension, Grace couldn't help but smile. She knew the text so well, and even under the grave circumstances, Alice's playfulness was infectious. So she did her best to sound aristocratic and proper, just like Lizzie Bennett.

"Heaven forbid! That would be the greatest misfortune of all! To find a man agreeable whom one is determined to hate! Do not wish me such an evil."

She tried to hold back a smile as she and Alice looked at each other. And then they both erupted into helpless rounds of laughter.

Chapter 12
"A Night Out"

He stood in the hallway for a moment, watching Victoria through the open door as she stood before the mirror. She was dressed in a low-backed burgundy dress...one that flowed in elegant proportion to her willowy figure. It was a beautiful garment. And yet, he could find little beauty in the woman wearing it. Her features were the same as they had always been. Nothing about her outward appearance had changed. But he could feel very little emotion as he looked at her now. There had never been love in his heart - only heated affection and desire. Now it seemed that the flame had gone out, leaving only a chilled feeling of emptiness when he looked at her.

A cold and quiet manner had taken over the house. They had not shared a bed in nearly two weeks now, since the night of the party. She had taken her things and moved to the bedroom across the hall, and somehow, he wasn't so disappointed about the change. It was taking some time to get used to an empty bed again, but he felt he was coping quite well. He wasn't about to go groveling to Victoria to come back to it. The only connection that seemed to remain between them was their relationship as employer and employee. It was mostly business as usual when it came to work, but even that relationship was strained. They hardly spoke, and when they did, it was with much petulance and arguing. It seemed she was intent on making his life as difficult as possible, and it was working. It didn't surprise him that she would be going along with John Langdon's invitation to dinner...just for spite.

"Need I ask why you insist on going to dinner?" he inquired. "Do you plan on making a public spectacle of yourself? Or is it just me you wish to humiliate?"

"Our neighbor has invited us to dinner," she answered, as she calmly donned a pair of ear bobs. "Is there something wrong with accepting his invitation?"

His eyes were cold looking at her. "What a cool liar you are."

She turned on a smooth heel and looked at him, her eyes flashing. "Why don't you stay home, if it makes you so uncomfortable?" Then she smiled a little...a sly, knowing gesture. "No, you won't stay home, will you? You're worried about what might happen when you're not around."

He only scoffed. "Are you really so insecure? You're intimidated by a little girl. A seventeen year old, for the love of Christ. I find that almost laughable."

Victoria glared at him, and he knew he had struck a sharp nerve with his words. But she had words of her own for him, and she did not mince them.

"What's laughable is a thirty-one year old man lusting after a child and making a fool of himself. That's the only reason you are going to dinner tonight, isn't it, Henry?"

It was true. He wasn't going to admit it to her, but it was true. Despite his best intentions, all he'd been thinking of was Grace. For the first several days after the incident at the pier, he'd buried himself in books and paperwork in an effort to erase her from his mind. And during the day the distraction had worked. But at night, his dreams were full of her image, and his imagination taunted him with happenings that went far beyond a simple kiss. It wasn't long before he realized that forgetting about her was an impossible notion. And discovering that, he knew he had to see her again. Only this time, he wanted to meet on friendly terms. He wouldn't tease her, or tempt her, no matter how wild his impulses became when he got close to her. His only trouble had been figuring out how to get near her without making her flee, as she'd been prone to do before and would certainly do now if he didn't tread carefully. But to his astonishment, and great delight, John Langdon had unknowingly opened a door of opportunity.

His only concern now was whether Victoria would behave herself. But any worry that he had he kept well concealed, especially as he addressed her remark about why he was going to the restaurant.

"Think whatever you wish. As far as I'm concerned, I'm having a meal with friends. If you want to misconstrue that, that's your business. I regret nothing that I've done, and nothing I'll do. Now if you're ready, I think we should go to dinner." He stepped back a step, and gestured for her to precede him. This she did, with head held high and defiant. He followed along behind her, and they set out to meet the neighbors.

* * * * *

They made their way down the street towards the restaurant. As they neared the door, Henry stopped and took Victoria lightly by the arm.

"So," he said, "Will you keep your claws drawn? Or will I have to haul you out like a child having a tantrum in a store?"

She looked at him with a cool, contemptuous expression. She pulled her arm free from his grasp.

"If you think I have such little class, then you are sorely mistaken," she declared, and she walked ahead of him into the restaurant, without waiting for him.

He knew he sat on a powder keg. He was no fool, despite what Victoria might have thought of him. She was plotting something, but he could not be sure what it was, and until she made a move, he had to be fully on his guard. In the meantime, he went through the motions of friendliness toward his neighbors. He shook hands with John and Alice, and smiled. But when it came to Grace, he put on his best air of detachment. He knew that everyone was watching, and so he kept his manner cool and polite. He gave no handshake, and only offered her a nod of his head as he greeted her.

"Miss Grace, it's a pleasure to see you again."

It was all he said. He sat down beside Victoria, and picking up the menu in front of him, pretended to browse it. But it was all he could do not to raise his eyes and search out the woman sitting across from him.

She looked better than he remembered, and that was saying something. Her hair was up, for one thing…gathered into an elegant twist at the back of her head. Her dress was a deep shade of violet, and the color suited her beautifully, bringing out the blue in her eyes. She looked so elegant, so sophisticated that it was hard to imagine how he'd once thought of her as a little bumpkin. How very wrong a first impression could be.

And as he'd been learning since that first day, she was impossible to ignore. He was quite certain she didn't intend to draw attention to herself, but she was a delight to watch with her endless curiosity and naïveté about the simplest things. He couldn't help but smile at some of her musings, and Jack and Alice were just as entertained by her innocent curiosity. He knew without looking at Victoria that she was not amused. But she was silent, and he let her remain so. He was still wary of what she might do, but he was so charmed by watching Grace, he found himself paying Victoria very little mind.

He watched as Grace turned the serving wheel slightly. "What is this for?"

Jack answered her with a little smile.

"When they bring the food, you use it to pass the servings around."

"Well if that don't beat all," she declared. "I wish we would have had one of those at home. Better than asking someone to pass the peas. If you want it, you just turn the wheel and take it from under their nose."

When the tea was brought, and her little cup was placed on the saucer before her, she looked at it with an odd expression. Sheepishly she asked, "Where's the handle?"

Alice looked at her. Taking her own cup in hand, she showed Grace how to hold it and sip it. Grace gingerly picked up her cup and followed suit, eliciting smiles from her three observers. Henry found her innocence so entertaining and appealing, he had trouble hiding his amused smile. On one hand, she seemed as if she couldn't help herself, and it showed in every little thing question and gesture she made. But on the other hand, she seemed hesitant each time she started to ask questions, as if someone might chastise her for doing wrong. Or ridicule her. At one point she looked at her brother, and saw him trying to suppress a grin. Henry was quite sure John meant his sister no harm. He was charmed, that was all. But Grace looked at her brother with a stern expression, and Henry felt a thrill run down his spine as he saw her eyes take on that wild flash of angry light he was coming to know so well.

"Don't laugh at me," she told her brother, her eyes blazing.

"I'm not!" Jack declared, though his grin was hardly suppressed, and Alice reached over to give his arm a firm slap.

"Leave her alone, Jack." And she gave him a sharp look, which he hardly acknowledged.

When the meat and seafood platter arrived, Henry could not keep himself contained any longer. He had to speak to her, even it was only to explain to her what the little flaming pot was in the middle of the wooden tray. She was staring at it intently, and he couldn't resist satisfying her interest.

"That's called a hibachi," he said, and he picked up a skewer of beef, putting it to the flame. "You let the meat smoke, and it enhances the flavor."

"Just like a campfire," she said with a slight smile, and she turned to her brother. "Remember that, Jack, how we used to sleep out at night, and cook the fish on the fire?"

"Yep, I do," he said. "Lord, it seems like forever since I've done that. Maybe we should take a trip somewhere and do that again. It would be fun. Hey, maybe we could all take a trip together, the five of us."

For the first time, Victoria spoke.

"No thank you," she said. "I'm not an outdoor kind of girl. But I do like to travel very much. In fact, I'm taking an extended trip very soon."

Henry looked at her. Something told him this was the moment. He could see the malice in her eyes - like the eyes of a coiled snake, preparing to strike. A cold hand of dread held his throat.

"I'm going to California," she said. "I'm going to be in pictures. My friend Hal has connections there, and he thinks I can make a name for myself."

Henry didn't know whether to believe her or not. The idea of her taking off on some wild flight to Hollywood sounded like a joke.

"You're ridiculous," he said.

"And you're an ass," she spat, and she jumped to her feet. "Why don't you just go ahead and sleep with her? That's what you want, isn't it, you slimy son of a bitch?"

Before she could say more, he shot to his feet and took her by the arm, dragging her out as she continued her rant.

"If you want him, honey, you can have him! But he's lousy in the sack, so what's the point in taking him?"

When he got her outside he shook her, though it hardly sufficed. What he wanted was to strangle her.

"That's what you call classy? Making a damn fool of yourself?" He gave her a slight shove...and she shoved him back, enraged.

"Go to hell, you self-centered bastard! Who needs you? I'll go to California and make my own way in the world!"

"You think so?" he spat. "You think you stand a chance relying on that crumb, Hal? Well don't come crying to me when it all falls apart. Women like you are a dime a dozen out there. You'll probably end up trading favors just to get by."

Her hand came up and slammed into his cheek, and he was momentarily stunned. It didn't particularly hurt, but it shocked him enough to render him still for several moments. In that time Victoria managed to hail a cab. Moments later it was speeding away, and he was left standing alone, feeling the eyes of passers by who had seen the whole thing. All he could do now was gather his pride, walk to his car, and go home. Alone.

* * * * *

"This is all my fault," said Grace, and she dropped her head into her hands.

"What do you mean *your fault?*" asked Jack. "And what the hell did Victoria mean by *you can have him?* Is there something going on with you and Henry?"

Grace just sighed, and didn't answer. She wanted to crawl under the table and hide and not have to face the round of questions and accusations she knew would come. Fortunately, Alice was there with her usual round of support.

"It's not her fault," she said.

"Whose fault is it then? Was it Henry? What did he do?" He turned to Grace. "Did he try something with you? If he did, I'll thump his skull."

As his voice grew louder, Alice rose to her feet and called for the check. She glared at him, her face flushed with mortification.

"Let's go before you make a total fool of yourself. We can talk about this in private."

Jack was silent just long enough to take care of the bill and escort the ladies out. But once back in the car, he immediately jumped back on the subject.

Grace sat in the back seat, listening and growing irritated at her brother's fatherly rambling. She loved him dearly, but to have him treat her as if she were a child, to talk to her as if she were his daughter rather than his sister, it made her want to reach over the seat and smack him, though Alice was doing a very fine job of scolding him. She sat back in the seat with her arms crossed, shaking her head, her voice laced with fury.

"That's why we didn't want to tell you anything. We knew you'd act like this."

"Wait a minute," Jack said, and he looked at her with wide eyes, his temper flaring fast. "You mean you knew about this, and you didn't tell me?"

"There's nothing to tell," Alice snapped at him. "Henry's had his head turned, and Victoria is green with envy. But your sister turned him down, and that's all there is to it."

His voice grew even louder. "And you didn't think I had a right to know? What if he crossed the line or something?" As the traffic came to a pause, he turned in his seat and looked at Grace. "And you," he said. "It's my job to look out for you, but how the hell can I do that if you're keeping things from me?"

Now it was Grace who found her temper rising, and she told him quite forcefully, "I don't need nobody's protection. I can take care of myself."

"Horse-feathers!" he snapped. "You're seventeen years old, fresh from the backwoods. You don't know a damn thing about the kind of men out there, ready to take advantage of a kid like you. Hell! Henry Shaw has been my friend and neighbor for years, and I wouldn't trust him more than any other dog out there."

"I'm not a kid anymore, Jack. I don't need you to boss me. I'm not ten years old."

"That doesn't matter!" he said. "And I don't want you to have anything else to do with Henry Shaw again. You stay away from him."

The traffic in front of them had come to a standstill, as they waited for the river bridge to come back down. Grace sat in her seat, her arms crossed in frustration. She wanted to scream and shout at him, fight with him and tell him how she was almost a grown woman, with her own mind and her own life to live. Then she thought...

He's just like any man. What's the point of talking to him? It would be like hitting my head against a wall

Suddenly she felt the need to be alone...to get away from him and his fatherly scolding. She wanted to run away and leave him stewing in his own juices, so he would know how it felt to be both furious and helpless at the same time. So just before the traffic began to move again, she opened her door and got out, slammed it behind her, and marched off down the street. She could hear him yelling at her to come back, but she kept right on walking. Soon she was lost among the crowd, and at that moment, there was nowhere else she would rather have been.

* * * * *

She roamed along the street for some time, and her great fury at her brother eventually diminished, though it did not go away entirely. The little shops along the street were turning on their lights for the evening, and she took her time looking in each window, lingering so that with each passing moment, she was certain Jack would be more and more worried. He deserved it, tyrant that he was.

It seemed funny to think that at one time not so long ago, she would never have questioned his lectures. He'd always been like her second father when she was young, but now that kind of control seemed stifling, and it reminded her very much of their father. Lord, if Jack heard her tell him that, he might lose his mind completely. To be compared to a man he despised, a man he'd left behind forever and vowed he would never, ever be like. Jack might never recover from such a blow.

As she ambled along the walk, her thoughts turned to the scene at the restaurant, and naturally, it sent her thoughts turning to Henry. She knew she shouldn't pity him. It was his own fault, losing Victoria and all, and with that came the possibility of his losing a great part of his business. He had brought it all on himself. And as for Victoria, she had to say she didn't blame her for leaving Henry and trying to make her own way. Grace knew all too well what it was like to be treated so coldly by a man.

And yet, it was Henry she kept thinking of more and more as she walked along. She should have thought him a beast for the way he treated Victoria. And she should have, if she had any sense at all, been condemning him for the common sinner that he was. But somehow, all of that now seemed like a weak flicker of light in the back of her mind. She knew it was wrong, and she knew it would probably be the ruin of her very soul - but, God help her, she adored him.

There, she had admitted it. It was like a weight lifting from her shoulders. And much to her own surprise, she felt no shame. What was so wrong about liking someone? And Henry was all the things she desired in a man. He was intelligent, and clever. He was devilishly charming when he wanted to be. She smiled to herself a little as she thought of him at supper. The way he held his glass with a light hand, and the way he ate casually and with small bites. He possessed manners. How wonderful it was to see a man who didn't shovel his food in his face as if it were his last meal. But of all the things about him, perhaps it was his honesty that most endeared him to her. He said just what he felt and what he was thinking, without wearing a false face or speaking too many pretty words. In a strange way, they were very much alike, the two of them.

In thinking of the things that she found so dear in him, she could not help but remember how he had looked at her that night at the lake, and how wonderful it had felt to know his kiss - the first kiss she'd ever had. How could she forget it, when she had lived it over and over again in her dreams at night? And she was beginning at last to understand that burning look in his eyes. The way it melted her will, and took her breath, she knew now it was a look of passion. She'd only read the word on paper, but until now she'd never known its all-consuming power, and somehow she was beginning to understand why human beings could succumb so easily to it's temptation.

But in thinking of it, she began to wonder how often he'd looked that way at Victoria - a woman he had shared so much of his life with.

A cloud of doubt came hovering over her then, and words came into her head to counsel her. She thought of Mr. Rochester, and how he talked to Jane of the mistresses he no longer cared for. How his feelings for them had dissolved into nothing. And then she thought of Jane, torn between the man she loved and the risk of a broken heart...

If I were so far to forget myself and all the teaching that had ever been instilled into me, as-- under any pretext--with any justification--through any temptation--to become the successor of these poor girls, he would one day regard me with the same feeling which now in his mind desecrated their memory...

What if, someday soon, Henry would treat her as he had treated Victoria? What if this fancy of his just up and faded away?

She shook her head at her own romantic musings. What did it matter if his feelings faded away? Those feelings, she was convinced, were not of the intensity that Rochester had for his beloved Jane. No man would ever love a woman that way. And so, what was the danger in being a friend to Henry? Friendship was not love, not passion - not commitment. It was just two people who enjoyed being in each other's company, and where was the harm in that?

Soon it was growing dark. But with the lights of the shops blazing, so warm and inviting, she decided she wasn't ready to go home just yet. So she slipped into a pretty little shop on the corner. It was a place of polished wood and shining glass, with leather booths and small tables, and a long bar that took up nearly one whole side of the room. It was an ice cream parlor. She could see that from the man behind the counter, who was filling a glass with chocolate soda, and the several people sitting around the place with their bowls and cones. But it wasn't the ice cream that drew her away from the door - it was the sight of a telephone on the back wall.

She may not have wanted to go home, but her conscience told her that she should at least call Alice and let her know she was all right. Alice could always relay the message to Jack, and then she wouldn't have to talk to him. She requested the use of it from the man at the counter, who smiled and nodded. When she called, Alice answered, and sounded quite concerned. It seemed Jack was still out looking for her, and he had called the house several times hoping she had come home. Grace assured Alice that she was well, and that she would be home soon, but would not say exactly where she was. She hung up the phone with a little sigh. She turned around and went to a seat at the bar, and the soda jerk came over to her.

"Is there something I can get you?" he asked.

She smiled shyly, unsure of what to do. She'd never been in a place like this by herself. "I don't know," she said. "I've never been here before. What would you have?"

"Try the banana split," said a familiar voice. "It's a classic."

She turned her head, and saw Henry sitting a few stools down. He must have come in while she was on the phone. He didn't look her way. He didn't get up and come to sit beside her. He just sat where he was, sipping a bottle of something. She looked at the soda jerk and nodded, and she waited as he went to prepare her dessert. She sat for several moments, wondering if Henry would come to her side, as he had before. She wondered if he would speak to her, as he had before. But he did nothing. So after several quiet moments alone, something within her drew her out of her seat. She knew in the back of her mind that she should not do it, but she found herself making her way down toward him, and the next thing she knew, she was standing beside him. Part of her wanted to flee, as she had before. But something made her stay. *I'm not a scared little bird*, she told herself. *It's time he learned just how brave I can be.* And as if to prove it to him, and herself, she took a bold stance and posed a question.

"Do you mind if I sit here?"

She couldn't believe she'd just invited herself to a place at his side. She'd imagined them forming a bond, but now it seemed she was telling him what she'd only had as a thought a few minutes ago. And she wondered, *Gracie Langdon, what are you getting yourself into now?*

Chapter 13
"Confessions"

He watched as she came his way, and his mouth cracked in a tiny smile. It wasn't so much that she was walking towards him, but it was the *way* she was doing it. He could read the tension in her face. And yet her chin was lifted…her shoulders were set, as if someone had dared her to approach him and she'd accepted, just to prove herself. When she came to stand beside him, asking to sit down, he couldn't help but tease her.

"Go ahead and sit. I won't bite…unless you want me to."

Immediately there was a disgusted curl of her lip. She started to turn away, but he reached out and stayed her arm.

"Oh for Pete's sake, I was only teasing."

As she cautiously sat down again, he rolled his eyes, letting out a breath. "Touchy, touchy. You good girls are all the same."

"So are all you flea-bitten hounds."

His little smile broke into a full grin…one he couldn't hide. And he wondered…

If I push her buttons just a tiny bit more, what will she do or say?

With amusement he asked, "How so?"

Her eyes flashed boldly. "If no one puts a good strong chain on you, you'll run around and chase every cat in the neighborhood."

And to that, he couldn't help but chuckle. "Touché," he replied.

From the look on her expression, he could see she was very satisfied with herself, and he let her have her little victory. If it meant she would stay there beside him, it was worth the little jab at his pride.

As she sat down, her dessert arrived. But before she could reach into her purse for a coin, he took one from his own pocket and put it down. He felt a sudden need to be generous, hoping it might soften any further resentment she felt. He was rewarded when she smiled slightly and nodded in thanks.

"So," he asked, wondering if they could manage a conversation without something going wrong. "What are you doing in here by yourself?"

"Running away from home," she replied

He smiled slightly. "I take it your brother wasn't too happy with the little show that Victoria put on."

"That's putting it mildly. I just wanted some time to myself, you know what I mean?"

He nodded. "That's why I'm here. Victoria is moving out of the house, even as we speak. So I'd rather be here than there. I think she'd like it that way too."

He watched as she slowly took little bites of her ice cream. She seemed like such a nervous creature at times, even in the way she ate. It was almost like she was afraid to relax, afraid to take a few moments and enjoy herself. Even with their topic of conversation, she seemed wary and self-conscience, as if the blame of the whole situation was supposed to fall on her shoulder.

"I'm sorry to hear that she left. I feel like it's all my fault."

Instantly he found himself trying to shield her, although he wasn't quite sure why he felt the need.

"Don't be ridiculous. It's her petty jealousy that brought it all about, but maybe it's for the best. I think we were doomed from the start. That's what happens when you get together with someone for all the wrong reasons."

She looked at him, concerned. "But what about your show? Will you be able to find someone to take her place?"

He waved a hand at her question. "I'll find someone sooner or later. It won't be easy, that's for sure. Victoria could sing and dance and look like a million bucks doing it. But she's gone now, so I'll just move on and find someone else. What else can I do about it?" He lifted the bottle to his lips and took a long drink.

"So what made you come here?" she asked.

He shrugged, letting out a breath. "A man can't drown his sorrows the way he used to. Not with the damned laws the way they are. Oh, I could go out and find a drink if I really wanted to. There are plenty of hooch mills in this town. But sometimes it's nice to pull back a little and enjoy the simpler things. Like a nice bottle of root beer."

She smiled a little, much to his surprise and delight. And he raised an eyebrow in curiosity.

"What's that smirk for?"

"I was just thinking about home," she replied. "If you gave a man anything but a jar of moonshine, you'd be laughed right out of town."

He smirked. "Moonshine? What would an innocent little thing like you know about that?"

Now she sat up slightly, looking at him, adjusting herself as though she were about to teach him a school lesson. She leaned an elbow on the bar, resting her head in her hand…and he found himself admiring how lovely she looked when she relaxed. It was hard to concentrate on what she was saying, but he did his best to listen.

"Well, down in the mines it's kind of like hell. And when a man gets out alive at the end of the day, I suppose the whiskey is a way to relax. But it's good for other things too. Like when I was a kid, Mama used to mix a little bit of shine with water and honey when we were sick. It don't really cure anything, but it's good to make you sleep."

She paused a moment, her smile fading away. She sat up straight, shifting her eyes away from him.

"Of course, there are folks who drink too much. Mama always said that drinking whiskey was like putting a thief in your mouth to steal your brain. And when Daddy used to go out and drink, she used to pray and pray because she thought for sure he wouldn't make it home."

What had started as a light conversation suddenly became covered in shadow. His own light manner became a bit less as he listened and remarked. "I take it it's not all sunshine and roses at home?"

She shook her head, and he felt the need to pose a question he'd long wanted to ask.

"You know, I've been wondering something about you."

She looked at him, her blue eyes full of curiosity.

"Why didn't you run away like your brother did? Surely the thought crossed your mind a time or two."

"I did run once," she replied. "When I was twelve I tried to, but it didn't work."

His eyebrow raised in curiosity. "What happened?"

She shrugged. "Jack sent me a ticket so I could come and stay with him. But I only got to the depot before I got caught, and Daddy came and got me. I remember it clear as day that on the way home, we came across this bridge that I was always scared to death of. It has big gaps in it and you can see clear down to the bottom of the river. And I remember that Daddy made me get out of the wagon and walk all the way across the bridge."

He didn't know what to say, except to think to himself...

What an evil old bastard.

He was suddenly angry on her behalf, thinking of how scared she must have been. But he'd admired her spirit before, and now he thought her to be one of the bravest young women he'd ever met, and he wanted to tell her so.

"You managed it, didn't you?" he said. "You walked right across, and I bet you didn't blink once."

He hoped to see her smile, wanted to remind her of how proud she should have been of herself. But there was no smile, and he felt a chill as he watched her expression grow darker than he'd ever seen it. Somehow he knew that in this story, there had not been the happy ending that he's hoped for.

"When I got home he blistered my legs with a switch off a birch tree. Then he locked me in the closet and I stayed there all night."

He had to swallow a sudden lump that rose in his throat. *Good God.* Looking at her, she seemed to change before his very eyes. She wasn't so childish to him now. She looked more like a woman, and he found that in her, he could now see something of himself. She had deep wounds that were bound only by the barest of threads. Those wounds were fragile...so easily capable of being torn open. The realization struck him deeply, and suddenly he wasn't just angry. He was livid.

How could anyone raise a cruel hand to her? Of course, he knew that she had sharp claws, which he found wickedly delightful. But she only brought out those claws in self-defense. She meant no real harm to anyone. And her defenses were no match for anyone who really wanted to hurt her. He had a sudden impulse to put his arms around her, to comfort her. He had a sad feeling that she'd never been held and soothed. She needed someone to care for her, to defend her from the cruel world. And he realized how much he wanted to be that person.

He was suddenly struggling with his own conscience.

How long has it been since I cared about anyone but myself? Am I just going soft? Or am I too stupid to remember how a woman can manipulate a man?

He didn't know what to be sure of. He only knew that when he looked at her, his heart swelled with something tender and profound. For a moment he met her steel-blue eyes and saw a look of pure vulnerability. But in a flash it was gone, replaced by that stubborn and willful look he was coming to know so well.

"I think I know what you're thinking," she said. "But I don't need your pity." She turned her eyes from him, taking a last little bite of her ice cream. When she'd swallowed it, she cleared her throat, and a thoughtful look came across her face. "You know, there's a passage from my favorite book. I'm pretty sure I'm not saying it right but..." She sat up a little straighter, her eyes slightly pinched in concentration, which he thought was quite amusing and lovely. But he didn't interrupt her as she recited the passage as best she could.

"Pity is a noxious and insulting sort of tribute, which one is justified in hurling back in the teeth of those who offer it. It is the sort of pity native to callous, selfish hearts. It is a hybrid, egotistical pain at hearing of woes, crossed with ignorant contempt for those who have endured them."

An impressed smile came to his face at her words. "Very well said," he declared. "And it's pretty impressive that you can remember all of that."

She only shrugged, saying nothing. He could have sworn she was blushing, but he kept the thought to himself, not wanting to embarrass her. And as he thought of her speech, he realized how well that passage reflected some of his own thoughts.

"I wish I'd had that written down when I came home from Europe."

He took a sip of his drink, sighing as he remembered the strange homecoming from the war. In all these years he'd hardly spoken of it at all. But in Grace, he sensed an understanding of pain and isolation, and he found himself speaking of things he'd long had buried inside.

"When I came back from France, it was like landing on another planet. I had all these people shaking my hand, patting me on the back, telling me what a great big hero I was and all that. But then, there were times when people said some of the stupidest things to me."

Hesitant, she asked. "Like what?"

He shook his head. "I actually had people say, '*It must have been tough.*' Christ sakes, what an ignorant ass thing to say. And then they would come back with something like, '*Good to have you home. Now you can get back to your life.*' He pursed his lips in disgust. "As if they had the foggiest notion of anything. They had no idea what kind of hell was in my head."

He knew she was watching him. He could feel her eyes. But the floodgate of memories had been opened, and he couldn't close it, even under a pair of watchful and innocent eyes.

"The military was so engrained in my brain. I just couldn't adjust. I had this kind of numbness inside that just wouldn't go away. It took years for it to wear off. But by then, Mary was long gone." He sighed, putting his drink down on the bar. "Casualties of war, I suppose." As he spoke, a sudden fog came over him. He didn't feel the world around him, or see the woman sitting next to him. He could hear distant voices, ones that cried out in terror and pain. The noise of battle echoed in his ears. And the smell of blood and waste filled his nostrils. And yet while his mind wandered on the bloody fields of France, his body remained in the present and his voice continued to speak.

"Some people know nothing of hell. They've never seen the blood and gore of other men mixed with the mud on your boots. They've never seen a land that's hacked to pieces by artillery and cannon fire. You sit in that trench, with your fingers and toes bitten to death by the freezing rain, and the stench of rot and death all around you, wondering if every moment will be your last. You live every day in the bowels of hell. Then, they suddenly snatch you up and away, and throw you in with 'civil society', and they expect you to go back to a happy life with a happy little job and a happy little home. And that's nothing but complete and total horse shit."

Something snatched him from his memory, and suddenly he blinked as if realizing where he was again. He glanced at her, seeing the way her eyes were wide with amazement and something close to fear. He wanted to apologize for his sudden loss of control, but at the moment he was still gathering himself together. He took a deep breath as he muttered a few more bitter words. "War does not determine who is right. Only who is left."

He took another deep, cleansing breath and felt his self-control being reigned in, enough so that he could relax and look at her without knowing how harsh his expression could be. When he glanced at her, those eyes were searching his face. He'd never seen such a tender and concerned expression on her face before, and it made his heart swell a little. But he didn't speak of it. He simply smiled, and was happy when she returned the gesture. There was something so warm and lovely when she let that pretty little mouth turn up, even in the smallest way. He turned and retrieved his hat from the stool beside him, putting it on his head as he stood.

"Let me give you a ride home."

In a flash the softness was gone from her face. It was replaced once again by that cool and defensive air, and she said quite firmly, "No thank you. I'll just walk."

"Don't be silly. I live across the street from you. Let me be neighborly."

She shook her head, and it occurred to him that despite the close little hour they'd just spent together, her guard against him had not come down at all. Perhaps the memory of that night at the pier was just too fresh. Perhaps they hadn't lingered long enough. If he had talked with her a little longer, would it have softened her at all? He had no way of knowing, and now it seemed too late to go back. He sighed, frustrated, a little at himself and a little at her for having no faith in him. But then again, he didn't blame her. If he were in her shoes, he would be suspicious too. And that was strangely troubling, which he didn't hide from her.

"Despite what you think, I do have a few decent bones in my body. I swear on oath that you'll get home with your reputation unharmed."

He turned and walked to the door, not looking back at her but hoping she would follow. He paused at the door and turned, waiting and watching. And much to his pleasure, a moment later she came towards him. He opened the door to let her precede him. As she passed by, he brushed the small of her back with his hand, guiding her. He had done it so many times before that it was simply a habit. But he'd never felt the reaction she had...a nervous kind of jolt as if she'd been electrocuted. He realized that whether or not she cared to admit it, she was still afraid of him. And while it bothered him now more than it ever had before, it made him quite determined to change the way she thought of him. He was a much better man than she gave him credit for, and he had her at just the right place, at just the right time, to prove it to her.

Holding open the car door for her, he winced slightly at how she hesitated. But when she got in, he smirked slightly and closed the door after her.

Now you can't get away so easily.

He went around to his side and got in, noticing the way she nervously pulled at her dress collar. But he didn't make mention of it as he started the car and drove away.

As they drove along, he kept his eyes on the road for the most part. But he saw from the corner of his eye how she pressed herself against the door...the way she kept subtly pulling at the hem of her dress.

Silly girl, he thought. *Do you really think I'm so low that I'd force myself on you? Of course if I wanted to, I could have you without a fight. You have no idea how persuasive I can be.*

But there was a deeper need he wanted to fill, and it went beyond temptation and lust. She triggered something profound inside of him, a feeling of caring and empathy he'd thought to be long dead. But she brought it to life, and he wondered what magic she possessed to make him feel this way. Whatever witchcraft it was, it was quite powerful. He was starting to feel a certain possessiveness when he thought of her. He wasn't much of a believer when it came to fate or destiny, but something told him she'd been sent to him for a reason. He had a faith in that reason. She needed someone to defend her...and that was just what he intended to do.

He pulled up in his own driveway rather than hers, mostly to keep his lights from shining into the Langdon house and arousing suspicion. He could sense the relief she felt in getting back home without incident. It troubled him that she still didn't trust him, when he'd been such a gentleman all this time. But he reminded himself that she had reason to be wary. Life had made her that way. And since they'd met, he hadn't always shown the best side of himself. But he was determined to change that. He saw her reach for her door handle, and he stopped her. He started to get out.

"Wait a minute and I'll get the door."

Her look, and her question, were both curious. "Why?"

He shrugged. "Etiquette," he replied. Quickly he got out and went around to her side of the car. Opening her door he extended his hand to her…and she looked at his palm as if it frightened her. He sighed at her hesitation.

"It's a hand, not a rattlesnake."

For another moment she looked unsure. Then at last she reached out and put her hand in his, and the thrill he felt was overwhelming.

Lord, her skin is so warm and soft. A fine tremor of heat went up his arm, radiating into his chest and spreading to every part of his body. For a brief moment he imagined pulling her close, holding her tightly against him to see what it felt like. But he kept himself from it, if only just. He'd always prided himself on his self-discipline, and he used it now to keep from doing more than just helping her from the car. He suspected she must have felt something too, especially the way she avoided his eyes as she spoke.

"I'd best get home. I'm sure my brother is pitching a fit."

He knew he shouldn't have touched her at all, but he couldn't help himself. He reached his hand out and lifted her chin, making her look at him. His voice was soft and kind.

"You know it might not be my place to say. But he's your brother, not your father."

She was looking at him, her beautiful eyes large and shining with surprise, and if he'd been less of a man he would have kissed her right then and there. But no, that wouldn't do for the moment. He'd been a gentleman all night, and to leave a firm impression on her mind, he wanted to remain one. He released his light hold on her chin, and putting his hat on his head, he pulled the brim to her.

"Goodnight, Grace."

He turned and walked away from her, only glancing back for a moment, at his doorstep, to see if she had gone. She had, and he felt rather disappointed that she hadn't lingered a little longer. He sighed.

Oh well. Tomorrow is another day.

* * * * *

Grace knew what she would find when she came in the house.

She stood on the stoop for several hesitant moments, letting out a little sigh before she opened the door. Before she did anything, she needed to gather herself together. The ride home had been one of the wildest experiences she'd ever had, even thought it had all been in her imagination.

All the way home she'd had insane flashes of things he might have done to her in the dark of his car. But he hadn't made a single move. He hadn't even said a word to her, until they were in the driveway and he was about to help her from the car. Then his hand had held hers so firmly, sending shivers down from her fingers to her toes. And when his fingers had held her chin, she'd thought for certain that he would kiss her again. And despite shaking all over with fear, she knew at that moment that she'd wanted him to do just that. She wanted to feel his kiss again.

The moment had been so perfect. But he'd let her go, leaving her trembling with strange feelings and a deep sense of loss.

But she had to stop thinking of that now. More pressing matters were waiting for her on the other side of the door, and she pressed her hands against her face for a moment, taking a deep breath. Then she opened the door and stepped across the threshold, the sound of the bolt clicking shut behind her. And when she looked up there was Jack coming towards her from the living room, his stride angry and his expression even more so.

"Where in the name of Christmas have you been?"

She started to speak. But then, she closed her mouth quickly. He looked so much like their father at that moment. The way he stood so tall and rigid - the way his feet were spread apart in his stance. Even the way the little muscle in his cheek twitched in fury. And his eyes were just the same - their soft brown had darkened to near black, they way their father's did when he was angry. And Henry's words flashed in her memory.

He's your brother, not your father.

Those words gave her courage, made her grow strong in defense of herself, and she knew she owed her brother not one single explanation. In fact, she owed him nothing, and as if to emphasize the fact, she gave him an evil glare and walked right past him.

"Where do you think you're going?" he demanded. "Don't walk away from me when I'm talking to you!"

But she did keep walking, up the stairs and into her room, where she slammed the door behind her. She fully expected him to come barging in like a force of nature, just the way their father would have done. But he didn't. In fact, there was a sudden silence behind her that she didn't expect. She stood for several moments, her arms crossed, still waiting for his entrance. But there was none, and her curiosity was piqued. She wondered if he might be playing some sort of trick on her, waiting on the other side of the door for her to come out, and then he would pounce. She moved cautiously toward the door, pulling it open quickly - and he was not there. She stepped out into the hall, and then she heard his voice. He was still downstairs. It seemed his voice, and Alice's, were coming from the living room. And both their tones were raised and angry. Grace went to the top of the staircase, sitting down on the step as she listened.

"She's not a child, so why are you treating her like one?"

"She's seventeen years old. She's not old enough to know what's good for her."

"Oh come on, Jack. Most girls like her are old married women with two or three brats. They're too stupid to know anything except lying on their backs and making babies. When they're not doing that, they're spending their whole damned lives chained to a house. Your sister knows exactly what's good for her, or she wouldn't be here."

"So she got out of being married," he snorted. "So what? That makes her an expert about the world? About men? She has no idea what she'll get herself into if she gets involved with someone like Henry. And damn it, as long as she's living under my roof, I'm not going to let that happen!"

"Oh for God's sake, Jack! You sound exactly like your father!"

Out on the steps, Grace winced as she heard that statement. In all of her anger at her brother, she would never have dared to say that to him. But she was not Alice, of course, who dared to say exactly what she was thinking, no matter what the consequences. And she could hear the absolute rage, barely repressed, in her brother's voice.

"Don't you ever, EVER say that to me again."

"Don't point a finger in my face, you hypocritical ass! You are acting *exactly* like your father!"

"Are you deaf, woman? I told you not to say that again!"

"I'll say whatever the hell I want to when you're acting like a total bonehead! If she were one of your brothers, you wouldn't question anything she does. But just because she's your sister…a woman…you think she knows nothing. Why don't you just do what your father would do? Take her out behind the house and beat her with a switch until she submits like a damn dog!"

The front door slammed as he stormed out of the house. Alice came to stand in the foyer, staring at the closed door for several long moments, arms crossed as she muttered furiously to herself.

"Stupid son of a bitch."

Letting out a short breath, she turned to go up the stairs. When she saw Grace sitting there, she smiled.

"Eavesdropping, were you?" She climbed the steps to sit down beside her.

Grace gave a sheepish smile. "I guess I was. Where do you think he went?"

Alice snorted, her smile dropping away quickly, replaced by an irritated curl of her lip.

"Oh, he didn't go anywhere. He's probably just sitting out there on the porch, pouting like a child." She turned to her with a serious, thoughtful expression. Her voice softened. "You know, it scares the heck out of him that he's getting older. And that you are too."

Grace sighed. "I think what you said scared him more. To think he's like our Daddy. He always said he'd never be like him."

Alice cast her eyes down in regret. "I know. And maybe I shouldn't have said that to him. But when he gets in a mood like that, he looks and sounds exactly like your father. He makes me so mad I'd just like to slug him right in the mouth."

Now Grace smiled a little. "You know something? You're the reason he's not a spitting image of Daddy. When that side of him comes out, you know just how to knock it back down to where it belongs."

Alice smirked. "It's a thankless job, but someone has to do it."

With a sigh, Grace rose to her feet.

"I should probably go talk to Jack before he does something ignorant, like going over there to start a fight with Henry."

"Good luck with him," Alice stated. "I'm tired of talking to the fool. I'm going to bed."

She left to go up, and Grace made her way down the stairs to the front door.

He was there, just as Alice had said he would be. He was sitting in the swing, slowly rocking back and forth. She looked at him for several long moments but he refused to say anything. She went to sit beside him, and still he said nothing. She couldn't tolerate it any longer.

"Well?" she demanded.

"Well what?"

He sounded like an out-of-sorts child, and she found the need to be quite stern with him.

"You *know* what. I know you're dying to say that you're right, and I'm wrong. That I'm too young to know anything. Am I leaving anything out?"

Crossing his arms defensively, he snorted with displeasure. "What difference does it make what I think? You're just going to do whatever the hell you want to anyway."

She grumbled in frustration. "Oh Jack, I'm not stupid. I know how to take care of myself. And if I make mistakes, they're my mistakes to fix, not yours."

He was silent for a moment, as if he were absorbing the things she said. Then he spoke, his voice low and disenchanted.

"So what am I suppose to do? It's my job to be in there pitching for you. Am I supposed to stand back and let someone else throw the ball?"

She nodded her head. "Yes, and that someone is me. I can think for myself. I can do for myself. You may not like it, but that's the way it is."

He sighed, mumbling something under his breath. It was the sound of acceptance…reluctant as it was, coming from him. She wanted to smile, but kept herself from it, knowing that it was difficult enough for him to accept defeat. Her gloating would just be salt in a wound. After a brief silence he sighed, the sound rather sad.

"So where does that leave me?"

Her tone became soft, trying to comfort him. "It leaves you in the same place you always were. I'll always need you around for one reason or another. You always come in handy, you know. You always did."

He didn't seem any happier, judging from his tone. "Do you remember when I taught you how to fight?"

She smiled. "You sure taught me how to give a good right hook."

He shrugged. "Yeah, well…I always hoped you could stand up for yourself. But now that you really can, I don't know if I like the idea so much. What good am I to you now? What's my worth?"

She didn't miss a beat in replying. "About ten or fifteen cents."

He looked at her and huffed. "Wise ass." She moved over to give him a peck on the cheek, which he immediately wiped away in disgust.

"Good Lord, Gracie, don't do that." He rubbed his cheek viciously. "You know I hate the mushy stuff."

She knew he was just putting on a show, and she smiled and laughed. She rose to her feet, declaring that she was tired and ready to call it a night. He agreed, following behind her. As they went up the stairs, he turned to her.

"Can I go over and punch Henry in the nose?"

She rolled her eyes. "No."

He grumbled. "Well I need to get something out of all this. Some bruised knuckles might be just the cure for my pride. Lord knows, there'll be hell to pay for that fight I had with Alice. I'll probably end up sleeping on the couch."

She gave him a sympathetic pat on the shoulder as they parted ways at the top of the stairs.

"Good night, Jack."

Chapter 14
"Ambitions and Old Ghosts"

He walked into the dark and silent house. Strange, he thought, how empty a home could suddenly be. And yet, the emptiness did not affect him as much as it might have. In a way, it was rather peaceful now. And he was glad to find that all of his belongings were as he'd left them. It wouldn't have been a shock to come home and find everything he owned broken, shredded, or on a bonfire on the front lawn. But she hadn't touched a thing, so he considered himself lucky. Now he could focus his thoughts and energy on what to do about Grace.

Tonight, it seemed he'd found one of the keys to unlocking the little puzzle she was. It seemed to him that she hungered for kindness...for simple human affection, and he could certainly see why. She was starved for it. But the lack of it had also made her thorny as a wild rose. Now he understood why shy shied away from him as she did. Oh, she put up a good fight when backed into a corner, but without primal instinct to strengthen her, she was fragile and soft. He'd seen the vulnerability in her. But it was like looking into a cage. He could see her in all her sweetness and beauty, but he couldn't get close to her. He couldn't touch her in any way, be it physically or emotionally. So what could he do to get past that barrier around her?

He went to the wall near the staircase. Hanging there was a painting, and taking it down off the wall, he opened a small liquor cabinet.

A fine thing, he thought, *When a man has to hide away his liquor from the entire world*. He wasn't much of a drinker, but there were times like now when a good bourbon seemed to calm his nerves. He poured himself a glass, setting it down on the credenza while he carefully realigned the painting on the wall. Prohibition, it seemed, had made criminals of the most common man, including himself. But what could one do but live with it? He took his glass, walking to the sofa and sinking down on it.

If he wanted to get to her, he knew they would have to spend time together. Surely time and tenderness would do the trick. But how could he convince the little skeptic to trust him, let alone spend more than a few hours in his company? Tonight had been a fluke...a mere coincidence, though a welcome one. He thought about courting her, and the idea was tempting. But he was quite certain she wouldn't accept him that way, even if he tried, and he knew for sure that her brother wouldn't allow it. Then, an idea came to him like a bolt from the blue.

Hire her as an employee.

It seemed like such an obvious answer. For a moment he let himself imagine the idea of seeing her every day, without worrying that she would flee at any moment. As her boss, he would have her in one place and she would be under obligation to him. But more than that, he could see her whenever he wished, instead of trying to steal little snippets of time. It made him grin to think of seeing her all the time, hearing her adorable little twangy speech. The warmth he felt at the idea, of being near her so often, made him wonder what to call this budding feeling. He dared not call it love. But it was more than friendship. He wasn't sure what to name it. Deep affection, perhaps? That seemed the only term that came close.

It was a strange feeling to care for someone after so many years of caring only for himself. Over the years he'd managed random acts of generosity, the Langdon wedding being one of them. Out of respect for an old friend and admiration for the great lady that Alice was, he'd not thought twice about giving them their start. But not since the first days of being with Mary had he felt the need to give on an emotional level. In a certain sense, he considered himself lucky that he'd had the means of exorcising his demons. He'd used women, used his wealth and standing to meet his own selfish needs. Selfishness had been a luxury he could afford, and he'd indulged shamelessly in it.

But poor Grace. She'd never known the joy of being selfish. She'd been too busy fending off the blows of life. Lord, it seemed so wrong for a seventeen-year-old girl to have suffered through such a miserable life.

Well if I have my way, there will be some changes made.

Only one thing needed to be done. He had to get her on his side. He wasn't sure how he was going to do it, but he was bound and determined to figure it out, one way or another.

* * * * *

The next morning as she came out of her room, dressed and ready to face the day, she saw Alice in the hallway, still in her robe and looking forlorn. Clearly she was still upset from last night's fight, but Grace did her best to be cheerful.

"Good morning," she said.

Alice tried to smile back, though it clearly wasn't true.

"Good morning, sis. Are you going down to fix breakfast?"

Grace nodded. But Alice put a hand on her arm.

"Don't fix him anything. I have something special in mind. I'll be down in a little while."

Grace shrugged. "If you prefer." She smiled at her again. Making her way downstairs, she wondered just what special treat was in store for Jack.

As she neared the bottom of the stairs, she heard a loud snore coming from somewhere in the living room, and she smiled. So it was just as he'd predicted. Alice had banished him to the sofa after their argument. She couldn't help but be amused, and her curiosity drew her quietly toward the source of the noise.

She found him lying there on his back, his mouth agape as he snored. One hand rested on his chest. The other hung down, nearly touching the carpet. One leg was bent, and one was straight. Most of the blanket covering him was on the floor. She shook her head as she looked at him, taking up the blanket to spread it over him.

He suddenly gave a jolt, as if electrocuted. With a cry of terror he jolted up, eyes wide with fear, his breath coming fast. He looked around as if not knowing where he was.

Grace jumped back in shock, standing away from him for several long moments. This was no waking from a bad dream, or anything of that sort. She had seen pure madness in his eyes.

"Are you all right?"

For another moment he was silent, still wide-eyed. But the calm and clarity had started to come back, and to her question he nodded.

"It's just an old reflex." As he sat up fully, straightening his shirt and smoothing his hair, he seemed to calm.

As he became at ease, so did she. And yet, she was rather upset with him for scaring her so, even if it was not intentional. And she scolded him.

"Lord, Jack, you nearly scared the pee out of me." She sat down beside him. "What was that about, anyway?"

He sighed. "A battle scar." He sat for several moments, lost in thought, running a hand across his weary face.

"From the war?"

He was silent, but after a moment he nodded his head.

There was a note of caution in her voice. "Jack, how come you and Henry are so different about the war? You seem so settled most of the time, so calm...well, except for what just happened. But you seem so happy. And Henry seems so...I don't know. Broken, I guess. Even though he's pretty good at hiding it."

At the mention of Henry, Jack turned to look at her with an expression both curious and dark. "How would you know about Henry's problems?"

She shrugged. "I talked to him a little last night." She knew he wouldn't be happy to hear that, but it seemed that his fatherly concerns didn't affect her as they once had. And yet she loved him as much as ever, and had no wish to rub salt in his wounds, even when he was chastising her like now.

"So that's where you were, out on the town with that crumb."

"Don't be ugly like that. And why are you so hateful about him now? I thought you were good friends?"

"We were until last night. Until he started sniffing around you. Now I have to treat him like any other mangy mongrel." He leaned back against the cushions, letting his head come to rest on the edge of the sofa. He smiled and chuckled as a memory came to him.

"Remember when Mama shot that old hound of ours for sniffing around the hens and stealing eggs?" He glanced at her, seeing her nod. "Maybe I should do that to Henry...That danged old dog."

She rolled her eyes. But she wouldn't let his friction with Henry deter her from the subject. "So why do you figure he's like he is? You both went through the same war, didn't you?"

Once more he was silent, seeming to think deep thoughts, but she didn't push for an answer. She knew her kind of questioning had to be approached gingerly, for the subject was such a sensitive one it bordered on being explosive. At long last he spoke to her.

"I was just lucky, baby sister. If there's such a thing as luck when you're in hell. And Henry spent a longer time in it than I did. So maybe that's why he is the way he is. But then you've got to figure what happened when he came home. I found my little honey when I got back, and his ran out on him."

She sighed sadly, thinking of the woman who had once broken Henry's heart. "I almost forgot about Mary."

Despite the fact that Jack thought ill of his old friend, Grace couldn't share in his animosity. At one time, maybe she could have. But now, her heart almost ached for him. "I reckon you don't believe it, but I figure he's pretty lonesome, and that's why he acts like he does."

Jack made a cynical noise. "So just because a man is lonesome, that means he should shack up with any pretty gal that comes along? Remember what I told you about his women?"

"But what difference does that make to me? I'm not one of them, and I don't plan on being one."

"I hope not," he declared. He leaned forward, running a hand over his face. "I don't want to talk about this anymore. I'd rather talk about breakfast, if you don't mind. I'm starving."

She suddenly remembered what Alice had told her.

"I almost forgot, Alice said she had something special for you for breakfast. What do you reckon she's making?"

The look on his face puzzled her. He almost seemed troubled.

"What's that look for?" she asked.

But he just shook his head. "It's nothing. Never mind."

He rose to his feet, following her, and they found the kitchen quiet and empty. While he sat at the table to wait, she went to the coffee pot and started fixing it.

"Do you suppose she'll mind if I make you some coffee?"

He only shrugged, letting out a sigh, and she could tell in his tone he was not happy. She couldn't speak for him, but she guessed he was none too pleased being at odds with his wife. And it was understandable, considering how well they usually got on.

At times, she'd been fascinated watching the two of them together. Even in the presence of other people they were open and loving, though restrained somewhat when being observed. It seemed they always needed to touch in some way, even if it was just the way one would bump the shoulder of the other. When standing together, they were always much closer than they should have been, and quite often she'd seen their fingers intertwining. Even when helping each other in some little task, they were always smiling and whispering with each other. But it was the unguarded times, when they thought no one was looking...those were the moments she found quite beautiful and moving. They liked to hold each other close, sometimes kissing softly and other times just looking in each others eyes and speaking in whispers. It was a deep, profound love they had for each other, and she could see how Jack would be in pain at the loss.

There came the sound of footsteps on the stairs in the hall, and she righted her expression, pretending to focus on the coffee. Alice came in, and Grace saw how she walked right past Jack and neither of them said a word to each other. But when Alice came to stand beside her, there was a smile on her face.

"Oh good, you made coffee. I'm dying for a cup."

"I could use one over here," said Jack. "And are we cooking something or not? I need to get to work in a little while."

She looked at Alice, seeing the slight sneer on her lip as she poured a cup of coffee for herself. Grace wondered...if she was so daring as to take a cup to Jack, would Alice be upset?

But it seemed her sister-in-law was occupied with her own thoughts. Grace watched, curious, as Alice opened the drawer to find a spoon. From the cabinet she took a bowl...from another cabinet she found a box of cereal. Taking them all over to Jack, she tossed them down in front of him. The bowl rattled with a noisy, almost angry sound. And Alice sneered at him.

"Eat up."

Grace looked at Jack, who looked up at his wife with a stunned expression. She didn't quite understand what that look was about, but if she didn't know better, she would say he seemed hurt. She turned to Alice, who went back to retrieve her cup of coffee.

"I'm going to sit outside to get some fresh air," she said. Taking her cup, she left to go out on the patio.

Grace looked at Jack again. He was staring at the empty cereal bowl in front of him...and then he suddenly rose to his feet.

"I have to shower and shave. I'll wait and eat later." He leaned over to give her a peck on the cheek, and then he was gone, upstairs to get ready for work.

Looking out the window, Grace saw Alice calmly sipping her coffee. After a few moments, she went out to sit with her. Almost before Grace's bottom touched the seat, Alice started ranting.

"Do you know he didn't even apologize for all that shouting and carrying on? He just tried to crawl into bed with me last night like nothing happened."

Grace raised an inquisitive eyebrow. "Is that when you kicked him out?"

Alice shook her head. "Not at first. He tried to talk to me, but I kept ignoring him. He even tried to put his arm around me, but I threw it back at him. That's when he got mad. He took his pillow and stormed out of the room."

"And that's why I found him on the couch this morning."

Alice nodded. Then Grace saw her turn her head, a little smile on her face.

"I know you didn't understand what the fuss was about the cereal box. But let's just say it's a little reminder of something from a long time ago. Yelling and screaming takes the pressure off. But sometimes, it's the little efforts that can really get a point across, and I think I made mine this morning." She looked down at the little watch hanging from her necklace. "I've got to run into town for a meeting about a library fundraiser. Do you want to come?"

Grace smiled, shaking her head. "No, I think I'll stay here and soak up the peace and quiet. You go on and do what you need to."

Alice returned the smile, giving her a kiss on the cheek. Then she left...and Grace was all alone.

It was a beautiful day out, and she considered just sitting there on the patio, enjoying the sunshine. But somehow, that didn't suit her today. What she wanted was a stroll, like the ones she used to take at home. She rose and headed for the door, but just before she got there, she paused, suddenly thinking of Henry.

What will I do if he sees me? Will I know what to say? Or will I make a fool of myself? How did I manage to keep my wits about me last night, and can I do it again?

Her head was high as she closed the door behind her. With purpose she focused her glance on anything around her...on the trees, the sky...anything other than the house across the street. At last she chose to focus strictly on the ground before her, trying to keep her mutinous eyes from looking where they longed to. She was afraid to look there, for fear that she might see him standing at the window. Or worse, she might see him on his front porch. Then he would come and speak to her, and the thought filled her with fear.

Or was it excitement?

Lately, she didn't know if there was a difference between the two. The idea of an encounter with him made her want to run and hide. And yet, the thought of looking into his beautiful eyes, of hearing his deep and melodic voice, sent tremors of anticipation down her spine. With a strange blend of trepidation and eagerness, she came to the end of the walk, standing still for a moment. Her eyes, with a power of their own, slowly rose up to steal a glance at the house.

There was no one about. She could see no one at the windows, and both the front porch and the yard were quiet and still. She breathed both a sigh of relief, and of disappointment. The thrill and fear had no grounds now, so she turned down the walk to begin a leisurely stroll down the street.

She had no shoes on as she went. She knew it would have been a strange sight if someone were watching, to see some girl walking down the street in her bare feet. But it seemed so uncomfortable to wear shoes at every occasion, having gone without footwear for so many years of her life. She was quite aware that decorum called for shoes in certain places, but this was no place of public gathering. Who was there to offend? So she simply strolled along, liking the rough but cool feeling of the pavement against her heels and toes.

To her amazement, not a single person seemed to notice her bare feet at all. An old gentleman sitting in a rocking chair was reading his paper. He glanced up for a moment with a friendly greeting, and then went back to his news. Several boys rode past her on their bicycles without taking notice of her. A woman in her front yard, tending her flower boxes, gave her a glance. Then she smiled, going about her work.

How grand it was to be free of expectations…everyone minding their own business, just as she was minding hers. Not like home, where everyone seemed to look at her with a strange sense of curiosity and expectation.

She is seventeen, and not married, those old crows of the church had always thought. She did not have to be a mind reader to know what they were thinking, for they whispered about her in the same way they whispered about all young girls without husbands. *She'll be an old maid, bleeding her family dry of their resources. Willful and ungrateful girl.*

So she might have been an old maid in their eyes. So what? As if those girls who had given up their youth for marriage were any better off. Most of them would be old women by the time they were twenty, burdened with a house full of children and a husband they were bound to for life, whether he was a good man or not. She thought of some of the women she had known in her life…how many of their men treated them like one of the animals they raised. How grateful she was to God that she had been spared such a fate.

Now, however, they had even more reason to talk ill of her, for in their eyes, she had dishonored her mother and father by being disobedient. She had abandoned her home and her family. And she was quite certain that even at this moment, most people in her hometown were condemning her wretched soul to burn in damnation.

But she did not give a hoot if they were condemning her or not. She was glad that she had broken all the rules to be here, even if it meant that her own flesh and blood might banish her from their hearts forever. She hoped and prayed it wasn't so…that her mother and father still loved her, despite her rebelliousness. But if they chose to forget her as their daughter, she would not bear them ill will. Whatever their state of mind, hers was to love them until the day she died, as was her duty as a daughter and a true Christian.

Love me then, or hate me, as you will, she thought. *You have my full and free forgiveness.*

Was it not the Lord's will that his people cherish the gift of life? Was it truly a sin to seek out joy and fulfillment in one's time on earth? Here with Jack and Alice, she was finding something of peace in her life. Surely, this happiness was God's doing, and what right had anyone to question that?

Before she quite knew it, she'd walked a complete circle around the block, and was soon nearing the house. As she approached, she saw a figure on the front stoop. There was something vaguely familiar about that figure…a man, dressed in a white shirt and dark trousers. It was not Henry, for this person did not have those dark features of his. The man was blond, she could see. And as she drew nearer, a sense of shock and dread began to wash over her, for her brain began to register who it was she was seeing. She stood frozen on the edge of the walk, and the man before her seemed to sense her presence, for he slowly turned to look at her. His voice was soft and pleasant.

"Hello, Gracie."

She thought she felt the world tilt a little, for she was looking at a face equally familiar and detestable.

It was Charlie Hillard standing there before her.

Chapter 15
"Friends and Foes"

Her response was instant, strong and firm.

"What are you doing here?"

He held up his hands defensively. "Gracie, please don't be mad at me for coming. Your Mama asked me to."

"Why?" she asked.

He gave her an odd look, as if the answer should have been obvious.

"She was worried about you. So was I. So was everyone. When you were gone a full day, she had the whole town looking for you. And when she heard you were here, she hoped you would change your mind in a few days and come home. But you didn't. So she asked me to come find you. We want you to come home, Gracie."

"I am home," she said, moving to pass him and go up the steps. But he lightly stepped in front of her.

"Don't run off now. At least talk to me for a few minutes. I've come all this way. Won't you at least listen to me?"

"No," she declared. "I'm happy here. I'm not going back to Virginia, and that's all I have to say about it."

"But you can't stay here. This isn't where you belong."

"It is now," she replied. "Go home, Charlie. Go home and find a wife who will jump when you bark and bring you a dozen sons. But I don't want to hear about it, and I don't want to see you around here again." She went up the steps, but only got as far as the stoop before he put his hand on her arm to stop her. There was something in his touch that repulsed her, and she shook him off. But he would not go. His tone was stubborn, his eyes narrowed in determination.

"I'm not leaving until you talk to me. I want to talk about what happened between you and me."

She shook her head. "There is no you and me, Charlie. Maybe there would have been, if you had been the man I thought you were. But you're not. And that's all I have to say about it." She turned to go in, but once again he held her arm.

"People change, Gracie. I know I said some things I shouldn't have. But I'm telling you here and now, I want to do right by you. Give me the chance to make it right."

She looked at him, seemingly so sincere. His green eyes were soft, pleading for her forgiveness. But she knew him better than he knew himself, for she had seen the other side of his personality...the one that she knew was hiding just beneath this veil of gentleness and warmth.

"Go home, Charlie," she said again, and then she turned from him and went inside, closing the door firmly behind her. She made for the living room, and was just about to sit down in a chair when she heard the door open behind her. She turned, and there he was...walking towards her. His step was not malicious, it seemed, but she was alarmed all the same. He had invaded her bubble of privacy, and her defensive instinct went on full alert.

"Get out of here, Charlie. Get out right now. If Jack finds you here, he'll kill you first and then ask questions."

"I'm not going home without you. I promised your Mama that I would bring you home, and I intend to do it. I don't want this to get nasty, so please just go on and get your things and don't fuss about it."

"I will not! This is my brother's house, and mine too, and I'm not going anywhere."

He tried to take her arm, and the first attempt she managed to dodge. The second time, he got a hold of her and tried to move her, attempting to drag her forward, but she dug heels into the carpet and refused.

"Let go of me!" She dug her nails into his hand.

He yelled in pain, cursing, but still he would not release his hold. Her control snapped...and she exploded in fear and rage.

"I said, let go!" Before she realized what she was doing, her fingers balled. Her arm came back. Then her fist landed into his jaw with all the strength she had. Spun aside by the blow, he landed on his knees on the floor, holding his face in pain.

She was in pain herself. It had been a long time since she'd hit anyone, and her small fist was not prepared for the impact. She stepped back, holding her throbbing hand and wrist. It distracted her so that she hardly noticed when the front door flew open.

Henry came rushing in. She glanced over at him for a moment, watching as he took in what he was seeing. She saw the change in his expression as he looked between her and Charlie. At first, looking at the man kneeling on the floor, he seemed angry and confused, probably wondering what in the world was going on. Then he looked at her, and seeing how she was holding her hand, obviously in pain, his eyes became soft with concern.

"I was on my way over here and heard the yelling. Are you all right?"

She nodded, wincing from her injury. "I'm fine." Then she looked over at Charlie, who was rising to his feet, still holding his jaw. "This is Charlie Hillard," she said. "He was just leaving."

Henry's expression changed again, now full of curiosity and surprise. "Charlie Hillard? This isn't *the* Charlie, is it?" He gestured his head towards the other man.

She nodded again. "The only one, thank heavens."

Now on his feet, his face dark with a scowl, Charlie took several steps toward Henry. "Who are you, walking in here like you own the place?"

Henry took his own step forward. He was taller, more confident...and he smirked, looking down at Charlie with a sneer. "I'm no one for you to worry about."

Though he wasn't equal to Henry's stature, Charlie hardly seemed intimidated. He sneered, turning to Grace in angry confusion.

"Who the hell is this? And why he is here strutting around like a Bantam Rooster?"

She sighed, wishing they would both go away so she could tend to her aching hand. But she knew she couldn't leave things as they were.

"If it's any of your business, Charlie...this is Henry Shaw. He's my neighbor."

For a moment, the two men just stood and examined one another. She wondered if they were about to throw punches. But Charlie suddenly gave a snort, throwing a hand up as if to wave Henry off like a buzzing insect.

"I don't give a damn who he is." He turned to her, determination is his every feature. "You get your things together right now, or I'll leave it all behind. Make up your mind. Either way, you're coming home with me, like it or not."

Lord, the man was thickheaded. She wanted to hit him again.

"Don't you hear good? I'm not going anywhere with you."

Henry stepped to her side with a confident little smirk. "She's right. She's not going back."

Charlie looked his opponent up and down. "Who the hell asked you about it? Mind your own business, mister."

The smirk on Henry's face was oh-so-confident. "Oh, I *am* minding my business. Miss Grace *is* my business. Because you see, I'm her boss."

Grace blinked for a moment, unsure of what he had really just said. Her mouth opened slightly, and then it closed again. *My Boss?* She thought. *That's the strangest choice of a lie I've ever heard.*

Charlie seemed equally as stunned...and completely skeptical. "What do you mean by boss? What kind of boss? For what job?"

Now, Henry's smirk was full and brazenly arrogant. "That's none of your concern, now is it? I think it's time for you to be on your way, Mr. Hillard."

Standing a little taller beside Henry, Grace looked at Charlie with her head held high.

"Tell my folks that I'm happy where I am, and that's all they need to know."

Charlie must have realized his time there was up. He moved towards the door...but at the threshold, he turned to give them both a dark look. His voice was cold...deadly serious.

"This isn't the end of this."

He stormed out, slamming the door behind him.

Grace turned to Henry, her figure relaxing with relief. She gave him a little smile. He gave her one in return. Then she noticed how he was looking at her, his eyes full of intense concern. She was about to say something...to assure him she was quite well...when the pain from her injury suddenly came back.

With a light touch he took her hand, lifting it up to look at it. His fingers were warm...very gentle, and she felt her breath quicken at the feeling of his fingertips. Her pulse throbbed as he brushed his fingers softly over her hand and her wrist, testing the extent of the damage, and she found she could not pull her hand from his grasp. The pleasure of his touch was much too intense. And his voice. It was like warm honey, rich and smooth.

"You've bruised your knuckles. And you might have a slight sprain in your wrist."

She found she could not respond, nor move a muscle. It seemed he had cast a spell around her, making her powerless. She felt weightless as he led her to the sofa, making her sit down.

"Wait here, I'll be right back."

She nodded, sitting there silently for several moments, feeling as if she were floating on a cloud. It was the same feeling she'd felt on that night when he had kissed her. But now, it was different. There was no feeling of guilt. No sense of shame, thinking that she was the force that might break apart a relationship. There was only a sense of pure joy...a great warmth that flowed through her entire frame.

A moment later he came back, holding a small cloth bundle in his hand. She wasn't sure what it was until he sat down beside her and pressed it gently against her skin. The feeling of the ice pack was sudden. She jumped slightly at its shock, gritting her teeth. It also helped her to regain her senses, for she could not ignore the numbing of her flesh as the cold pressed against it.

"Thank you," she said to him, giving him a grateful smile. He returned it with a slight upturn of the corner of his mouth.

"You're welcome." Then he chuckled. "Here I was, thinking I had to rush in and rescue you again, like I did before. But you manage to clock the bastard all by yourself. Gave him a good one, too, from the way he was down on the floor when I came in." He still grinned slightly, but then he forcibly dropped the smile, trying to give her a look of disappointment. "Thank you so much for stealing my thunder."

She laughed a little. But then, her own expression sobered a bit as a lingering question surfaced.

"Why did you come over, anyway? And what did you mean by saying you were my boss?"

He shook his head, waving off her questions. "Don't worry about that now. I'm just glad I *did* come, even though you made me useless." The smile returned to his face. Then he sighed. "I hate to leave good company. But I have to get to work. Just keep the ice on your hand and the swelling will go down before you know it. And have fun explaining it to your brother."

She nodded, watching as he rose to his feet. She felt a kind of disappointment in seeing him walk to the door, and secretly she longed for him to stay. When he paused at the threshold, turning to her, she felt a surge of happiness at the sight. Maybe he would not go, after all.

"I'll see you at the club tomorrow morning," he said. "Noon sharp, if you please."

Her happiness turned to bald shock at his statement. Surely he was still joking. He had to be.

"Noon?" she repeated, the pitch in her voice slightly raising in question of what he was talking about.

"Please do not be late," he said. "I expect my employees to be punctual." And without further words, he smiled at her and walked out.

She sat there with her jaw slacked, utterly astonished. By the time she came to her senses and hurried after him, he was gone. And she was left alone, bewildered, and completely unnerved about what she would do now.

* * * * *

"I'll kill him," said Jack. "I'll hunt him down and stomp his guts out."

Alice rolled her eyes in disgust at his manly prowling, for that's what it seemed to be as he stalked back and forth across the living room. "You're not going to do anything, Jack."

"Well I need to do something, and I think it involves a good ass kicking."

Alice looked at Grace and smiled. "Looks like that's been taken care of." She handed her a fresh wrapping of ice. "You must have hit him pretty hard."

Grace just shrugged, as her mind replayed all that had happened in the last few hours.

Jack had not been pleased at all to come home and find her with a sprained wrist. And when he found out what had caused it, the explanation left him red-faced and ready to kill. He wasn't the least bit appeased to hear that she'd defended herself, and quite well. He was furious about Charlie having been in his home, in his own living room…and the fact that he was still out there somewhere.

Jack and Alice were still angry with each other, judging from the tone of their voices as they argued over her. Jack snorted in contempt and gestured a hand at his sister.

"So you can take care of yourself, can you?"

Grace said nothing, looking away. But in her usual way, Alice had plenty to say to him and she didn't mince words. She turned on him with her green eyes full of fire.

"Will you please shut up? You play that tune so much the record is worn out! She socked him in the face and he left. What the hell more do you want?"

"Woman, who are you telling to shut up? I wear the pants in this family!"

"Jesus H. Christ, if I hear that one more time I'll punch you in the mouth myself!"

Trying to be a peacemaker, Grace chimed in. "He's probably on his way home already."

Finding Grace

Jack turned on her fast. "And hell is just a sauna! What the hell was Henry doing over here? What was he doing the whole time Charlie was in the house? Was he just standing there watching?"

"They're not all Neanderthals like you!" Alice spat at him. "Your sister took care of herself. She didn't need Henry to beat the hell out of anyone."

"It was the least he could have done!"

"Well if that's made you mad, you'll love this!" Grace said. "Henry wants me to work for him."

Jack and Alice both looked at her, their faces stunned. Then Jack turned on his wife. "This is all your fault! You're the one who encouraged her!"

"Don't blame me, you horse's ass!"

Grace watched the battle. It was almost scary to watch a married couple fighting so badly...and yet, it was fascinating in its own way. They were like two brawlers taking shots at each other. She might have worried, if she didn't know that eventually, they would settle down and make up. It might have been interesting to see how far they would take it before the making up began, but she found she was too tired to stay any longer. Her wrist was still tender as well. Without saying anything, she made her way up to her room. Halfway up the stairs she heard the front door slam, and she knew Jack had gone outside again. Alice was in the living room, probably buried in a book or one of her crossword puzzles. So she left them to sort out their differences, heading into her room to nurse her hand and to think about what a day it had been.

An hour or so went by as she lay on the bed, book in hand, trying to calm herself with a bit of reading. From downstairs she heard the sound of music coming on. It wasn't so strange. The radio or the record player was always on, especially at night. But listening, she could swear it was Jack's voice she heard singing the song, and curious to know, she went to the door and opened it so she could listen. It was indeed him. He'd never been the most grand of singers, but he had a nice voice and it made her smile to think of him now, trying to entertain his wife with a love song. He really was a ham when it came to her...

Why do I do, just as you say
Why must I just, give you your way
Why do I sigh, why don't I try to forget

It must have been,
That something lovers call fate
Kept me saying: "I have to wait"
I saw them all,
Just couldn't fall 'til we met...

Grace walked out into the hall and sat on the steps to listen. Last night she'd heard them fighting as she sat there. Now she hoped to hear them making amends.

Finding Grace

It had to be you, it had to be you
I wandered around, and finally found
The somebody who
Could make me be true,

And could make me be blue
And even be glad, just to be sad
Thinking of you…

She heard Alice say, "I'm not talking to you, Jack-ass." But in her voice, there was a hint of amusement. And still he kept singing to her.

Some others I've seen,
Might never be mean
Might never be cross,
Or try to be boss
But they wouldn't do

For nobody else, gave me a thrill
With all your faults, I Love you still
It had to be you, wonderful you
It had to be you.

Now she heard Alice telling him what a big foolish idiot he was, but it was clear that she didn't mean a word of it. The sound of laughter and whispering was now distinct, and Grace knew that the two of them had made up. She smiled with delight at the thought of it. She turned and went back upstairs, closing the door to give them their privacy. They had made up, so now she could think of other dilemmas that needed solving.

She drew a hot bath and relaxed in it, thinking for the longest time about Henry's offer, and at long last she decided she would take him up on it.

It wasn't just the idea of being him more often…although, that thought had made her smile to herself with pleasure. It was the idea of doing something that no one thought she would do, or should do. Jack would hate the idea, simply because of Henry. Had they known of it, her parents would have deemed her a devilish child indeed, for women were not suppose to work outside the home. And the idea of her working in a club…a den of evil, they would have no doubt called it…would be their equivalent of their daughter giving herself to Satan.

The more she thought of it, the more she found herself excited by the idea of working for him. What she would be doing there, she was not for certain. Maybe she would be helping with costumes, or something else in the backstage area. It had certainly looked exciting and interesting when she had seen it that night a while back. How wonderful it might be to be a part of the whole working of things, to be useful and important, and not confined to a house as she was now. As much as she loved living here with Jack, and much as she adored Alice, she knew there was a loftier purpose awaiting her out there. Perhaps this was her chance to find it.

Henry looked at his watch. *Twelve Forty-Five*, it read. He clicked the lid of the watch shut, feeling a knot of frustration tighten in his belly.

He had told her noon sharp, and that was what he had meant. But she was not here, and he began to fear that she might not show. He had left her house yesterday, feeling a great sense of triumph along with the spring in his step. It had all fallen into place so easily…much more easily than he would have imagined, or could have planned. Charlie Hillard, as much of a worthless dog as he was, had provided the perfect means for him to get just what he wanted from Grace. There had been no need to make a fool of himself in asking her to come and work for him. He had worried about that, for he was almost certain that she would have refused him, for one reason or another. But with his sudden declaration of being her "employer" in order to give her a front of protection, it had all been done in one quick moment. His method was unorthodox, it was true. But now he might have her, in his own little way. The only question now was, would she come to work for him or not?

What a woman, he thought, as he remembered the sight of Charlie on the floor, holding his jaw. Her passion and intensity were all there, and he could not deny that it thrilled him to think of her fiery nature, and how it might be put to good use in other ways. Ways that were not at all polite and pure, and he felt his blood warm and stir at the thought. He had felt that same torrent of feeling yesterday, when he had examined her slender hand for injuries. How soft her skin had felt beneath his fingers. How difficult it had been not to press his lips to the tender place on her upturned wrist, where he knew he would have felt her pulse throbbing. He had seen the warmth in her eyes, and knew that if he had taken his time and done things slowly, he might have nearly had his way with her. Of course, he might well have ended up with a swollen jaw. But behind the want in her eyes, he had also read fear. She was an innocent…a thing of purity and goodness, despite the fact that she had been kissed before, and by him. That had been his doing, not hers. He was fairly certain that she didn't know much about sexuality, despite the fact that she had probably seen more pregnant women and babies than he ever would in a lifetime. He would take his time with her… make her trust in him, for what was a relationship without trust?

He had once vowed never again to fall in love, or to engage in a real relationship with any woman. But there was something about her that was breaking down that barrier he had built around his heart. And much to his own surprise, he wasn't afraid of it. Truthfully, he welcomed the thought of such a change, for it had been far too long since he had known love. And wasn't it the right of every man…or woman…to be loved?

Finding Grace

He only half-listened to the rehearsal of the band and some of the singers and actors working on the stage. He sighed, taking out his watch again to check the time. As he did, one of the crew members called out from the hall behind him.

"Anybody know this kid?" he shouted, his voice echoing in the empty hall. "She says she works here. Did somebody hire her?"

Henry turned in his seat, and saw her standing there. So she had come, after all. A surge of delight went through his frame, and he did his best to suppress the smile that threatened his expression. He rose from his seat, straightening his collar...and made his way towards her.

Chapter 16
"With the Band"

She stood at the entrance to the ballroom, looking around at the activity...the juggler doing repetitions, the magician practicing his tricks, the dancers each stepping in time to their own beats. And as she watched them she wondered...

What place do I have with these people?

She'd made the trip all on her own. Jack and Alice had both asked several times if they could take her. But she had declined. *I can manage on my own, but thank you all the same,* she'd told them. To which Jack had grumbled, saying how tired he was of hearing that turn of phrase. But before he left for work, he came around and told her they would all go out to dinner that night...maybe go to a movie, to celebrate her first day on the job. She had smiled at him, kissing his cheek, and he had muttered something utterly childish and grumpy in response...which only made her smile all the more.

Now she stood, watching as Henry came towards her. He was smiling slightly. Gloating, actually. Clearly he enjoyed the idea that she'd come to work for him. *Men,* she thought. *How they love being right.* But his smug expression was becoming too familiar. And she found that her reaction now wasn't what it was before. At one time, she would have found it infuriating. Now, that smirk was one of the little things she was beginning to love. But she wasn't about to tell him so. His pride was beastly enough as it was, and there was no need to make it worse. When he came near, he nodded at the worker to send him on his way. Then he looked at her.

"You're late."

She shrugged. "So sue me, then."

Now he smiled in that cheeky way of his. "I knew you couldn't stay away."

When he was being this way, she found it much easier talking to him. His love of himself was easy to battle, and she had to say she rather enjoyed taking him down a notch or two. She stepped close to him, pointing at his neck. "What's that swelled up thing between your shoulders?"

He looked a bit worried. "What swelled up thing?"

"Oh, never mind, I know what it is...It's just your head." She smirked, mimicking his impish trademark, and she liked the look that came to his face. It was like a balloon deflating. And yet, he seemed gracious in his defeat, giving her a kind of sheepish look.

"You are a cold, cold woman," he replied, and he sighed. "So how's the hand?"

"Kind of sore, but otherwise fine. I can take a little pain." She saw him smile as they began to walk together towards the stage, and she couldn't help but smile a little too. How different the place was now, so calm and quiet, except for the sounds of the band playing low in practice, and the light hum of voices from the stage and all around. "So what am I doing here?" she asked. "Sewing? Washing windows? What?"

He only chuckled in response. "Not exactly. No, I think you're of more use working with the band. Singing with the band, actually."

She stopped. So did he, turning to look at her. She waited for him to say he was only joking. A long moment went by as she waited for him to say it. But he didn't, and she felt a nervous little laugh bubble up from inside.

"You want me to sing?"

"What did you think I wanted you for?" he asked. Then he scoffed. "Sewing and cleaning - please."

She took a slight step back, shaking her head. "I can't sing in front of crowds like yours. I just can't." She turned to leave, but he grabbed her hand and started pulling her along.

"You can do anything you set your mind to."

She tried to pull away, head still shaking. "No, I can't."

He stopped, but retained her hand, looking at her intently. "Yes you can, and you will. You're here, and I've already told my people about you. They want to meet you. And besides, I don't have the time to look for someone else. You're all I've got."

She tried to speak, to give further fight, but couldn't find words for aid.

You're all I've got, he'd said. How could she refuse, without seeming selfish and petty? She couldn't, and she knew it. But she wanted to, and she would've done anything if he would just let her out of it. Just the thought of standing there, in front of whole room of people with their judging ears and eyes on her, was terrifying. But looking at his face, she knew he wasn't about to give up, and her shoulders sank in defeat. She groaned slightly, and he seemed to take pity on her, for he gave her hand a little pat.

"Before you curl up on the floor in a ball, why don't you come over and introduce yourself? You should meet everyone."

He let go of her hand, gently taking her by the arm. He led her across the floor and up to the stage. She felt her stomach knot up a little as everyone turned to look at her. Meeting new people was not one of her strong points. In her life, there had been few strangers who crossed her path, and the rare occasion of meeting someone new was something she still hadn't mastered. The tension beat strong in her veins, but she did her best not to show it, raising her chin in an attempt at confidence. Henry called for everyone's attention.

"People, this is Grace Langdon. For today, she's here to observe. And if you're nice enough to her, maybe she'll consider staying."

While the men in the band started chattering, pushing forward in an attempt to introduce themselves, Henry introduced her to the ladies and gentleman around them on the stage. They were pleasant, but their words were brief, as they were more interested in getting back to their work. The band seemed more eager to meet her, and as Henry led her down to them, she felt his hand holding her arm a little tighter...his body moving a little closer, as if he were trying to protect her. The men were certainly a rowdy bunch, all trying to talk over each other. It wasn't until Henry raised his voice that they finally quieted.

"Settle down, you bunch of monkeys. I know that respectable women aren't the kind you're used to, but try and control yourselves."

That sent them into another outburst of noise, many of them playing at being offended by their boss's insult. Henry led her through the crowd, bringing her to the piano, where a white-haired gentleman rose to greet them with a kind smile. Henry introduced her to him...the leader of the band.

"This is Thomas. Bandleader, piano player, and all around good egg. If you need anything, he's the one to go to."

They shook hands, and she smiled shyly.

"I have a brother named Thomas," she said. "But he can't carry a tune in a five gallon bucket."

Thomas chuckled. So did the other men, and one pushed his way to the front of the crowd. He was a baby-faced trumpet player, ginger-haired and hazel-eyed, and she recognized him from that first night she'd been to the club. As he took her hand, she smiled.

"I remember you. You were in the show, dancing and singing. You play in the band, too?"

He nodded, a boyish grin on his face. "Call me Toby." He raised her hand to his lips, kissing it lightly, his eyes twinkling with playfulness. "Let me say, Miss Grace, that you are aptly named."

She wanted to be skeptical about all of the attention. They were just men being men, after all. But they were all so charming. Toby in particular. He had just a little bit of the devil behind his eyes. But his face was so angelic, his way so endearing, she couldn't help but be charmed by him. Still, she tried to keep a bit of sense about her. She shook her head, giving him a sly little smile...and the first remark that came into her head.

"I ain't seen so much ham since I left Virginia."

The men all laughed again, and even Henry managed a chuckle. But then he was suddenly called away on a matter of business. He seemed reluctant to leave her there, and she felt a little nervous at the prospect of his going. But Thomas kindly offered to watch after her.

"Don't worry boss. I'll protect her from these hounds." His smile was gentle...his way almost grandfatherly, and when he asked her to take a seat at the piano, she only hesitated for a moment before accepting his invitation. He leaned on the piano's closed top, looking kindly at her.

"So...The boss says you play. Is that right?"

She nodded, feeling a bit shy. "A little."

"Would you play for us?"

She opened her mouth to protest...but before she could speak, the men all gathered around, encouraging her to perform for them. Her cheeks flushed pink with embarrassment. But when they asked her repeatedly to play, she felt it wouldn't be right to turn them down.

With their eager eyes watching, she played the first piece she could think of...one of Chopin's most famous nocturnes. Her fingers flew through it much faster than she wanted them to. But when she was done, the applause they gave her made her feel as if she'd given the best performance of her life. She thanked them, and started to leave the piano bench, thinking she had remained too long. But Thomas urged her to stay where she was. He sat down beside her.

"You have a real gift, Miss Grace. And lovely piano hands, I might add. But have you ever played Jazz?"

She shook her head, and he smiled.

"Well then, let *these* hands show you what they can do."

He began to play, and the moment she heard the infectious melody, she was captivated by it. He spoke as he played, punctuating his words with rhythmic movements of his fingers on the keys.

"Jazz is a feeling. It's a frame of mind...a state of being. It comes from deep down in the soul. It radiates out through the fingers, almost like they're under a magic spell."

Toby came hurrying to her side, an eager smile on his face. "It works with the feet, too." He took her hand, pulling her away from the bench. "Come on. I'll show you what I mean."

As quick as he moved, it was difficult to put up much of an argument. And he was so eager, so full of energy, she found that she had little will to resist him. He led her up on the stage, pulling over a chair for her to sit on. He smiled at her, straightening his tie as if preparing himself.

"Let me show you how it's done," he said. "Observe the wonder that is me in action."

She sat there watching as he took several steps back. He cued the band to play a tune. And then he danced, moving with athletic grace like nothing she'd ever seen before. His feet moved so fast she could hardly believe her eyes. And when he finished, he went down on one knee in a flourish...kneeling right before her. She was awestruck, her voice almost a whisper.

"That was amazing. How do you do that?"

He grinned, clearly pleased with himself. "Natural born talent," he replied.

She smiled. He certainly wasn't shy, that was plain to see. Neither was he modest about his talent. And yet, as confident as he was, he wasn't the least bit offensive. Under his bravado there was an underlying sweetness that shined through, and she couldn't help being impressed by him. She liked him very much, as she found she liked everyone she'd met. They were such a close knit group, and so friendly, even to her. They didn't know her, and yet they'd welcomed her as if she was one of their own. It made her forget the doubts she'd had just a little while ago. It made her want to be one of them.

* * * * *

After settling some small matters with his bookkeeper, Henry went out in the hall to listen to the music coming from down below...and to see how Grace was getting along. Leaning his hands on the railing, watching her as she sat in her chair on the stage, he was quite surprised at what he saw.

She smiled. She laughed. The light of joy shined in her every movement. How beautiful she was when she was happy...and seeing it, he was stung with envy.

Why can't she be that way with me? He wondered.

She'd known his employees less than half a day. And yet, she smiled and talked to them so freely, particularly with Toby. With growing unease, he watched the two of them onstage. Toby danced for her, showing off the way he always did with pretty girls, especially new ones. But there was something about him showing off for her...and her obvious enjoyment of it...that made his temper rise.

Toby was just a boy, nineteen years old, with a baby face and a head of ridiculous curly hair. What was so damned special about him? He could sing and dance, but so what? And as for Toby himself, why did he have to chase after *her?* He'd always been a notorious rascal, flirting with and charming all the women in the place. But why couldn't he leave this one girl alone?

Surely she wasn't so unwise as to be fooled by such a display. She was bright... intelligent. Could she really be moved by such false flirtations? He didn't want to believe she would fall for such an act...and yet, there she was, clearly taken in by it all.

He stood up straight, his fists clenched at his sides. Who did they think they were, fooling around as if they were mingling at a party? They worked for him. This wasn't playtime...and maybe they needed a reminder of just who was running this show.

* * * * *

She was having a ball. The music was delightful, but the company was even better. Toby wasn't just a great dancer and a sweet-natured soul. He was quite possibly the funniest person she'd ever met. He told the most awful jokes, but the way he told them, she couldn't help but laugh. He had a great gift for mimicry, doing spot on impressions of Thomas and other members of the band. But when he started to do an impression of Henry, she found herself covering her mouth, feeling a bit ashamed for finding it rather funny. She was actually quite relived when Henry suddenly appeared. Like a no nonsense teacher, coming into a room full of rowdy students, he commanded instant attention.

"Are we on a break, people? I'm paying you to work, not to sit around. Get to it before I bust some heads."

Everyone scrambled to get back to business. Unsure of what to do, she went to stand beside Thomas at the piano. Feeling he was the best person to inquire after, she started to ask him what she should be doing. But before she could say anything, Henry came over with several sheets of paper, handing them to her.

"These are lyrics," he said. "They're the songs you'll need to learn for the show. Thomas will teach you the words, the rhythms. Singing jazz isn't what you're used to. It has a very different feel. Very unique. So you'd better get to work on it right away."

Looking down at the papers in her hand, she was overcome with sudden apprehension. Thinking of who she was replacing...knowing what Victoria would have thought of her for it...she wondered if she'd made a mistake in coming here. She sighed sadly.

"I feel awful," she said, turning to Thomas. "I feel like I'm stepping in someone else's shoes while they're still wearing them."

He just smiled kindly. "She's in California, doing what she wanted to do. She left us in the lurch, and if you don't take her place, someone else will. Out with the old, in with the new."

She frowned at that. "That seems kind of cold."

Henry shrugged. "That's this business. And by the way, you'll only have about two weeks to be ready. I hate to rush you, but I can't keep my patrons in limbo. Like they say, the show must go on."

She sat down on the bench, her shoulders slumping at the daunting task before her.

"Two weeks," she said. "I don't know if I can do this."

He came to stand close to her. She slowly looked up, and saw him smirk. He shook his head.

"Don't be so insecure. It doesn't suit you. You're capable of a lot, you know. You just don't give yourself enough credit."

The warmth of his compliment touched her...and as she watched him turn away, a smile slowly crept across her face. With just a few words, he'd eased her nervousness. How did he do it? What magic did he possess, to sweep away her doubts the way he did?

She watched him as he walked along the front of the stage. He was talking to one of his directors, reviewing a paper in his hand. There was something so beautiful about him. The way he moved, the way he stood...especially in profile. His presence alone was enough to render her speechless. As she had so often, she wondered how she could keep her senses being around him.

Henry Shaw, she thought. *If you only knew the power you have over me. You'd never let me live it down.*

* * * * *

After such a great day in their company, she was sad at the thought of leaving. She watched Toby as he cleaned his trumpet and put it in its case, preparing to leave for the night. He turned to her with a sweet smile.

"What are you doing for dinner tonight?" he asked. "If you're hungry, maybe you and I can grab a bite."

She blushed, both honored and stunned at his asking. He was, after all, still just a stranger to her. And yet, part of her wanted to accept the invitation. She liked him very much. But she regretfully declined his offer.

"I'm sorry," she said. "I can't go. My brother and sister-in-law are taking me out tonight."

He shrugged. "Maybe tomorrow night."

She smiled shyly. She didn't want to hurt his feelings, but she shook her head.

"No thank you. I don't think my brother would like it. He's a little bit protective." At first she was a little worried how he would react. She wondered if he might get mad, but he didn't. He was kind about it, smiling as he teased her.

"Have a good time then, for me. I'll be at home, broken hearted that I wasn't invited."

She laughed, saying goodbye to him as he left with the others.

She did not see Henry, who had been standing nearby the entire time. When she turned around, she was surprised to find him there, looking at her with a rather dark expression.

"Is something wrong?" she asked.

There was a long pause before he answered. "Nothing." He turned away for a moment. Then he turned back. "Do you need a ride home?"

She shook her head, a little nervous quiver fluttering in her belly. The feelings she had were so very confusing. She feared being alone with him. And yet, if he had only insisted a little harder about taking her home, she might actually have gone. But she remembered her plans with Jack and Alice.

"My brother and Alice are meeting me here. Matter of fact, they're probably waiting for me right now."

From the back of the room, there came a familiar voice calling. She turned to find Jack waiting.

"Sis, are you ready to go?"

She looked back to Henry for a moment, and saw him walking away. Why did she feel as if she were abandoning him? She could have sworn that just before he turned away, she saw a hint of disappointment in his face. For some reason, it pained her to think that her refusal might have hurt his feelings. She wanted to go to him, to ask if he was all right. But she knew she couldn't. He wouldn't have admitted to having his feelings hurt, even if they were. So she turned to Jack and made her way towards him. As she neared him, she heard Henry's voice behind her.

"Tomorrow, at noon?"

She turned to him, nodding her head. He nodded back, and disappeared from sight.

* * * * *

In his office, Henry tried to distract himself by picking up papers and studying them, but he found it useless. His mind was too full of other matters. He tossed the papers aside as he sat down in his chair, letting out a deep sigh.

His hopes had been high at the start of the day. Then his plan had backfired on him. He'd brought her here, wanting her close so he might interact with her, even if it was only on a professional level. But he'd also hoped that by being her boss, she would depend on him in some way…and maybe in time, her dependence on him would grow into closeness.

He couldn't have imagined how she would blossom so suddenly. He wouldn't have thought that others, men in particular, would be as enchanted by her as he was…and that she would be so charmed in return.

How the hell could he have known that someone would ask her out on a date? And worse, she might have accepted, if it weren't for having a prior engagement. In truth, he'd been quite fearful that she would accept the invitation…and even after he'd heard her decline, the fang of envy still bit him hard.

It had been so long since he'd been envious of any man, and he'd forgotten how bad it could be. The sting of it made him want to smash something with his fist.

He shook his head at his musings, wondering just when he'd become such a hopeless fool. He rose from his chair and left the office, walking down the hall and down the stairs toward the front doors. He needed to think and clear his head, and he was glad his important matters had been settled for the day. Any other small things could wait until tomorrow. Quickly he locked up the place, and took a slow walk towards the El-Train.

He wasn't quite certain what he would do about her. Not yet, anyway. It would come to him in time. But between now and then, he didn't intend for her to be swayed by someone else. He couldn't have everything his way, but he was still the boss. He had authority, and he damn well intended to use it…even it was to his own advantage.

Chapter 17
"New Heights"

The early morning sun shined through the living room window. It was a lovely, quiet morning, except for the low volume of the music coming from the record player. Standing with sheet music in hand, Grace went over the song lyrics, quietly singing to herself as she practiced. All was melodious, flowing quite nicely…until she stumbled over a word for the third time.

"Damn!" she cried, stomping her foot.

The stomp made the record player jump, which made the record skip and screech. She rushed over to shut it off, and when the silence fell so did her head, coming to rest in her hands.

The week had started with such promise. Being with the band had been so wonderful, and she found herself looking forward to each day with them. And she'd anticipated seeing Henry every day. But as it turned out, his manner as a boss was very different than his usual persona. He was quite serious, even stern at times, particularly with Toby. At times he seemed very irritated with him, always telling him to do more work and less socializing. She wasn't quite sure why Henry would single Toby out, when the whole atmosphere of the club was so very relaxed. Everyone chatted and goofed around a little in between practicing their music or routines. It seemed rather strange to her. But then again, he was the boss. He must have had his reasons for his behavior, so she didn't do more than wonder about it.

Stern as he was when he was working, she found herself watching him more and more with fascination. His presence commanded respect, and from the way he moved, it was clear he knew he was the top dog. And oh how she loved to watch him move about. His strides were smooth and confident, his eyes a brighter shade of blue when he was deeply involved in matters of business. At times she would be looking at him and those eyes would turn to her. A few times he gave her a little smile when he caught her staring, and she would turn away with a blush. At those moments she was certain he'd come to her, ready with a sly remark.

But he didn't. In truth, he didn't speak to her very much at all, except to ask her how her work was progressing or how she was getting along with everyone. Part of her was glad he was being a gentleman for once. But another part of her wondered at the change in his behavior.

Is he bored with me? She asked herself. *Has he lost interest in me already?*

She wouldn't have blamed him if he had turned his interests elsewhere. In all honesty, she wanted a deeper relationship with him...but fear and uncertainty kept her from pursuing it. He was so much older, so much more experienced. She was so unschooled in so many ways. If he did want more from her than friendship...if by some small chance, he might think of engaging in a romance, he would likely be disappointed by her naiveté in even the smallest matters. Maybe it was better not to hope for something more.

If there was a consolation to Henry's seeming lack of interest, at least Toby and the boys in the band were there for her. Toby was quickly becoming a good friend, always ready with a joke or some way to entertain her. Thomas was like the grandfather she'd never known, so patient and easy-going as he taught her. It was he who had suggested she practice at home with the aid of a record player, to help her learn the lyrics. So she had. But she'd hardly started practicing before she found herself having to begin again, for she missed a word here or a phrase there. She tried not to look at the paper in her hand, but found her eyes consulting it again and again. At first, she had remained calm about her mistakes, telling herself not to mind it and start over. But with each practice came more slips and small mistakes, and they began to chip away at the confidence that had just started to build within her.

Early this morning she had risen at her usual time, but instead of going to the kitchen to cook, she had gone back to the record player and turned it on, though she kept the volume low. Alice came in a little while later, watching her for a moment. Grace apologized for not starting breakfast, but Alice waved it off and left her alone to work.

Several times, she listened to the record all the way through without singing, to let the words and music soak into her brain. Then once again she began her vocals. When she got through the entire thing without a mistake, she felt her confidence soar. But when she began again, and her tongue slipped over a word, she wanted to pick up the record and slam it down. Instead she cursed out loud.

"What's with the cussing, baby sister?"

Jack stood, leaning against the doorframe, dressed in his work clothes. She looked at him for just a moment before turning away again, and she grumbled in frustration.

"I'll never get this in time. They'll have to find someone else."

Jack pursed his lips and rolled his eyes. "Oh come on, now. You started this, and you'll finish it. We're not quitters, are we?"

She slumped in defeat, moving to the sofa and falling on it in a heap of discouragement. She flung her arms over her eyes, as Jack came to sit in the chair beside her.

"Oh buck up, will you?" he demanded. "I can't stand a weak woman."

She sat up a little, her brow crinkled in irritation. "A little while ago you were fussing at me for wanting to do this. Now you're mad at me for NOT wanting to do it. Make up your mind!" She flopped back down.

"Don't get all huffy with me," he snapped at her. "You're the little hothead who insisted on doing what you wanted to do. Now you're stuck with it. It's your bed, sister. You'll have to lay in it."

She curled up on her side and tried to hide, but he just laughed at her. Then he took her by the sleeve, pulling her up to a sitting position. And a moment later, he was dragging her to her feet. She protested, insisting that she be left alone. But he ignored her.

"Quit your bellyaching." He went to the record player and turned it on. She stood there for a moment, and watched with a raised eyebrow as he began to dance and sing to the song. She tried not to smile, forcing the muscles of her face to remain composed. Then, he tried to dance with her.

She pushed him away. "Get away from me, you idiot." But she couldn't help smiling a little.

"This is not an incestuous thing," he declared, holding her at a distance from himself and leading her into a dance.

The smile fell from her face. "That's disgusting!"

"You're the one with your mind in the gutter, not me!" he shouted back. "Now shut up and move your feet. If you're going to sing, you should know how to dance, too."

She reluctantly consented to the lesson, and found that it came to her quite naturally. All the time they moved, Jack kept looking at the floor, perhaps fearing that she might smash his toes. But she didn't. It seemed to all come to her quite easily, and it helped ease a little of the fears she had on other matters. When the song was over, there came a round of applause from behind them. They both turned to look.

"Nice," said Alice. "Very smooth."

Jack came forward, smiling. "What can I say? I'm the best."

"I was talking about Grace," she replied, now with face straight. But it turned back into a little smile as he came to stand before her. He leaned in and kissed her, an ardent expression on his face.

"Evil woman," he said, smiling wickedly. He made for the door, putting his hat on his head. He paused for a moment to tip his cap at Grace, and then he was gone.

Alice, still smiling, went to stand next to Grace, who had turned and picked up her lyric sheet again.

"You aren't thinking of quitting, are you?"

Grace looked up at her. "How did you know I was?"

"I heard you taking to Jack."

Grace shrugged. "I don't know. I don't think I can get out now. I already promised to be part of the show. I don't know what I'm going to do." She sighed again.

"Well I say, don't miss the brass ring."

Grace looked at her with a blank expression, and Alice smiled.

"It's an expression," she said. "When you ride a carousel, each time you go around, you have a chance to grab a ring made of brass. If you catch it, you get a free ride. So the meaning of the saying is, don't miss your chance. This is your chance, Gracie. Don't let it go by."

She gave her a light touch on the arm, and left her to her thoughts.

Grace reached out to turn the record player back on, but paused when she heard a knock on the front door. Somehow, she knew who it was even before Alice went to answer it. Her heart beat a little faster, and she anxiously reached up to tuck a loose curl of hair behind her ear. Why her appearance suddenly mattered so much to her, she didn't know. It was almost like a reflex... something involuntary that she could not control. A moment later she heard that warm, familiar voice falling on her ear, and she could not suppress a thrill that ran over and through her.

"Sis, you have a visitor," said Alice, who flashed a sly little smile as she left the two of them alone, retreating into the kitchen.

Grace turned slowly, and felt her breath catch slightly as Henry set eyes on her and gave her a slight smile. He came near, his hat in hand. He looked from her to the player a moment, reading the label on the record, then back to her again.

"Working at home, I see. Very smart of you. But then again, you don't have to try very hard in that department, do you?"

She lowered her head, feeling a blush come to her cheeks at his compliment. She tried to hide her smile. Much as she wanted to bask in his sunshine, there was something within her that held back. But he was making that rather difficult, with the way he looked at her at times, and the way his voice was so soothing and rich. If only she could believe in him, without having a memory that warned against it...a memory of Victoria, in particular. Had he spoken to her like this, at some time in the dim and distant past? Had he smiled at her in this way, and sent the same warm thrills down her spine, just at the sound of his voice? Her smile fell away as she realized that Victoria most probably had felt those very same feelings, and in the end, they had all been for nothing.

Henry must have sensed the change from joy to doubt, for she heard him sigh bitterly. She looked up, and saw that his smile had gone as well.

"I see it's too early in the morning for compliments," he said. "My apologies. I'll just skip the flattery and get to the point." He lifted his chin slightly. "I wanted to thank you for being a help to me. For putting yourself out there against your will, etcetera, etcetera. So I wanted to know if you'd like to take a little trip?"

"A trip?" she exclaimed, shaking her head. "I don't know. We have to be at the club soon, don't we?"

Now he smiled again. "I'm the boss, aren't I? I can show up whenever I please. It's one of the many perks of owning a business. So, are you coming along?" He turned from her, almost as if he expected her to follow. And strangely enough, she did. She paused just at the front door.

"Where are we going?"

He clucked his tongue as he put his hat on, and he smirked at her. "Don't ask so many questions. Sometimes a journey is better when you don't know the destination."

Alice appeared in the kitchen doorway, watching them. Henry turned to her with a smile.

"Don't worry. I'll bring her back safe and sound, along with her reputation."

Grace watched as Alice smiled and wagged her eyebrows. Then, Grace turned her eyes back to Henry. He opened the door, waiting for her. Hesitant, and yet willing, she stepped out before him, feeling his eyes upon her as they moved down the sidewalk. She was headed towards the streetcar stop on the corner. But his words made her still her steps.

"We're driving," he said. "Where we're going is a little outside of the city."

She paused a moment, feeling a shiver of anxiety at the thought of being alone with him again, and in the close quarters of a car. And as before, he seemed to sense her feelings, as the look on his face told of his irritation. But for the moment he was silent on it, and she moved with him across the street to his car, where he opened the door for her and waited. She took her seat, waiting for him. When he came around to his seat, and the door closed, she expected him to say nothing about her nervous ways. Though she'd often wondered if her wariness offended him, how could she know? It had seemed to be his way to wear a look of irritation, and then to let it pass away as if it had never been there. He had never voiced his feelings. But this time he turned to her, his expression serious and slightly dark.

"Look," he said, his tone sharp. "I'm no angel, but I'm not a heathen devil either. I'm not dead set on jumping you, if you must know."

She stammered shamefully, trying to defend herself. But his words kept her from it.

"I've been as pleasant as I know how to be. And I thought it would be nice if you and I could spend some time together, outside of work. Away from the clutches of your brother and sister-in-law. But if you're that afraid of me, maybe this isn't a good idea. Maybe we should stop associating with each other at all."

He waited, as if allowing her the chance to get out of the car and go home. She put her fingers on the door handle, but then she paused.

When did I become such a coward? She thought. *I adore this man, but I try to fly away like a nervous little bird whenever he gets too close.*

She turned to look at him, seeing his handsome features marred by the scowl he wore. He stared straight ahead, his hands resting on the steering wheel. He was silent. It hurt her to imagine what he must have thought of her. She had wanted him to see her as strong and independent...able to make her decisions with intelligence and maturity. But now she realized how small her behavior was...how her mistrust in others made her seem flighty and weak. If she said nothing now, just opened the door and walked away, his suspicions about her would be confirmed. And that she could not allow.

"I'm sorry. I don't like to be mean. I just can't help how I am." She looked at her knees, trying to keep her composure by focusing intently on something. She felt the burn of tears, but fought to keep them at bay. He already thought her weak, and tears would only confirm it for him. At long last, she heard him speak…and his voice turned calm and soothing.

"We all have our ways. Change is never easy for any of us."

Her voice wavered slightly.

"No, it's not." She reached up to wipe away a tear that had escaped, hoping he didn't take much notice of it. If he did, he said nothing. He just reached his hand forward to turn the key in the ignition. And without speaking he backed out and slowly drove away.

* * * * *

They rode in silence for some time, each thinking their own separate thoughts. She was focused on the road ahead and the passing of the scene outside her window. They were leaving the city, as he'd said, and with great curiosity she wondered what he had in store for her. There was no way of knowing, even if she asked him, for she was certain he would never tell until he got her where he wanted her. So she just sat quietly and waited, as they made their way down a small town road, and soon turned down a long and winding drive. It wasn't long at all before she realized they were at a small airport. She'd never actually seen one before, but it wasn't difficult to figure out. Looking out at the numerous aircraft before her, she felt a nervous knot starting to form in her belly. She looked over at him, seeing the hint of a smile on his face. She narrowed her eyes at him.

"What are you up to, bringing me here?"

He pulled the car to a stop. "Did I ever tell you about my love of flying? I've become quite good at it over the last few years."

Her heart beat fast with anxiety at what he was hinting at. "You're not going to make me get in one of those, are you?"

His reply was calm. "I'm not going to make you do anything. But it won't hurt to take a look, now will it?" He got out and came round to her side of the car, opening the door and waiting patiently. She sat still for a moment, unsure of what to do. Her fear of the unknown was strong, but so was her curiosity. It was the chance to do and see something that so very few people got to do. Still she hesitated. Then she heard him sigh.

"Coward," he said…and her response was an indignant cry.

"What did you call me?"

"Oh I'm sorry. Chicken…that is what I should have said. Something you can relate to, little farm girl."

"I am not a chicken!"

He nodded. "Yes you are. They don't fly. They run away at the slightest little thing. So that *does* make you a chicken."

She was no fool. She knew he was just baiting her. And yet, she could not stand the thought of his being right about her cowardice. Yes, she could probably take the high road and not give in to his challenge. But that seemed so dull, and her rebellious nature got the better of her.

"Fine," she said. "I'll go. But if I die of fright, it'll be your fault. And when I'm in heaven I'll be looking down laughing while my brother sends you to meet me."

His smile was impish. "Who says that's where I'll end up?"

They walked together to one of the hangars, where a man was coming forward to meet them. He shook Henry's hand, and hers, and the two men had a brief conversation about the plane that sat nearby. She hardly heard the words, as madly as her heart was beating at the thought of flying. From what little that registered in her head, she learned that Henry had been a pilot for some years. There was also a comment about someone named Charles Lindbergh, but she had no idea who he was and what he had to do with anything.

The man handed Henry two pairs of strange looking eyewear…goggles, he called them. When he placed them on her head, covering her eyes with the lenses, she tensed at the strange sensation.

"What are these funny things for?"

He smirked. "They're a fashion statement."

Beneath the goggles, her eyes rolled.

Just moments later she was being helped into the little pit in the front of the plane, and Henry was getting in the one behind her. It seemed strange to sit in front.

"I'm not supposed to operate this thing, am I? There's no steering, no dials. How does it work?"

"Don't worry," he replied. "I'm running the show. This rig operates with a backseat driver."

That hardly calmed her. Her heart beat so that she feared it might leap from her body, and when the engine and propeller roared to life, she nearly jumped out of her seat and fled. She felt a little tap on her shoulder, and she turned her head as far as she could, for the way she sat it was impossible to turn all the way around. She could only hear his voice.

"Relax," was all he said.

She turned back, her reply bitter. "Thanks for the advice."

He laughed, though she could hardly hear it over the noise. She closed her eyes, and clutched the cross at her throat. Then they began to move.

She opened her eyes, realizing how slow they seemed to be going. And, they were still on the ground. Her shoulders slumped a little in relief, thinking that maybe it had all been a trick. He couldn't get this contraption up in the air…all he was going to do was drive around the place, and that was just fine with her. They stopped then, and she waited. Nothing happened. She shouted over the noise.

"Is that it?"

He didn't answer. Then a moment later they were suddenly racing forward at a terrifying speed, the ground and the land around them whipping by her in a blur. Her breath caught, for she knew that something monumental was about to happen, and a moment later she felt her stomach rise up near her throat as they escaped the bonds of the earth. She ducked her head down and closed her eyes, terrified for her very life. Then she heard him shouting from behind her.

"Open your eyes, little chicken! See the world the way the real birds do!"

She felt the air across her face, and she sat up, eyes still closed. But very slowly she allowed them to open, and she gasped as she saw the earth falling away beneath them, the blue of the sky all around. They seemed to float in the very air, and her fear faded into wonder as she looked around at the heavens. For a time they drifted along the sky, peacefully and calmly. Then the plane ducked down, and she gasped at the motion of it...terrified that they were descending into a crash. But as they came up in a smooth motion, she caught the sound of his laughter on the wind.

He'd dipped the plane that way on purpose. And she wanted to be mad at him for it...but it was impossible. This moment was too thrilling to feel anything but absolute joy and excitement. With him, she was safe...and free.

When they banked in a turn she found herself gasping not in fear, but in delight.

So this is what it is to be a bird, she marveled.

How she had so often dreamed of such a freedom, watching hawks and sparrows take to wing and soar though the sky. Now, here she was...and the feeling was beyond anything words could describe.

All too soon they were drifting down to the ground, and she found a great disappointment in coming to the end of the marvelous journey. She clung to every last moment, until the wheels hit the pavement and the reality of the earth was brought back to her. How heavy and oppressive it all felt now, after soaring so freely in the clouds. Yet, she could not be melancholy. Her entire being felt alive and exhilarated from the experience, and as she stood when the plane stopped, her legs wobbled slightly. She watched Henry put his legs over the side and slide easily to the ground. Then he came to her with open arms to help her down. Almost without thinking she leaned in to rest her hands on his shoulders, and she felt his hands grip her waist and easily lift her down. She could feel nothing but elation, even as he leaned in close to her and smiled. She could not help but look up at him and return the gesture. For the first time, she looked in his eyes and felt no fear, no mistrust. All she could feel was happiness, and a realization that she would never love anyone in the world as she loved him. He reached up slowly, running his fingertips along her cheek.

"Tell me the truth." His voice was almost a whisper. "Is there anyone else who can make you feel like I do?"

She could not answer, could not speak. Her eyes were locked with his, rendering her motionless. Of their own power her eyelids closed, as he leaned against her, gently but insistently. Then she felt his lips pressed to hers, and the memory of that first kiss came to her with all its force and fire. In another moment she found she could not think of anything but leaning her own figure into his, bringing her arms and hands up around his neck, kissing him back with all the passion and feeling she'd been holding back for so long.

Finding Grace

* * * * *

He slowly pulled away from the kiss. Not that he wanted to…oh no, quite the contrary. He had so often recalled the softness of her lips, of how they felt so warm against his own. And they *were* soft and warm…yielding, pressing to his firmly after only a slight hesitation. He could have kissed her again, and yet again, held onto her for longer, relishing in the feel of her arms around him. But deep down he knew that he must pull back, if only to give them both the chance to take a breath. When he released her she swayed, declaring that she thought she might faint. He smiled as she leaned against him for support. She rested her head against his shoulder, letting out a little sigh, and he felt her cheek pressing there, warmly and insistently.

This was the woman he wanted. This warm, tender being…loving and unafraid of being loved. He took in a deep breath, pressing his cheek upon her hair. For quite some time they remained that way, quietly holding one another. When one of them spoke, it was he who broke the silence first.

"What are you thinking about?"

It was a moment more before she replied, and her voice was soft. "You." She kept her head against him, but he knew she smiled. He heard it in her voice.

"I was thinking of the first time I saw you, that day at the station. I thought you were the most beautiful thing I'd ever seen in my life." She leaned back in his arms, looking up at him… and her smile lessened somewhat. "Until you spoke".

He looked at her with a raised eyebrow. "Until I spoke?"

"Well," she said, "It wasn't what you said, so much as how you said it. You had this kind of look about you, like you couldn't be bothered with anyone. Especially someone like me. You looked at me like I was a stray dog or something."

Knowing that he risked triggering her temper, or worse, being on the receiving end of her hand, he grinned at her statement. And he took further chance by saying, quite boldly…

"You know, you were something like a stray dog."

At that, her eyes widened indignantly and her mouth fell slightly open, but still he spoke. "You were kind of cute and shabby, and a total pain in the neck. And then there was the way you came running after me, begging for help, looking at me with those great big eyes. All you needed was four feet and a wagging tail." Even as he said it, he knew she would come back at him with something sharp and direct, like a duelist whose sword hits mark for mark. She did not disappoint.

"All you needed was a long bushy tail, four shod hooves, and a pair of long ears." She thrust her finger into his shoulder for emphasis. "You jackass in a man's suit."

He laughed softly. It was one of the things he so adored about her…the way she could match him beat for beat. Most women had never understood the wickedness of his humor. With them, he risked hurting their feelings and seeing them fall into a fit of misty eyed dramatics. But not with her. If by chance he did ever hurt her feelings, he knew she would come back and hurt his as badly, and failing that, she would have blackened his eye or bloodied his nose. But under that tough as nails demeanor, he saw a fragile spirit, yearning for acceptance and love. She wanted...hungered for...the simple contact of a human touch. One that was not brought against her in harm or coldness, but in warmth and gentleness. He wanted to be the one, the only one, to give her that. Gently cupping her face in his hands, his smile fell away. His eyes burned with an intense light as he looked at her.

"I know you've been hurt before. Not just by Charlie, but by others. People who were suppose to love you, to take care of you as best they could. They shook your faith, made you afraid to trust. But I swear to you, here and now, that I will never do that to you."

Once more, he slowly brought his lips to hers. He leaned into her, thrilling at the feel of her body against his, and now she did not seem to hesitate as before. She pressed against him eagerly now, kissing him back, and caressing the back of his neck with warm hands. But somewhere in their fog of passion, a glimmer of reason asserted itself. She was so young, so inexperienced with these feelings, and he knew all too well how overwhelming they could be. He knew, too, that if he wanted to take advantage of such naiveté, it would not have been difficult. How ardent and generous a lover she would be! Pure passion was in her nature, and the thought of it sent a tremor of excitement through him, making him cling to her more closely. But such delights of the flesh would only be for a time. When reality came crashing down, she would despise him as much as he despised himself for such thoughtlessness. And he wanted so much more from her than a meaningless tryst. He wanted her heart and soul, as he would give her his, and only through complete honesty and trust could they achieve such a union. Agonizing as it was to do, he pulled away from the kiss. Leaning his forehead against hers, breathing deeply to calm himself, it was a long moment before he spoke. At last, he took mastery of his voice.

"Will you spend the day with me?"

He knew from the look in her eyes, the warmth and longing he saw reflected there, that at that moment she would do most anything he asked. But somehow, he sensed a bit of uncertainty in her. Or was it fear? As overwhelmed as he himself was, he knew she must have been ten times as unnerved by what she was feeling. And just as he had thought only moments before, he realized that in some corner of her mind, there was a concern that his intentions were not honorable. He did not want her to think of dishonesty and wrong when she thought of him. He had come so far to win her affections, and he would not destroy it all now with mere selfishness.

"I have promised you. I won't have you against your will. I won't lead you astray. You have my word on it."

As though sealing the pact, he softly kissed her temple, and holding her close, he rested her head against his heart. He made his request again.

"Will you spend the day with me?"

She looked up at him. "What about the rehearsal?"

He shrugged. "Hmm." He smiled a little. "Well, it seems I have an all day business meeting, and you are spending the day rehearsing at home. At least, that is what my employees have heard." He leaned back to look at her, his eyes mischievous. "What do you think?"

She shook her head…but smiled. "I think you're an awful sinner, Henry Shaw."

He smiled back, and he was greatly tempted to kiss her again. But something caused him to look out of the corner of his eye. Something told him they were being observed. And a slight glance away from them let him see two of the workers watching them, obviously enjoying the sight of two people in each other's arms. He stepped back slightly from her, re-establishing something of formality in their being together, but he could not resist bringing her hand up to his lips, kissing it. Then he took her hand in his own, and hurried away with her.

Chapter 18
"Romance"

Driving along, his eye continually looked to her. The corner of his mouth rose up at the shy way she wouldn't look at him. But it was a different expression she wore now. Shyness, but not fear. If he didn't know better, he'd say she was blushing. He would have liked her to be beside him, leaning softly against his side. But he could sense her uncertainty. She wasn't sure what to say or do, despite the fact that she'd just been in his arms.

Her naiveté only made her more endearing, and it was all he could do not to stop the car right then and there. He might have moved close to her, to look in her eyes, to gently brush his fingers across the flush of her cheeks. He longed to press his lips to her skin, moving slowly, softly brushing light kisses on her forehead and nose…her sweet little mouth. But he kept those impulses in check, at least for now. There were better places for romance. Pulling to the side of the road…that seemed so juvenile, though it was very tempting. If she'd been less important to him, he would have done it without a thought or a care. But she wasn't a fling…a moment in time that he was killing. As though needing to assure her, and himself, he settled for gently reaching out to take her hand. It evoked a shy and tender smile from her, and for the moment, that was pleasure enough.

* * * * *

The Field Museum of Natural History.

Typically speaking, it wasn't the kind of place he would've chosen to court a woman. But then, she was no ordinary girl. He knew that her curious little mind needed to blossom. And maybe in touching her mind, he could touch her soul as well.

At the bottom steps of the building, she stood rooted to one spot, staring up at the huge stone facade. Her eyes were large. "What is this place?"

He just grinned. "The kind of place that fits you to a tee." Taking her arm, he led her up the steps.

As he'd suspected, she was fascinated by the Egyptian mummies and dinosaur skeletons, and all the other artifacts the museum housed. Too fascinated, in a manner of speaking. She hardly looked at him at all, and when she did it was when she asked one of her multitude of questions, which he tried his best to answer.

Finding Grace

He knew that seeing all these things was hardly enough. They might have done for the moment, but he wanted to do more. He imagined taking her with him to far off places...to London, Rome, or Paris. Places that were tangible, and not just some collection of things behind glass. But he kept those thoughts locked securely in his mind, for he knew if he suggested such desires now, she might think him a dreaming romantic fool. And it would be foolish to express such wild wishes, for their bond was only at its start. Perhaps in time, he could express such desires to her. But for the moment, he would have to be content as they were. And contentment was a small kiss he would steal in the shadows of the hall. Or the loving way she leaned against him, sometimes without seeming to realize she was doing it. Just being with her, he was so happy. It had been so long since he'd known such a feeling of peace, and he hated the thought that at the end of the day, they would have to part.

But he didn't want to dwell on those thoughts. He'd had enough of cynicism. And thinking of that, he swiftly took her by the hand after hours spent in the stillness of the hall. She gave a little smile at the way he seemed to rush along.

"Where are we going now?"

He looked back at her, delight in his features. "I think we should get some fresh air. It's a little stuffy in here, don't you think? And sunshine is good for the soul."

As they came out of the building, he turned to her, and she to him. It moved him to see her that way, her face full of joy and love. It was the soft kind of expression he'd so longed to see, and he leaned forward, anticipating a kiss. But suddenly she darted away, and the next thing he knew, she went sliding down the brass railing of the museum steps. She landed soundly on her feet at the bottom, where she waited for him with a grin. As he came down to meet her he wore an amused smile, shaking his head.

"Sometimes I forget that you're only seventeen."

She just shrugged innocently. "Alice always said our inner child should never die, and mine is alive and well."

When he came to her side he couldn't resist taking her hand, pressing his lips to her palm. He would have preferred something more, but he could see how her cheeks turned a lovely shade of pink at his caress, even though she didn't pull away.

One little step at a time, he reminded himself.

He linked her arm with his, walking away towards the lushness of Grant Park. The sun was so warm, the air so pure. He knew that she wasn't defined just by her brilliant mind, but by her earthy nature. She may have loved all that the city had to offer, but she needed to see the green of trees and smell the scent of grass. The park was the best he could offer her, though he was quite certain she would be content anywhere if she had to be. She was young, and despite being knuckled about by life, she was still impressionable. He studied her as they walked by the newly built Buckingham Fountain, which she was staring at with fascinated eyes. The fountain hadn't been officially opened yet, and was not turned on, but her inner child was at play again as she climbed up to walk along the edge. It was the contrast between her innocence and intelligence that made him watch her so. As she had done so often, he was struck by a remark she made…one that revealed her intellect.

"This looks a little like the fountain at the Palace of Versailles…built by Louis the Fourteenth."

He smiled. "How would you know about that?"

"Jack showed me pictures of the palace. I would love to go to Paris some day."

Taking her hand to help her down, they walked to the park. From a vendor they bought food and drinks, and sought refuge under a tree while the cool lake breeze drifted softly. While she sat with her back against the tree trunk, he stretched out beside her, resting his head on his arms. He thought about resting his head in her lap. It would have been delightful if she would've run her fingers through his hair. But that kind of affection seemed a bit too daring, so he settled for just being close to her. And he thought about what she'd said.

"Why Paris?"

It was a moment before she replied. "Jack used to write to me about it. He said it was the prettiest place he'd ever seen. He told me about the Eiffel Tower, and the River Seine. And that shopping street…I can't remember the name."

"The Champs-Elysees," he answered. "The most beautiful avenue in the world, so they say. I wasn't in the city long enough to find out."

Her voice was low, a little sad. "I wish I could see it, and a lot of other things out there. But I don't suppose I ever will."

He moved forward to rest his chin on her knee. That didn't seem like too much of a liberty. "Never say never," he replied.

You and I will go there someday, he thought, but he didn't say so out loud.

"Think of all you've done on your own. Leaving home, finding your brother…catching me, hook line and sinker." He smiled when he glanced at her from the corner of his eye, seeing how she shook her head, which only amused him all the more. "I'd say you've done well. So traveling to Paris? It doesn't sound so far-fetched to me."

Turning his head toward her, he saw her watching him. He moved close to her, sitting up. Their faces were nearly touching. He leaned in closer, his eyes full of fire, his pulse increasing its tempo in anticipation. But she backed away. Not much, but just enough to give him pause. And it hurt a little. It was the second time she'd avoided his kiss, and he had to wonder why. His look was puzzled.

"Is something wrong?"

She shifted her eyes. "No…Well, yes. I mean, I'm not sure."

His look was curious. "There is something troubling you. I can see it in your eyes." He paused, waiting for a reply, but she turned away and wouldn't look at him. He sensed that she feared saying what was on her mind. But he wanted her trust, no matter what the confession might be, or how it might affect him. Gently he reached his hand to her cheek, turning her face so she would have to look at him. "Tell me."

It was a moment before she answered, and reluctantly, it seemed. "I'm not sure about all this."

His expression grew solemn, his voice pained. "Why?"

Was she rejecting him already? Did she have no faith in him at all? Then, as if to answer, she reached up to touch her hand to his cheek.

"It's not that I don't like you. I do, more than anything." She dropped her hand, casting her eyes down. "But I'm worried what people will think if they see us together."

He shrugged. "Who cares what they think? They don't know us."

"Maybe they don't know me. But they know you. And if they see us being sweet on each other, I know exactly what they'll think. They'll figure I'm just...well, another notch on your bedpost."

His mouth fell slightly open, and he gave an indignant snort. "That's ridiculous. How could anyone look at you and believe that? And if I ever heard someone say such a thing, I'd wring their neck."

Now she smiled, amused by his chivalry. But still she shook her head, and that troubled him even more.

"People will figure what they want to figure. And I don't want people telling lies about me."

He looked down, afraid to meet her eyes. He was fearful she was ready to cast him off. The thought of being pushed away, when he'd tried so hard to win her, was nearly too much to bear. The hurt became a lump in his throat, briefly stealing his voice.

"Henry? Can I ask you something, and will you tell me the truth?"

He could only manage a small murmur in reply. Then her question stunned him back to life.

"Am I just the next name on your list? Is that all you really want from me?"

His head came up, his eyes meeting hers, the light in them almost frantic. "God no, why would you think that?"

Now she gave him a skeptical look, her eyes holding a light of concern. "I don't mean to upset you by asking, but you can't blame me for thinking about it."

"Don't think about it," he said quickly. "They meant nothing to me. I didn't care about them the way I care about you." He wanted to kiss her deeply, to express to her the intensity of his feelings. But he thought for a moment of what she'd said, the revelation of her fears. It was true that not so long ago, he might have been satisfied with a meaningless romp. And she was aware of it, clever thing that she was. But that was then, and he wanted her to be sure of it.

"I'm not the way I used to be." He took her hand, clutching it tightly, pressing his lips to the soft warmth of her palm and fingers. "But I'll admit, I'll never be a saint." A moment passed, and he sighed while he held her hand in both his own. "So what will I do? Deny myself completely?"

He felt her draw close, resting her other small hand over his. "Just when people are watching."

If only in a way, he became content. At least she wasn't being *too* cruel. He was allowed to give her his affection, but on her terms. Terms of discretion, which he hadn't followed since he'd courted his wife. It made him smile with amusement.

"To think of me…being discreet about a relationship. If that got out, my bad reputation would be ruined forever."

To that she smirked, and leaned her head against his shoulder.

That evening when he drove her home, he was careful to look about for prying eyes when he pulled up in the driveway. He sighed as he looked at her sitting beside him, and he forced himself to look away. The pull of her was so strong, he feared he might take her in his arms and kiss her the way he truly wanted to, breaking his own vow of being a gentleman. His sense of self-discipline was greatly tested…but it was not broken, especially when she spoke in her gentle way, reminding him of her innocence.

"I'll see you at noon, then?" she asked. "Tomorrow?"

He looked at his watch. "That's nineteen hours, twenty-four minutes, and some number of seconds," he declared bitterly.

"An awfully long time, don't you think?" His face grew dark and morose. But a moment later he was taken by surprise when she moved quickly, taking his face in her hands, kissing him full on the lips. It was so sudden he hardly had time to react. Her soft "Good night" he just managed to hear, and when he reached for her it was too late, for she was already gone.

* * * * *

She hurried up the steps into the house, a giddy feeling rushing all through her. Coming in, she leaned back against the door with a sigh of joy. She felt positively wild. She'd lost control of her facial muscles…a smile breaking out despite her weak attempts against it. Bringing her hands up, she tried to gain some sense but found it impossible. She closed her eyes, taking a deep breath.

Just get on upstairs before someone sees you. Then you can giggle like a fool to your heart's content.

She passed the living room, and saw Jack and Alice on the sofa. They were speaking softly to one another, sharing and discussing a book. They were smiling at one another. There was nothing strange in that. And yet, they had a glow about them she could not describe. She approached with a wary step, but was smiling.

"You two look very happy. What's going on?" She looked from one to the other. Alice noticed her first, looking up…and there was a dreamy smile on her face.

"Oh, nothing much. We're just sitting here thinking of baby names."

Grace took in a little breath. Her voice grew soft with wonder. "Are you serious? When will it be?"

Alice's face was all aglow. "Around the first of January, give or take a few weeks. What a wonderful way to start the New Year, don't you think?" She looked at Jack, her eyes growing misty. He was looking back at her intently.

"We've waited so long for this."

She didn't hesitate in rushing forward to congratulate them both. "I'm so happy for the two of you. But I think I'll go on up and leave you alone to celebrate." She kissed both of them on the cheeks. "Good night, mommy and daddy. I'm so excited!"

She ran upstairs, wondering how life could possibly get any sweeter.

Happily she drew a bubble bath, and relaxing back in the steaming water, she looked up at nothing in particular, just thinking deeply and dreamily.

Oh, to be in love! What a blessing to know such contentment. She might have wondered at the loss of her senses, but at that moment, such caution seemed a faint whisper in the corner of her mind. She imagined seeing him in the morning, how he would smile in his little way. They would look at each other, knowing they shared a little secret. Of course, they would have to pretend that nothing had changed. But they would both know the truth, and she wondered how they would get through the day without running to each others' arms.

She was humming to herself as she slipped into her pajamas and got into bed, pulling the sheet up over her, for it was too warm for a blanket. Not that she would have needed it, for she felt warm and tingly all over. All of life seemed in order, all of life seemed right. She was happy, and those around her were equally so. How incredible it was that by the start of the New Year, Jack and Alice would be parents, and she would be an aunt. The thought made her sigh with wonder. And yet, a dark thought crept into all that was bright.

Would her parents ever see their grandchild?

Would Jack try to make amends, even for the sake of his child? And would Mama and Daddy even want to make up?

She bent her head, folding her hands to pray for a miracle.

* * * * *

She stood in front of the stage microphone for the very first time, her heart drumming madly beneath her ribs. She tried to swallow, but the lump seemed firmly lodged in her throat. At her left was the new stage manager, Bill, watching her expectantly. The music began, flowing to a crescendo, leading to her cue...and from her lips came only a tiny whisper. The music stopped. A murmur went through the room, and Bill approached her, his eyes quizzical.

"Is something wrong?"

She shrugged, trying to smile. "I'm so nervous, my voice is stuck in my throat. My legs are like Jello."

He gave her a kind pat on the shoulder.

"Just relax. You're doing swell."

He turned to the band, cueing them to begin again.

Again, the music rose, and her cue came...and as before, her voice was barely audible. Her shoulders fell, and that same murmur was heard again. She wanted to run and hide behind the curtain. She felt tears stinging her eyes. Looking about, she searched for Henry, longing for the comfort of his presence, but he was conducting business in his office. She was alone, even with the band sitting there in front of her. But then, a voice came from among the men. It was Toby, who stood and came to the stage. With an athletic leap up to the platform…forgoing the stairs altogether…he came to her side, approaching as though a hero to her rescue. He glanced back at the band.

"I think we need to try something new, boys."

He leaned down to put his trumpet on the floor, and rising with a little smile, he gently took Grace by the hands.

"Why Miss Grace, I do believe you're trembling." Leaning slightly towards her, he whispered…"I have that effect on women."

From down among the band, several of the boys good-naturedly jeered him. Pete, one of the guitar players, cupped his hands around his mouth and stood up. "Boo! Get that idiot off the stage! His act stinks!"

The boys in the band laughed, but Toby seemed to pay them no mind.

"Shut your pie holes, all of you." He turned to Bill. "Why don't I stand with her? Have her look at me now and then, instead of just the crowd."

"But that will look pretty dumb come show time, won't it? You, standing there next to her, for no particular reason."

"But I'll be playing, and the lights will be down. They won't even be looking at me. And as long as she gives a little look out to the audience once in a while, no one will be the wiser. What do you think?"

While Bill stood rubbing his chin, thinking, Grace stood close to Toby. She loved the idea of him being there. Then she wouldn't have to face the crowd alone. It would be almost like having Jack beside her for support. She turned to Bill.

"I would feel so much better if Toby stood next to me. I want to try it. Please, Bill?"

He shrugged. "Okay, Miss Grace, we'll give it a shot. What's there to lose?" He cued the band, and the music began.

As Toby played, Grace kept her eyes moving between him and the lyric sheet, and when her cue came, the words of the songs began flowing from her. They were soft at first, as they had been before. But quickly her voice found its strength. It was like being there with Jack and Alice, as the lyrics flowed out with smoothness and beauty.

At the end of the song her eyes closed, and she kept them that way for a moment more. Then she heard the applause, and she took in a cleansing breath of air, full of relief and happiness. Something made her turn her head to her left, and standing there behind the curtain, she saw Henry in the shadows, watching. Even with his face in shadow, she could see his smile. She longed to run to him, to throw her arms around him. A feeling of joy coursed through her. For a moment she was lost in her thoughts, until Toby's voice brought her back.

"That was excellent," he said with a smile. "See what happens when you have me around? Now let's do something more upbeat, to keep the good mood up."

She wanted to go on. But then a troubling thought came to her. Would the other acts in the club think she was hogging the stage and the spotlight? She would not blame them if they thought that, and it made her shake her head at Toby's suggestion.

"I don't want to take over the stage. I should let the others work up here for a while."

He balked at that, grinning. "The stage is yours." He turned to Bill. "Isn't that right?"

Bill nodded. "The boss wants you to work here. The others work downstairs, in a private stage area. This is where Victoria used to work, so now it's where *you* work."

"But the other day, I saw the girls out here practicing," she said. "Are you sure I won't be invading their space?"

He shook his head. "Not at all. They were just out here because they knew Victoria was gone. But now they know you're here, so they're back on their regular routine. And everything is as it should be. So let's do something fun. Do you know 'My Blue Heaven'?"

She shook her head, and he smiled.

"Well then, I'll sing it for you." He took her lightly in his arms, leading her in a dance as he sang the song. The words were sweet, his moves and manner playful. She smiled along with him as he led her and sang.

Day is ending, birds are wending
Back to the shelter of,
Each little nest they love

Nightshades falling, lovers calling
What makes the world go round?
Nothing but love

When whippoorwills call, and evening is nigh
I hurry to my Blue Heaven

I turn to the right A little white light
Will lead you to my Blue Heaven

A smiling face, a fireplace,
A cozy room
A little nest that nestles where roses bloom

Just Molly and me and baby makes three
We're happy in my Blue Heaven

A smiling face, a fireplace,
A cozy room
A little nest that nestles where the roses bloom
Just Molly and me and baby makes three
We're happy in my Blue Heaven

She was laughing a little as he sang to her. His voice was so pleasant to the ear, his way so warm and enjoyable. It reminded her a little of Jack. She was quite caught up in the happy moment, and it seemed he was just as lost in the fun. Then the voice of Henry came from the side of the stage. His tone was calm, but it was firm...and somewhat serious.

"Toby," he said. And at that, the pair stopped, turning to look at him. "I think you should get back to work."

"Right, boss." Turning to Grace, Toby gave her a little smile and a wink. He hurried to pick up his trumpet from the floor. They started another song she had amongst her lyric sheets, and the flow of rehearsals resumed once again.

After they resumed their work, she didn't see much more of Henry. The day had been busy, both of them going about their business. Her main focus had been on getting the words of her songs into her head.

What a lovely day it had been, with Toby there especially. He was such a good soul, so kind and generous. He loved being the center of attention, if his showing off was any indication. She even wondered if maybe he was a little sweet on her, especially when he asked her out again.

"Why don't you let me take you to dinner?" he asked. "We're partners now. Why don't we get to know each other a little better?"

She blushed, flattered by his invitation. But she shook her head. "That's really nice of you...but I already have a sweetheart."

For a moment he seemed disappointed, and she hoped she hadn't hurt his feelings. But he smiled sweetly. "Well it's good to hear you've got someone. Whoever he is, he's a very lucky man."

She smiled...and her thoughts drifted back to Henry. She wished it had been he who had danced with her, and sung to her so sweetly. But he had been true to his word and kept his distance. Now that the day was done, she wondered if that might change in some way. She knew he felt as she did...that he wanted to be with her, as much as she wanted to be with him. If only they could defy the rules and be with each other as they wished. No fear of scandal, or judgment. If only he could be her husband.

The thought came to her so suddenly, it nearly took her breath. He hadn't so much as hinted at such a union, though she had seen such love and desire in his eyes, she did not doubt his feelings. Then it occurred to her that he might not want to be married again, even to her...not after the failure of his first marriage. Such a wound was deep, and not always healed, even with the passage of time. Then, of course, there were her own worries and fears. Marriage had always seemed like a life-long prison sentence to her. Now, she felt a great temptation to gamble on it...to gamble on love, and hope that he would dare to do it too. But she would not demand it of him. She would let things be as fate intended, and trust in time.

* * * * *

As things were winding down for the day, Thomas came to her.

"The boss wants to talk to you."

Her eyes widened a little. A pulse of anxiety ran through her, but she tried to appear calm as she went towards the stairs, going to the office above. She was not in the hall alone. There were two gentleman in the office with Henry...she saw them talking to him as she stood outside the open door. But they might have been invisible, for he glanced at her briefly, and the warmth in that tiny moment spoke volumes. He was speaking to his partners, but clearly it was each other they were both thinking of. She waited several moments, and when the two men left, she saw him rise from his chair and come towards her with flashing eyes. She took a brave step forward into his office, careful not to stray too far beyond the doorway. Before he spoke, he looked about. It seemed they were quite alone, but still they were cautious, and he did not touch her. He stood just before her, almost nose to nose. He inclined his head forward, his voice a whisper.

"I've missed you."

A tremble of excitement seized, her face flushing with warmth. She was surprised at her own ability to maintain her voice. "I've missed you, too."

He sighed in frustration. "When can we be alone again? Really alone, and not like this. Stealing a moment, wondering who might come along."

She sighed in return. "I don't know."

She felt his fingers, a light touch, on her jaw. He lifted her chin, and she gazed into his eyes, seeing how they sparkled with mischief. He was plotting something. She could see it in his look. And she gave him a little smile, which he returned as he revealed his thoughts.

"Maybe we can meet somewhere, just the two of us."

After a quiet moment, he leaned back to study her face...and his smile deepened at seeing her cheeks flushed with color.

"You are blushing. Are you thinking of being with me, but afraid to say so out loud?" She did not answer, and it seemed to amuse him all the more. "It is not a sin to enjoy being with someone."

"I know," she said softly. "But being near someone, and not being able to show them how you feel..." She sighed in frustration. She knew she should not, but she felt drawn to him more than ever. In a moment, she was leaning against him, pressing her cheek against the warmth of his chest.

His arms went around her, his cheek firm against her head. "I know we promised to be sensible. But this may be the most difficult promise I've ever kept."

She sighed, feeling his heart beat against her ear. "There must be something we can do."

He nodded. "I'll come up with something. I'll leave you a letter when I think of it." They lingered together for as long as they dared, but all too soon they knew they had to part, at least from each other's arms. To remain in an embrace was too risky. And yet, that element of danger only heightened their longing for one another. As she turned to go, he took hold of her hand and pulled her back quickly, placing a brief but heated kiss on her lips.

"Go, quick," he said, his voice a low whisper. She nodded, smiling, and hurried away.

* * * * *

On the street outside, she started walking towards the stairs of the El. She knew she could easily ride home with Henry. He would want her to, and she would have relished the chance to be so alone and close with him. But she had decided it would not be wise, as they were trying to maintain a sense of decorum. The time on her way home, alone, would be a quiet time, to think and reflect on her day. As she reached the stairs, she was stopped by the sound of a familiar voice…and it chilled her to hear it.

"Gracie," he said.

She turned slowly, and there he was. Charlie, standing with his hat in his hands, looking nervous at best. It was not the expression she knew so well on his face. There was something forlorn about his look. But she did not dwell on what his appearance was. All she knew was that he was standing in front of her, when he should have been far away from here, and she felt the urge to flee. He must have sensed it, for he spoke almost instantly.

"Don't run away. I promise, I won't do anything. I just want to talk to you, that's all. Please, give me five minutes."

She looked at him, seeing his sad eyes. She could not help but pity him, despite what she knew lurked under the surface. And part of her wanted to hear what he had to say. If anything, he owed her an explanation. So she sighed, and relented to his request.

"All right Charlie. There's a little coffee shop across the street. We can go there and talk. I'll give you a little time, but if you try anything, I swear I'll call someone for help. The police, maybe. Or my brother. He would love to have some words with you, or worse." She walked past him across the street, and he followed quickly.

* * * * *

"The church set me up at the YMCA," he said, sipping a cup of coffee. "That's where I've been staying since I got here. I just couldn't make myself go home."

She sat across from him at a little table, watching him as he talked. He looked a little thinner, she realized. The last time she'd seem him, she'd been too rushed in her actions to notice it. There was a change in his face…a look that seemed desperate and gloomy.

Somehow it troubled her more to see that, rather than the angry side of his personality. In its way, there was something darker about his gloom. But she tried not to dwell on it. He had come here to talk, and she wished him to be done with it.

"Charlie," she said gently, "Why are you still here? If it's to make me change my mind, I'm sorry, but it's not going to happen. I'm happy here, and that's not going to change."

"But I want to talk to you about the night I proposed," he said quickly, before she could stop him. "I was angry. I was hurt. You don't know what it was like for me, growing up with Uncle Robert. I had all this anger inside, but I wasn't supposed to express it. I was supposed to believe that God meant for everything to happen to me, and that I should accept my suffering with humility."

He was rambling...and making her nervous...but she let him go on.

"Sometimes, with all that anger bottled up, I just lose my temper. But I didn't mean to talk to you that way. If I could take it back, I would in a second."

She wanted to believe him. And she was sure that somewhere in his soul, he really did regret the things he had said. But what did that matter now? Their lives were set on different paths. And she realized that this was the point where they needed to part, perhaps forever.

"I forgive you Charlie, for everything. I think all we can do now is move on. I think it's the best thing for both of us."

He looked down at his hands, his voice low. "I was still hoping we could go on together." He turned to her, placing his hand on hers. "I love you, Gracie. I always have, ever since we were kids. You were always the one good thing in my life. Like my own little angel."

She pulled her hand from his...his touch sending fearful tremors up her arm.

"I'm no angel, Charlie. I'm not perfect. No one is. Besides, there are plenty of other girls out there. And you have a lot to offer them."

A light of hope seemed to light his eyes.

"Oh, I see what this is about now. You're thinking about my inheritance. That's something else I have to talk to you about. There was a rumor going that I only wanted to marry you to get my hands on my father's property. But that's not true. You're the only woman I've ever wanted to be with."

All of these revelations were too much. And now she feared that if she told him what was in her own heart, he might not be able to accept it. But if she did not tell him, he would only be lingering on. No, the best thing to do was to tell him the truth, and hope that this time, he would understand and do what was best for the both of them.

"I'm sorry Charlie. This has to be goodbye." She tried to say more, but could not find the words. She rose to her feet, and though she heard him say her name pleadingly, she hurried out of the restaurant before he could stop her.

Chapter 19
"Anticipation"

Sitting at his desk at home, Henry held his pen over a sheet of paper, prepared to scribble out the details of a secret rendezvous. They would meet at the Oriental Theatre...a grand movie house, where once the lights went down, they could sit as close as they pleased and few would notice them. And yet as he held his pen in his hand, something kept him from writing the words.

He had so anticipated the night to come. He imagined sitting beside her, feeling her slight figure leaning warmly against him. Holding her hand, so warm and soft in his own. Kissing her. He felt a deep, wild thrill at the thought.

And then a great sense of shame.

It was that shame that kept him from writing, and he put the pen down, folded his hands together, and leaned his mouth against his knuckles with a deep sigh.

Had he not promised her, and himself, that they would keep their relationship tame? Yet here he was, about to plan out a secret meeting, while his wicked mind conjured up thoughts of the two of them entwined in each other's arms, sharing heated kissed and whispers...all while in the dark, hoping not to be found out. Grace was not like the women he had known before, and yet he was treating her as he had treated them... thinking of himself first, of his own burning needs and desires. He had made a promise of chivalry to her, and already he found himself near to breaking it. And what galled him more was the idea that she might allow it. He had so admired her strength and stubbornness...and her resistance to him had been proof of it. But despite her strength, she was young and vulnerable. Sweet words, soft affections...after her initial struggle, she had given in to those temptations quite willingly, and he had so delighted in every moment. But therein lay the rub.

She was a pure woman, a good woman, better than any he had ever known. Better than he deserved. He would not treat her like a cheap plaything. He swore he would not, and as he vowed it to himself, he rose up from his chair to pace the floor, as yet another troubling thought came to him.

How would he keep his word? He wanted to keep it. He wanted to be a good and decent man for her. And yet, it was so difficult to restrain himself when she was near. His weakness had been proven earlier that day, when they had embraced in his office. She had initiated it, which he had not minded at all. But then he had taken it a step further by kissing her, which was proof that neither of them were quite in control of their feelings for one another. There had to be a way to solve their dilemma. For one wild and thoughtless moment, he entertained the notion of just running away from her. He could flee temptation, and it would free her from his clutches. But then he realized such an idea was not only cowardly...it was utterly ridiculous.

He could not leave her, ever. She was the woman he wanted, and giving her up was not an option. How would that look to her, to have him wild for her one moment, and then abandoning her the next? No, he would not go the route of a coward. He sighed deeply, and thought, *If only I could make her my wife.*

The idea hit him like ice water, shocking him with its suddenness.

His *wife*? For a moment the word petrified him, as it had for so long. The idea of committing himself to someone, body and soul, for the rest of his days? He had tried it once, and failed. He shook his head, trying to dislodge the whole stupid theme from his brain.

But it would not go. And the more he tried to fight it, the more his resistance to it was worn away. His *wife*. How he had loathed the word for so long. But as it was churning again and again there in his head, he began to partner the word with the person who had occupied his thoughts for weeks. He began to imagine how it would be to spend every moment of his life with her. It would never be boring, that was for sure and for certain. And thinking of her, he marveled at the idea that he could be the only man ever to have her. She would be his, and only his, and the thought seemed so heavenly. Almost too heavenly, it seemed. What if she refused him, as she had refused Charlie? But nearly in an instant, he banished that idea from his thoughts. She loved him. He could see it in her eyes, could feel it in her kiss and her touch. They were meant to be together.

To know he had found his mate was a revelation that words could not describe. Yet he knew their path to happiness was still paved with stones. Her tender age, her admired reputation in the circle of the club, her brother...all were potential landmines, and had to be handled delicately. And as to marriage, it was something he vowed not to take lightly this time.

Fools rush in, he reminded himself...and he vowed *not* to be a fool with this second chance.

* * * * *

She hadn't "consulted" with Jane in quite a while. The whirlwind of activity she'd been in lately had left her little time for her mentor, but now, it seemed that a perfect opportunity had come along. The night was quiet. She was calm, and yet too excited to go to bed. The day at the club and her progress there...the glorious moments alone with Henry. Then, to come home and learn about the baby. All of it was too much to allow sleep. She was selective about one thought...that of Charlie. She wanted to erase him from her mind, preferring to only dwell on happy things. So she brought out her well worn copy of *Jane Eyre* opening it to one of the loveliest of scenes...Jane and Edward, newly engaged and deliriously happy. The words held a new and deeper meaning for her, as she understood at last what it felt like to be so much in love. She was sitting against the pillows, reading, when there came a soft rap on the door.

"Come in," she said, raising her head, and she smiled when Alice appeared.

"I saw your light under the door. I thought I would come in for a minute."

"I'm glad you did." She put her book down as Alice came to sit beside her on the bed. She smiled at her. "How are you feeling, little mother?"

A great beam of delight came to Alice's face. Her hand came to rest on her belly.

"I'm wonderful at the moment," she replied. "I was sick those few times in the morning, and even though I hoped it was good news, I was scared to believe it. You'll never know how shocked I was when the doctor confirmed it was a baby." She smiled and chuckled at the memory. "I know it won't be long now before I'm dealing with swollen feet and backaches, and all the other joys of pregnancy." She paused, letting out a little sigh, and yet she smiled still. "But even that, I don't think I'll mind, especially when I think of the end result."

Grace leaned against her sister-in-law, sharing in her joy, while deep in the depths of her own. She let out her own little sound of contentment, which Alice took note of.

"You sound as happy as I am," she declared. "And I, being a clever creature, have to wonder if my suspicions are correct. You are a woman in love, aren't you?"

Grace nodded, and Alice tilted her head in a little triumph. "I saw it on your face when you came home. So will we be planning a wedding as well as a baby shower?"

Sitting a little straighter, Grace's joy lessened. "I don't figure that far ahead. I'm almost afraid to."

"Because of the other women?"

She nodded. "I want to believe him when he says he cares for me. But I'm no fool. I don't know much, but I know that all men aren't loyal like my brother. And I can't help wondering. Did Henry say the same things to me that he said to all the others?"

Alice put an arm around her, drawing her close for comfort. "You know, sometimes you just have to go on faith."

She sighed again. "Maybe. Or maybe I should just enjoy it while it lasts." Now the sunshine came back, warming her expression. "He does make me happy."

Alice smiled. "You deserve that, sis." She kissed the top of her head and withdrew, bidding her good night.

"Good night," Grace replied. She watched Alice go, and as the door closed behind her, she leaned back against the pillows again. Burrowing down a little under the sheet, she opened her book again. She came to the last words of the chapter, and read...

My future husband was becoming to me my whole world; and more than the world: almost my hope of heaven. He stood between me and every thought of religion, as an eclipse intervenes between man and the broad sun. I could not, in those days, see God for His creature: of whom I had made an idol...

Finding Grace

She knew it was silly to imagine Henry as her husband. But then again, it was just that...her imagination. Anything was possible there. And besides, who knew what the future might bring? Stranger things had happened.

And I'm living proof, she said to herself.

* * * * *

A memory came to her as she stood behind the stage curtain, watching the dancers in their glory. Not so long ago, she had been wandering where she did not belong, seeing these people prepare for their work, and she had tried to imagine what it was like to be among them. Now she knew the excitement of seeing people she was coming to know as family, in their element on the stage and bringing the full crowd to their feet at the end of each performance. Would she have that power over the people, when she took the stage in only five days? She might have been more frightened, were it not for the thought that Toby would be there. Sweet, wonderful man. With his constant spirit and encouragement, he was quickly becoming a dear friend to her. If only Henry could see it that way.

This morning, when she'd been on the stage with Toby during rehearsal, she'd seen Henry standing as he had before, in the shadows behind the curtain. But his face had not been soft and loving. His look was troubled. Maybe even a little angry. She didn't understand why he looked so, until she was sitting at the edge of the stage, and he came to stand just before her. His face had softened. He even smiled a little, as he talked to her about her work. They were both all politeness and civility, as they had to be in the public eye. It seemed he was trying even harder now to be a gentleman. In the brief moments they'd stolen earlier that day, he'd told her that he'd changed his mind about a secret meeting. It was too risky, he declared. And though she was disappointed, he had promised to think of something more sensible. That put her at ease, knowing that he was being so considerate.

As he stood there in front of the stage, he asked her how she felt about her upcoming debut, and if she thought she was ready.

"I think I'll be fine. Everyone is so sweet, just like a big family. And you're here, even when I can't see you. I know you're around, thinking of me." He smiled at that, and she returned the gesture. "Toby will be next to me for support, so I'm not as scared as I was."

She did not see it at first, but his expression darkened. "Hmm," he said, low and almost bitterly. That little sound made her look up. His mouth was set in that familiar line, the one he wore when he wasn't happy. A womanly instinct told her what that meant.

"I think there's a green-eyed monster in the room." She kept her tone casual, for who knew what ears were listening? But she knew *he* was, and if he needed soothing, she would give it. "Slay that beast, white knight...Because there's only one Lord for this Lady." She looked in his eyes, reassuring him with a smile.

After a long moment, she finally saw the corner of his mouth turn up, and she felt a great triumph in his reply.

"One Lord for the Lady, and one Lady for the Lord."

"That's right," she declared. "Now go, good sir, and let me be."

He seemed reluctant, but left her side. She could sense the resistance in him, for she felt the same pull of frustration in her own breast. If not for watching eyes, she could easily have fallen into his arms and reassured him of her love in a much more pleasant way. And she knew he would have done the same. But he was gone from her sight in a few moments, and she hardly saw him the rest of the day.

Now it was the middle of a busy evening, and she wondered where he was. Likely he was mingling among his guests, shaking hands and greeting familiar faces as he always did on busy nights. She longed for a look at him, and moved from the backstage to the hall, where she stood looking for his face among the crowd. She did not see him, but she smiled when she saw Jack and Alice at a table. They waved when they saw her, and she went to them. She kissed each of them on the cheek and sat with them, listening to the music. The selection was a slow one, a selection of stringed instruments and piano that was romantic and soft. As she sat there, listening, she wished that Henry would come and ask for a dance. She was still not very good at dancing, having only done it a few times, but she knew he was strong and could lead her, and the thought of being in his arms was thrilling. If only he would come to her. But still she did not see him, and disappointment filled her through.

Then a cheerful voice came near, and she looked up to see Toby at their table.

"Hi Gracie. Won't you introduce me to your company?"

She smiled, and though still longing for Henry's company, she was happy to see her friend there. She introduced him, and he shook hands with Jack. Taking Alice's hand in both of his, he greeted her warmly.

"A pleasure, truly. Beauty runs in both your families, I see."

Alice grinned, a knowing look in her eyes. "You're a smooth one, aren't you?"

He flashed a rascal's smile. "I was born way before whipped topping," he replied. "Can I have your sister for a minute? I'm on a break, but I think I can get one more dance in before I go back. Do you mind?"

Jack just shrugged. Alice nodded, but Grace hesitated for a moment. She looked once more for Henry, but a moment later Toby was leading her out to the dance floor, and she felt she had to turn her attention to him to keep from hurting his feelings. She smiled politely as he moved with her, helping to watch that she didn't miss her steps, and she did enjoy his light conversation and usual charm. But it was Henry she thought of, and she wondered where he could be. Surely he wasn't hiding. As the number ended, and she stood with Toby, applauding the band, she sighed. He looked at her, concerned.

"Are you all right?" he asked. "You look a little down. I didn't step on your feet, did I?"

She shook her head, trying to put on a happy face. "No, you didn't. You were just fine. And thanks for the dance. I think I'm getting pretty good at it."

He smiled, looking at his watch. "I better get back. I'll see you later, Gracie." He gave her hand an affectionate squeeze, and left her side.

Her smile fell away as he went. She turned to go back to the table. And as she did, she came eye to eye with Henry. Dressed in his best suit, he took her breath away, and she could not keep the deepest smile from coming across her face.

"And where have you been?" she asked.

"Around," he replied. "Watching my patrons enjoy themselves. Watching my lady dance with someone else, while I have to wander about shaking hands and putting on airs."

She smirked. "Jealous, are you?"

"I think we established that earlier."

"We did," she said. "And I told you there wasn't any reason to be. So should you ask me to dance, or should we stand here and talk about it?"

He did not ask her to dance. He simply took her hand and drew her to the floor. With his arms and hands guiding her, somewhat closer than they should have been, he seemed to be saying without words that she belonged to him, and no one else. Even though so many were around them, they seemed the only two in the whole world. In the circle of each other's arms, on the dance floor, they could be together, and for several glorious moments they savored the closeness of each other's company.

Words seemed incapable of expressing how it felt being held. And the way he was watching her, his eyes and smile full of fire, it seemed he felt the same. But in the back of her mind, she knew their heated expressions were on public display. Even in the whirl of romance, her better sense remained.

When the dance ended, and they stood giving applause, she took a breath to steady her nerves, so she might speak clearly. Still her tone was soft.

"Will you do something for me?"

He looked delighted, smirking in that way of his. "Maybe."

"I want you to find the prettiest girl in the room and dance with her."

His response was a shrug, and a cheeky grin. "If you insist." He took her hand as the next number began, but she rolled her eyes and withdrew from his grasp.

"I mean it, Henry. Find the prettiest girl. I know you're good at that. Dance with her, flirt with her. Put on a good show."

He looked baffled. "Are you serious?"

She nodded. It wasn't easy pushing him away, but it had to be done. "They all need to be fooled. And we're in show business, right? It's what we do."

Without waiting for a response, she turned towards the table. A sharp hurt rose in her breast. She tried to suppress the feeling, but it only dug itself deeper as she watched him do as she'd asked. Her manner was low as she sat there...the sting of jealousy biting bitterly into her heart. Jack and Alice came from the dance floor to sit with her, and both saw her morose expression.

"Well," said Jack. "You two looked mighty cozy out there. If you're trying to hide your romance, you're doing a hell of a lousy job."

She sighed. "That's why I sent him away."

Both Alice and Jack looked out and saw Henry with a petite little blond.

Alice snorted in disgust. "Who is that tramp?"

Grace couldn't resist a chuckle. Alice certainly had a way with words. "I don't know who she is."

Jack scoffed at such thoughtless behavior. "What a romantic," he sneered, "Flaunting other women right in front of you. If he were a real man, he would be shouting out to the world who his girl is. He wouldn't give a turkey what other people thought."

"I made him do it," Grace insisted. "It has to look like I'm no one particular. Just the girl he happened to dance with once, and that was it."

To that, Jack just shrugged. "If you say so."

"You know it, but you still look so down," Alice declared. "Are you really all right with the method to this madness?"

Grace sighed. "I suppose I have to be…but knowing it is one thing, and seeing it is another." For a long moment, she kept her eyes cast down, not wanting to look over and again and see Henry with someone else. Then, she took a deep breath and squared her shoulders.

"Maybe I'll do better with some fresh air," she declared, rising from her seat.

"Do you want us to come with you?" Alice asked.

But Grace just smiled and shook her head. "No, I'll be fine. I always do fine on my own."

Being careful to stay away from the dance floor, she made her way downstairs to the lobby, and outside to the sidewalk in front of the club. The street was calm and quiet, compared to the hustle and noise found inside. For several long minutes she walked up and down the sidewalk, looking at the lights and sometimes looking up at the summer sky that twinkled with bright stars. The serenity of the night calmed her, and she thought of Henry and what had occurred just now. And she shook her head at her own silliness.

He loves me, and no one else, she thought. *I see it in his eyes, and I felt it just now, in his arms. I owe him my trust.*

She wanted to trust him, as he had asked her to. She had seen in his expression that he did not want to hurt her…that he would rather have stayed with her, and only her. But she was aware that sometimes, the best was brought with great pain, and this it seemed was one of those times. She sighed, feeling the weight lift a little from her heart. When the night was over, he would certainly come to her and offer a comfort, perhaps an apology. And she smiled to herself then, thinking how she might tease him a little just for fun. It gave her spirit an uplift, and with fresh energy, she turned to go back inside.

As she reached for the door someone came out first. And when she looked up her breath caught. A figure appeared before her, one she had not thought to see again. And the look in his eyes struck her cold with fear.

"Charlie," she said, her voice a whisper. "Why are you here?"

Before she could ask more, he suddenly gripped her shoulders and pushed her back against the wall. Her eyes grew wide with fear.

"They've ruined you," he said.

Her voice squeaked. "Ruined me?"

"I saw you in there, Gracie. I saw you dance with those men. In this place. This evil place, full of sinners. You used to be such a good girl. What have they done to you?"

"No one has done anything to me." She wanted to be strong, but his face was intense and wild, and it struck her to the core with fear.

"Yes, they have," he insisted. "You're not who I thought you were. They've shown you their wicked ways." He backed away, shaking his head. He continued to slowly retreat, and as he moved from the light into the dark of the street, she saw him turn his back on her and disappear into the night.

Chapter 20
"Someone to Watch Over Me"

What was she to do?

Her hands shook a little as she opened the door and went back in, and though she tried to calm herself, the encounter with Charlie had left her shaken. His look had been so frightful, almost mad in its way, and now she just wanted to go home where she could escape to the security of her room...where she could think, and decide what to do. She did not want Jack to know, for if he found out he would be furious and might do something foolish. Henry would be just as angry if he knew, of that she was certain. No, neither of them could know. And as for Alice...well, it would only cause her to worry if she knew, and in her condition, stress was the last thing she needed. Somehow, she would deal with this herself. Maybe she could find a way to go to where Charlie was staying and talk some sense into him. There had to be a way to end this without anyone getting hurt.

She was looking back towards the door, thinking of Charlie, when she neared the stairs. In her mind, she was hoping not to run into Henry. If he saw her in this current state, he might ask one too many questions, and she might not be able to keep from hiding the truth. She turned toward the stairs. It was not Henry she saw, but Jack and Alice.

"There you are, baby sister. We were wondering if you got lost."

She just shook her head, trying to smile, but was hardly able to. They looked at her curiously as they came down the stairs, and she hoped they would associate the look on her face with the Henry incident. But Alice had always been able to read her better than almost anyone, and she knew something else was amiss.

"You're white as a sheet," she said. "What's wrong?"

"Nothing, really," Grace insisted. "I'll be fine."

"You're hands are shaking," Alice noted, taking Grace's hands in her own. "Jack, look at her." She looked worriedly at him, then at her again, and wanted an explanation. "Grace, what is it?"

Jack was staring at her, his eyes intense, and Alice was gripping her hands firmly. She knew she would have to say something, or they would never let her be until she did.

"I saw Charlie," she confessed.

Alice gasped, and Jack did what she knew he would. His eyes widened, his mouth opened, and he cried, "What? Where?" He looked ready to kill, but Grace just sighed.

"It doesn't matter right now," she said. "I just want to go home."

Alice nodded, as did Jack, and he hurried to open the door, ushering them out.

* * * * *

She was all wrong, and he felt it.

Even as Henry smiled at the feminine face before him, he couldn't keep himself from silently picking out all her faults. Too much makeup, for one thing, especially around the eyes. It made her look like a raccoon. Her breasts were flattened to make her look more waif-like...it was the style of the times, though he had never understood how men were attracted to that. He certainly wasn't. But if her appearance was false, her intentions were quite truthful, and written all over her face. The way she looked at him through half-closed lids...the way her hand pressed a little too firmly on his arm. He knew an invitation when he saw one.

But she wasn't who he wanted. She didn't feel as warm, not nearly as soft. Her scent was not the sweet smell that set his senses to reeling, heating his blood with excitement. No matter what way she looked at him, this woman could never compare to the one he wanted, the one he needed. And he couldn't maintain the pretense any longer. He'd played this part for one dance, and that was all he could stand for the time being. Placing a light kiss on the woman's hand, he turned away from her, catching the look of disappointment she wore at his sudden departure, but he didn't give another thought to her. All he wanted was to go back to the arms of the one he loved. Maybe he could persuade her to go for a little late night stroll. Perhaps they could find a quiet little place somewhere, away from prying eyes. Lord, how his heart beat fast at the thought of her sweet lips on his. He knew he was rushing, but at that moment he could think of nothing but being back with her.

He approached the table where the Langdon's had been sitting...and saw it was empty. She was gone. Why had she left? Where had she gone? He looked around, as if needing to confirm it, and she was nowhere to be seen. A feeling of dread fluttered in his heart. *Be calm*, he tried to tell himself. *She must have gone home.* And yet he couldn't be calm, no matter how he wanted to be. Moving towards the stairs, he didn't give a thought to who was watching him. Was she angry at him? Had she changed her mind about his being with another woman, even if it was under false pretense? He had to go to her and find out...

* * * * *

At home, Jack paced furiously across the living room floor as Grace told them what Charlie had said. And his fury was only driven further when he learned of Charlie's previous encounter. In telling her brother the truth, she had found herself confessing all. She didn't want to tell him, knowing how upset he would be, but it just came tumbling out. Jack crossed his arms and stared at her, his tone deadly calm.

"Where is he staying?"

She scoffed at his demand."You think I'm telling you that? I won't have you ending up in jail for murder while your wife is sitting here carrying your child. It's ridiculous, Jack. We just have to hope Charlie comes to his senses and goes home."

He jeered at her suggestion.

"Oh, that's a great idea. That worked well the last time, didn't it?"

There came a knock on the door, and Jack threw his hands up in frustration. He cursed at the interruption."For the love of God! Who the hell is it at this hour?"

He went to open the door. And seeing it was Henry who stood on the stoop, he grumbled impatiently.

"What do you want?" Henry looked surprised by the reaction. But his voice was calm.

"I saw that you all left early, and I just wanted to know if everything was all right. Is it?"

"No, everything is not all right," Jack said. "In fact, I'd like to slam the door in your face right now. But I won't, because you're a part of all this mess. So come on in here and join the party."

Henry gave him an odd look, slowly stepping across the threshold. "What are you talking about?"

Grace looked up and saw him. Their eyes met, and she seemed to sense why he had come. He wanted to know why she had gone so quickly, and he was looking for answers. But now it seemed he would get more than he bargained for. Before they had a chance to speak to one another, Jack went on in his tirade.

"Charlie is back. He met Grace outside of your club."

Henry's mouth opened slightly. "Are you serious?" He turned to look at Grace. "What happened? What did he say?"

Jack stood between them. "He scared her to death, that's what happened. And it's all your fault."

Henry's brow raised, his expression stunned...and growing upset. "My fault?"

"You're the one who made her come and work for you."

Grace rose to her feet before they could argue further. "I don't want to hear anymore of this." She fixed her eyes on her brother. "I went to work for him because I wanted to, and I still want to. Charlie isn't going to scare me out of it, and neither are you."

Henry became calm. He tried to be a voice of reason.

"He's just looking out for you."

She turned to him with a firm look. "Well I don't need anyone else fussing over me." Then she turned to Jack. She pushed a finger in his chest. "You should be worrying about your wife and your baby. They don't need to hear all of this, and neither do I." She turned to Alice, giving her a kiss on the cheek. Then she hurried out of the room and went upstairs.

Finding Grace

* * * * *

Henry wanted to hurry up the stairs after her, but he held back that impulse with a strong force of will. She had been through a bad night, and wanted to be left alone, so he would grant her that wish. Besides, it would be ridiculous to make a scene in her brother's house, and make fools of them both. So he sighed, turning around, and looked in the face of John Langdon. Once, they had been rather close. Now, it seemed, they were on the verge of becoming enemies. It was not what he wanted in the least...not when Grace was so close with her brother. He did not want to fracture that bond. But neither did he want to go on battling with this man. They were at an impasse, it seemed. For a moment, the two of them just stared coldly at one another, until it was Alice who at last spoke.

"I think this would be a good time to make myself scarce." She smiled at Henry, and then turned to her husband, laying a hand on his chest. "I'll go up and see if I can talk to Gracie."

"Are you all right?" he asked, his tone concerned as he rested a gentle hand on her abdomen. "No pain or anything?"

"Just you," she replied, smiling, as he squeezed her hand and kissed it. She leaned in to kiss him on the cheek, and then turned towards the stairs. Before she went up, she turned to him again with a little smile. "Jack, please don't get blood on the rug. It's a hell of a stain to get out."

Henry smiled in amusement. Alice reminded him a lot of Grace, and in a way, he envied the loving relationship between Alice and John Langdon. He hoped that maybe someday, he and Grace might be such a couple. But before he could even attempt the start of such a dream, he would have to overcome a few things, namely her brother, who was now staring at him with a kind of loathing in his eyes. The smile fell away from Henry's face.

Jack gestured towards the living room. "Sit down, why don't you?"

Henry went in, taking a seat on the sofa. He watched as Jack went over to a cabinet, rifling around. He produced a bottle of liquor and two glasses. Setting it on the top of the cabinet with a kind of force, he pulled the cork out of the bottle and poured some drink into each glass. "I'm not a big drinker," he grumbled. "I should have been, considering where I come from, but their ways have never been mine. Still, sometimes the occasion calls for it, don't you think?"

Henry nodded and accepted the drink, giving the liquid only a slight sip. He eyed Jack over the rim of the glass. He watched him down a gulp of his own drink, and then drop himself heavily into a large armchair.

"So," Jack said. "What are your intentions with my sister? And don't you give any bull, either. I ain't in the mood for it."

Henry sighed, an irritated sound. This interrogation seemed so stupid and pointless. He wasn't some teenager looking to court a girl, hoping for a father's approval.

"No offense, John. But I don't really think it's any of your business. Why should you concern yourself with it? And while I'm thinking about it, why do the two of them call you Jack, and everyone else calls you John?"

"John is my given name. Jack is the name I let people use when I'm close to them. And I'm close with very few. Now don't try to change the subject. We were talking about my sister, who happens to be right behind my wife in a line of importance. Whether you like it or not, she IS my business. Always has been, always will be, no matter what anyone else says."

"And why, exactly is that? Why are you so afraid to let someone else take care of her?"

Jack's reply was grim and firm.

"Because...besides me, my wife, and my Granny, no else ever gave a damn."

He took another sip of his drink as he spoke. "I was ten years old when she was born. Clear as crystal, I remember the morning she came into the world. Me and my two brothers were sitting there with my Uncles while Granny was in with the doctor and my Mama. Daddy came out of the room. And do you know the first thing he said, after he told us it was a girl? He said, 'Maybe we'll get it right next time.' Then he just walked out of the house and didn't come back until after dark."

He reached over to put down his drink on the end table. Leaning back in his chair, he crossed his arms as he let out a deep sigh.

"We all went in to see the baby. Mama had this look on her face. Not the kind of look a mother has when they hold a new baby...all soft and glowing. But she had the kind of look people have when they open a present, and it's something they don't want."

Henry nodded. "So you came in and took over."

"No," Jack said quickly. "I didn't think much of Gracie the first time I saw her. I saw her the way most kids see babies. She was all red and squished up. She looked kind of like a little turnip, and she was squalling at the top of her lungs. But Granny was tickled pink about her. She paid more attention to her than my Mama did...holding her all the time, talking to her. She even named her. My folks didn't even have any girls names picked, if you can believe that. And Granny got me interested in her. She didn't look so bad to me after she got some regular color, and filled out a little. I started to like her more and more, sort of like a stray puppy I might have found. And pretty soon, I was attached."

"So you adopted her, in a way."

Jack shrugged. "If you want to put it that way. The whole point is this. I've been taking care of her since she was born. Alice was there to help when I met her, and Gracie has learned to do all right by herself. But damn it all, women aren't supposed to count on themselves. We're men. We're supposed to take care of them, not the other way around. That's why God gave us big shoulders."

Henry rose to his feet. "I *will* take care of her, if you'll give me the chance. When the time comes, she will be my wife. I'm willing to wait, for her sake, but we will be together. When we are married, I'll make her happy, I promise you that. And as for that Charlie Hillard..."

Jack rose to his own feet, his face a new mask of fury at the mention of the name. "That worthless piece of gutter trash. First thing in the morning, I'm going to go out and look for him. When I get my hands on him, I'll rearrange his face." "I'll give you a hand. If I meet you over here in the morning, we can go together and find him out. Two heads are better than one. And as for your sister, I'll make sure she's never alone at the club. If he shows his face around my property, it'll be the last thing he ever does."

Jack raised an eyebrow. "Do I have your word on that?"

Henry reached out to offer his hand, and Jack firmly shook it.

"I swear it on my life," Henry declared.

"If you hurt her, it will be your life," Jack replied. "That's my promise."

Just giving a slight nod, Henry released the handshake and went for his hat. He felt a slight weight lift from his shoulders as he let himself out. He and John Langdon might never again be the best of friends, but now at least, they had made their peace with one another…and they were both on the same side. With the same goal.

He silently berated himself again and again as he made his way into the house, wishing he had just gone ahead and stomped Charlie's guts while he'd had the chance. Instead he had let the man go, and now this. What if he came around again, when they had their guard down? Desperate men were so often dangerous, and who knew what Charlie was capable of? It terrified him to imagine Grace at the hands of anyone who might harm her, and though he knew she had defended herself on that one occasion, what if Charlie had become violent? Yes, she was strong, but not strong enough to fend off a man driven to desperation. A momentary image came to him, of Grace being struck down by Charlie's hand, and it both frightened and infuriated him, so much so that he nearly left right then and there to look for the bastard. But he stopped just short of the door and took a deep breath, trying to calm his raging feelings.

He had to remind himself…she was safe at home now, and her brother would never let anything happen to her.

✳ ✳ ✳ ✳ ✳

A chaperone. That was what Jack now called Henry. According to the sudden announcement he'd made at breakfast, the two of them would be taking turns in watching over her. But she balked at the term he'd chosen.

Chaperone my foot, she thought bitterly. *Warden would be a better word for it.*

She knew their intentions were good. And in all honesty, she knew there was a certain danger in not knowing where Charlie was or what he might do. But still, she was not happy. According to Jack, she wasn't even allowed to take a simple walk without having someone at her side. She found it very difficult to accept her loss of freedom…and harder still was the idea that Henry was in on the whole scheme. He would be escorting her to work each day, driving instead of taking the streetcar. He and Jack were convinced it was safer to use private transportation instead of public means. But when Henry picked her up that morning, she found it hard to even look at him, much less speak to him. Upset with the entire situation, including him, she kept her eyes away from him, staring silently out her passenger window. He tried talking to her, maybe in the hopes of easing her temper. And she listened to him…but she would not answer or look at him.

"We went to his hotel early this morning, and found out he checked out last night. He could be anywhere, you know."

There was a long pause, as if he was waiting for her to say something back. Still she was silent, and he tried again.

"I know you think we're treating you like a child, but we're not. Your brother and I only want to do what's best for you."

They arrived at the club, parking at the rear. Before he could come around to open her door she opened it herself and got out, walking on ahead of him. She fully intended to get to the club door before he did, wanting very much to leave him behind. But he was too quick, stepping in front of her first. She tried to turn away from him, but he wouldn't allow it, holding her chin firmly in his hand.

"Please don't give me the cold shoulder."

She pushed his hand away, narrowing her eyes at him. "I don't need a guard dog." She moved past him towards the door. "I shouldn't have said anything to either of you." She reached to open the door, but he pushed it closed with his hand and stood there, blocking her path.

"Are you saying you would rather not have my company?"

When he looked at her that way…his eyes so soft, his tone so gentle…it was hard to stay upset with him. And yet she could not let go of her anger altogether.

"How would you like to be told where to go and what to do? How would you feel if you were watched every minute of every day? You wouldn't like it either, would you?"

He shook his head, his eyes lowered.

"No, I wouldn't like it." He took her hand, holding it gently in both his own. "But this is different. And for my own peace of mind, will you let me do as your brother asks?"

He paused, a look of fear flashing across his face…fear for her, she realized.

"I couldn't bear it if something happened to you."

Her heart swelled at his tender confession, making her sigh as her defenses crumbled around her.

"All right then," she said with a defeated tone. "If it makes you happy, I'll let it be. But you have to promise me not to be silly about it. No following me every single moment of the day. There are plenty of people around besides you, and they can be on watch just as well as you can."

"Good," he said, starting to smile. "And think of it this way. Having me as a chaperone, we can spend time together without causing much suspicion. I would say that's a good way to look at it, wouldn't you?"

She shrugged, trying hard not to smile. She hadn't really thought of things the way he'd just put them.

"I suppose so," she replied, trying not to meet his eyes. But he moved his head so that she had to look at him. He chuckled softly, probably quite pleased with himself for defeating her. Then he kissed her softly, breaking down the last of her defenses.

* * * * *

In the days that followed, the need for worry seemed to wan. Charlie made no appearances, and though Jack and Henry checked his hotel each day and made inquiries to other establishments he might have been staying in, there seemed to be no sign of him. They could only assume he had gone back home where he belonged, though they remained constantly wary.

Despite the precautions, Grace found those days to be some of the most pleasant she had ever known. Now that Henry and Jack had declared peace, they, Alice, and she spent time together as a little group, going on outings. They went golfing, and though she found the sport itself rather dull, she enjoyed walking along the greens and taking in the calm, quiet air. She found baseball much more fun to watch. At least it was a game she understood and could participate in, even it was only as a spectator. She found a strange affection for Wrigley Field, with its beautiful bright green grass and rusty red dirt...and its wild horde of fans. Jack and Henry were among them, being bigger fools than she'd ever seen. But in a good way.

When the weekend had passed, she immersed herself in her work, rehearsing for her singing debut which was only a few days away.

She knew her solo well now, and found she was singing it to herself quite often. As well as her progress, she discovered another pleasantry in her singing that she had not given a thought to before, and that was her salary. When Henry handed her a paycheck, she did not quite know what to say or do. She had never seen a check before, and felt silly in not understanding what she was to do with it. But as she knew he would be, he was generous and patient in explaining the whole process of finance to her. Her sharp mind caught on very quickly, as he helped her set up a bank account in her own name, taught her how to write a check and make withdrawals and deposits, and explained both the joys and pitfalls of money. He cautioned her that a woman with her own means was not always taken politely by society, but she brushed that thought aside. All of her life she had been fighting those sorts of backward ideals. What was one more to her now?

She'd always thought of herself as independent, but now she felt a kind of power in herself like she'd never known. She realized it was the power not just of financial freedom, but of personal freedom. With her own money, she had the freedom to go anywhere, do anything, and buy anything she pleased. It was overwhelming to think of it, and if she had been a lesser woman, with less strength of mind, she might have started imagining all the ways she could spoil herself. But it was not herself she thought of at all.

Sitting on the sofa one afternoon, waiting for Henry to arrive for supper, she looked through the Sears and Roebuck catalog as she had done so many times before in her life. But this time, there was no sense of disappointment as she looked through it, seeing things and knowing she would never have any of it. Now, she had the chance to have whatever her salary could bring. She was so wrapped up in her thoughts, she hardly heard the knock on the front door, or heard the sound of Alice greeting Henry as he came in. It wasn't until he came in and placed a kiss on top of her head that she even looked up, and she smiled at him, and then looked back to the catalog.

"What are you looking at?" he asked, and he slid into the seat beside her.

"Sears and Roebuck," she replied, moving closer to him. She pointed to the page before her. "Look at these tractors. If my Daddy had one of these, he'd never have to hitch up a mule to a plow again. And these washing machines. If Mama had a washing machine, she'd never make her fingers bleed on a washboard ever again."

"They sell generators too, for hooking up all of those newfangled gadgets," he said, pointing to another page. "But do you think your folks would even take such things? Don't you think they might look at it as charity?"

She closed the catalog, thinking about what he had said. "I didn't think about that." She folded her hands on top of the book, sighing. "I suppose it doesn't matter anyway right now. It would take me a long time to save up the money for all these things. I suppose I'll just have to be patient."

He reached out to touch her hand, gently toying with her fingers.

"What about you? I'm sure you can afford to treat yourself to something in this book."

She shook her head. "I don't need anything for myself. I've got everything I need right now. Everything I want." She leaned against him, resting her head against his side to emphasize her words. He smiled.

"You think you have everything, do you?"

She sat up, looking at him curiously. She saw the little smile that had formed on his face. "What are you up to?" she asked.

He withdrew from her hold. "You'll have to wait and see." Standing up, he turned to her and told her to close her eyes.

"I don't like surprises," she said.

To her protest, he gave her a stern look.

"For once in your life, will you please just humor me? Why must you always make everything a contest?"

Taking up a couch pillow he hit her over the head with it. Laughing, she hit him back as a tussle ensued. But it was brief, and in a moment he demanded that she be still and close her eyes as he had asked. She sighed, and finally relented. A long minute passed, and she felt something warm and soft put into her hands...something that moved and squeaked, and a smile came across her face before she had even seen what she held. She knew the feel, the smell, of a dog.

"Open your eyes," he said.

She did, and sitting in her lap was a grey and white little thing that wiggled and leaned its head against her in a plea for attention.

"Oh my goodness," she replied. It was all she could think to say at the moment, she was so overwhelmed.

"The salesman called him a little greyhound. He's a lapdog, so won't get nearly as big as the farm dogs you're used to. But I thought you would like him all the same."

She looked up at him, her eyes radiant, and she wondered how she could love anyone more than she loved him. "How did I ever find such a good man?" His grin was typical of him. So was the reply.

"Luck. Pure luck."

Chapter 21
"Truth and Consequences"

She felt her hands tremble as she stood at the side of the stage, listening to the music from the band, and from where she stood she could see the people dancing out on the floor. The sound of a crowded house had become so familiar to her, and now every noise reminded her that in a few short moments, she would be standing out there in front of them. She started pacing back and forth, but she didn't get to pace for long. Toby reached out and put a hand on her arm, and she smiled nervously.

"Are you going to make it?" he asked.

Her voice trembled. "I hope so."

"Just breathe deep," he reminded her. "And remember, I'm there with you. You'll be just fine."

She nodded, hoping against hope that she didn't pass out on the stage.

As she resumed pacing, Jack and Alice appeared in the hall, and they came towards her with smiling faces. She felt a certain weight lift from her shoulders, knowing that she had such love and support around her. The only downside was that Henry was not there. He did not always mingle around the backstage, as it was not his place. He was out there, among his guests. But she knew that he was watching, from wherever he was, and that was comfort enough.

Jack and Alice both embraced her, and Alice reached into her purse to take out a little wrapped package.

"We got you something for good luck," she said, opening the box. It was a braided gold bracelet, which she put on Grace's wrist. "It's not exactly a brass ring, but we thought it could serve the same purpose."

She wanted to cry, and she felt the tears well in her eyes as Alice kissed her cheek. But Jack, in his usual way, had the antidote to any bouts of weepiness, even while he was kind about it.

"Lord, you women and your tears," he said. "Now's not the time to fall apart. Wait until afterwards, and then you can cry and blubber like a baby."

Standing near them and watching with a smile was Toby, and the three at last seemed to notice him there. Alice went over to give him a kiss on the forehead. "Thank you for being there with her."

Jack reached his hand out, and they shook.

"Take care of her out on that stage. Don't let her fall on her face."

Toby grinned. "I'll try not to."

A moment later, they heard Thomas on the microphone, announcing Grace's name. She felt her breath leave her body, and a wave of dizziness came over her. But then, she felt the warmth of Toby's hand on hers. He smiled at her for a moment, and suddenly she felt a kind of peace steal over her entire being. He went out on the stage and a moment later she followed. The backlights went down as she stood before the microphone, enveloping her in darkness. The curtain rose, and she cast her eyes on the floor as the music began. Then the spotlight came on her. She lifted her head, seeing the audience shadowed in the dimness, waiting. With a little glance over at Toby, she smiled. And she began to sing...

Pack up all my care and woe,
Here I go, Singing low,
Bye-bye blackbird,

Where somebody waits for me,
Sugar's sweet, so is he,
Bye-bye Blackbird!

No one here can love or understand me,
Oh, what hard luck stories they all hand me,
Make my bed and light the light,
I'll be home late tonight,
Blackbird bye-bye...

The words of the song flowed out of her with such smoothness that she hardly knew the sound of her own voice, and when it was over, the room erupted in applause, and she took in breath after cleansing breath as relief flooded her body and soul. She looked at Toby, who stood smiling and applauding. She looked over at Jack and Alice as they clapped and smiled as well. And out in the audience, at the back of the room, was Henry. He stood with arms folded, and she could not see if he was smiling. But a moment later she saw him bring his hand to his lips, and he sent her a kiss across the room as the curtain came down.

Behind the curtain, she hardly had time to recover before Bill, the stage manager, was at her side demanding that she give an encore.

Her eyes grew wide with fear and confusion. "An encore? What's that mean?"

"It means they love you, and they want to hear more."

"What do I do?" she asked. "What will I sing? It took everything I had to learn that one song. I don't know any others that they like."

"Sing anything," Bill declared, looking a little afraid himself. There was a long moment as they looked at each other, unsure what to do. They looked to Toby, who just shrugged his shoulders. Then, from the side of the stage came Henry.

"You have to get out there before they rush the stage."

"But I don't have any other songs," she replied.

"Sure you do. Sing the 'Wabash Cannonball.' That's a great song."

She looked mortified at the idea. "They don't want to hear an old country song like that. That's not what they listen to."

"Everyone knows that song. They play it on the radio all the time. Believe me, they'll be putty in your hands. Now get out there and do your thing." He took her by the shoulders, turned her around, and gave her a little push towards the stage.

Bill went out on the stage to make another introduction as the curtain went up again, and the applause rose a little. A moment later she was before the microphone again. Still a little nervous, she spoke in a soft and unsteady voice as the audience calmed down. When she asked them if they wanted to hear more, a round of cheer went up, and she smiled shyly, encouraged and delighted that they wanted to hear her.

As the song spilled out of her, the audience responded with spontaneous applause. As she played the last notes, she felt an urge to jump up and down with excitement, thrilled by the love she was feeling from the whole room of strangers. And almost before she struck the last note, the place went wild and rose to their feet, cheering and yelling their approval of her. She took her bow, feeling as if she were floating on air, and then she turned to Pete and threw her arms around him in a hug of appreciation, and then looked at the audience and smiled, nodding her head in thanks. The curtain came down, and she rushed off the stage in a wild leap of joy.

"I did it!" she cried, throwing her arms around Henry's neck and laughing at the same time, not caring who might be watching. Only the slightest bit of mental strength kept her from kissing him full on the lips, as she wanted to do in a most ardent expression of joy. Instead, she went to Pete and hugged him again, then to Toby, who was standing nearby with a proud smile, and then to Jack and Alice. It was the greatest night of her life, and she wanted the whole world to know just how happy she was.

In the hall, she walked along surrounded by the people she loved, and her step had a certain kind of spring to it. Everyone seemed to be speaking at once, but Henry's voice soon carried over all the others. He took her by the hand.

"There are some people I would like you to meet." She started to go, and then looked back at Jack and Alice. Jack waved her away.

"Go on, sis, go meet your public. We'll see you later at home."

"But you're not leaving now, are you?"

"We really should," Alice replied. "I'm not feeling so well. I think I need to go home and lie down. But you stay and mingle. I'm sure someone will see that you get home safe." She looked pointedly at Henry...and Jack narrowed his eyes, though the corner of his mouth threatened to turn up.

"He better make sure."

Henry nodded. "I promise, she will be home safe and sound, and very soon. Now come on." He took her gently by the arm. "There are people waiting."

She managed to give Jack and Alice each a small kiss before she was whisked away to the main floor, where person after person waited to speak to her and shake her hand. The praise was all very thrilling, but quite overwhelming as well. Most of the names she knew she would not remember, but she still managed a polite word or two and genuine smiles to all who were so kind to her. One couple stood out from the rest...an elderly couple, dressed in much finery, who seemed to know Henry quite well. She learned they were his Great Aunt Melinda and Great Uncle Andrew, who were proprietors of a bed and breakfast in Florida. They gave her a card, declaring that if she ever wanted to escape a frigid Chicago winter, she could make herself welcome as their guest. She was certain she might never use the invite, but she took the card all the same, thanking them for their kindness.

After all the commotion had died down, she was glad to escape to the peace and quiet of the little dressing room she'd been given. Henry was busy tending to some last minute things before closing up for the night, so she waited there for him, trying to gather her wits after all the night had brought. She had just put her head down on the dressing table when there was a knock on the door. She expected Henry, but it was as pleasant to her to see it was Toby who had come instead, and she smiled at him as he entered.

"I just wanted to check on you before I go home for the night," he said. "How do you feel about all of this?"

She sighed, but smiled at the same time. "I'm tired. I'm happy. I'm stunned. I can't believe I got through the whole thing without making a fool of myself."

He grinned and chuckled. "Well you did, and you were wonderful. You should be very proud of yourself."

"I owe you everything," she declared. "If it wasn't for you, I would never have been able to do it." She came to his side, kissing him on the cheek. "You're the best friend I ever had, and I mean that."

He seemed overwhelmed, and she was sure she saw a blush on his face, which made her smile. "Good night, Grace," he said quickly, turning to go.

But as he turned, the door opened. And Grace gasped as she saw Charlie appear before her.

"Charlie, what are you doing here? Get out now, before Henry sees you and skins you alive."

"Who is this?" Toby asked her.

"Nobody to worry about," she replied. "Charlie is someone I used to know, but not anymore."

She looked at Charlie, who was standing with his eyes on the floor, shaking his head. There was something eerie about the way he was doing that, but she told herself it was nothing. All she had to do was get him out of the room, and everything would be fine. "Go, Charlie, or I'll call someone. The police, if I have to."

At last he looked up at her, and his eyes shined with a strange, frightening light. "I loved you so much, Gracie. When we were kids, you were the only one who didn't laugh at me or call me names. When I left, I told myself I would come back someday and marry you. But you didn't want to marry me. You didn't want me. Nobody has ever wanted me." His words became mumbled as he began to cry a little, and he reached into his pocket and pulled out a small pistol, which he raised to his head.

Toby gasped, backing up. "Jesus, Mary and Joseph." He stood in front of Grace, who had her hand covering her mouth.

In a wild voice, Charlie cried out. "With righteousness shall the Lord God judge the poor, and reprove with equity for the meek of the earth! And he shall smite the earth with the rod of his mouth, and with the breath of his lips shall he slay the wicked!"

Two shots rang out, piercing the quiet of the room…and an eerie quiet fell.

* * * * *

As his last associate left his office, Henry sat back in his chair with a little sigh. He reached into his pocket, and smiling at himself, he opened the little box he'd been keeping hidden all day. There was the little ring he had purchased. Through Jack, he had discovered the right size of her finger. He looked at the shining little object…a gold band with a small diamond and sapphire setting, not too large as to be ridiculous, but not so little as to go unnoticed. For a moment he imagined her reaction to it, wondering if she might cry, as most women would when accepting a proposal. But then, he knew she hardly acted as other women did…so her reaction would probably be something delightfully unusual. It made him grin just thinking about it, and he rose from his chair in anticipation of meeting her downstairs.

He would take her to Union Station, in the great hall, where they had first met. What more perfect setting could there be than where it all began for them? He flipped off the office lights, and just as he closed the door, he heard a distant sound of two loud popping noises, almost like the sounds of firecrackers…or the sound of gunfire.

Instinct made him rush down the stairs towards the source of the noise. As he rounded the banister, he suddenly heard screaming and shouting. He saw people rushing towards the back hallway behind the stage…and a sick feeling began to come over him. He moved faster, seeing the little crowd that had gathered. He looked for Grace, searching the crowd for her face…and a cold sweat broke on him as he realized she was not there. Then a voice, shrill and feminine, cried out from near the dressing room door.

"My God, they're dead! They're both dead!"

He shoved standing bodies aside, muscling his way into the little room…where he found Grace and Toby lying near each other on the floor. Both were still and pale…white as death, lying in pools of blood. Pete was next to them, moving from one to the other, saying their names and giving them a shake in a futile attempt to stir them. Henry went forward just a few steps before he fell to his knees beside her.

"Jesus, God Almighty!"

The blood was all over, her entire midsection soaked with it. He put his fingers to her neck, trying to find a pulse. It was there, but faint.

Pete was beside Toby, looking for the same sign of life, his voice trembling. "I can't feel anything! Boss, I think he's dead!"

Henry looked up, seeing the people staring with terrified looks, and his anger and panic exploded.

"Why are you just standing there like dumb sheep! They're bleeding to death, for Christ's sake! Somebody call an ambulance!"

He looked down at Grace, terrified at the thought that she might be dead before help could arrive. Her still, silent body made it all the more frightening, and where he had been afraid to touch her a moment before, now he found himself lifting and holding her, hoping to feel some movement.

Oh God, she's going cold!

Each passing second was draining the life out of her…and he knew it. But he refused to give in to death.

"Get me something to cover them with!"

Someone rushed out and came back with two blankets. He snatched one up and wrapped her in it…and he heard a little moan come from her lips. It was the sweetest sound he'd ever heard. Her eyes opened slightly.

But then he saw the blankness. The lifeless stare. He shook her, breathing fast…verging on madness.

"No, don't do this. Don't go."

Another little gasp. A flicker of hope…and he clung fiercely to it.

Finally he could hear the sound of sirens, but he took no moment to relax. He lifted her fully in his arms, her weight so incredibly slight. "We have to get them out of here. Somebody help him, quickly."

He nodded towards Pete, and Thomas rushed forward to help lift Toby from the floor. Together they hurried to the stairs and down them, where ambulance workers and policemen were just coming through the doors. With Pete and Thomas right behind him, Henry rushed to place Grace on the stretcher. Feeling her weight slip from his arms, he felt a cruel pain at the sudden empty sensation. Now the feeling of helplessness began to set in. He followed along as they carried her out the door to the waiting ambulance. The other stretcher carrying Toby was loaded already and on its way to the hospital. A moment later Grace was put in the other ambulance.

Just as he was about to jump in with her, someone called his name and he turned to look. It was an officer he'd seen around the neighborhood, though he could not recall his name at the moment. The man looked anxious, his breathing rapid.

"Mr. Shaw, they have a man in custody. He turned himself in right away. He was begging for the police to take him in."

A violent urge welled up inside him.

"Where is he?" He did not have to hear the name to know who had done this deed

"They're taking him to the station right away," the officer said.

"Take me to him, now."

The officer nodded, leading him to a police car. He wanted desperately to ride to the hospital. But she was in the hands of doctors now, and there was nothing he could do to help. But he would avenge her, even it meant murder. He asked himself...Should he make it slow and painful, or just snap the son of a bitch's neck like a chicken? Either way, Charlie Hillard would pay for what he had done, and he would find joy in every minute of the suffering.

* * * * *

At the station, he stood at the desk as an officer took down his statement. "I want all contact through me," he told them. "Miss Langdon's sister-in-law is expecting, and I do not want her to answer the phone and hear any of this. Anything they need to know, I will tell them."

Even as spoke, all he could only think of was getting his hands on Charlie.

The bastard is here somewhere.

He ran a weary hand over his face, turning his head to look around...and a distance away, he saw him - being led by two officers. He did not pause for the slightest moment. He moved with animal speed as a leopard in the grass would swoop in on its prey. His attack was so swift the officers hardly had time to react. He spoke no words, letting his fists beat out their brutal message several times before the men managed to peel him away, and that with superhuman effort.

"This son of a bitch shot two of my workers, and I want him dead! I'll kill him myself!"

He fought the hands that held him back, watching as the other men took Charlie away. Just before they took him around the corner towards incarceration, he shouted at the top of his voice.

"She was mine first! No one else will have her! Not you, not anyone!"

Henry tried to lunge forward, but was held back...and then Charlie vanished from sight. Seeing him taken away, the madness in Henry seemed to fade enough for him to gain some control, and he shook off the hands of the officers. Having seen for himself that Charlie was locked up...having had a brief taste of physical vengeance, he was ready to finish his business here and be gone to the hospital. And, he realized with dread, he would have to tell the Langdon's what had happened.

The officer gave him a ride back to the club, where the crowd of employees were waiting for information. They surrounded him, asking question after question. But as they closed in on him, he suddenly boiled over in anger.

"What the hell happened in there? How in God's name can some nutcase walk in a building full of people and not one God-Damned person notices anything! Tell me! HOW!"

Their faces were awash with different expression. Concern...confusion...fear. Deep down, he knew they weren't to blame. He shook his head, eager to escape their questions...and yet he told them what he could.

"I don't know anything yet. I've got to get to the hospital. As soon as I find out anything, I'll let you know." He gave orders for one of his partners to see that the place was closed for the night. Then he got in his car and drove away.

* * * * *

Before making the evil journey to the Langdon's, he had to pull himself together. When he got home, he went upstairs to bathe his face and change out of his dress clothes. Standing before the sink he looked in the mirror and saw his own appearance. The paleness of his face was almost staggering. But it was what he saw on his shirt that nearly buckled his knees.

There was blood all over him. *Her* blood. Suddenly he saw it on his hands too, from where he'd picked her up. Yanking furiously at the buttons of his shirt, he worked to get it off fast, and if he'd had a fireplace he would have burned it. Then the sight of his stained hands took hold of him, and he turned on the faucet and seized the soap, scrubbing his skin until it was raw. But after a few mad moments, the soap suddenly fell from his grip. He let the cold water run through his fingers before burying his face in his hands, tremors shaking him as he pressed his face against his palms.

Oh God, what if she died?

Just the thought of it nearly brought him to his knees. In his mind he tried to envision a world without her, and it was like looking into a fog. All he could see was a gray emptiness, devoid of life and sound, and his head spun from the disorientation. And if she lived, then what? How could he face her again when he'd failed her so miserably? His fingers clutched at his hair, pulling it in agonized frustration.

I've nearly killed her. I was supposed to take care of her, and now she lies helpless because of me.

He was hateful in his own eyes.

He wanted to sink to the floor and weep. But he knew there was something more important that he had to do.

Five minutes later he stood on the Langdon's front stoop. For several long moments he paced back and forth, holding an anxious hand over his mouth. A light in the living room was on. It glowed through the front window, but instead of being a welcome, it was now just a chilling reminder of what he was about to do. He let out a breath that trembled, lifted his hand, and knocked. There was a long moment of silence, and then the door opened, and it was Jack. They looked at one another...and Jack could read the trouble in Henry's eyes.

"What's wrong?" he asked, fear in every line of his face.

Henry knew he could not delay the truth, and stepping forward, his head lowered slightly, he heard himself say, "Grace is in the hospital. She's been..." He paused, unsure of how to continue.

Jack's expression grew darker, more frenzied. "What? She's been what?" He seemed to know what Henry would say, and needed only to hear it.

"She's been shot. Charlie's been arrested for it."

He watched as Jack took a slight step back, shaking his head in denial. For several moments he just stood there, staring with empty eyes as the words registered. Henry looked over Jack's shoulder and saw Alice appear in the foyer behind her husband.

"Jack, what is it?"

He turned to her, looking at her for a long moment, before he went to her.

Henry watched as Jack took his wife by the hand, telling her that something had happened to Grace, but not wanting to give all of the truth at once. But Alice demanded the truth, and as Jack slowly spoke the words to her, Henry saw the lady's hand come up to cover her mouth. He waited for the explosion of tears, the doubling over of agony, or the cry of denial that would come from her lips. But he was stunned and amazed when she rushed forward and demanded that she be taken to the hospital immediately. But Jack refused.

"I don't want you there, seeing her that way! I won't have you putting yourself and the baby through that hell!"

"Better there than here, waiting and worrying myself crazy!" Alice shouted back at him. "That is a kind of hell, Jack Langdon, and I won't stay here for it. Now you either take me to that hospital, or I'll take myself!" She meant it. Henry could see it in the set of her jaw, the firmness of her stance, and for a moment he fell in love with her.

"Get dressed as quick as you can," he said. "I'll drive you." He turned and hurried out the door, across the street to his car, and pulled it quickly to the curb of the house. A few minutes later the couple was rushing out, Jack helping his wife in and then climbing in to sit beside her. A moment later they sped away towards the hospital.

* * * * *

Henry's foot was nearly on the floor as he drove, his eyes intense and focused on the road ahead, and his voice was raw as he told Alice what had happened. Jack sat silently beside his wife, refusing to look anywhere but out the window. He was quiet and still as the grave, and no amount of questioning or prodding could get him to speak. But in his eyes there stirred a deep, black fury, and both Henry and Alice could feel the tension and anger emanating from him.

Henry's rage had simmered down into a deep, painful, and numbing worry. What would happen when they got to that hospital? What soul shattering news would be waiting for them? All he could do was silently pray, over and over, for a miracle, as the helplessness dug deep into his soul like sharp claws.

Inside the hospital, the three of them hurried to the desk where a nurse was sitting, and Jack was the first to demand her attention.

"Nurse, excuse me," he said quickly. When the woman did not turn right away, he began banging on the desk impatiently. "Nurse!" he shouted, and now the woman turned to look at him with an odd expression.

"Can I help you?"

"My sister was brought here and I want to see her."

"The name, sir?"

It was Henry who stepped forward now.

"The shooting victims from the theatre. The lady and gentleman were brought in about an hour ago."

Instantly the woman's face lit with recognition and concern. "Oh, yes. Dr. Brown has been asking about relatives or friends. I'll get him right away."

She hurried away, and the three took to walking to and fro in front of the desk. Alice took a seat in a chair, her hand resting on her belly, and Jack came and quickly sat beside her.

"Are you all right?" he asked, the concern on his face intensifying.

She reached up to rest a hand on his cheek. "We're fine. And Gracie will be fine. I know she will be." Jack put his arms around her, and they held each other close.

Henry listened to her encouraging tone of voice, and shook his head. He had seen what she had not...the blood, the coldness and paleness of her skin. The image was seared in his mind, and as he thought of it again and again, his hand came up over his mouth to stifle a shudder of fear and horror. For what seemed like an eternity he paced the floor. Then at last, they heard the tread of heavy footsteps, and looked up to see the doctor approaching. Jack and Alice rose to their feet, coming to stand beside Henry as he reached out to shake the doctor's hand.

"How is she?" he asked.

"Are you a family member?"

"We are," Jack declared, stepping forward with Alice next to him, and he moved Henry to the side so he might speak to the doctor more closely. "I'm her brother."

"And you, sir?" he asked Henry.

"What does it matter?"

"Only family members are being allowed in at this time," the doctor stated. "We've been turning people away left and right over the last hour or so."

"This is Mr. Shaw. He's family," Alice lied. "Now, what about Grace?"

"She will recover in time, but right now she's in poor condition," the doctor said. "The bullet did not strike any major organs, but it both entered and exited the body through her left side, causing a very serious wound. The loss of blood was extensive, but we've brought that under control. What we're concerned about now is the risk of infection. We've given her medication to ward it off, but there is always the possibility of complications."

"How is she now?" Alice asked. "When can we see her?"

"I'll take you in now," the doctor said, leading them down the hall. "She's asleep, and may not wake up for some time." They approached the room. "The shock to the body was extreme, and she has been heavily medicated."

He opened the door to the room, and Jack and Alice went in quickly. Both gave slight, soft cries as they saw Grace lying there in her hospital bed. Henry felt a wave of nausea hit him as he looked at her.

She was a sickly shade of pale...so much so, he almost swore she was dead. Lying on her back, her eyes closed, she was eerily still. Her dress had been replaced by a stark hospital gown. Her hair, removed from its decorative upsweep, was clean and combed down smooth. Her little sequined hair combs were lying on the bedside table, along with her little gold bracelet.

Sweet Jesus, why have they left her this way?

It all looked so cold, so set...so final. As if they were making her ready for the grave.

Standing in the doorway, he couldn't bear to take a step closer to her. If he did, he feared he would fall at her side and weep. It was all he could do to remain upright as the doctor came near, preparing to go. Henry placed a hand on the man's arm.

"What about the gentleman who was brought in with her?" he asked. "How is he?"

The doctor shook his head. "I'm sorry Mr. Shaw." His voice was low. "The gentleman was dead on arrival."

Henry felt himself lean heavily against the door frame, his whole body feeling like a massive lead weight. He brought his hands up to cover his face and slowly sank down to a spot on the floor, feeling as if the whole world was coming down around him

＊ ＊ ＊ ＊ ＊

For nearly an hour Jack and Alice remained at her bedside, as Henry remained sitting on the floor near the doorway. After a long time, a nurse came into the room, and Henry rose from the floor and followed her.

"Excuse me, Mr. and Mrs. Langdon," she said. "It's nearly dawn. The doctor asks that Miss Grace be left alone for a time, so we can tend to her and allow her time to rest."

Jack, who had been sitting beside Alice and holding her hand, grumbled a curse under his breath.

"How soon can we come back?" Alice asked for him.

"This afternoon will be fine," the nurse replied kindly.

Alice nodded her head, rising to her feet, and gently she prodded Jack to do the same. Reluctantly he stood, leaning down to place a kiss on Grace's forehead. Alice did the same, and together they turned and walked past Henry into the hall.

Henry gave a last long look into the room at Grace, then slowly turned and followed the couple out.

＊ ＊ ＊ ＊ ＊

The drive home was a silent one. Not a word was spoken between the three of them, even when Henry pulled into the driveway to let Jack and Alice out of the car. It wasn't until Jack got out and slammed his door, and headed around to help his wife out on her side that Alice finally turned to Henry and spoke.

"This isn't your fault. It just happened, and that's all there is to say about it. Grace would not want you to blame yourself. Remember that."

Such words were of little comfort to him, though he nodded his head in response. As Jack helped his wife out of the car, Henry saw from the corner of his eye that the man stood waiting for something. Something told him that Jack was waiting until his wife was out of earshot, and Henry braced for what he knew would come next. A moment later, Jack stood by the car door, waiting, and Henry stepped out to stand before him. Neither man looked at each other, until Jack turned with blazing eyes of fury.

"You have no idea what it would mean to me to break your neck right now." His hands were clenched in fists of rage. "You promised to take care of my sister, and you didn't." He clenched his jaw, and the muscle in it throbbed a little. "But I will not put my wife through anything else. And my sister, sick as she is, would be angry at me for trying to get rid of you. So you're going to do something to make it up to her."

Stunned, Henry looked at him. "What?"

"I want you to get the best lawyer you can find, and see that Charlie Hillard never sees the light of day again. If he is shot by a firing squad, or strung up from a gallows, all the better. Just see that he gets exactly what he deserves."

Without another word, Jack turned and walked across the street into his house. Henry turned to his own door, and as he did, the housekeeper came to meet him, telling him he had an important phone call. He hurried inside to answer it, and it was a policeman on the other end.

"Mr. Shaw, this is Detective Taylor at the Cook County jail. We have some urgent news about Charlie Hillard."

Henry snorted. "What about him?" he asked.

"We're calling to inform you that Mr. Hillard is dead. He hung himself in his jail cell last night."

Chapter 22
"The Shadow of Death"

She could hear voices. She knew the familiar sound of Jack's voice, speaking to Alice. Henry's voice too, deep and soothing. They were all speaking, and yet she couldn't answer them, and there was darkness all around. Then a voice she didn't know started giving her orders, commanding her to wake up and open her eyes.

Who are you? She wondered. The voice became more demanding. She grew frustrated and angry. *Why won't you go away and leave me alone? All I want is to sleep.*

But the voice was unrelenting, and her muddled and throbbing brain began to stir. She couldn't ignore the commands any longer. Her eyes started to perceive light as they opened heavily. All she wanted was to sleep, but a great burning pain seized her left side, knifing from front to back. She groaned, whimpered, and then she felt a presence at her side. Her eyes opened fully and she saw Jack standing there. Alice was beside him, and at the foot of the bed, she recognized Henry. She tried to speak, but her mouth was as dry as cotton. Jack came to her aid.

"Get a glass of water, quick."

It was Alice who brought it to her, holding it to her parched lips, and she drank heartily. But before her thirst was quenched, the nurse ordered the water away.

"Only give her a little, or she'll bring it back up."

Almost at the moment the nurse said it, Grace felt her insides do a violent summersault. And then her nose was burning with fluid, her mouth tasting vile as she emptied her stomach into a pan put before her. A wet cloth was put to her, helping her wipe the mess from her face. But feeling mortified, she pushed the nurse's hands away.

"As I said," the nurse told them. "The medication has an effect on the stomach. Too much water will do this. But the symptoms should ease with time."

It was meant to sound kind, nurturing. But all Grace could feel was resentment.

Evil witch. I wish she would get away from me.

Almost as if sensing the hostility coming from her patient, the nurse excused herself for a moment, and Grace was glad to see her go. She looked again at Jack, Alice, and Henry. At long last, she found the will to speak.

"What happened?"

Jack stepped forward. "You've been here for over a week. But you're awake now, and the doctor says you'll be fine."

She looked at him, sensing that he was keeping something from her. She asked her question again.

"What happened?"

They all looked from one to another, and she sensed with great frustration that they were *all* keeping something from her. The pain in her body and mind was so intense, it made her temper very short. "Don't try to fool me," she whimpered.

It was Alice who finally spoke up, in her soft and calm way. "You were shot, Gracie. By Charlie."

Shot? How can that be?

And yet the pain tearing through her body seemed to confirm it. With every breath she took, she felt the sharpness of her wounds. Then another kind of pain came to her, one of the mind and heart, as she remembered who had been with her in those last moments.

"What about Toby?"

There was a silence, and she saw how they all looked at each other. It was all she needed to hear. She closed her eyes, feeling a deep hollowness opening up inside her. But tears didn't come. All she felt was numbness. Nothing seemed real, and reaching down at her side, she pinched a random piece of her own flesh to see if it hurt. The pain from it was real. And the gravity of everything fell together, hitting her like a slap to the face. She felt Jack reach up and brush his hand over her forehead, and it took everything in her not to knock his hand away. Part of her knew he wasn't to blame, but she could barely control the tempest raging inside of her.

"Please leave me alone."

They looked at her, seeming wounded. And it only made her angrier. And yet, she managed to hang on to a sense of kindness, if only by a tiny bit. She asked them again. "Please go away. I'm tired and I want to sleep."

The nurse, who had stepped out for a moment, came back. "We need to check the bandages and tend to her other needs."

Jack and Alice both kissed her on the forehead. "We'll be back first thing in the morning."

Good God, why? She wanted to ask. She didn't want to see them. At that moment she didn't want to see any of them, not even Henry, who stood at the foot of the bed, never saying a word. He hardly took his eyes from her the entire time, and when it came time to leave, he seemed reluctant to do so. But gradually he moved out, following Jack and Alice. And she was glad to be rid of them. But there was still the nurse, who soon had a companion to help her. Their cold hands forced her up, and she gasped in agony and fought back tears of pain. They were methodical in their work, removing the wrapping and cleaning the wound, then re-wrapping it and letting her lay back and rest. But the reprieve was only for a moment, for they came back to her with fresh water and sponges, cleaning her from head to toe. And finally they finished and let her be. Exhausted and hurting, inside and out, there was no need for the medicine they gave her, though she was forced to take it. Only moments later she was falling into darkness again, and into the blissful realm of knowing nothing.

* * * * *

For several days more, she drifted in and out of darkness. The medication kept her in a swirl of lost time, and she didn't care to change it. But there were moments she couldn't ignore, particularly when the doctor and nurses came to tend to her. She hated the three of them. All they did was cause her pain as her body was manipulated and her wounds were tended to, and it took all of her self-discipline not to strike them every time they touched her. After suffering at their hands, she longed for the potent medication that took her away. Only sleep seemed to be a way to find peace.

Flower arrangements were brought in for her and placed around the room, gifts from various friends and well wishers. Pete and others from the club came once with wishes for her recovery, as did various members from the church. Even Mike, the milkman, stopped by for a visit and a word of good will, and he left behind a little stuffed cow as a gift. She tried to be polite to all of her visitors.

But behind the little smiles she managed, she was tormented by darkness and guilt. Absorbed in her pain, and consumed by heartbroken thoughts of Charlie and Toby, she silently wished that she did not have any visitors there to hover over her. All she wanted was to be alone in her grief and suffering, but she knew they would never leave her side. So she found some comfort in the numbness of sleep, and though she hated the idea of being out of her own control, she let the oblivion of the medicine take her away from everything.

* * * * *

The sun came through the window and she blinked, and her brain protested the invasion of light. She wanted to get up and rush to the window to draw the curtains, but when she tried to move, the pain in her side screamed otherwise, and she gritted her teeth and groaned. Alone in the room with nothing but her pain and her thoughts, the feeling of sorrow began to return to her, deep and anguished. In sleep, at least there was some relief from the physical pain. But even there, she could not escape from the memory of Toby. He was there in her dreams, smiling in his wonderful way, so sweet as he had always been.

Had been, she thought. It made a lump form in her throat, and free from any witnesses, her eyes filled with great burning tears. Though she could not remember the inflection of her wounds, she could still recall how he had stepped in front of her, as if to shield her from harm. But how could he have known that he would make the greatest sacrifice? Good God, how it hurt to think to think that an innocent man, a good man, had given his life for her. If only it had been her, and not him. She had been prepared from an early age to go home to God, and if she had been able to choose, she would gladly have taken his place. But it was not to

Finding Grace

be, and she wept bitterly at the cruelty of it all. And that cruelty seemed to have seeped into her very bones. Even as she wept for Toby's loss, she mourned the loss of her freedom. The simple abilities of moving, of going where she wished, were both impossible in her current state, and she wished with all her heart that she could just disappear.

Footsteps came toward her room, and she fought for mastery of herself, not wanting anyone to see the misery that had overtaken her. It turned out to be only the nurse, who came to administer the morning medications and do routine examinations. The woman looked at her, and there was a light of concern in her eyes, but Grace turned her head away, and the nurse seemed to sense that she was not wanted. She gave the meds and did her physical checks, and left quietly. But Grace was not left to mourn for long. Before she could quite fully compose herself, Alice appeared in the doorway. She had raised her hand to knock, but paused when she looked in and saw Grace, who turned her head and tried not to look at her.

She came in, slowly, carrying a fresh bouquet of flowers and a teddy bear, which she placed on the dresser beside the bed. For a moment, she tried to sound cheerful as she came near.

"That brother of yours is something else," she said. "He almost refused to go back to work today. But I told him it wouldn't be fair to have his family starve, on top of having a sister in the hospital. He finally listened, as long as I promised to come and stay with you. It seemed like a fair bargain."

As she sat down beside the bed, Grace was sure that she would start spouting some words of wisdom and support. Wasn't that what everyone tried to do when they came to see a sick person? And as much as she loved and adored her sister-in-law, the idea of hearing bouts of sentiment was enough to make her ill.

But she was surprised when Alice took her hand.

"Feel this," she said, placing the hand on her abdomen. "It's like butterflies. I started feeling it yesterday."

For a few blessed moments, she let herself think beyond her pain. The flutters she felt beneath her fingers made her forget, even if it was only for a little while. Alice's voice was calm, so soothing. It helped to hear talk of something normal, something of hope.

"As soon as we get you out of here, we're going to start work on the nursery. You won't mind helping with colors and things, would you?"

She shook her head, and even managed a little smile. She should have known Alice would know just what to say, how to act. How silly she felt thinking that Alice would have come with useless words and false hope. She knew the balm would not last...that once Alice left, the pain would all come back. But for the moment, she felt something like a sense of peace.

The nurse walked in, but this time instead of being there for patient care, she was carrying a vase of red roses.

"These just came for you Miss Grace. Aren't they beautiful?" She put them down on the dresser, and after she left, Alice turned to look for a card, but didn't find one.

"No card," she said. "But I think I know who they're from."

Both of them knew the flowers were from Henry. Alice looked at her, the light in her eyes a little sad.

"You know, I think he's blaming himself for what happened."

Grace's eyes widened a little. "Blaming himself? Why?" She suddenly recalled the times she'd been awake long enough to see those around her. And each time she'd looked, he had been there. Only, he had kept away from her bedside. He always remained at the back of the room, and at times, even confined himself to the hallway, where she'd seen him walking back and forth.

Alice shrugged. "I can't say for sure. But I think he feels like he let you down. He didn't get there in time to keep you from getting hurt, and he feels like it was his fault."

She sighed, feeling a sudden welling of tears. "That's just silly. It wasn't his fault." She knew she shouldn't feel so, but hearing of his sorrow only added to the burden in her heart. It seemed everyone was insistent on reminding her of how close she'd come to danger. She knew their intentions weren't to harm or hurt. But every look of pity, every word of regret or condolence, made her feel like an animal on display in a zoo. She heaved a shuddering breath, desperate for a change of subject.

"When can I go home?"

A familiar voice answered from the hallway. "Just a few more days."

They looked up, and there he was, watching them. Alice smiled in her special way.

"How long have you been eavesdropping, Henry Shaw? We were just having some girl talk."

"I just stepped in," he replied. "I only heard the part about going home. And I just talked to the doctor in passing. He said a few more days should be it."

Grace sighed, relieved to hear she would soon be free. But now, the way Henry was watching her, she knew the time had come for them to be alone. To talk about what had happened, and how they felt. It was the last thing in the world she wanted. If there had been a way to keep from bending heartstrings, she would have gladly done it. But she saw in his eyes that he needed peace. There was a tempest in his look, and though she was tired of deep emotions and heartache, she couldn't quell the need to comfort him. She looked at Alice, one woman to another, and neither had to speak to know what the other was saying.

"I think I'll go," Alice said. "Jack and I will come by after he gets off of work." She leaned forward to kiss Grace's forehead. Then she turned and left them alone, giving Henry a comforting touch of the arm as she went out.

For a few moments they looked at each other. Then he came quietly to her bedside, and she gave him a weak smile. In all honesty, she was so glad to see him, and happy to have him closer than he'd been in a long time. When he was at the bedside, he knelt down and wordlessly took her hand. But he did not look at her directly. His eyes were cast down, his mouth drawn in a grim frown. He glanced up at her for a tiny moment, and she saw his eyes shimmer. His mouth quivered slightly as he tried to remain composed. But in a moment more he put his head down next to her, and brought her hand close to his lips. "God, I'm so sorry," he said, and his voice trembled. "If I had been there, none of this would have happened."

She knew, without his saying so, that he needed her reassurance. He feared that she was broken somehow and couldn't be fixed. That he was responsible, and that maybe she blamed him in some way. He'd promised to never let her be hurt, and yet there she was, lying injured and weak.

But how could he think she would drop blame on him? He'd done so much more for her, thought more of her, than almost anyone ever had before. She reached out a gentle hand to touch the crown of his head, running her fingers through his dark hair, and she spoke to him soothingly.

"Even knights in shining armor aren't perfect." She heard him give a tiny, half-hearted laugh. Still he did not raise his head, and for several moments she continued to caress his hair with her fingertips. Then at long last he lifted his eyes to hers, still holding her hand. He let out a trembling breath.

"So you forgive me?"

"There's nothing to forgive," she replied. "There was nothing anyone could have done. It was just one of those things."

"But if I'd been there a little sooner..."

She lifted a finger to his lips, trying to smile, knowing that humor would sooth him so much more than sentiment. "Don't be so insecure. It doesn't suit you."

His own expression warmed a little, and at last he managed something of a smile. He came forward, bringing his lips to hers. For a long moment they remained so, sharing the warmth and comfort of a kiss...until a pain seized her, making her wince. He pulled back, a shameful look on his face.

"I'm sorry. Are you all right?"

She spoke through clenched teeth. "I'll be fine."

"Should I call the nurse?" His voice was troubled.

"No, don't," she replied hastily, shaking her head. "They'll just force me to take those awful medications, and I'm tired of being out of my head." She sat back, lips pressed together for some moments, and breathing deeply, she at last felt the pain ease a little. Letting out a deep sigh, she turned and looked into his eyes.

"Henry, will you do something for me?"

He nodded. "You know I will. Just name it."

"There are two things, actually. First..." She paused, as if hesitating. Then she found her voice again. "I want you to bring my folks here for me."

He looked at her with a baffled expression, and she knew that her request seemed outrageous. To have to ask for her parents, rather than knowing they would come on their own. She knew an explanation was due. "I want to see them, but I know a phone call or a letter won't make them leave that blessed hill, even for something like this."

"And even knowing that, you want them here?"

She shook her head, and it made him shake his in amazement.

"You're certainly a better soul than me."

"I wish it was a noble cause, but no. It's not."

"Why bring them now?"

She sighed, a sad sound. "I just want to know what will happen. If they'll come and see me, even if I ask for them. It sounds stupid, but I want to know. And if they can't love me enough to do that, maybe they can make peace with Jack, at least for the baby's sake."

He frowned, shaking his head. "I don't like it. I don't like the idea that they can hurt you again."

"Don't fret for me, no matter what happens. I'm much tougher than I look."

He cracked a little smile. "I know that for a fact." He leaned forward to place a soft kiss on her temple. "So what is the other request?"

"I want you to take Charlie home."

He leaned back, looking at her with stunned eyes. "What?"

"I want him to be taken home where he belongs. I doubt if anybody's even told his family what happened. His Aunt and Uncle are his only kin, and when they find out he's dead, I don't want that poor old couple to have to come all the way here. Charlie's remains should be taken to them, not sitting here in some cold storage place."

Henry looked at her with something like wonder. "After all of this, you still find it in your heart to be kind to him?"

She nodded slightly. "He was not a monster," she said. "He was a poor soul who lived a wretched life. It's only right that he be sent home to rest in peace."

He sighed, smiling at her. "I'll go first thing in the morning." He leaned forward, kissing her head again. "But before I think any about that, is there something else I can do? Something to make you more comfortable?"

She had her answer right at hand. "Can you take me outside? I find it hard to breathe in this place, with these walls closing in and only one little window, which I can't even see out of from here."

He nodded, giving her hand an affectionate squeeze. He left the room for a moment, returning quickly with a wheelchair, and he lifted her gently from the bed and placed her in it.

Once outside, they found a quiet place in the little park next to the building. It was shaded with thick trees, and birds flocked on the ground, unafraid of any human presence. All was still and quiet, until she remarked with some sadness and a little sigh, "Sometimes I miss Virginia."

"Do you?" he asked. "Haven't you been happy here?"

She nodded. "I've been very happy. It's just that I miss the wildness of it. When I was unhappy, I could wander far away into the hills and never see another soul. Sometimes it felt like the only beings in the world were me and God. I wish I could be there now. All alone." She lowered her head, not wanting him to see the sadness in her eyes. "That's the only place I want to be right now."

She didn't say all that was in her heart...that she wanted to hide from the world, and everything in it. Even him. The shooting had finally convinced her of a simple fact.

Some people weren't born to live a happy life...and now she knew was one of those people. Whatever happiness she'd ever known, it had always been taken away from her at one time or another. All she'd ever had was herself, and it seemed that it would always be that way.

But for the moment, she tried not to think of it. The separation would come soon enough, and she didn't want to rush it. So she tried to smile as she met his searching eyes, which examined her face with a look of great concern. She reached out to touch his hand, comforting him. If she could not find the hope in herself, at least she could give it to him...for just a little longer.

* * * * *

That tone in her voice...something about it struck him cold. Even while she looked at him, trying to smile, her hand softly brushing his, he felt a sense of deep foreboding in her manner. But when he asked her about it, she just shook her head, saying she was tired and beginning to hurt again. He helped her back to her room, listening to the names she gave him of those he needed to contact in Stones Mill. Even as she spoke, her eyes grew heavy. He lifted her gently, placing her in the bed, and she was already sleeping by the time he drew the blanket up around her. Brushing the hair back from her forehead, he examined her face...so pale, even now. There were dark circles below her eyes. She was still so frail. So vulnerable. And yet, he knew her mind was as sharp as it had ever been. Which brought him back to that chilly tone he'd heard in her voice.

What is in that mind of yours?

If he'd been just anyone else, any casual observer, he might have chalked it up to depression over what had happened. She certainly had great reason to be distressed and sad. But he was no fool. He could see there was something going on in her head, as if she was plotting something.

He wanted to stay by her side until she woke, even if it wasn't for hours. He wanted to talk to her, convince her to confide in him. But she'd asked him to go, to see to things that were important to her...and so he did, reluctantly, leaving her with a gentle kiss and a promise to come back as soon as he could.

That night, he contacted the preacher, Mr. Clay. According to what Grace had said, Jack had not been in contact with his parents, and didn't intend to tell them what had happened. But she wanted them to know. And yet, Henry himself was reluctant to inform them right away. He explained himself to the preacher as they spoke on the phone.

"It won't be right to have them worrying for days before I can get there. I'll explain everything when I arrive." Even as he said it, he wondered if it would even matter to them. But he did not know for sure, and so he would spare them the details until he got there.

He boarded the train just before dawn, and set out on his way.

It was a quiet and lonely journey. His first class ticket had given him access to the dining car and sleeping car, so he did not lack for comfort. But he ate little, and slept fitfully. His mind was too full, too troubled to rest. Grace was lying back home in the hospital, and he would rather have been there with her, at her side. Again and again he had to remind himself...this journey he was making was on her request and behalf. But rather than being a consolation, it only served to bring him more concern.

He kept thinking of her parents, and below his calm outer surface, his anger simmered. Over and over he thought to himself...

If I were a father, neither hell nor high water could keep me from my child.

It made him furious to think that any parent would need convincing to come and see their ailing daughter. When she'd first asked him to fetch them, his immediate impulse was to say no. Something inside him had said there would be no storybook coming together for her and her family...that she would have her heart broken all over again, and he prayed that he would be wrong. But if he was right...and dear God, he didn't want to be...he hated to think what it would do to her. But in the next moment he realized, she was made of much tougher stuff than that. When all was said and done, she would still be standing. His strong, stubborn girl.

His girl. Thinking of her, he reached into his pocket and took out the little velvet box that held her ring. He'd been robbed of that first chance to give it to her. And now, he was almost afraid to ask for her hand. He wanted to make her his own, in every way. But he'd let her down once. What if he failed her again in some way? And what if she didn't want to marry him? The thought of her rejection was terrifying. She was so independent, so unwilling to let anyone else care for her. She wanted to do everything on her own. Truthfully, she didn't think she needed anyone. But he needed her, and he was willing to do whatever it took to convince her that they belonged together.

* * * * *

It was late afternoon when the train reached its destination. For what had seemed like an eternity, Henry had been looking out his window and seeing nothing but dark, thick clusters of trees, and that view was only broken on occasion when the land dipped down into some great green valley or river, and then the trees closed in again.

He stepped down from the train to a small rail platform. No grand station here. In fact, there was no station at all. There was just a little depot with a ticket window. He looked about, expecting to see the preacher and an elderly couple, who had arranged to meet him there. He did not have long to wait.

"Mr. Shaw?" said a small man with thinning brown hair and glasses. He was wearing the collar of a cleric, and so Henry knew he'd found the right person. Following behind the preacher was the couple, looking stunned and shaken.

"I am Henry Shaw," he said, kindly extending his hand to each of them. He turned to the preacher. "You're Mr. Clay?"

"Brother Clay," the man corrected him. "And these are the Browns. They'll be taking care of Charlie."

Henry nodded, and they all walked towards the baggage car, where a small group of men were waiting. The doors opened, and the men helped lift the casket out and carry it to a nearby wagon. Despite his best intentions against it, Henry felt a bit of a lump rise in his throat at the sight. It was something he had never gotten used to, and perhaps would never get used to, seeing a young man brought home to his final resting place. He had to turn his eyes away, and focus on his other task at hand. He turned to the preacher.

"I'd like to see Mr. and Mrs. Langdon right away. I don't intend a long stay, seeing as I have business to attend to at home."

"You wouldn't like to stay over at the boarding house? A small meal, maybe?"

"No," said Henry. "Just a ride to the Langdon place will be enough."

They walked to a waiting horse and buggy. He hadn't been in anything but a car for years, and it was an odd experience traveling so primitively. It was like taking a step back in time. But as he looked around, he realized that everything around him seemed frozen in a past era.

Most of the journey was spent in silence. His eye roved over the green and brown wilderness that surrounded them. The road was rough, unpaved. It didn't even have the luxury of being graveled. It was just a narrow path of soft brown earth. Along the way, there were very few signs of human existence…Only the occasional white-washed farmhouse and barn, and mile upon mile of barbed wire fence behind which herds of cattle and horses roamed. How strange it was to see not a single living soul, and a memory of Grace came to his mind, of what she'd said about being lost here. One truly could be lost in this place, and feel as if they were the only being in the entire world. This was her world, the place where she had come into being, and something moved in his soul at the wonder of it.

They turned off the main road, and the path became two thin dirt tracks, rougher than the main way had been, if that were possible. The trees closed in overhead, forming a dark green arch that blocked a good deal of the sun, and along the sides of the trail the ground dipped down in deep slopes of rock and earth, littered with fallen logs and limbs. As they moved along, Henry caught a glimpse of motion among the trees to his left. Two shadows seemed to move, and then disappear in a flash. He tried to tell himself it was just his imagination, and for a moment, he thought it might have been. But then he saw the same ghostly movement again, this time to his right. His senses went on alert. His head lifted, his eyes dancing as he tried to determine who or what it was he'd seen. His wary stance caught the attention of the preacher, who looked at him with a strange expression.

"There's something out there," Henry said in a low voice, looking around suspiciously.

Mr. Clay glanced about, not seeming to be concerned, but in a moment he pulled the reins and brought the horse to a stop. Slowly, he rose to his feet, cautioning Henry to be still. Mr. Clay stood, cupped his hands together, and blew into them gently, and as he moved his fingers he imitated the sound of a dove.

Then a voice…the soft, slow drawl of a young man…called out.

"Is that you preacher?"

Mr. Clay slowly sat down again. And he called to the young man.

"Come on out here, boy."

The young man emerged slowly. As he came from the shadows, Henry could see that the boy might have been twelve or so, if he was that. And a moment later another young man appeared behind that one. This boy was a little older, but not by much. Both boys were armed with .22 caliber rifles. The preacher shook his head.

"You Langdon boys sure are gun happy, ain't you?"

"I'm sorry sir," said the younger boy. "I didn't know if it was you or not, with that stranger there beside you."

Henry heard the snap of twigs, and his head whipped to the right. Almost from nowhere came another pair of young men, these two older than the others. They might have been in their late teens or early twenties, and like their brothers, they carried rifles in their hands. Henry felt as if he might be under an ambush, as quickly and quietly as this quartet had come upon them, and armed to the teeth at that. But the preacher seemed quite comfortable with it all.

"Boys, this is Mr. Shaw," he said. "Mr. Shaw, these are four of the Langdon men." He named them from oldest to youngest. "This is Raymond, James, Thomas and Matthew. The youngest boy is at home, I take it?"

"Yes sir," said James. "He's out playin' somewheres. He ain't old enough to go rabbit huntin' yet. Maybe next year."

"So what brings you out this way?" asked Raymond. "And what's your friend's business here?" He eyed Henry suspiciously.

"Mr. Shaw is a neighbor of your older brother," said Mr. Clay. "He's come to see your folks about Gracie."

Almost in unison they stepped closer, and Henry felt his muscles tense. At the mention of their sister's name, he saw a quick flash of change in their faces, as if hearing her name so suddenly was a way of telling them something was wrong. They were now like a wary pack of wolves, these four, seemingly ready to tear him apart, should the need arise. He wasn't afraid to admit, at least to himself, that he was a little worried.

"What's wrong?" asked Matthew.

"She ain't hurt or anything is she?" asked Thomas.

There was a pause, as Henry debated with himself whether or not to speak. How did he know one of them wouldn't point a rifle at him and fire? But he knew they would have to hear it sooner or later, and he decided just to let it out of the bag quickly.

"She's in the hospital," he said.

All at once they began talking furiously, but the preacher intervened before things could get out of hand, and with his calm and soothing voice he quieted them.

"Boys, take it easy now. Your sister's gonna be all right."

James stepped closer. "Well what in the hell happened, then? Why is she in the hospital?"

"She was shot," replied Mr. Clay. "By Charlie."

They erupted into something like an angry mob, and Henry shrank back a little as Raymond came up close to the wagon, which he slammed with his fist in a fit of rage.

"I'll kill that son of a bitch."

"He's already dead."

They all fell silent as they heard Henry's reply. They looked silently to him, eyes wide with anticipation and hungry for more information, and Henry gave it willingly.

"He's dead, gentleman. He killed himself in his jail cell, so there will be no torches and pitchforks necessary."

Mr. Clay nodded. "Your brother Jack has been seeing after her health. And so has your Aunt Alice. But your sister needs family around her, so Mr. Shaw is here to take your Mama and Daddy to see her."

"Oh they won't go with you mister," said Raymond. "Daddy was so mad when Gracie left. Mama cried all the time, but he said he didn't want to hear no more about her. He said she was with Jack, and they could stay with each other as long as they wanted, and he didn't care if either one of them ever come back."

So there it is, thought Henry. As he had suspected, at least where Mr. Langdon was concerned, they had washed their hands of her. He wanted to turn around and leave right then. But no. He had promised Grace, and he was determined to at least give it his best try. As if thinking along the same lines, Mr. Clay spoke up.

"Well," he said, "Me, Mr. Shaw, and the good Lord are going to do our best to change their minds."

There was a long moment of silence as they all looked at each other. Then the preacher took up the reins and slapped them, setting the horse in motion, and the boys followed along behind the wagon as it made its way down the path.

They pulled out of the dark woods and into a clearing, where Henry saw the house for the first time...a one and a half story structure, white-washed but in terrible need of a new coat of paint. There were even places where the paint was so faded that the wood itself could be seen. It had a sad-looking front porch that looked like it might fall down at any moment. He wondered how such a structure could be holding up the swing that hung there. Personally, he would have feared sitting in the thing.

Several geese roamed the yard freely, when they weren't scattering away from the small pack of dogs that had come running, surrounding the wagon before it had even stopped. They leaped and barked until Henry thought he might go deaf, but the two older boys jumped down and began commanding them to silence. In a moment they were under some kind of control, though they still milled about with curiosity for the stranger in their midst. Most of them kept a short distance, buffing, but one of them came right up and began sniffing his pants and shoes, and the dog's stubby tail wagged fast and furious.

"That's Pilot, Gracie's dog," said Thomas. "He's been so lonesome since she left. He misses her something terrible."

Henry reached down to pat the dog on the head, and the sudden attention spurred something in Pilot, who whined excitedly and leaned against Henry's legs, rubbing like a cat. Smiling, Henry reached down to scratch the dog's ribs, and Pilot pressed himself further until he had slid down and rolled over on his back, his tail still wagging madly.

"I can see why Grace is so fond of him," he said. "Maybe I should take this old fellow back with me to visit her."

"I don't think so mister," said Raymond. "Pilot's an old country dog. He's hardly set foot in a house, and never been in a cage. He'd go plum crazy if you tried to cage him, and Gracie wouldn't want that. If she wants to see her dog, she'll have to come see him when she gets better."

If I have my way, she might never set eyes on this place again, he thought. But of course, he did not voice his thought. Instead, he looked up at the front door of the house as it opened, and a lady came slowly out. She was a thin, worn looking woman with mousy brown hair that was swept up in a loose knot. She was wiping her hands on a towel as she came out, and she put it over her shoulder as she saw them.

"Come for supper, Brother Clay?" she asked. "And who's this gentleman with you? Is he hungry too?"

Wordlessly, Henry and Mr. Clay walked towards her. This was Grace's mother, Henry realized without hearing her name. He just knew it, and looking at her, he had a sad notion that this might have one day been the woman he loved. Tired eyes, worn hands, a battered figure...the scars of living a life of servitude. Grace had once said that her mother was married at fourteen, and Jack was her oldest boy at age twenty-seven. So that meant Mrs. Langdon must have been about forty-two. She looked much, much older but he didn't dare say so, and he politely introduced himself.

"I'm Henry Shaw. And I'm here to talk to you about your daughter."

Mrs. Langdon's eyes widened. She seemed to look to the preacher for understanding. He took her lightly by the arm and ushered her into the house, with Henry following. As they came in, a small boy came rushing from the kitchen towards his mother.

"Mama, I'm hungry, when are we gonna eat?"

"Not now, Robert Langdon!" she scolded harshly. "Go on outside and play until I call you back in."

Pouting his lip, the boy did as he was told, as Henry realized he'd met yet another member of the family, albeit briefly. But he didn't linger on the thought, as there were more important matters at hand.

At the kitchen table the three of them sat, while the four older boys stood listening near the doorway. Henry looked at them for a moment before turning to their mother.

"Mrs. Langdon, I am a neighbor of your son, Jack."

At the mention of that name, her eyes widened and lit up.

"My son? You know my son? How is he? Does he ever ask about us?"

Henry shook his head. "Mrs. Langdon, I'm not here to talk about him. I'm here to talk about your daughter."

"Oh," she said.

It seemed to Henry that she seemed disappointed. It bothered him, but he ignored the feeling and went on.

"Mrs. Langdon, your daughter was working for me recently, and was quite happy in what she was doing, until she ran into an old friend. Do you know who that friend was?"

She nodded, still looking calm and unconcerned. "Charlie?" she answered. Then she nodded. "We were hoping he might get her to come home with him."

"Well he *has* come home," Henry said, and at the mention of Charlie, his voice took on an angry tone. "He's come home in a pine box. He killed himself, Mrs. Langdon. He killed himself in his jail cell, after nearly killing your daughter."

At last, her calm broke. Her hand came up to cover her heart. "She's dead? My daughter is dead?" She rose up slightly in her chair, horror in every limb.

Sitting close, the preacher reached out to put his hand on hers. "No," he said. "She is not dead, thank the almighty. But she is confined to a sick bed for some time, and she has asked for you and your husband to come to her. Mr. Shaw is here to take you there."

Mrs. Langdon's frame wilted in relief, and she let out a shaking breath. And then, the worry that had just been there was wiped away, and the calm returned. "Thank the maker for that," she said. "I'm just glad her brother was there. I'm sure he took care of her. He always thought of her like a pet of his. And God rest poor Charlie."

Poor Charlie? Henry thought furiously. *I've just told you your daughter nearly dies, and Charlie is who you talk about?* He wanted to curse the woman. Grace should have been the one, the ONLY one, she was thinking of. He wanted to shout it to her, but somehow, he maintained his polite manner and tone of voice.

"I have bought two tickets for the both of you, and I would like you to come with me first thing in the morning. The sooner you get to her, the better."

There was a long silence, and Henry quickly realized that she was thinking about it. *Thinking about it?* His brain cried out, though it didn't extend to his voice. *What in the hell is there to think about, woman?* He almost shouted it at her, but kept the impulse down by the strongest force of his will. Still, he had an edge to his voice when he asked, "Will you come?"

"I don't know," she said. "John is still so angry about Gracie leaving like she did. I don't think he'll go to see her, even if she's sick."

Henry rose to his feet, furious almost beyond words.

"Would he see her if she was dead?"

He could not keep that question from his lips, enraged as he was with her response. He paced the room, choosing to ignore the wounded look on her face, and the reproachful glance of the preacher, who seemed to sense that some divine intervention was needed. He reached out his hand to her, and he spoke kindly but firmly.

"Rachel, she is your daughter," he said. "It is only right and Christian that you forgive any wrong she has done. Remember, to err is human, to forgive divine."

"I know the words well enough, Brother Clay," she said calmly. "But if John don't change his mind, I can't change it for him. He's my husband, and I have to honor and obey him."

Henry gritted his teeth, doing his best to restrain himself. He wanted to reach out and strangle her. She obviously couldn't think for herself. Maybe her autonomy had been drained out of her by her husband, the way a dog is broken by its master and forced to submit. He wondered how in the hell this woman and Grace could be of the same flesh and blood, as different in character as they were.

The door to the kitchen opened, and looking over, Henry realized he was looking, for the first time, upon John Langdon. He was not a man of great height or stature. And yet, his presence filled the entire room. There was something in his movement, something in his deep set brown eyes that was dark and forbidding. There was nothing of friendly feeling about him, though when he spoke, his voice was calm and cool.

"Brother Clay, how are you," he said. Then he looked at Henry, eyeing him up and down. "Who is this?"

"John, this is Mr. Shaw," said Mrs. Langdon in her meek way. "He's Jack's neighbor in Chicago."

John's face drew into a grim, dark scowl, and he turned and removed his hat and jacket. "Is that a fact? And what in tarnation is that to me?"

"John, Gracie's been hurt," the preacher said. "Charlie shot her. And then he committed suicide."

For a moment, John was silent, his face almost grave.

"Is that a fact? Well, God rest his soul. And I'll say a prayer for Gracie."

He started to walk away…but Rachel came to stand before him.

"John," she said, and though her voice was small, there was at last a hint of determination. "Gracie wants to see us. I don't ask much of anybody. Will you at least think on it?"

Henry watched as they looked at one another, and for a moment, he swore he saw a flash of real feeling in Mr. Langdon's face. But John said nothing. He just turned and walked away, past them into the hall, where he went into another room and closed the door. Rachel turned to Henry and Mr. Clay, looking nervously from one to another.

"You'll stay for supper, won't you?" she asked.

Henry glanced at the preacher, who looked back at him as if to say, *It's your decision.* Henry turned to look at Mrs. Langdon, and nodded his head. Then he looked again at Mr. Clay.

"I think I'll go out and stretch my legs a bit, and get some fresh air."

"I think that is a fine idea," said the preacher. "I'll stay here and see what I can manage."

With a slight nod, Henry turned and walked away, passing the brothers as he went. And one by one they filed out after him. Raymond was the only one to say anything.

"You ain't gonna get lost out there on your own, are you mister?"

Henry smiled. "I think I'll manage to find my way, thank you." Looking at the four young men, he noticed that they still clutched their rifles. Being a former military man, he couldn't help but comment on their weapons.

"Those are fine looking guns you have there. Maybe when I get back, if there's time, we can all show each other what kind of marksmen we are."

They all just looked at him blankly, but he said nothing more, setting out on his walk. It was his thought that he might be related to these men someday, and if a few hours were all he would have to know them, he might as well relate to them on some level. Socially, mentally, and in so many other ways, they were worlds apart. But if they could relate, even over something as small as knowledge of weapons, then so be it.

The long walk took him across open green fields, by pastures of cows and horses. And as he went, he thought of course, of Grace.

It was so hard to believe that someone such as her could be born of two people like John and Rachel Langdon. In only two small respects could he see a similarity, and that was in the stubbornness of John Langdon, and the temper. But though she was stubborn, Grace did not fly into fits of temper for no good reason. He had often sensed that she did not like confrontations, but when backed into a corner with no choice, she came out swinging. As for Mrs. Langdon, the only similarity between the two women was just that...they were both women. It gored him to think that, if Grace had remained in this place and given in to marrying Charlie, she might have eventually become just as beaten down in spirit as her mother. He sent a little prayer of thanks, then, for Jack and Alice who had fostered her strong spirit, and he prayed that as she was lying there in her bed back home, she was doing well and thinking of him.

Soon, my love, I will come back to you, he thought. *With or without your family, I will come back to you.*

Chapter 23
"Promises"

Upon returning from his walk, Henry found the four brothers in a field near the house, target shooting. He came up to them and watched for a while. Then Thomas looked at him.

"Are you any kind of shot, mister?"

"I'm been known to fire a round or two," he replied.

Thomas handed him the rifle. And he proceeded to show them just what had made him a crack shot in the infantry.

They were impressed with his abilities. So much so that they started competing with each other, trying to see who could outshine who. And while they shot, they talked to him, telling him about Charlie and all the things they would have done to him if he hadn't taken his own life.

Charlie was a bullied kid, they said. He'd lost his mother and been abandoned by his father. But that didn't excuse anything he'd done. On that, they were all in agreement. And while Henry had certainly wanted revenge for Grace, he had nothing on her brothers. Some of their ideas for justice were so violent and gory, he had to shake his head in amazement. They were a protective bunch, he had to give them that.

They got on so well, they were reluctant to go into the house when their mother called them in for supper. But they did as they were told, chatting with him all the way back to the house.

John Langdon was noticeably absent from the table, and Henry was privately glad of the fact. He knew it would give him a bit of time to work his charms on the rest of the family, and as it seemed Grace's brothers had already accepted him, he now turned his attention to their mother. As the plates and bowls of food were being passed around the table, he eyed it all with interest, and looked to Mrs. Langdon.

"Are you of Irish decent?"

Of course, he already knew the answer. He smiled as he remembered a certain person swearing at him in Gaelic. But he wanted to make an impression, and certain that she would take interest in having a fellow Irish native at her table, he used it as his angle. He watched her as she took her seat slowly, looking at him with curiosity.

"Most folks around here are of Scotch-Irish blood. Most are from poor folk who came over from the old country. How'd you guess it?"

He smiled a little, thinking quickly. "The food. I remember my grandmother used to cook heavy foods this way. Cabbage, for one. And potatoes. Always potatoes, usually boiled like you have them here. I suppose working men needed hearty meals in the old country, much like they do know. My grandfather spent many a day behind a plow-horse."

Surprise was written all over her face. "Your grandfather was a farmer?"

He nodded. "Until he was nineteen. Then he left with his new bride to come to America. His father and mother had survived the potato famine, and he swore he wouldn't let his children live a life of poverty. So he and my grandmother packed up what little they had and migrated to New York. After a few years they left there and went west to Chicago. The railroad was a source of steady work, especially with the huge meat industry there."

"So you work for the railroad, then?"

"No ma'am," he replied. "My father was a very ambitious man. The railroad didn't satisfy him, so when he and my mother met, he found a job working for her father as a bookkeeper. He eventually took over their theater business. After he passed on several years ago, the business went to me." Lifting his drink to take a sip, he looked at her over the rim of the glass and she was watching him, hanging on his every word. Just as he'd intended. He smiled slightly. "I'm now a man of great means. But no matter where the journey of life leads, there are certain things are always important. Things we shouldn't forget. Like where we came from. And more importantly, our family. Don't you agree?"

She nodded, looking rather perplexed. And he wondered if his subtle hint about "Family" had the intended effect. But maybe it was better to just let her sleep on it. Let the thought sink in during the night.

When the meal was done, he walked towards the door with the preacher, who was preparing to leave for the night. He turned to Henry.

"Will I be taking you to the boarding house for the night?"

Henry was about to speak when Mrs. Langdon came in from the kitchen, in a bit of a rush it seemed.

"No, no," she said to them. "Mr. Shaw don't need to go way back to town. He come all the way from Chicago. It wouldn't be fittin' if we didn't give him a place to sleep for the night. Don't you think so, preacher?"

Henry and Mr. Clay just looked at each other. Then a moment later, reading the answer in Henry's eyes, Mr. Clay nodded. "I'll get your things."

"I'll walk with you and see you off," said Henry.

The preacher bid goodnight to everyone. Henry followed him out to the buggy, thanking him for taking care of everything so quickly. He watched as he drove away. Then he turned back to the house, looking forward to the promise of a good night's sleep. The past few days had been so long.

As he stepped up on the porch, a voice came from somewhere nearby...a deep voice, and he recognized it as Mr. Langdon, who had come around from the back of the house.

"Who do you think you are, boy?" He came up on the porch, leaned against a post, and folded his arms, staring intently. "You think can come in my house and try and rule my roost? Well you've got another thing coming, son. There's only one rooster in this hen house."

God-awful old man, Henry thought. But he kept his tone calm and cool.

"Mr. Langdon, I'm not trying anything of the kind. In fact, coming here was the last thing I intended to do. I thought it was a ridiculous idea, but your daughter seems to think otherwise. She asked me to come, so here I am."

"Yes, there you are. Thinking you're going to trick me into leaving my place to go up north. Why should I waste my time going to see a couple of ingrates?"

Hells bells, Henry thought. *I would love to sock you right in the mouth.* Instead he shrugged. "Mr. Langdon, you can do just as you please. But my end of the deal is done. In the morning, I'm going home either way. So if you don't mind, sir, I would like to say good night and turn in. It's been a long few days for me."

With nothing further to say, he went back inside. Mrs. Langdon was sitting on the sofa, with her youngest son lying beside her, asleep. When she saw Henry, she gently removed herself from her son's arms and came to stand beside him.

"I'll talk to him tonight," she said. "I don't know if it'll do much of anything, but I'll try."

Again, he shrugged. "That's the most any of us can do, isn't it?"

She did not reply. She just looked down, even as she moved past him towards a little side door, which she held open.

"You can sleep in here for tonight, in Gracie's old room. And in the morning, if we have to, we'll figure out a way for you to get back to town."

He nodded as he crossed the threshold, into a small and plain room...one that reminded him of the Spartan dwellings of the Army barracks he'd once slept in. There was a bed with a trunk at the foot, a small dresser against the wall, and a washstand. Otherwise, the room was bare. It felt to him like a prison cell or a dormitory room, but he knew it would be rude to speak such a thing, and so he was silent.

"I'll fetch you a light," said Mrs. Langdon, and she left for a moment.

He stood in the little room, feeling a deep and profound sadness as he looked around. This was the miserable little place Grace had spent so many a night of her life. How many times had she rested here, dreaming of something better? It made him want to be with her...made him love her...more than ever, if that were possible. If he had anything to say about it, she would never be without a comfort ever again. He was bound and determined to make sure of it, after seeing all he'd seen this day.

Mrs. Langdon returned with a small kerosene lamp, which he took from her with a small word of thanks. She bid him goodnight, and left him alone.

228

Finding Grace

It was quite warm in the room, even with the window open. He longed for the humming sound and light wind of a ceiling fan. He had trouble sleeping without it. But with no electricity, of course, there was no such comfort. And all he could do was lay there and try to relax. His mind was full of thoughts, but mostly he was thinking of Grace.

Secretly, he was hoping that Mr. Langdon would refuse to go back with him. Then he could remove the element of danger that the man brought. Grace's mother, in her meek and quiet way, would not be much trouble as far as he was concerned. But her father seemed so vindictive and cold, and one had to wonder if would go along just for spite. Or just to keep control of the situation, most notably his wife. He certainly had her pressed well under his thumb.

He grumbled and groaned, turning on his side and pressing his cheek against the pillow, trying not to think of anything but Grace and how all of this trouble he was bringing on himself was, in the end, for her. After hours of tossing and turning, the wear of two days travel took their toll, and he fell into a deep and heavy sleep.

* * * * *

The smell of food and coffee brought him awake, and he rose and dressed quickly. He washed and shaved in the cool water of the deep basin, and went out in search of a meal.

From the kitchen doorway, he watched Mrs. Langdon as she rushed about in her preparations. He imagined that at one time, Grace would have been in this kitchen, helping her mother...lifting some of the burden from this weary woman's shoulders. For a moment, he actually felt sorry for her and the burdens she carried. Then he reminded himself that part of her suffering was her own doing. And he thought...

If you'd just been good to your daughter, maybe you wouldn't be playing the slave. But then again, maybe I should thank you for your blunder. Your loss of your daughter will be my gain of a mate.

As if sensing his presence, she turned to look at him. Wiping her hands on her apron, she bid him good morning as she moved from one project to another.

"Would you like some coffee Mr. Shaw?"

"Please," he replied. "But don't trouble yourself. I'll get it." He saw the cups hanging on a hook by the sink and took one, and as he went to the stove to pour his own coffee from the pot, he noticed the strange way she looked at him. He looked back at her, as if to ask why she examined him in that way.

"Is it a crime for a man to pour his own cup?" He took his coffee and seated himself at the table.

"I suppose not," she replied. "I just never saw it done before."

He smiled. "I'm a bachelor, Mrs. Langdon. I do have a housekeeper, but at times I'm forced to manage for myself. Although, I do let her take care of the cooking and cleaning. Those are two feminine duties that remain beyond my ability."

She smiled, and for the first time, managed a little laugh. He watched her as she went about, bringing biscuits out of the oven to cool, setting glasses on the table and pouring milk, frying sausage and eggs in a heavy cast-iron skillet. The smell was heavenly. But even the prospect of food did not keep him from thinking of Grace. As he sat there, watching her mother, he wondered if she was thinking of her daughter. If so, she was most certainly thinking of her son as well. The son she had lost long before her daughter had gone.

"Mr. Shaw," she said, her voice low and small. She turned the fire down on her skillet, turning slowly toward him, and she came to sit in a chair beside him. She looked at him with sad, shining eyes. "Will you tell me about my children?"

He cleared his throat, feeling a sudden tightening there. He wondered for a moment if she might cry, and he prayed that she would not, for he could not bear to see such an outpouring of emotion. He had never been entirely comfortable with such sentiment. Although, where Grace was concerned, he was starting to change his ways. But he knew it would be cruel to deny this woman answers, and so he spoke, trying to remain cool and collected as he gave them.

"Your daughter is well, or as well as can be expected. She's been happy until the last few weeks. And despite what you might think, she doesn't speak ill of you or your husband."

There was a pause, and a moment of silence. "What about my son?"

He sighed, knowing that what he was about to say was bittersweet. But she had asked, and he would tell.

"John has been very happy, until this recent bad luck with his sister. I've been told that you and your husband weren't happy with his choice of a wife. But let me tell you, Mrs. Langdon. Alice is a good woman. Maybe the best I've ever known. And as a matter of fact, she will be blessing you and your family, despite the bitter feelings you've had towards her."

Mrs. Langdon raised an eyebrow, her face alight with curiosity.

"She's having a baby, Mrs. Langdon. In January, you will be a Grandmother."

The look on her face was indescribable. She and her husband had wasted so much time in their bitterness, and were probably aware of it, whether they wanted to admit it or not. But if ever there was something to make them realize it was time to come to their senses, the prospect of being grandparents might just be it.

"A grandchild," she said, almost in a whisper. "My sweet Lord."

Had it put her doubts to rest? He couldn't say. But it had certainly gotten her attention. Perhaps fearing she might burst into tears or otherwise lose her composure, she rose to her feet and went back to her cooking.

The back door opened. Henry turned to look. There stood Mr. Langdon, carrying an armful of thick firewood. He paused for a moment as he eyed Henry, and then wordlessly he walked to the stove to put the wood on the fire. He turned to leave, but Mrs. Langdon stopped him, placing a hand on his arm. She looked at him, but spoke to Henry.

"Mr. Shaw, would you mind leaving us alone for a minute?"

Henry did not question why. He simply nodded, picked up his coffee cup, and stepped outside.

For several minutes he sat alone on the back porch. It was a lovely morning out, full of sunshine and the smell of the damp earth. He might have felt quite at peace, were it not for the turmoil he knew was going on just inside the house. The moment of truth was upon them all, and all he could do now was wait.

It was several moments later when the door opened, and he looked over to see Mrs. Langdon there. He questioned her with his eyes.

"Breakfast is ready," she said.

"And the other matter?" he asked.

She waited a long moment before she answered, her voice small but firm in its tone.

"We'll be leaving whenever you're ready, Mr. Shaw."

* * * * *

The room was dark, except for the light of the moon stealing in from between the curtains. Unable to sleep, Grace longed to go to that window and throw the curtains open so she might see the moon and stars. The doctor had urged her to remain in bed and rest, but she had been resting in that infernal bed for too long. She couldn't stand it anymore. Throwing back the blanket she took a deep breath, and turning herself to put her feet on the floor, she felt the pain of a body still healing. She gritted her teeth, sat very still for a moment, and waited until the pain subsided a little. It never went away completely - it was always there, even if it was only dimmed down to a slight throbbing sensation.

She tried to rise, and suddenly found that her legs, weakened from lack of movement, would not support her, and she fell back into a sitting position. But in a moment she was up again, determined to stand, though she had to cling to the bed stand for support. After a few moments of bearing her own weight, at last her legs began to stabilize, and she managed several wobbly steps before collapsing against the chair. The arm of the chair kept her from falling down to the floor, and with a great effort she pulled herself up and into the seat, where she sank with both relief and pain against the cushioned back.

Such a small thing, she thought, *To go from a bed to a chair.* And yet, it felt like the greatest triumph. To move again…to regain some small degree of independence. No one, not even some highly educated doctor, could keep her from such a personal victory. Now that she had made the adjustment from one place to another, she found that she was quite exhausted from the effort. But she had no wish to get up and return to the confinement of the bed. So she leaned against the arm of the chair and looked out the window, where the moon was shining full and the stars were twinkling like diamonds.

She knew, or at least she hoped, that Henry might be looking up at the sky at that same moment, thinking of her. And she hoped that when he came back to her, he would bring good fortune with him. Yet as much as she hoped it, she was equally fearful of it. She thought of her mother and father, whom she hadn't seen in nearly six weeks. Just thinking of them - imagining them walking into her room and looking at her - it made her feel like a very small child, returning to the house after a temper tantrum to face punishment. And yet, there was a part of her that welcomed the chance to stand and face them - to show them that she was not that scared little girl. But what if nothing changed with their coming? Or, what if they did not come at all?

She wanted to convince herself that she didn't care either way, so she might spare herself further heartache. Then again, she knew that deep inside, she wanted them to be there because they loved her, and not just because someone had made them come to her in her hour of need. Oh, how the two feelings of fear and hope waged war within her heart! In desperation, she bowed her head and folded her hands, and uttered a prayer so familiar to souls in need.

God, grant me the serenity to accept the things I cannot change; the courage to change the things I can; and the wisdom to know the difference.

Her strength overtaxed, and weary from her thoughts, she felt her eyelids growing heavy. Soon she drifted into a deep sleep, and she never knew it when two of the nursing staff came in during the night and found her there. She never felt it when they picked her up and put her back in bed. All she felt was the cool of the pillow against her cheek, and the softness of the blanket as they pulled it up over her.

Early the next morning, she woke to find herself back in the bed, and for a moment, she could not understand how she had gotten there. Then the nurse came in with her breakfast - which it could hardly be called, since it was only a small piece of bread, a cup of apple juice, and a cup of chicken broth. Almost looking like she was enjoying telling the tale, the woman explained how they had found her in the chair the night before, and how they had placed her back where she was suppose to be. She was starting to detest the nurses, and the doctor, for that matter. They talked to her like she was an idiot - but she sensed that they probably talked to all of their patients that way. It was just how health care was given. It was a routine for them. No personal attention was thought to be of use, or so it seemed to her. Still, as much as she disliked them, she did her best to be polite. And she was surprised but happy to hear that message had come from Henry, via a phone call.

"You were asleep, so we took the message down for you. The doctor thought it would be best if you weren't disturbed. Here it is."

Grace took the note from her hand, and she read...

Grace,

We will be on the noon train today. We will be in Chicago by Thursday afternoon. I Hope all is well.

Henry

Simple and to the point. What else could it be, sent by phone to a stranger? She wished they had let her talk to him herself, but the fools had let her sleep through it instead. There were so many things she wanted to ask, and most of all, she longed for the sound of his voice. Now, she would have to wait another few days, and the idea did not sit well with her. But what could she do, except sit and wait for either the doctor on his daily check, or wait for a visit from Jack and Alice, who had been there each and every day? Rather than lying there and thinking of it, she finished her bland meal, and lying back she closed her eyes, trying to lose herself again in sleep. She did not have much trouble, and as her eyes weighed heavy, she had a thought that the nurse had likely put some medicine in her drink. She had been refusing the stuff, and stubbornly, even though they insisted she needed it. So they had done what a parent would do to a naughty child, and slipped it in without her knowing it. *Evil woman,* she said to herself. She hated this place...couldn't stand the people in it, and her last thought before she fell into oblivion was that as long as she lived, she vowed she would never let herself be put in a hospital ever again.

* * * * *

She felt a hand shaking her shoulder, and for several moments she protested the disturbance. But the shaking kept on, gently but insistently, and she opened her eyes to see Jack and Alice standing beside her.

"Good afternoon, sleepyhead," Alice said with a little smile. "Your doctor has some good news for you."

Grace moved to sit up. Jack came to her side to help her, though she insisted she would do it on her own. He insisted that she would not, and helped her anyway. The doctor came forward, a little smile on his face.

"I think it's safe to send you home today, young lady. But you have to promise not to pull until funny business, like you did last night."

"What?" Jack and Alice said together.

"Very early this morning, we found her asleep in the chair by the window," the doctor said. "She's a rascal, this one. I suggest you keep an eye on her, to keep her from injuring herself before she's completely healed."

Just like a danged old doctor to run his mouth off, Grace thought with more than a little malice. She looked up at her brother, who narrowed his eyes at her suspiciously. As for Alice, she just smiled in her usual way and shook her head.

"Well, they say the strong and stubborn heal faster than the weak and timid."

Jack folded his arms. "That may be true. But if she tears her stitches, she won't be so sassy when they have to sew her up again."

"Speaking of stitches," said the doctor, "I'll be by the house at the end of the week to check them. Just try to limit your activity as much as possible. Now if you'll excuse me, I'll sign the discharge papers and you can be on your way."

"Thank you doctor," said Alice. She turned to Grace, who sighed. "So, young lady, are you going to behave?"

"Yes, yes," Grace muttered. "Please, just get me out of this place, will you?" She started to turn her legs and put her feet on the floor, but Jack stopped her with a firm hand.

"Oh, no you don't. You may have a fit about it, but you're going out of here in a wheelchair." He wheeled the thing up to the bedside, but stubbornly she pushed it away.

"I don't care what the doctor says. I still have use of my legs. I'm not a child. Why do you always have to treat me like one?"

"I'm treating you the way you're acting!" he shouted back. "Now get in this chair or I swear I'll hog tie you to it." He reached for her arm but she flung it away. She would rather have crawled out of the place on her hands and knees instead of wheeling out like an invalid. But she wanted to get out of that cell they called a room, so she complied. But she did not go quietly. Even as she was being taken to the car, she protested against her brother and the nurse, who both lifted her from the chair.

"I'm not helpless. If you'd leave me alone, I could take care of myself."

"The doctor says you can't overexert yourself," the nurse replied as she helped her into the car.

Grace spat, "The doctor can kiss my foot." And she slammed the door closed. Sitting in the back seat, she grumbled to herself as she watched Alice get in the front, and Jack come around to his side and get in.

"Someone got up on the wrong side of the bed this morning," he said, starting the car.

She dropped her head into her hands. "Oh hush up and leave me alone."

The rest of the way home, nothing more was said. They all spoke little as they helped her out of the car. She had the feeling that Jack fully intended to carry her in if she showed the slightest weakness. She was determined not to be so fussed over. So she took the arm of Alice and no one else, even though Jack tried to take her other arm as they went up the walk. She pushed him away, and when she reached the stairs, she pushed Alice's hand away as well, although more gracefully than she had her brother's. Leaning heavily on the banister railing, she took the stairs slowly but surely, and when she reached the top step, Alice came quickly and took her arm again, helping her into her room.

Jack followed, ready to assist if need be, but Grace waved him away as she collapsed in exhaustion on the bed. With gritted teeth she pulled herself up a little to a more comfortable position against the pillows. She let out a deep breath. She looked at Jack, and realized that the time had come for him to hear what she'd been dreading to tell him. He had to know, and so she would tell him now. She looked at Alice, and tried to smile kindly.

"Alice, can you leave us alone for a few minutes? Please?"

Alice nodded, and quietly left the room. As she went, Jack watched her go, and then he turned and looked at Grace.

"Why so nice to her, and not to me?"

"She's an expecting mother, so I have to be nice to her. You're my brother. I can be mean to you if I want to be."

"What did I do to you?"

"Nothing!"

"Then why are you yelling at me?"

"Because it makes me feel better!"

She crossed her arms, locking her eyes on anything but him, and she heard him sigh in frustration.

"Look," he said. "I know you've been through hell lately, so I'm not going to get too mean with you. But I've only been trying to take care of you, so don't treat me like a worn out shoe you're done with."

She felt a stab of guilt at his statement. She hadn't meant to be so mean to him, but she was frustrated and impatient with her slow recovery, tired of her nagging pain, and nearly mad with worry over what would happen with her parents. She had become so tense and frustrated that she could no longer contain it, and he had seemed the easiest person to target. But he didn't deserve to be so persecuted, after all he had done for her, and she was shamefully aware of it. She also knew what she had to do, and the moment was upon her now.

"It's not you," she said to him. "And it's not everything that's happened to me. I can take that, believe it or not."

"Then what is it?" he asked. "And why do we have to be alone to talk about it?"

She avoided his eyes, knowing that he would not be happy with what she was about to tell him. But she spoke all the same. She took a little breath, and said, "Mama and Daddy are coming."

"What?!" he cried instantly, a look of both shock and fury crossed his features.

She had known he would probably act as such, but still she went on. "Henry went to get them, and he'll be here with them on Thursday."

"No they won't," Jack said firmly, shaking his head. "I don't want them in this house."

"But Jack…"

"I said no!" he shouted. "I don't want to see them, I don't want to look at them. Either of them."

"It's too late," she said with a sigh. "They left this morning."

His face dark, he paced back and forth for a few moments, before he went to stand by the window. He leaned an arm on the sill, and wordlessly he stared out, saying nothing.

"Believe me, I know how you feel," she said. "But think about your son or daughter that's on the way. Mama and Daddy are the only grandparents that child will ever know. Do you think it's right for a child not to know their family? It's best to set things right, right now. If you can't do it for yourself, do it for your child."

He was silent, and remained so for several long moments. She wondered if he was considering what she had said. It was impossible to tell from his expression, which was blank and stony. Then at long last, he spoke in a chilled, deep voice.

"Do you remember when you were a kid, and you broke the kitchen window playing ball?"

She nodded as the memory came back to her, and as it came back, she felt a cold shudder pass through her. She knew then just what he was thinking of. It was a fearful memory for her, but for him, she could not imagine what he was feeling as he relived it. She was shocked at the weakness of her own voice. "Daddy came out there. And then he tried to take me out for -"

"A beating," Jack finished for her. "You were hardly seven years old, and he was ready to switch the blood out of your legs over a damned window. Devilish old bastard." He swallowed, and after a pause, he went on. "But he didn't get to beat on you that time, did he?" She shook her head, unable to speak as he went on talking in a cold, almost mechanical way. "I told him to leave you alone. That he should fight someone his own size. He just turned and walked away. He never said a word. And like a dummy, I thought he'd forgotten the whole thing. Then later that night, he caught me coming around the side of the house, and the last thing I remember was seeing him swing at me with something heavy in his hand. I didn't know at the time that it was a brick coming at me."

Tears rolled down her cheeks, and her heart broke as she felt the pain of a memory she had not had in almost ten years. Clearly, time had not healed his wounds. It was evident in his every word.

"I remember telling Mama that if he ever came after me again, either I was gonna kill him or he was gonna kill me. And she cried and told me not to hurt him. She said to run away from him. Just run, as fast as you can. I remember the last day I was at home. Me, Raymond, and James were cutting tobacco all day. Thomas was working in the barn. It was so hot that day, so I went in the house to get a drink of water, and he started fussing at me for being in the house and not out working. I was in such a rotten mood that day, slaving out in that danged old tobacco patch and sweating like a hog. I started to go back, and I saw Matthew there by the porch, playing in the dirt. I stopped to say something to him and here comes the old man, hollering and cussing. He said to me, 'Get on out there like I told you and don't you tear a single leaf in that patch or I'll knock the fire out of you.' And then I spit water right in his face."

She remembered how their father had raged about the insult. How he had cursed Jack, saying he never wanted to see his face again. She remembered crying endlessly in her pillow, having lost the most important person in her life.

Grace looked at him now. Not the young man, full of rebellion, that she'd idolized as a child. But a fully grown man. A husband, and soon to be a father. He was in full control now, his life all his own and in the hands of no one else. That determination showed in his eyes as he turned to look at her. He came to stand just before her bedside with his arms folded.

"If you want him here, that's your decision, and I won't keep you from it. But don't expect me to stick my hand in the fire again. I've been burned enough, and I don't need no more reminders of how much it hurts."

Calmly, he turned and walked away. As he left, Alice appeared in the doorway. He kissed her cheek as he passed by her, and gave her tummy a gentle touch. Then he was gone.

"Is everything all right?" Alice asked, coming to the bed.

Grace shrugged."We'll know soon enough." She cast her eyes down for a moment. Then she looked up, into Alice's eyes. "Mama and Daddy are coming. Henry is bringing them to me. But I'm so worried about what might happen, not so much with me, but with you and Jack. And the baby. I'm worried that if something bad happens, you might get sick or something."

Alice smiled and shook her head. "I'll be fine. We both will be. This needs to happen, and better now than decades from now, when one or both of your folks are gone, and Jack is sitting around wondering what might have been."

Grace nodded her head, knowing that Alice spoke the truth. She sighed, and felt the gentle arms of her sister-in-law go around her in a warm hug.

"Now, get some sleep," Alice said. "And after that, I'll see that you get some decent food in your belly. I think they make hospital food bad on purpose. Who wouldn't want to get well and go home after eating that stuff?"

For the first time that day, Grace smiled, and even laughed a little. Then she fought a yawn, and nestled down against her pillow. If there was one small thing to be happy about, it was her own bed in her own room. And feeling something like contentment, she slept.

Chapter 24
"Resolutions"

The clock in the hall struck noon, and Grace felt her heart skip. Unless something dire had happened, they would be pulling into Union Station at that very moment. She felt her hands tremble a little at the thought, and clasping them together, she sat back in the living room armchair and shifted her weight uncomfortably. She felt a little movement beside her, and she looked down at her little dog that Henry had given her. The pup was curled up in a ball, sleeping contentedly, and she smiled slightly at the sight of him. As all puppies tended to be, he was quite a handful at times, and Jack wasn't happy about having to occasionally clean up after it. But the dog was sweet and he helped to keep her mood up. In her current state of mind, any kind of lightheartedness was welcome.

Since coming home, she had remained mostly quiet and undisturbed in her room. She'd tried to read and take her mind off of the impending visit. But she'd never been sedentary, and each morning she got up early like she'd always done. Using the furniture for support, she made herself walk back and forth across the room to bring the strength back into her limbs. For several days now she'd been moving about. And this morning, she had come down the stairs completely on her own, clinging to the banister for support, and she had walked into the kitchen by herself, supported only by the use of a cane.

Since she had come home, Alice had been making her meals and bringing them to her when Jack was not home. But she felt mortified by the idea of a pregnant woman trying to care for her. Even Jack had chastised his wife for her actions, insisting that she get one of the neighbors to come and assist her in her daily tasks. But Alice, in her ever stubborn way, refused any help, insisting that the things she was doing were small and not a burden to herself or the baby. Still, Grace was insistent on getting back her independence. She had walked into the kitchen, unassisted, and though her movements were slow they were steady...performed all on her own.

The joy of that triumph was overshadowed by the anxiety she felt in thinking about the visit. They all felt it. Alice sat at in a cushioned armchair beside the sofa, working a crossword puzzle. Jack was sitting next to her on the couch. He had refused to go to work that day, insisting that he would not leave his wife and sister there alone. And yet, Grace knew that he would have rather been anywhere but there. She wondered and feared how he would react when their folks came walking through the front door. He sat on the sofa, reading his newspaper, though she sensed that he was probably not reading anything printed on the page.

Lately he'd been unusually quiet, but that was understandable. He had vowed to never have his mother and father in his house or in his sight again. But Grace was sure he had heard what she'd said about the baby, even if he hadn't acknowledged it. And she was quite certain that Alice had been thinking along those same lines, for last night she had overheard part of a conversation between the two of them. And as she listened, she was sure she heard the sound of him walking back and forth across the floor as his wife talked to him.

"When this baby comes, it will be a Langdon," she said. "He or she deserves to know their family. My family is long gone, Jack. Yours are the only Grandparents the baby will ever have. Think of those brothers of yours…all five of them. I'm sure they would all be tickled to pieces to have a little niece or nephew. And what about Nathan, and Emily, and all of their children? They've always been so good to you, Jack."

Grace had not heard him give an answer, and she had gone to sleep wondering. *Even if he had heard their words, had he listened?* She could not be sure, even up until the moment when he sat in the living room that mid-afternoon. She had imagined him leaving the house altogether, or maybe hiding somewhere in it to avoid seeing their parents. But he had remained, and she could only wonder what would happen when they finally came through the front door.

When the knock on the door came, all three of them froze. Then they all looked at each other for several long moments. To the surprise of both Grace and Alice, it was Jack who stood at the sound. Grace watched him as he set his broad shoulders and went to the door, and then he reached and opened it. It was Henry who stood before him, and as he stepped aside, Mr. and Mrs. Langdon came forward.

From where she sat, Grace could see them clearly. She also caught a glimpse of Henry. For a moment she wished he would come rushing to her side. She wanted to feel the warmth of his arms around her. But he seemed to sense, as she did, that such a display would ruin the fragile peace of the moment. This wasn't the time to declare affections, when they both knew her mother and father would frown upon it. So he stayed in the background, and after several moments he turned to go. She wanted to call out to him. But before she did, Alice stepped over to him and took his arm.

"Don't go just yet. Why don't you stay for lunch?"

He seemed hesitant. "I wouldn't want to impose. You have your family here."

"Don't be silly. You've been so sweet to go to all this trouble. The least we can do is offer you something to eat."

Grace felt some of the burden lift, comforted by the reassurance of his presence. When he came to stand close to her, it was all she could do not to rise up and bury her head in his chest. But she kept her face composed, reigning in her feelings, while he clasped his hands behind his back and spoke in a very civil and polite way, as if they were mere acquaintances.

"Are you well? You look a little pale."

She nodded. "I'm fine. For now..." They both turned to watch her folks, particularly her mother, who had started crying as she put her arms around Jack. Grace noticed how, at first, he stood stiffly in her arms. But he had always loved their mother, and he'd always had such a soft-hearted soul underneath his tough exterior. Gradually he relaxed, and he even managed to give her a slight caress on the back. But when he spoke, his tone was cool. He sounded like a parent talking to a child.

"Mama, stop crying." He carefully disengaged himself from her grasp. And then Grace watched as Jack turned their mother in her direction. She rose slowly, slightly unsteady, and Henry tried to help her. But she shook her head.

"It's all right. I can do it myself." She leaned on her cane, but kept her balance. The last thing she wanted was to look weak and needy in front of them, especially her mother, who came and gave her a light kiss on the cheek. There was a light of concern in those eyes, but it didn't reflect in her expression. But Grace hadn't expected it, and so was not disappointed. At least there was an inquiry after her health.

"Are you all right?"

Grace nodded. Suddenly she felt lightheaded, and she wavered a little. For a moment she dared to wonder if her mother would reach to support her. But it was Henry who gave her an arm to lean on. He helped her sit, sitting on the stool beside her, and as she sank into her chair, it was then she noticed her father and her brother standing beside each other. They hadn't been so close in years.

But watching them, it was nothing like she'd imagined. In her thoughts she'd pictured a scene of extremity...either of sudden rage and swinging fists, or of anguish and tears. But she found no such sight before her eyes. Neither of them spoke. They just stood side by side, looking everywhere but at each other. And both of them seemed to be silently saying the same thing.

I don't want anything to do with you, and you don't want anything to do with me. So we'll leave it at that.

It was all very strange, as if no one knew at all what to do or say. Then Alice, who had been standing quietly aside, stepped forward.

"Well let's not all stand around like this. The baby's hungry and so am I. Why don't we eat? You all must be so hungry after the trip. Rachel, would you mind giving me a hand?"

Without waiting for a reply, she turned and walked into the kitchen. And Grace watched her mother, whose eyes widened a little in surprise...but she followed after her. Grace looked over at Jack and her father, who hadn't said so much as a word all this time. He glanced around, seeming rather uncomfortable.

"I'm going out for a breath of air. It's too dadblamed hot in this house."

He went out on the front porch. And Jack, who had been left to stand alone, turned and looked at her.

"Sis, are you all right?"

She nodded, letting out a small sigh. "Don't worry about me. Why don't you go on in the kitchen and be with Mama? She needs you more than I do."

He looked hesitant, but after a moment more he went. She and Henry were left alone. And almost before Jack was out of sight, Henry let out a little sound of anger. It sounded almost like a growl, and then he rose to his feet and paced in front of her chair.

"You don't know how hard I'm biting my tongue right now. If I came all that way to visit my daughter…my sick daughter, no less, I think I'd have a little more of a reaction. Somehow, I can accept the fact that your father's an old devil. But your mother…good God, what is wrong with that woman?"

Grace shrugged. "That's just how she is. And it's about how I figured it would be. But I got what I wanted out of it."

He looked curious. "What's that?"

"Jack and my folks are in the same house together. Mama has her boy back. And even Alice has gotten something good. She's getting along with her mother-in-law. So it looks like all is right with the world. At least for now."

He came to her side, pulling the stool up close. Taking her hand, he threaded their fingers together.

"But what about you? You've been giving all this talk about what's good for everybody else. You deserve a lot more attention than you've been getting, especially from those jackanapes you call your parents."

She shook her head. "I'm not ignorant. I know what I am to them…what I'll probably always be. But there's this tiny little part of me that wants to see it for myself. It wants to know if they will really treat me like they always have, even after all of this."

He shook his head. "You want to know if they'll break your heart one more time? Damn them both, I know that's what they'll do. And I can't stand the thought of it. How can you let them do that to you? I just don't understand it at all."

She lowered her eyes, saying nothing. His sigh was deep and troubled. He reached up, gently touching her cheek.

"Sometimes I wish you would do what other women do…weep and wail, or babble on about how unfair your life is. Then I would know what to do to ease your pain. And don't try to tell me it's not there. Not matter how hard you try to hide it, I can see it in your eyes."

She met his gaze, seeing the anger and frustration there, the concern. But the last thing she wanted was for him to be worrying himself silly over her. He'd done enough of that already. She reached up and clasped his hand, gently moving it away from her face.

"I'm tired. Very tired. I've been up since early this morning, but I don't have the energy to get through the day anymore."

He smiled a little. "Well I can't imagine why."

She started to get up, and right away he was there to support her. For once she let him, feeling it would hurt his feelings if she pushed him away. When she was steady on her feet, helped by the use of her cane, she looked at him and tried to smile.

"Maybe you should go home and get some rest yourself. I'm sure you're exhausted after these last several days. I'll make excuses to Alice for you not having lunch."

"Are you sure you don't need me to stay? I hate the idea of you being alone with those people. Excuse me for saying it like that, but I can't help it."

She shook her head. "I'll be all right, I promise. Besides, Jack and Alice are here if I need them. They've always been my champions when I've needed them, especially where it concerns my folks."

His eyes were full of doubt. But his frame relaxed, signaling his consent to her wishes. Glancing about, seeing no watching eyes, he leaned in close, his voice soft. "I'll stop by in the morning." He kissed her sweetly. Then with a reluctant expression, he left her.

It was painful to watch him go. And yet it was a relief to know he wouldn't have to watch all of this, worrying as much as he did. Now all she wanted was to rest. Without calling for anyone, she went to her room to lie down, losing herself in a few hours of sleep.

* * * * *

That night, supper was a rather quiet affair, except for some polite talk between Alice and Rachel. Grace could see the rift between the two women was mending, and though she was glad for them, she couldn't help wondering where her place was in the entire peace process. She watched her mother as she asked questions about the baby. And all the time she wondered. Why can you make nice with your daughter-in-law, but not with me? But it was useless to voice such a question. She knew the answer would only lead to more disappointment, and she'd had her fill of that.

As for her father, he hardly said anything. He seemed nervous, always fidgeting and pulling at his collar. When he silently let himself out into the back yard, where he sat on the step and smoked a pipe, Rachel turned to Jack with an apologetic expression.

"He's never been in a place like this. I think he feels cooped up, like a critter locked in a cage. He'll feel better when we get on back home."

Grace found a steady enough voice to ask, "How soon will that be?"

Rachel's voice was meek. "Tomorrow."

"Isn't that a little soon?" asked Jack.

Rachel looked down at her hands, which rested around the cup she held. "There are so many things to do at home. We can't stay away for long."

"There's time for work, but no time for your daughter, is that how it goes?" His tone was sharp. "Nice to know some things haven't changed." He rose to his feet swiftly, leaving the room before his mother or anyone else could stop him.

Grace waited to hear her mother's reaction, part of her hoping that his words had prompted her to say something about the shooting. She wanted to hear her mother say how badly she felt about it, give some sign of deep concern to let her daughter know that Jack wasn't the only person she was thinking of. Yes, her mother had a right to hope for healing in that relationship. Jack was, after all, her firstborn child. And wasn't that part of what you wanted? Grace asked herself. Isn't that why you had Henry bring them here?

It was part of the reason. And yet, some desperate part of her soul wanted to claim some of that affection for herself. A little light of hope flickered in her, and she looked at her mother in anticipation, hoping she would look at her in return.

"How he must hate the both of us," replied Rachel.

Grace sighed, feeling that little light of hope dim. Even now, it was all about someone else...all about Jack. As much as she adored her older brother, she couldn't help but feel a sharp pain of jealousy.

To Jack's words, Alice spoke up. "He doesn't hate you. Jack can't hate anyone, no matter how he tries to put on an act."

Rachel nodded. "He's a good boy," she said. "He always was. And I'm glad he has a woman who makes him happy, and a baby on the way. He deserves such good things in his life."

Grace scooted back slightly, the noise disrupting the sentiment of the moment that threatened to drive her mad. But she kept herself collected, her face calm and her voice cool. "I'm really tired, so I'm going to bed. Good night."

Her rest was fitful. Once, she heard footsteps at her door and she shut her eyes, pretending to sleep. Jack and Alice were in the doorway for a few moments, and then they were gone, and in all honesty she was glad. Not that she was angry with them. But she didn't want them coming in with sweet words of understanding. The idea of it was nauseating, and the last thing she wanted was to feel worse. Sometime in the night, she found she couldn't lay still anymore. She needed fresh air, to clear her head from all her troubled thoughts, and she wanted to creep out to the front porch swing and sit in the dark. As she crept down the stairs, she heard voices coming from the living room, and quickly realized it was her mother and father. They had chosen to sleep on the living room floor on blankets, almost as if they were sleeping outdoors on a hunt, rather than sleeping in a strange bed. As she neared the bottom of the stairs she listened. She quickly realized they were talking about her.

"Doc Smith could have taken better care of her," said John. "I don't trust no big city doctor for anything. None of this would've happened to her if she had stayed at home where she belonged."

"I just praise God she's all right. But if she'd just gone on and married Charlie, instead of making such a fuss about it, she would've never been hurt in the first place. She always was bull-headed."

She sat there listening. Then after a few moments more, she turned and went back to her room, sinking back to her bed.

She was sick of fighting the good fight. Tired of fighting for their love and her own independence. Worn to the bone from all that her life had become in these last weeks...weak of heart and soul, she dropped her arms on her pillow and cried, the sound of a soul broken in two. For many long minutes she wrung her heart dry. And when it was over, a little voice spoke inside her head.

Love me then, or hate me, as you will. You have my full and free forgiveness.

And they *did* have it.

Clarity washed over her soul. A strange kind of peace descended on her heart as she came to a great conclusion…

They would never love her as she needed them to, no matter how much time went by. And after all the misery she'd endured, she just didn't give a damn anymore.

It was time to lift all the burdens from her soul. To clean out her life, in a manner of speaking. She needed to go away…far away, where there were no memories. She needed to be alone, to find happiness for herself. On her own. Looking to others for happiness? Bah! It was like trying to grasp sand, only to have it slip through her fingers.

Sand, she thought. The word triggered a memory. With some effort she sat up. Reaching over to the bed stand and pulling open the drawer, she rifled through it and pulled out a little card…the one that Henry's Great Aunt and Uncle had given to her the night of the show. It had been in her pocket the night she'd gone to the hospital. The day she'd come home, she'd thrown it in the drawer without a thought for it. Now she looked down at it, reading…

The Little Palm Inn
350 Ocean Drive
Key Largo, Florida
Mr. and Mrs. Andrew Stanton, Proprietors

* * * * *

She could smell breakfast cooking, but she didn't get out of bed. She imagined her mother downstairs cooking. Alice was probably there with her, showing her mother-in-law the ease of a modern kitchen…just as she'd once done for her. Part of her wanted to see it.

But then she remembered last night. And thinking of it, she ignored the impulse to get up, turning her head back into her pillow and squeezing her eyes shut.

There was a light rap at the door. Then Jack's voice called to her.

"Baby sister, are you coming down to eat?"

She was silent, ignoring him in the hopes that he would go and leave her alone. But a moment later the door opened, and he poked his head in.

"They're leaving after breakfast. You should at least come to say goodbye. Or good riddance. Whichever you prefer."

Still she didn't answer. Perhaps sensing her feelings, he left with a quiet closing of the door. After he'd gone, she lay there for some time, wishing she could just hide under the covers and disappear.

It was sunrise before she finally moved. *I'm not going to hide up here like a scared rabbit,* she thought. She got up, and slowly she washed and dressed, all the time wondering if someone would come to check on her. No one did. And she said to herself, *No one cares.* For a moment she wallowed in self-pity. There was a burn of tears in her eyes. But she took a deep breath, shaking her head.

I've never felt sorry for myself for long. Why should this be any different?

For courage, she thought of passage from her favorite book. It had always served her in times of crisis. She turned to it once again…

I care for myself. The more solitary, the more friendless, the more unsustained I am, the more I will respect myself…

Soon she was standing by the front door. Jack was about to leave to take their folks to the train station. Standing beside him, she watched as their mother came forward, and a moment later she felt a light kiss on her temple. But it was strange to feel so disconnected to someone. The gesture felt so empty, like kissing herself in the mirror. Her father's response was even cooler. He didn't bother with a false gesture of affection. He just nodded his head, and nothing more. Somehow, the brutal honesty of his feelings was rather satisfying. It gave her closure where he was concerned. And now, it was all over and done. Before she quite knew it, they were driving away and out of her life. Not for the last time, she was sure. There would come a day when she would see them again.

But never again would there be a bond there to hold them to each other. It was as if she'd been severed from them with a sharp object. That wound was deep. Maybe it would never heal completely. But she vowed she wouldn't bleed to death from it. And starting now, maybe she could at least dull the pain of it…with time, and distance. A lot of distance.

Standing next to Alice, they watched the car as it drove away. Alice sighed.

"I never thought to hear it," she said. "But last night, Jack agreed that at least once a year at Easter, we would bring the baby to them for a visit."

Grace felt miles away, but managed to respond. "No fooling?"

Alice nodded. "He made it clear that he was just doing it for the baby. But I think there's a tiny spot in his soul that knows it's good for everyone."

Grace nodded, and tried to smile, though it was forced and weak.

"That's as it should be."

She felt Alice's eyes searching her, and she took a little breath and spoke before Alice could.

"I'm still not feeling so well. I think I'm going to lie back down for a while."

Alice sounded concerned. "You didn't come down for breakfast. Are you sure you wouldn't like something to eat?"

Grace shook her head. "I'm not hungry. Just tired."

When she turned and went back into the house, she could not hold back the sigh that escaped her, and Alice put a gentle but firm hand on her arm, turning her to look at her face.

"Something is on your mind, and don't try to tell me otherwise. I know you too well." She waited a moment for a reply, and when none came, she gave voice to her own assumption. "It's your parents, isn't it?"

Grace sank down on the sofa and put her head in her hands, letting out a deep and trembling breath. "It's them, it's Jack, it's Charlie...it's everything."

She felt Alice's gentle touch on her shoulder, but now, even that was little comfort. There could be comfort in only one place, and it was in solitude. She could not recall the last time she had been alone and at peace. At home, she had found peace in her long walks through the woods and hills, with only herself and perhaps her dog, who was ever the blissfully silent companion. Now she felt trapped, and the need to escape was overwhelming.

"I'm going away for a little while." She lowered her hands from her face and brought them into a folded position under her chin.

"Away?" asked Alice, a note of concern in her voice. "Where?"

"Key Largo."

Alice's mouth fell slightly open. "Are you serious?"

Grace nodded, and Alice began grappling for answers.

"How in the world did you decide on that? Do you know how far away it is?"

"I do. I found it on a map. It was Henry's Great Aunt and Uncle who invited me to come when I felt the need. They have a little hotel there. And as for being far away, that's exactly what I want right now."

Alice rose to her feet. It was clear from her tone she was flustered. But she was calm when she spoke. "How long will you be gone?"

All she could do was shrug. "I don't know. However long it takes, I suppose. I just need to be by myself."

"But what about Henry?" asked Alice. "You're not leaving him behind forever, are you?"

Grace shook her head. "I hope not. Maybe. Good Lord, I don't know." Her head fell back in her hands. "I thought about it all night long. Maybe I should just give him up."

"Give him up? Why?" Alice came to sit beside her.

"I don't want him feeling like he has to be bound to me. The poor man's had enough trouble in his life. Why should I cling on to him and make his life more complicated?"

Just as Alice was about to say something, the doorbell rang. Grace's expression paled, knowing who was on the other side of the door. Alice turned and looked at her.

"Do you want me to send him away? You look a little pekid."

Grace shook her head. "No, don't send him away. Let him come in so I can talk to him. It's better to say what I have to say and be done with it." She looked down at the floor. Alice nodded and went to let him in.

As he stepped across the threshold, his eyes immediately met with hers. Alice left them alone, and he came to stand before her. She felt a great melding of excitement and fear at the sight of him. In his hand he held a bouquet of flowers. She felt a little part of her heart sink at the sight. *Oh Lord*, she thought. *How can I go through with this?*

She tried to smile as he came close to her. He bent down and pressed his lips, warm and tender, to her temple. He handed her the flowers.

"They're beautiful," she said. "Thank you." She buried her nose in them for a moment, and then set them down on the table in front of her.

He sat beside her, and thinking about what she knew she had to tell him, she was suddenly nervous. Unable to know just what to say, she began with the first thing that came to mind.

"How are things at work?"

His face turned rather glum, and she wondered at that downturn of expression.

"My partners are pushing me to fill your place. I told them they should wait and see how long your recovery will be, but they're insisting on finding someone else right away. Selfish bastards."

"But you can't afford to lose money, can you? And all because of me."

He took her gently by the arms and turned her to face him. "Don't blame yourself for that. Besides, it's my business. They're just partners in the investment. I can do whatever I please, and I say they can wait until you're well again."

She couldn't hide the frown that came, and she couldn't hide it from him.

"What is it?" he asked, looking concerned.

"I think you should find someone else."

She looked up at him. His eyes were bright, almost fearful, seeking explanation. "I don't think I can go back on that stage," she told him. "Not after what happened. And not without Toby being there." A look of great pain came to her face, and she felt it in her heart as well.

"Are you sure?"

She nodded sadly, looking down at the floor.

He sighed. "Very well, if that's what you want."

For a few moments they were both quiet, and sensing that a change of subject was necessary, he gave it. "So what happened with your mother and father?"

She let out a slow, deep sigh. Her tone was calm, but sad. "Nothing like I hoped, but just about what I figured. But Jack agreed to bring the baby home for a visit at Easter. He wants to be a good father."

Henry shook his head as he looked at her. "There you go again, trying to deflect the attention from yourself. I didn't ask about your brother. I asked about you."

Without quite thinking about it, she leaned her head against his shoulder. She sighed, a slight tremble in it.

"I think they're over my 'rebellious streak' as they like to think of it. So now, we're right back where we started. I'm their daughter, and to them, that's a wrong that won't ever be righted. So it's just something I have to learn to live with."

He said nothing to her words. What good were words, anyway? He put his arms around her, and she let herself lean against him, taking comfort in his warmth and strength. She felt the sudden urge to break into tears, but a deep and cleansing breath kept her from it. Her head against his chest, she took in the scent of him.

He smelled of soap and the slight spice of his cologne. His presence was so calming, his fingers lightly rubbing her back, so soothing. She didn't want to think of her parents or any other troubles. She certainly didn't want to think about leaving him. But she knew that if she didn't go, if she stayed here, with all the memories so fresh in her mind, she'd soon go mad. She took another deep breath.

"Henry?"

"Hmm?" he replied, seeming very content to remain in silence and just hold her, rather than talking. But she knew she had to speak while the thought was strong in her mind.

"I have to go away for a little while."

At that, she felt him tense a little, and she feared what he would say. It hurt her to think that she would wound him in any way, but she knew it was something she could not keep from doing, and she hoped he would somehow understand. But when he pulled away from to look at her, his eyes were so full of pain that she almost hated herself.

"Go?" he asked. "Go where?"

She wasn't sure how she managed it, but somehow she answered, her voice more calm than she would have thought it would be.

"I'm taking up your Aunt and Uncle's invitation. I'm going to Key Largo for a little while."

"When?" he asked, almost demanding it.

"In a few days. As soon as I see the doctor, and he gives me my medical clearance."

He slowly rose to his feet. She watched as he turned away from her and went to stand before the window. He drummed his fingers on the sill, almost as if he were angry, and she wanted so much to know what he was thinking. For the longest time he was silent, and she feared she had made him so upset that he wouldn't talk to her at all…and that she did not want.

"I promise, it's not forever," she said. "I just need to get away from everything for a little while. A complete change of scenery. I need a place with no memories of any kind. And I need to do that on my own."

Still he said nothing. He just brought his hand up to cover his mouth for a moment, and he let out a tense kind of breath.

"Will you say something to me?" she asked. "I feel like you're about to walk out of here in a fit of temper and never come back."

He scoffed at that. His voice was cool and calm, but full of bitterness. "I'm not Charlie. I'm perfectly capable of controlling my temper, even when someone is about to walk out on me."

She had known this moment would come. She told herself that she was strong enough to see herself through it. But now she felt close to tears, so remorseful was she for hurting his feelings. "I'm sorry, Henry."

And then she found she could say no more. The lump in her throat had grown much too large, and she put her head in her hands. Then, a few moments later, she felt his presence before her. She felt him take her hands and move them gently away from her face. He sat beside her, and she found herself trying to look down and avoid his eyes, as the guilt she felt threatened to overwhelm her. Then she felt his hand on her chin, and he lifted her face to make her meet his eyes, which were shining with tears. He gently cupped her cheeks with his palms, placing a soft kiss on her lips. He looked at her with a tender and loving gaze.

"Do what you have to do," he said softly. "Don't worry about me. I'll be here waiting when you get back." He smiled slightly, brushing away a tear that had escaped her eye. Gently he brought her head to rest under his chin, and for a long moment he just held her close.

"Will you promise me one thing?"

She could not speak, but she nodded in reply.

"Let me take you to the train station when you go. At least give me the chance to see you off. To say goodbye."

She nodded again, words failing her. All she could do was press her burning eyes against his shoulder as her silent tears fell. She felt herself growing calm as he held her close, and soon her tears had ceased. She sighed against him, glad to have her fears subsided by his tenderness and understanding.

"I was so worried that you would be mad."

In his reply, there was a hint of amusement. "You think I'm that insensitive?"

"No," she said. "But I was worried that you'd think I was being like..." She paused, anxious about the thought on her mind, but she made herself go on. "Like Mary."

They had hardly spoken about his wife. She knew it was a painful subject for him, and rightfully so. And for a few chilling moments, she'd worried what he would think of her. Would he think she was like that? Just another heartless woman?

But he was every bit the good man she knew him to be. He proved it even now, replying to the confession of her fear.

"Don't compare yourself to her, not ever again. Mary was good-hearted, but she was a child in so many ways." He set her back a little in his arms, and looked down at her with a serious expression. "You're more of a woman than she could ever be."

She looked into his eyes, nodding. She started to smile. But then, she saw a flash of pain cross his features. The look was only there for a moment, but she had seen it just the same, and she felt a sharp ache in her heart. She had caused that hurt - she knew she had, and guilt began to shake her again. She started to speak, but he gingerly pulled himself from her embrace and turned away from her. For a moment she was afraid that he would turn and rush out, wounded and crushed, and leave her there to suffer in her shame for hurting him. But when he moved away he was strangely calm, his movement smooth and unhurried. She didn't know what to make of him.

"I should be going," he said. "I have some business matters to attend to, and a meeting with my accountant."

She wasn't sure if he was telling the truth or not, but that didn't mean much to her at that moment. She didn't want him to go, and as he went to retrieve his hat, she hurried to move close to him.

"Do you have to go so soon?"

He nodded his head. "I'm sorry I can't stay." He wore a half-hearted smile, and he reached out and caressed her cheek with his palm. "I'll see you soon." Then he turned, and in a few moments more he was gone.

Chapter 25
"At Last"

Lying on her side, she closed her eyes and gritted her teeth as she felt the stitches being taken out. The pain was only momentary, and she was thankful, because it was a sign that soon, the only pain she would have would be a memory. A small part of her independence had been given back to her. Despite the gloom that had been with her for these long weeks, she felt some comfort in knowing she was no longer confined. The doctor smiled down at her.

"You're a fast healer, young lady. There will still be some soreness, but as far as the physical aspect goes, you've healed over quite nicely. There will be a scar, of course, but I don't think it's something to make a fuss about."

She said nothing to his comment, remaining quiet as he applied a healing salve and a fresh bandage. When he'd finished, she quietly thanked him for all he had done. Then Alice led him out of the room, leaving her alone.

She did not take much time to dwell on the doctor or his comments, or even on the prospect of her recovery. She rose almost immediately from the bed and went to her closet, taking out the dresses hanging there. Laying them on the bed, she went to her dresser and emptied it. As she went about the room, collecting her things, there was a knock on the door. Jack appeared behind her a moment later. In his hand, he held a leather suitcase.

"I brought you this," he said. "I think it would be better than that old flour sack you came here with."

She smiled, for the first time in a long while, and took it from his hand. "It's very nice, Jack. Thank you." She took it and put it on the bed, opening it. "So you didn't like the poke I brought from home?" A little grin turned up in the corner of her mouth.

"Well, I think a lady needs proper travel gear. And you're a real lady now I think. Not that you weren't one before, mind you. But I think…" He paused, searching for the right words. "Well, I don't think of you as that little country girl who came here a while ago. I think you've turned into a grown woman somewhere along the way. I don't know if I like it much, but what can I do?"

She smiled. Then a light of mischief came into her eyes. "You're not going all soft on me, are you?"

He snorted. "Hell, no." But still he was smiling.

She found great comfort in seeing him more pleasant than he'd been in some time. He was starting to seem more like the old Jack, and she was glad of it. Now, it seemed, it was her turn to go find that part of herself that she'd lost. Jack stood just at the door, looking at her.

"Are you sure you don't want me and Alice to go with you to the station?"

She shook her head. "I promised Henry that he could take me. But now I'm not sure if he'll even want to. I haven't seen him or talked to him in a week. It makes me wonder if he's changed his mind."

"I don't think he'll miss the chance to say goodbye," Jack replied. "I saw him in town a few days ago. He didn't look so good. And when I told him what day you were leaving, I swear his face lost every bit of its color."

She didn't look up. "Do you think he's sick? Maybe you should go check on him."

He shook his head. "He's lovesick, that's what he is. And I'm not the one to cure it."

Her heart was struck by the idea that he might be suffering because of her. But she'd made her decision, and would stand by it. "He'll be just fine without me. Let him live his life in peace. He doesn't need me like a millstone around his neck."

Jack sighed and rolled his eyes. "I'll never understand the way you women think." The doorbell rang, and he looked towards the sound. Then he looked back to her. "Speak of the devil." Turning away, he headed out and down the hall.

She trembled a little at the sound of the doorbell. But gathering her courage, she took up her suitcase and followed Jack down.

When she came into the foyer she saw Henry there. Jack and Alice were beside him, waiting for her. She came down slowly, and at the door, Alice put her arms around her in a warm embrace. She lovingly kissed her cheek.

"Let us know the minute you get there." She nodded and smiled. Then she turned to Jack, who leaned forward to kiss her on the forehead. "Don't stay away too long."

She smiled, giving him a gentle hug. "I'll be back to bother you before you know it." She pulled away from him and turned to meet Henry, who was looking on with a cool, unreadable expression.

On the way into town, he hardly said a word. But then again, she hardly said anything to him either. How could she, when she knew that in a very short time, she would be parting from him? She began to sense that he might have been thinking along those same lines, and she understood why he would have wanted to remain quiet.

She felt miserable as they got off the streetcar and walked down the sidewalk toward the station. As he led her through the doors and down the stairs to the great hall, she couldn't help but recall the first time she'd seen this incredible place...how it had so overwhelmed her. Thinking of that, she couldn't help remembering the first time she'd seen him there. She wanted to cry at the thought of leaving, but somehow she managed to keep her tears held back.

Don't make a fool of yourself now, she told herself. *When you get on the train, and are out of sight, you can pour your heart out, but until then, be strong.* She took a very deep breath to steel her nerves. Then she heard the announcement come from overhead...the call for her departure. She rose to her feet and Henry followed, walking with her toward the platform.

They walked together under the soft white light of the glass atrium. She hardly noticed the milling crowds or the hissing of the train as it waited. In that moment she thought of Jane, leaving Thornfield in the middle of the night...fleeing from her beloved Rochester.

He who is taken out to pass through a fair scene to the scaffold thinks not of the flowers that smile on his road, but of the block and axe-edge; of the disseverment of bone and vein; of the grave gaping at the end.

She turned to Henry, but found she could hardly bring herself to look at him. As hard as she tried to suppress them, she could not keep tears from pooling in her eyes. He reached out to give her the suitcase, and with a trembling hand, she reached for it. Then she felt his other hand come and close over her wrist - a warm and potent touch that sent a thrill up her arm. Then she heard his voice, deep and soft.

"Stay."

She began to tremble, inside and out, as he took the suitcase from her hand and put it down. He closed one hand gently around hers.

"I can't be noble about this...not anymore. Since the day you came into my life, you've been trying to turn me into something better...trying to make a good man of me. And damn your soul, you almost did it."

She opened her mouth, tried to reply, but he cut her off.

"I'm not noble. Just saying the word makes me sick. I'm self-centered and selfish, and when I want something enough, I'll do whatever I have to in order to get it. And I want you."

Her heart raced madly. She watched him reach into his pocket to search for something.

"You think you don't need anyone. You think you can waltz through life on your own and carry everything on your own shoulders. But you don't stop to think about anyone else. Maybe you can do without me, but what if I can't do without you?"

Oh Lord, she thought, sensing what he was about to do, and she began to weep when he unclenched his palm, showing her the ring.

"The first time I was going to attempt this," he said, "Some fool ruined it by trying to take you from me. And then I tried it again the other day, but you had to break up my plan by saying you were running away from me. But I won't let you go." He gingerly lifted her hand, carefully sliding the ring on her finger. Then he looked into her eyes, the corner of his mouth rising in a devilish little grin. "I won't give you time to think it over. And if you say no, I'll just follow you wherever you go and keep asking until you give in. And you know how stubborn I can be."

She leaned her head against his chest, smiling. "You've been a stubborn fool since the day I met you."

"That's beside the point," he replied, lifting her chin, making her shining eyes meet his. He brought his lips close to hers, whispering. "Just say yes."

She didn't say anything. She just threw her arms around his neck, kissing him. And he kissed her back with equal fervor. It was all the answer he needed to hear.

* * * * *

"Why do you want to marry me?"

Henry's eyes widened a little, surprised. For two days they had been traveling. And for most of those two days they had sat close, as they did now. They'd talked softly and exchanged many a loving look and caress. But now, for the first time since she'd accepted him, her expression was all seriousness. Those steely eyes of hers were full of concern. But he was in too grand a mood to answer a real question. He just smiled and took her hand. He pressed his lips to her palm, delighting in its warmth. For a moment he dared hope that the caress would distract her. It didn't.

"Why?" she asked.

His lips trailed from palm to wrist. "Why not?" A moment later he was stung when she carefully pulled her hand away. Her brow became stern, her eyes silently declaring that she wouldn't be put off further. A small sigh fell from his lips. "I love you. What more reason do I need?" He leaned forward to kiss her, giving a groan of frustration when she leaned away. Her tone was firm.

"You could have any woman in the world. A beautiful woman. One with lots of money and high-born qualities. What am I but a little old country girl?"

"Are you trying to say you're not good enough for me? Because if that's what you think…"

She shook her head. "I know what I am, and where I come from. And I'm proud of being me. I wouldn't want to be someone else."

He gave her an odd look. "What is it you're trying to say? I'm having trouble understanding."

"The truth is, we're from two different worlds. Worlds that weren't meant to meet and get together. Why do you want me? Everyone will figure you've come down in the world if you marry me."

"You should know by now. I don't give a damn what anyone thinks."

"You're not answering the question."

He sighed, more deeply this time. In truth, it was hard to put into just a few words what he loved about her. But she wanted a reply, and for a moment he struggled to find one. When at last it came to him, he leaned in close to her. His voice was soft and tender. "Sometimes, you just know when something is right. And when I'm with you, it's like I've found a missing puzzle piece. Everything fits, just like it should. And I'm happy."

Now she smiled, and it held a hint of mischief. "Do you rehearse these speeches ahead of time, or do you just make them up on the spot?"

He didn't answer. Instead he stole a kiss, as he'd wanted to do from the first. And now, he sensed a change in her…as if she finally understood that she was his, and he was hers, for she kissed him back with as much fervor as he felt for her. I'm happy, he'd told her. It felt so marvelous to say those words. And yet they didn't seem adequate to convey the joy she'd brought to his life. He didn't know if words would ever fully express what he felt for her…but he intended to show her his feelings, every day, for the rest of their lives.

*****

They spent several weeks at the seaside. In all honesty, he would have preferred to be married straight away. But she was still in need of recovery, and her health mattered to him more than rushing her to the altar.

He was also aware of her inexperience with relationships. In her life, she'd hardly gone more than a few days without some sort of chaperone to watch over her. He wanted her to be at ease when she was alone with him. And in those weeks before their marriage, she seemed to grow quite confident and content being at his side. It delighted him to witness the change. And after they were wed, he hoped they would always be as happy together as they were in those first days.

She was such a contradiction…and he absolutely delighted in it, much as he always had. But now, the pleasure it gave him was all the more intense, when he could act on his feelings. She was so young, so innocent. And yet, she carried herself like a woman twice her age. She could be so sweet and shy, and a moment later she could be wild-eyed and as fiery as a little devil. It was hard to decide which side of her personality he liked better, because both were tempting in equal measure. And whichever side he dealt with, there was one point he was certain of…her heart was always true, whether she was devil or angel, woman or child.

That contradiction was made startlingly clear to him the morning after their wedding.

He stirred from his sleep just as the sun was rising. As he came awake, he felt her presence in the bed beside him. Looking down, he smiled at the sight of his lovely young wife, who was lying on her belly, her face turned to him as she slept. Her skin was a rich golden color, more so than before. Her long honey-toned hair was spilled over her back and shoulders. A beautiful memory came to him as he recalled how softly her hair had spilled through his fingers the night before. Looking at her now, he knew it would be kinder to let her sleep. But the sight of her was too strong a temptation. Aching to press his lips to her warm bare skin, he reached out and swept her hair away.

He froze. There between her shoulder blades, faint but still evident, were several long marks. They were pale in color…too pale for him to have seen them last night, in the dimness of candlelight. But with the bright sunshine now streaming in, the scars were all too clear. All at once he was angry, brokenhearted, and disgusted.

Not by the imperfections themselves, but by what they implied. He knew what she'd endured at her father's hands. But to see it...to think of someone actually striking her...leaving her branded this way. It sent a fierce surge of fury, of protectiveness, pulsing through his veins. He wanted to snatch her up in his arms, clasp her to his heart and swear to her that no one would ever harm her again. But closing his eyes, taking in a deep breath to calm himself, he knew he couldn't act so impassioned. How would that seem to her, especially on the morning after their wedding?

As he tenderly looked at her, she stirred slightly. Her eyelids fluttered. She looked at him...and smiled the most beautiful smile.

Her beauty moved him, so much that he wanted nothing more than to draw her into his arms, to express all the love and desire he felt for her. But the memory of seeing her scars was overwhelming. To keep from troubling her, from letting her see the anguish he still felt, he needed to step away for a moment. Gently, he grazed a knuckle over the soft slope of her bare shoulder.

"Stay here and rest," he whispered. "Have a hot bath, if you like. It will help...the tenderness." Her cheeks went pink as she sensed what he meant, but he just smiled. "I'll find some breakfast and bring it up." Reluctantly moving away from her, he went to wash and dress.

Before he went out, he turned at the door to glance back at her. Her eyes had closed again, her look so peaceful. And he left her so.

Coming down to the lobby, he went out to the veranda where he walked for some time, calming his nerves. When he felt his temper had cooled enough, he went to the front desk and ordered a tray of fresh fruit.

He came into the room quietly in case she was still sleeping. Walking across the threshold, he caught sight of her before she noticed him. She was out on the balcony, in a light summer dress and bare feet, looking over the railing at the sea below. Her hair billowed lightly in the breeze, and he smiled as he thought how child-like she seemed. And yet she was a woman. And his wife. The very thought of it sent a flood of warmth all through him, and he wasn't content any longer to stand and watch her. Coming quietly through the open door, he put the tray down on a table and walked up behind her. Gently he put his hands on her shoulders, and he felt her jump.

"I'm sorry if I scared you," he said.

She shook her head, looking back at him and smiling. Then, to his delight, she leaned back against him. "You didn't scare me. My mind was just way out there while I looked at the ocean."

It was clear to him that she was content with his closeness. He had worried for a moment that she might shy away, still being a new bride. But the way she relaxed against him, letting out a small sigh of joy, he didn't think it wrong to move his hands from her shoulders to her waist. Bringing his arms around her, he pulled her tightly against his body and pressed his cheek to hers. And she contentedly sighed again.

"I could stay here like this all day...with you."

"And I with you." He brushed a delicate kiss just behind her ear, feeling her shiver. It was enough to turn his thoughts wicked. But as eager as he was for her, he wasn't some hasty youth, demanding immediate indulgence. He was a grown man, and now a husband. He intended to be the best one he could be, which meant taking care of the woman he loved. And not just in matters of a sensual nature. He forced himself to let go of her, difficult as it was. He took her by the hand and led her to little table. But he wasn't ready to be parted from her completely. Sitting in the chair, he brought her close and pulled her down to sit on his knee. Close as she was to him, he felt her tense a little, and a flush of pink came to her cheeks. He smiled at seeing it.

"You're blushing. Does sitting like this make you nervous?"

She shrugged, and leaned her head against his shoulder. "I don't figure nervous is the right word. Overwhelmed, maybe. But in a good way."

Reaching for slices of orange, he handed her one and nibbled on one for himself. "You're imprinted, I suppose, with the idea that intimacy is evil. I'm sure your mother and father never sat together like this."

A tiny laugh escaped her. "Most likely not." As she finished her bit of fruit, her face blushed again. He was about to ask why when she cleared her throat, rather nervously and spoke. "You know, one time I asked Mama what is was like to have a husband."

He raised a curious eyebrow. "I can only imagine her answer. What did she say?"

"She quoted the bible, of course. She said, 'A husband is the head of his wife as Christ is the head of his body, the church; he gave his life to be her Savior. As the church submits to Christ, so you wives must submit to your husbands in everything."

He had a livid memory of seeing the marks on her back. And now he was seeing that, because of her mother, her mind was nearly as scarred. Good God, where did it all end? He clenched his teeth in fury. There was an urge pulsing in his veins - the urge to destroy something, to spend his outrage and wish it was John and Rachel Langdon he was punishing. They deserved to burn in hell for the way they'd nearly ruined their daughter. He thanked God that by some miracle, they hadn't fully succeeded in their task.

His temper just under control, he nonetheless couldn't hide the seriousness of his voice when he turned his eyes to her and spoke.

"Some men may like that in a woman, but I don't. I want a wife, not a pet. I don't want to be married to someone who rolls over at my command..." Just as he was about to say more, she reached out her hand and placed it over his mouth. And she gave him a little grin.

"Since when have you known me to be like that?"

When she looked at him that way...smiled in that way, he found his anger melting away fast. And he couldn't help but smile back at her.

"I know you're not like that. And I'm so thankful for it. But I know there has to be some little part of you, like a little voice in your head, that wonders if it's wrong to enjoy marriage. And I mean in every way."

"What could be so wrong about loving someone?"

Before he could respond, she put her arms around his neck and brought her lips to his, kissing him deeply. All other thoughts fled from his mind, and all he knew was the nearness of her...the feel, the scent. And especially her sweet taste. Briefly, she held him back to catch her breath. And she gave him a saucy little smirk.

"I have to be honest. Thanks to my folks, sometimes there are those little voices in my head. I'm sure that once in a while, they'll try to sway me from your wicked ways."

Chuckling, he trailed warm lips along her collarbone, and kissed the little hollow at the base of her throat. "And how will you answer them?"

She let out a warm sigh. "I don't know, because I'm just not listening right now...

*****

"I wonder if this is what Eden looked like."

She sat with him on the soft sand. Leaning back against him, his arms around her, they watched the afternoon sun as it slowly descended into the sea. There were other visitors from the inn watching as well, but most of them were at a distance, away in their own little places. She didn't notice anyone except her husband, the dazzling sunset, and the soft sound of the waves rolling in and out from the shore. To her words about their paradise, Henry didn't say anything. But she felt his lips in her hair, and it made her smile. Words weren't really necessary.

As the sun dropped below the waterline, she let out a little sigh of contentment, and made to rise. It had been a long day in the sun and the water, and feeling happy but rather tired, she wanted to retire for the night. She reached for his hands, thinking he would rise and go with her. But he pulled her back down, and though she was getting sleepy eyed, she found his invitation impossible to resist. But to her surprise, instead of embracing her, he reached into his pocket and brought out a small velvet box. He placed it in her hand, and the moment she looked at it, she let out a sound of protest. She knew he wanted to spoil her...he'd said so several times in the last few days. But accepting gifts was something she just couldn't get used to, no matter how he tried to change it. She opened her mouth to tell him so, but he put a finger to her lips to quiet her.

"It is a husband's right to give a gift now and then. And I think you will like this one very much. It's more symbolic than anything else."

She sighed, knowing he would argue with her all night long if he wanted to, and she was simply too happy with him to fight. So she relented and opened the box. It turned out to be a silver compass, and her eyes sparkled with delight. Without him saying a word, she knew just what his gift implied. She said nothing, and just smiled at him, as she cradled the trinket lovingly in her hand. Then it was he who rose to his feet, and pulled her to hers.

"The mainland is to the north," he said. "But let's look in other directions." They faced the water, which still shimmered with the lingering red light of day. She lifted the compass and showed it to him. "Now we're facing the west," he said. "Across the gulf is Mexico, if you want to take that direction. Personally, I found it much too hot." Taking her by the shoulders, he turned her so she looked down the stretch of the sandy shore. He reached out and lifted her hand, asking her what the direction read.

"South," she replied.

"And somewhere out there is the Caribbean." With a smile he turned her again, this time in the direction of the inn and the open evening sky behind it.

"That's the east," she said, looking at her compass.

He nodded. "To the east is the Atlantic, and if you go as the crow flies, you wind up in Africa." She looked up to see him smiling at her, and she couldn't help but smile back when he asked, "So, Mrs. Shaw. Which direction would you choose if you could?"

She sort of tilted her head to one side, thinking. A moment later she left his side, holding the compass and turning until she had found a direction she desired, and he came to stand close behind her, where he bent his head and placed a kiss on her shoulder. "So? What did you choose?"

She lifted the compass to show him. "North, Northeast. I think you know just what lies in that direction."

A little grin turned up the corner of his mouth. "I expected as much," he said. "Which is why, in three days, we will board a ship to New York. And after a day or two of visiting that most American of American cities, we will travel across the Atlantic to Europe, and you will finally get to see all those far-away places you've been dreaming of."

She slipped the compass into her pocket. Then she slid her arms around him and rested her head against his chest. She sighed in contentment. "Sometimes I wonder if this is all my imagination." She looked up at him, seeing his sly little smirk. It was a look she was coming to know very well, and to look forward to.

"Let me assure you," he said. "This is all very real." As if to prove his words, he kissed her firmly and she responded in an instant, snaking her arms around his neck, pulling him as close as she could. When he broke the kiss she whimpered in protest, but he just gave her another wicked smile and replied, "I don't think you're completely convinced. We'll have to remedy that, won't we?"

She nodded, her head spinning slightly as he took her hand and they walked back to the inn.

Chapter 26
"Epilogue"

After two days in New York, they traveled by luxury liner to England. Her sea-legs were not as steady as his, but she managed to enjoy the shipboard entertainment and the constant attention of her doting husband, despite her seasickness.

They spent a whirlwind month in Europe, taking in the cities of old and loving every moment of it. Paris had been her favorite, as she had always known it would be. It was truly the city of romance, and she found that it was not only a romance of the heart, but of the mind and soul. It seemed the whole city was overflowing with great writers, poets, artists, and musicians, and she could not help but be inspired by the creative spirit and beauty. As she and Henry walked along the Champs-Elysees, she told him of the thought that been swirling in her mind since their arrival.

"I think I will be a writer...I think Paris has inspired something in me that I have to express. A kind of creativity that needs to flow from my mind, and I think a pen and paper will be the only way to really express it."

He smiled at her, giving her a knowing look. "I didn't think you would be content for long with just being married and settling down. Just keeping a home and family never did seem like something that would suit you. You're much too independent for that."

"You're right. But I do want to keep a home and children. And I just love being married to you. But I want something else in life. Something that is my own...all my own. I think being a writer will give me that."

She kept a journal of their travels, writing her thoughts and feelings about Europe and all of its wonders. All in all, it was filled with treasured memories. But one memory she chose to keep locked safely in her head. For the rest of her days it would remain there, to serve her time and time again...

She often thought back to that first night in Paris. It had been a long and tedious journey, and they retired early, both exhausted. When they slept, it pleased her to rest with her back against his chest. His solid warmth made her feel safe and secure, and his arm around her was only an added pleasure, and that time was no different.

Until, sometime late in the night, he began to shudder strangely in his sleep. His arm moved away from her as he rolled to his back. He murmured words she couldn't understand at first, and for a moment she thought he was just talking the gibberish of dreams. She tried to brush off the nonsensical words. But when they became clear and frantic pleas for help, she realized he was having a severe nightmare. A war memory, she sensed, from the terrified way he cried out. In his state he flailed his arms about, and on her knees beside him she tried to shake him from his sleep.

"Henry, wake up!" She reached out and gave his cheek a light slap, and he jumped so violently that she moved back slightly to give him a bit of space. He lay very still for several moments, though his chest rose and fell sharply, his eyes wide with fear. For a second or two she hesitated touching him. The sight of him was fearful. But the need to comfort him was overwhelming, and though her heart beat fast with fright, she reached out and put her hand on his shoulder. He jumped slightly at the touch of her hand, but she didn't withdraw it. And after a few passing moments, he seemed to calm under her touch. She looked down at him and spoke softly.

"Are you all right?"

Though he was calm in the physical sense, his breathing slower now, his eyes were still wild. To her question he gave no reply, and she didn't press him for answers. Instead she slowly sank down beside him and put her head on his shoulder. They lay silently that way for some time, until in a swift gesture he rolled over and put his arms around her. Now it was her shoulder that cradled his head. She felt a trickle of moisture on her skin, and realized they were tears that fell from his eyes. Her heart broke, and she wanted so much to ask what shook him so. But something within her said he needed her to listen, and not to speak. It was a long time before he said anything, and when he did, he sounded to her like a frightened little boy.

"I've tried so hard to forget it. But in the middle of the night it comes back to me, and it's like I'm there all over again. It's like the years since then have never really been. And I'm so afraid I won't make it home."

She let him go on as he needed to. She just held him soothingly, stroking the curls of dark hair at his temples. When a good deal of time had passed, she heard him give a shuddering sigh. And he muttered sadly.

"What you must think of me. A hopeless shell of a man, that's what you've married."

Moving slightly, adjusting her position so they were nose to nose, she gently kissed his forehead, his eyes, his lips. She brushed her fingers through his hair, speaking softly to him.

"So neither one of us is perfect...but maybe together, we can be something better."

Even in the dark, she could see how he tried to smile, despite his sorrow. He whispered lovingly. "So the whole may be greater than the sum of our parts?"

She didn't say a word. Taking his head in her hands, she kissed him softly. Then she gently brushed her thumbs under his eyes, wiping away his tears. In moments such as these, she realized that deeds were more powerful than words. The comfort of her arms, her body, was the very thing he needed to ease his pain.

Finding Grace

* * * * *

In early October, when they left the continent, she was sad to depart from it. But she was also happy to be coming back to Jack and Alice…and to the home that was now hers as well as her husband's.

Jack was there to meet them when they arrived at Union Station. Delighted as she was to see him again, she was a bit disappointed not to see Alice. Many times she'd smiled to herself, thinking of the day she and Henry had arrived in Key Largo, when she'd called Alice and told her what they were planning. She could still recall the delighted squeal over the other end of the line. And she'd imagined how they would dance around in girlish delight when they saw each other again. But Alice wasn't there. And after she kissed her brother's cheek, greeting him, and he and Henry shook hands with some polite words, her first question was about her sister-in-law.

"Why didn't Alice come with you?"

Jack sighed, and the look on his face was that of a weary, frustrated man. "She's home taking a nap. She's having an awful time sleeping lately."

"Why? Is something wrong with the baby?"

He shook his head. "The doctor says everything's fine. But Alice is having back spasms that wake her up in the middle of the night. It's gotten so bad that sometimes she has to sleep in the armchair."

As it turned out, the back trouble was the least of Alice's concerns, as far as she said. When Grace came into the living room, where Alice was resting on the sofa, they exchanged great smiles and hugs. Then, Alice told the men to go away and leave them alone so they could talk. And when they were gone, she turned to Grace and beamed.

"You little devil, running away and getting married like that. Did you have that planned all along?"

Grace shook her head. "Not at all. I was just as shocked as you were. I still can't believe all this is happening. I pinch myself every morning." She reached out a hand, placing it on Alice's. "Enough about my little life. I heard your back is giving you trouble."

"Yes, it hurts. But I'll live. What's really driving me crazy is your brother."

Now Grace smiled. "What's he doing?"

"What's he doing? He's won't leave me alone. I'm surprised he even went out of the room with Henry. Do you know that he calls me two or three times a day from work? He won't let me lift the smallest thing. And I can't even make the slightest moan or groan without him asking me what's wrong. He's like a mother hen from hell."

Grace couldn't help but be amused. She knew how much Jack wanted to be a father, and how much he adored his wife. The idea of something happening to either of them was probably what motivated his nervousness. And until the baby actually arrived, that wasn't likely to change.

* * * * *

It was an odd thing, having her own house to run. But it was even harder getting used to the idea of having a housekeeper. It was the source of the first real argument in her marriage.

"I don't need nobody to cook and clean for me. I've been doing those things since I was five years old."

"But you're not a poor little mouse anymore. You don't need to slave away like your mother. I pay my housekeeper a salary, so let her earn it."

"That's the silliest thing I ever heard. Why should you pay some poor little old lady to work when I can do it?"

"Because that's how she earns her living. She's a widow. She has no family to care for her, and she has no other source of income. What should I do, throw her out on the street?"

She knew he had a point in that. And Mrs. White was a kind-hearted soul. The last thing Grace wanted was to cause trouble for an elderly lady. And so they all reached a compromise. Mrs. White would stay, but as a helpmate to the lady of the house. Henry wasn't at all thrilled with the idea, but Grace would not budge. If she was forced to have a housekeeper, she insisted on sharing in the work. And for the first time in her life, housework was a choice, not a burden. She was proud of keeping a tidy home, and looked forward to entertaining visitors, though she knew Henry balked at the idea of guests invading his privacy.

"I don't like people traipsing in all the time. I'd rather it be just the two of us."

Jack liked to slyly remark that Henry never liked having company because he wanted his wife all to himself.

"No argument there," Henry would reply. Then he would look at his wife and give her a wink, which always made her smile but roll her eyes at the same time.

Of course, Jack and Alice were their most frequent guests, just as they were theirs in return. While Henry was gone working, Grace spent much of her time helping Alice around the house. By December, she'd grown so large with the baby that she had to accept any help she could get, for it was difficult to manage some of the smallest tasks. Just getting up from the sofa was a chore, but Grace was there to lend a hand whenever she could. And when she left, Jack gladly took over, and was happier still to have his help accepted, if grudgingly so.

When he wasn't fussing and clucking over his wife, he was busy buying toys and setting up the nursery. There was much arguing back and forth over whether to paint it pink or blue, but they finally settled on more neutral shades of white and soft yellow. It was all done just before the holidays, and all that was left now was for the baby to make its entrance into the world.

* * * * *

A soft snow fell a week before Christmas, coating everything in a glistening white blanket. Everyone was in the holiday spirit, but as Grace helped Alice decorate the tree, Jack was rattling on about slippery sidewalks and icicles that kept forming on the edge of the roof. As she and Alice hung ornaments, he and Henry were sitting nearby and they were supposed to be playing chess, but Jack wasn't concentrating on anything except his worries.

"What if one of those icicles fall on someone's head? A person could really get hurt. And honey, what if you step out on the sidewalk and hit a patch of ice?" He looked panicked, but it wasn't a new thing. Grace couldn't help but be tickled by him. Lately, he'd been worse than she'd ever seen him. Every time Alice made a noise, he was convinced it was time to go to the hospital. And by now Alice had gotten so use to it, her reply was a familiar phrase. "False alarm, Jack. Go back to what you were doing." She spoke it quite calmly, for it was pointless getting upset anymore or arguing with him. It was easier just to make her remark, and then ignore him.

He rose from his chair with a determined look. "I'm going out to salt the sidewalk again and clear the overhangs. They're driving me crazy." He threw on his coat and went out, and Grace looked at Alice, who sighed but was smiling.

"I hope he's not like this with all of our babies. I might end up in a rubber room by the time the next one's born."

Grace chuckled. She glanced out the window and saw Jack knocking ice off the roof with a broom, and it made her smile all the more. Then she looked over at Henry, who was moving Jack's chess pieces.

"What are you doing?" she asked. He didn't look up as he replied.

"Cheating. He's not paying attention anyway."

She started to laugh. But then she heard Alice make a noise, and a moment later...

"Oh my."

Grace turned her head quickly. "Oh my what?"

"Oh my, oh my," Alice replied, and she gave a knowing look as she rested her hands on her belly. But neither of the women panicked. Grace was calm as she turned to Henry, who was still concentrating on the game board.

"Henry, will you go start the car so it will be warm?"

"Start the car for what?"

After a moment he looked up, and seeing Alice's state, his eyes grew wide with understanding. He rose quickly, moved quickly, but was quite relaxed. It wasn't until he stepped outside and spoke to Jack that any kind of pandemonium ensued, and all on Jack's part. He came running into the house and to his wife, but Grace pushed him away.

"Go get her suitcase, dodo bird. Make yourself useful."

He ran off to fetch the bag, while Henry came hurrying back to help get Alice into the car. A few minutes later Jack came rushing out the front door, and promptly he slipped on the sidewalk and fell backwards into the snow. Grace called out to him as she turned and saw what had happened.

"What are you trying to do? Put the both of you in the hospital? Come on, you bug dumb-bell. We have to get going."

He managed to get to his feet, and after he got in the back seat with Alice, she closed the door on him and grumbled. "He's a bigger baby than the one that's coming." She got in the front seat beside Henry, and they were off to the hospital.

* * * * *

"He's the most beautiful baby I think I've ever seen in my life."

Grace looked down at her nephew, so small and delicate in her arms, wrapped in a blanket with only his tiny hands and pink face showing. His eyes were closed now, and his hands were clenched close to his face as he slept. But just moments before, she'd seen his beautiful eyes, and they were big and brown just like his father's. Thinking of that, Grace looked up at Jack, who was standing close by, and she seemed to sense that he was eager to have his child in his arms again. He'd been fascinated with his son from the moment he'd seen him, and she couldn't remember ever seeing such a look of love on her brother's face. She smiled, gently handing the baby back to him, and she watched with joy as he walked about the room, unable to take his eyes off of his boy.

They'd decided to call him Toby, for as Alice explained, she wanted the name to be associated with joy and not sadness.

"Besides," she said with a smile. "I think it's only right to name him after a good man."

Grace couldn't find a reason to argue with that. And as she stood with Henry at her side, watching Jack, she could not help but imagine that one day, her husband would be holding a child in the same loving way.

It was on her mind later that night, as she and Henry lay together. He was nearly asleep, and though she was quite exhausted from the events of the day, her thoughts kept her from closing her eyes. She looked upon her husband, admiring the rugged beauty of his face, so peaceful in repose. She did not want to disturb him, but her curiosity overwhelmed her, and she gave his shoulder a gentle shake.

"Henry?"

"Hmm?" was all he said.

"When we have children someday, do you want a boy first, like most men do?"

"I think I'd prefer girls to boys," he replied, his voice mumbled with sleepiness.

She smiled, curious. "Really? Why is that?"

"Boys are nothing but trouble," he said. "Don't you think I'm proof of that?"

Even as his voice grew softer, the corner of his mouth turned up a bit in that way she loved so much. She smiled, bringing herself up close to him and kissing him softly on the lips.

"I love you."

"I love you too," he replied, and a moment later, she knew he was asleep from the sound of his deep and even breathing. She smiled again, resting her head against his shoulder, her heart full of contentment and hope for the future.

Just before she drifted off, she heard the sound of Jane's voice in her head, and it was her own voice as well.

I know what it is to live entirely for and with what I love best on earth. I hold myself supremely blessed - blessed beyond what language can express, because I am my husband's life as fully as he is mine.

She could not forget where such blessings came from, and she sent up a silent prayer to heaven, thanking the maker for all she had been given. Her eyes grew heavy, and soon they closed, and her breathing soon fell into rhythm with his... deep, even, and peaceful.

Made in the USA
Lexington, KY
04 October 2011